Welcome. It's your third trip to the mean streets of Memphis. By now you know that when the sun goes down, shit starts popping off. The three major female gangs still ruling the gritty Mid-South are the Queen Gs, who keep it hood for the Black Gangster Disciples; the Flowers, who rule with the Vice Lords; and the Cripettes, mistresses of the Grape Street Crips.

The stakes are at an all-time high and blood has a whole new meaning. Here, bad things happen to good people all the time and survival is not guaranteed. Memphis's gangsta divas play by their own set of rules and they're as hard and ruthless as the men they hold down. Only love can destroy them.

Also by De'nesha Diamond

Street Divas

Hustlin' Divas

A Gangster and a Gentleman (with Kiki Swinson)

Heist (with Kiki Swinson)

Heartbreaker (with Erick S. Gray and Nichelle Walker)

Published by Kensington Publishing Corp.

Gangsta Divas

DE'NESHA DIAMOND

Kensington Publishing Corp.
http://www.kensingtonbooks.com

DAFINA BOOKS are published by

Kensington Publishing Corp.
119 West 40th Street
New York, NY 10018

All Kensington Titles, Imprints, and Distributed Lines are available at special quantity discounts for bulk purchases for sales promotions, premiums, fundraising, and educational or institutional use. Special book excerpts or customized printings can also be created to fit specific needs. For details, write or phone the office of the Kensington special sales manager: Kensington Publishing Corp., 119 West 40th Street, New York, NY 10018, attn: Special Sales Department, Phone: 1-800-221-2647.

Dafina and the Dafina logo Reg. U.S. Pat. & TM Off.

First trade paperback printing: January 2013

ISBN-13: 978-0-7582-4759-9
ISBN-10: 0-7582-4759-1

10 9 8 7 6 5 4 3 2 1

Printed in the United States of America

This is dedicated to those surviving the Memphis struggle.

Cast of Characters

Ta'Shara Murphy was once a straight-A student with dreams of getting the hell out of Memphis, but she took a detour on her dreams when she fell in love with Raymond "Profit" Lewis, the younger brother of Fat Ace. The war between the Vice Lords and her sister's set, the Gangster Disciples, puts her between a rock and a hard place. When she failed to take her sister's warning to heart, she was unprepared for the consequences.

LeShelle Murphy is Queen G for the Memphis Gangster Disciples. Not only does she love her man, Python, but she loves the power her position affords her and there is nothing that she won't do to ensure that she never loses any of it—that includes doing whatever it takes to keep her younger sister in line and handling the many chicken heads pecking at her heels.

Willow "Lucifer" Washington is Fat Ace's right hand and as deadly as they come. A true ride-or-die chick to her core. The latest explosion between the sets will have her true feelings bubbling to the top, and when she's forced to step up to lead, she proves that you don't need a set of balls to wash the streets with blood.

Qiana "Scar" Barrett is a Vice Lord Flower and the younger sister of Vice Lord soldier Tombstone. She's long been in love with Profit and will do anything to see Ta'Shara removed from his arm. She's also crossed enemy lines to forge a deal with Queen G LeShelle to erase Python's baby mama, Yolanda.

Maybelline "Momma Peaches" Carver, Python's beloved aunt, believes and acts as if she's still wildin' out in her twenties. With an arrest record a mile long, Peaches is right in the thick of things and when old family secrets start coming home to roost, her partying days may be well behind her.

Alice Carver is Momma Peaches's baby sister and mother to rival gang leaders Python and Fat Ace. She has escaped the mental hospital to settle old debts. She is tortured by regrets and loss, and her demons may lead her tragic life to a tragic end.

Shariffa Rodgers is the ex-wifey of Gangster Disciple Python, who was thrown off her throne and nearly beaten to death after getting caught creeping. Now married to Grape Street Crip leader Lynch, Shariffa not only wants payback, she wants her new crew to take over the entire street game.

Ja'nay "Trigger" Clark, Shariffa's right-hand chick, proves that there's nothing she won't do for her girl. But one hit in Vice Lords' territory lands her in Lucifer's crosshairs—the last place anyone wants to be.

Detective Melanie Johnson is the daughter of the most decorated and crooked cop on the Memphis Police Department payroll. Unfortunately, the apple doesn't fall too far from the tree. She has her own skeletons in the closet, but none bigger than being the lover of both leaders of the dueling gangs, Python and Fat Ace.

Yolanda "Yo-Yo" Terry is an ex-drug mule turned stripper turned Python's latest baby momma. Convinced that she's the smartest chick on the block, her ambition has led her to cross paths with Python's real wifey, LeShelle. Her recklessness has already cost her her best friend, Baby Thug, but this time, she stands to lose a whole lot more than she bargained for.

Essence Blackwell, Ta'Shara Murphy's best friend and once the lone voice of reason, now finds herself tripping over the same pitfalls that snared her friend. Of all things, she finds herself a pawn between the two biggest bitches in the game . . . with just a hope and a prayer of getting out alive.

Aftermath

1

Lucifer

"**N**OOOOOOOOOOOOOOOOOOOOO!"

The light. Where is the light in Mason's eyes? The world tilts off its axis as my brain forces my heart to accept the unbelievable. *He's dead.* The leader of the Memphis Vice Lords . . . my lover, my best friend . . . my life—dead. Flipped upside down in a black Escalade on the side of the highway, I'm twisted in an awkward position. It feels like every damn bone in my body is broken. Still I scream until my voice fails and my lungs beg for oxygen.

My world.

My rock.

Since we were kids, I've been Mason's ride-or-die chick—not because of the shared allegiance with the Vice Lord family, but because I loved the air he breathed and the ground he walked on.

Until recently, he didn't know about the torch I carried for him. To him, I was his right-hand bitch, blasting and carving niggas up who dared to cross the Vice Lord family. I never realized that my brother Bishop had cock-blocked my ass and made it clear with his best friend that I was off-limits. All that shit changed when that crooked-ass cop Melanie Johnson got murked and all her secrets fell out of the closet. The bitch had some kind of hold on him—and apparently Mason's life-long sworn enemy, Python, too. She had even convinced Mason that she was carrying his child.

I knew the bitch was no good and was more than thrilled when Mason realized where his heart truly belonged—with me.

His world.

His rock.

A couple of hours ago we made love for the first time. Hell, there's still a sweet soreness throbbing between my legs that if I close my eyes I can still feel him.

Rare tears fuck up my vision and splash over my lashes as I try to accept the unacceptable.

He's gone.

This shit wasn't supposed to go down like this. We had planned everything. Everything.

Hit the Pink Monkey, blow that shit up.

Hit Goodson Construction, mow down every Gangster Disciple in sight.

The hitch: Python's ass was nowhere to be found.

Bishop fucked up. He was the one who'd been in charge of tagging that nigga. Instead of hitting the chief, we got his second-in-command, McGriff. Turned out his ass was cutting his own deal with their supplier behind Python's back, tryna come up. We did that muthafucka a favor takin' them out.

That shit didn't sit well with Mason.

Hyped on a murderous high, we made up a new plan on the fly and drove our murder train toward the heart of the Gangster Disciples: Shotgun Row.

The shit was bold. Any other time, we would've known it was a suicide mission. We were picked off a few miles out. Bullets flew like we were in the Middle East. By chance we spotted Python. We chased that ass going the wrong way on the highway. We were gaining ground until a near head-on collision with an eighteen-wheeler spun and then flipped us off the road.

"Muthafucka, answer me! What the fuck is your real name?" Python, the chief nigga of the Gangster Disciples, roars at Mason. They are inches outside the flipped vehicle where the nigga was just wailing his meaty fist against Mason's jaw. Both gangsta chiefs are physically intimidating men. Their major differences are that Python is covered in tats and has a surgically altered tongue so that it resembled one of a snake. Mason, a little bulkier, a little darker, shiny on top with a goatee and one fucked up eye that he lost in a gun battle years ago. Despite these differences, I'm suddenly hit with the realization that at this angle these two look eerily similar.

"ANSWER ME," Python roars.

"G-get away from him," I spit, ignoring the taste of my own blood. However, the pain ricocheting throughout my body intensifies to the point that I know I'm on the verge of blacking out. I don't care. I need to protect my man at all cost.

Then this nigga does something that surprises the shit out of me. The muthafucka starts crying. I ain't talking about a few bullshit sniffles either. It's a gut-wrenching roar of a wounded lion.

BOOM! BOOM!

The heavens crack with thunder and lightning flashes across the sky. A second later, rain falls in torrential sheets as Python tucks his head into the crook of Mason's neck and weeps.

"I didn't know," he croaks. "I didn't know."

I'm numb all over except where my heart feels like it's being chiseled out of my chest. I don't understand what the fuck I'm looking at and I ain't too sure that I'm not imagining this shit. Tears? From this big, overgrown nigga who thinks his ass is a snake?

Nobody is going to believe this shit, especially since the war between the Vice Lords and the Gangster Disciples has been raging decades before any of us burst onto the scene. But no two gang leaders have ever beefed harder than Mason and Python. It's like the world demands that there can only be one.

"Forgive me," Python sobs. "Please forgive me."

BOOM! BOOM!

This nigga has lost it. I redouble my efforts and after a hell of a lot of huffing and puffing, I'm able to move my arm about an inch. It's not much, but my fingertips brush the barrel of Mason's TEC-9. *I can do it. I can do it.*

I don't know why this muthafucka is crying and I really don't give a shit. I'm more interested in street justice. An eye for an eye. A life for a life.

I take pride in being the baddest bitch breathing so it's killing me that the pain seizing me right now is getting the best of me. Darkness encroaches my peripheral and a new desperation takes hold of me. *I can't black out now. I can't.* I know at my core that I'll never be able to forgive myself if I don't take this human reptile out.

BOOM! BOOM!

Chugging in a deep breath, my nose burns from the stench of gasoline. *Is this muthafucka about to blow up?* It takes everything I have to twist my head around, but everywhere I turn, the smell grows stronger until it feels like my nose hairs are on fire.

Fuck it. If it blows, it blows. The three of us can blaze up and that shit is just fine with me. In fact, I prefer it. I won't have to return to Ruby Cove with my tail tucked between my legs and buzzing whispers about how my gangsta wasn't tight enough to protect our leader. Niggas will look for any excuse to try to knock a bitch off her throne. But if we all go out together, we'll become legends in the streets. I close my eyes and allow death to seduce me.

A sob lodges in my throat, forcing me to choke on the son of a bitch. Hell, I can't tell what hurts more, my broken body or my broken heart.

Regardless, if death is coming, the bitch is slow.

BOOM! BOOM!

A spark. My eyes fly open. I need a spark to set this shit off. My gaze darts around again for something—*anything* that can make a spark.

"I didn't know. I didn't know," Python sobs again, clinging tighter to Mason.

What the fuck did this nigga not know? My gaze returns to the two gangstas, but what I see does nothing to clear up my confusion. Either I banged my head too hard or I'm seeing that this nigga really is broken up about taking his long-time enemy out. Soaked to the bone, Python has wrapped Mason in his arms and is rocking back and forth—much like I would do, if I could get my ass to move.

BOOM! BOOM!

My brain flies back to the TEC-9. If I can get one shot off, I can end all this bullshit. I draw in another deep breath to build up my resolve, but the strong scent of gasoline now has waves of bile crashing around in my gut and burning up my esophagus. Choking on my own vomit is not the way I'd pictured exiting the game.

At the last second, I'm able to roll onto my side and hurl. But even that shit feels like I'm hawking up gobs of broken glass. Before long, I'm swimming in acidic bile.

"I'm taking you home," I catch Python saying through the booming thunder and hammering rain. Next, he awkwardly struggles to pick Mason up.

"Wait. No!" I choke on more bile. "What are you doing?"

He ignores me as he struggles to stand on the wet earth. After splashing around, he hooks his arms underneath Mason's and then locks his fingers across his chest so that he can drag him away from the vehicle. If he succeeds it will fuck up my plan.

BOOM! BOOM!

Clenching my jaw tight and holding my breath, I force myself to calm down. For my troubles, my stomach revolts and cramps up.

Move your ass! Move your ass! I thrust my hand up again to reach that damn semiautomatic. Again, my fingertips brush the barrel.

"C'mon, Willow. C'mon." I twist and squirm while Python succeeds in dragging Mason from view. "NOOOOOOO!" Fat tears roll over my lashes at a clip that blinds my ass. I redouble my efforts, but I . . . just . . . can't reach this muthafucka.

BOOM! BOOM!

I can't block out the horrific images of what the Gangster Disciples will do to Mason's body once Python gets it back to his home turf. Everything from chopping him up, pissing and shitting on him and even sexually molesting him, crosses my mind. I know how the GDs get down and that's not the way Mason deserves to be taken out.

"Oh God, baby. I'm so sorry." Something snaps within me and tears that I've been holding back for decades pour out of me. I'm not a crier. I never cry. But this shit has broken me. I can't imagine a world without my nigga. I never thought I had to.

BOOM! BOOM!

I close my eyes and hear the opening and closing of a car door. Less than ten seconds later, an engine roars to life and tires squeal in a growing pool of wet earth. My sobs grow more pathetic and no mental military barking can get my ass to stop.

I fucked up.

I fucked up.

I fucked up.

That shit repeats in my head for I don't know how long before I hear another vehicle pull off to the side of the road. Even then I don't know or even give a shit who the hell it is. I

want to be left alone in my own private hell until I die from
my car injuries or from my shattered heart.

"WILLOW," Bishop yells, cutting through the bullshit clut-
tering my head. "Willow, are you fucking in there?"

BOOM! BOOM!

I battle myself on whether to answer. To try and save myself
after this colossal fuck-up seems too much like a bitch move.

"WILLOW!"

I squeeze my eyes tight and will my brother to go away.

"WILLOW!"

The desperation in his voice tears at me. The sibling beefs
we've had in our lives are so fucking small in the grand scheme
of things. If a gun was pressed to my head to name someone
who has loved me unconditionally my entire life, the name I'd
spit would be: Bishop. I followed him and Mason into this
game like an irritating pest and I forged my moniker in the
street with the big dawgs—not the Flowers. I didn't want to
just lock down a big lieutenant and play wifey. I wanted to be
the big lieutenant and tell the world to suck my balls.

I succeeded. My people love me but more importantly
they respect my ass. There's never a question of whether I can
hold shit down. But after tonight, will that change?

BOOM! BOOM!

"Death, where are you?" I beg softly. "Take me out of this
place."

"Here she is," Bishop shouts.

My eyes spring back open and I see Bishop's scared face
through the shattered glass of the front window. The second
our eyes connect, I see hope ripple across his chiseled face.

"Don't worry, Willow. We're going to get you out of there."

That's what the fuck I'm afraid of.

"Hold on." Bishop hops back onto his feet and calls out to
the other members of our fam. "Y'all niggas, c'mon over here
and help me get her out of here!"

"No." Weakly, I shake my head. It's all I can do since I lack the strength to beg him to let me die.

BOOM! BOOM!

As the storm rages on, I pick up the faint sound of wailing police sirens.

"C'mon, nigga. We need to hurry this shit up," Bishop barks.

"Grab her feet and pull her out this way," Novell, I think, shouts.

When he grabs the bottom of my foot, I roar, "AAAAAR-RRRRGGGH," and nearly burst my own damn eardrums.

"NIGGA, STOP!" Bishop snatches Novell back. "What the fuck is wrong with you?"

"What?"

"Are you blind or some shit? Look at her fuckin' leg. Can't you see that we can't pull her out that way? Look at her leg."

BOOM! BOOM!

What the hell is wrong with my leg? I try to peek, but I can't even swivel my head around. I need to rest. *I'm tired—so fuckin' tired.* My eyes lower and though I can still hear the shit that's going on around me, I can't say that I give a fuck about any of it.

Sirens grow louder while the booming thunder shakes everything around me.

BOOM! BOOM!

"Kick out the front window and grab her that way," Bishop yells. A second later, I hear their Timberlands attack the glass. Next, several hands grab my arms and drag me out of my gasoline-drenched coffin and into the freezing downpour where my tears blend in with the rain.

2

Ta'Shara

"DIE, BITCH! DIE!"

Enraged, I plunge the large knitting needles deeper into my sister LeShelle's chest. Blood sprays everywhere. I want this bitch erased so I can piss on her fucking grave. If she thinks she's the baddest bitch walking because she's the leader of the Queen Gs, I got something for that ass. We have the same blood coursing through us and I can play this fucking gangsta bullshit with the best of them.

LeShelle's bloody hand slaps against my face as she tries to push me off, but I ain't going nowhere. I stab again and growl in her face. "I hate your fucking guts!"

Her eyes bulge.

All this shit was because LeShelle felt that I violated the law of the streets when I fell in love with Profit, a member of the Gangster Disciples's sworn enemies: the Vice Lords. In Memphis, GDs and VLs don't mix. I was never a part of that world and their fuckin' rules shouldn't have applied to me.

Until *she* dragged me into this shit. "DIE, BITCH! DIE!"

Snapshots of that awful prom night flash in my head. LeShelle ordering her thugs to hijack our limo and then take us to some abandoned part of town. There, she had those nig-gas beat and rape me. I'll never forget how she stood there and watched as one dirty nigga after another climbed on top of me. I can still hear Profit, yelling and fighting to break free from the muthafucka that held him down and forced him to watch. They even carved the initials GD into the side of my ass like I was some fucking animal. The pain was more than anything I can describe.

When I thought that it was over and I was covered in blood, cum, and bruises, LeShelle turned toward Profit and unloaded an entire clip. Time stood still as I watched him sink to his knees and then collapse.

A waterfall of tears flows over my lashes as I snatch the needles out of LeShelle's chest and plunge them back in. "I hate you. I hate you. I hate you." I lean down and gnaw on her ear until the lower lobe falls into my mouth.

"Aaaaaargh," LeShelle roars.

I sit up with her blood dripping from my mouth and then spit that muthafucka in her face.

"How do you like my fuckin' balls now, big sis?"

Shock covers LeShelle's face as the needles go back in deeper than before.

"DIE! DIE! DIE!"

LeShelle's eyes glaze over, but it tickles the shit out of me. Big bad LeShelle is finally getting what she has coming to her. I laugh—and once I start, I can't fuckin' stop. I sound like a crazy person—but I don't give a shit. I want justice. For me. For Profit.

High-pitched hysterical screams whirl around me as a herd of people rush into the room. Before I know it, several hands and arms grab and drag me off LeShelle. "Noooo! She's not dead yet! She's not dead!" Still wielding a weapon, I stab the closest arm in hopes to win back my freedom.

"AAAARGH," a man howls. "Get those damn things away from her!"

The second the needles are snatched out of my hands, I fuckin' lose it. Kicking and screaming, I claw my way through the piles of bodies that are trying to hold me down, but these muthafuckas got me pinned.

"Ta'Shara, baby. Please, stop. You're hysterical," Tracee, my foster mother, screams. Fat tears race down her face. There's love there, I can see it, but that shit don't matter right now. She can't and will never understand the rage boiling in my veins. How could she? Tracee and her perfect husband, Reggie, with their perfect jobs and perfect suburban house, had done all they could to shield and protect me. They had planted seeds of hope and endless possibilities in my head on how I can rise above my parents' abandonment and the horrors of the State's foster care system and it was all *bullshit*.

I'm never going to get out of this fuckin' city.

I'm never going to become a doctor.

I'm never going to escape LeShelle and her street politics. *Not as long as she is still breathing.*

"I want her dead! I want her dead!" I shove Tracee away and send her stumbling back over the edge of the bed. Launching forward like a locomotive, I fight to get at LeShelle's bleeding ass again, but another team of quarterback-looking men dressed head to toe in white tackle me. "Let me go, goddamn it! Let me go!"

"I thought you guys had her pinned?" another man yells.

"We're trying. Look what she did to my arm!"

These big niggas grab my bruised body and intensify my rage. In my mind's eye, they are LeShelle's goons, ready for another round at my bruised pussy. "LET GO!"

"Please, please," Tracee wails. "Don't hurt her."

"LET GO!"

I jack up my knee and hit a nut sack so hard that this miscellaneous brothah can forget about having babies.

"Awwww, shit."

At least one pair of hands fall away and I redouble my efforts to break loose, but I don't get so much as an inch off of the floor before being tackled back down again. *They're going to rape me! God, no. Please not again.* Terror seizes me.

I can't let LeShelle win. I can't!

"Ta'Shara, sweetheart. They are just trying to help you," Tracee yells above the scuffling. "Please don't fight them."

"No! No!" I don't believe her. She's a liar. They are all liars.

There's a painful prick on my right arm. I wrench my head around to see a nurse inject me with something. "What are you doin'? What is that?"

"Don't worry. This is going to calm you down," the woman says, smiling.

I open my mouth to tell her that I don't want to calm down, but the words get lost in the journey from my brain to my mouth. A second after that, my tongue swells to the point that it feels like it's too big for my mouth. My vision is the next thing to go as the bitch in front of me blurs. I blink several times, but then my eyes grow heavy. Before long, I can barely keep them open.

What the fuck?

"Get the jacket," someone shouts.

Jacket? What jacket?

"Be careful. Don't hurt her," Tracee sobs.

"Sorry, ma'am, but we're more worried about her hurting someone else," an attendant tells her.

"Ta'Shara, baby. Everything is going to be all right," Tracee wails as I'm being strapped into something. There is no need for it now since the horse tranquilizer shit they gave me has kicked in.

"How's the other one?" a woman asks.

Even though I'm sinking into a black hole, I wait with bated breath for the answer.

"We have a pulse!"

LeShelle is still alive.

NOOOOOOOOOOOOO! My scream ricochets inside of my head as I tumble into darkness in despair.

3

Qiana

"**W**HAAAAAH! WHAAAAH!"

Out here in the middle of nowhere on a hidden rocky gravel road, I lift a baby out of its dead momma's belly as bile rushes up and burns my throat. I choke that shit down. I ain't no punk-bitch. When I set out to do a job, my ass follows through. I'm taking one hell of a risk doing this job for Queen G LeShelle. After all, Queen Gs and Flowers don't mix—*ever*.

But I'm the one who brokered this deal. I wanted that pip-squeak Essence to stop sniffing around Profit. After all, he is Vice Lord royalty. That's something that even he forgot when he dipped his dick in that GD trash, Ta'Shara. I'm playing a dangerous game aligning with LeShelle on this hit. After all, word on the street is she's the deadly bitch that put both her sister and Profit in separate hospitals, but sometimes the enemy of my enemy is my friend.

I dropped dime that Essence was two-timing the sets—which was true. The lil blood clot had struck some kind of deal with our main gangsta bitch, Lucifer, and in turn, the VL fam was ordered not to touch her. However, I learned a long time ago that there is a way around everything—but there's also a cost.

LeShelle didn't waste a second blazing that snitch, Essence, but in return, she wanted me to get rid of one of her man's jump-offs, Yolanda. Problem was: LeShelle failed to mention that the bitch was pregnant—and not just kinda pregnant. This yellow heifer was due to shit this baby out any day.

That's when it hits me that my ass needs some insurance. I trust that LeShelle about as far as I can throw her ass. Any bitch that will order her own sister's rape is a bad bitch and one you'll have to constantly look over your shoulder for.

"WHAAAAH! WHAAAH!"

My God, this damn thing has the strongest set of lungs I've ever heard. "Somebody get me something to wipe this shit off."

My Flowers, Lil Bit, Tyneshia, and Adaryl, who'd been standing back while I carve this bastard out of this dead bitch, slink farther away. I glance over my shoulder and stare their asses down. "Are you bitches hard of hearing or something?"

At seeing the grayish black umbilical cord stretching between momma and baby, Adaryl slaps a hand over her mouth, turns, and then spills her guts all over the dusty, gravel road.

Fuckin' pussy. I roll my eyes. Sometimes I wonder why the hell I even bother with these tricks. "Just look in the backseat. I got some clothes back there."

"WHAAAAH. WHAAAAAH."

"Damn, muthafucka. Shut up." I slice through the spongy cord and more shit splatters everywhere.

Lil Bit is the first to toss up her hands. "Yo, Qiana. This shit is foul. You didn't say shit about this bitch being pregnant and you *certainly* didn't say nothin' about cuttin' no baby out."

"WHAAAAAH! WHAAAH!"

"Whatever. The shit is done now. Put on your big girl panties and move your ass."

Their shifty eyes look everywhere but at me. I jump up and step away from the dead bitch on the ground as thunder booms overhead and lightning lights up the night sky.

"Awww shit. This is a bad muthafuckin' sign," Tyneshia

says, backing away. "This is some demonic cursed shit. Our asses is gonna go to hell for this. You can miss my ass with all this shit."

"I don't fucking believe you scared-ass pussies. You call yourselves Flowers—the baddest bitches locking down the VL family?" I stare each one of them down, including Adaryl's puking ass, to let them know how disgusted I am. "All y'all ever talk about is how y'all want to be big bitches that did big thangs. Now here's the chance of a lifetime and this is how you act—pissing in your panties and emptying your guts?"

"Nuh, uh. Don't pull that reverse physiological shit on us," Lil Bit protests.

This dumb bitch here. "The word is *psychological.*"

"Bitch, you know what the fuck I meant. This ain't no sanctioned hit. This is you doin' a favor for that Queen G LeShelle and *that* shit alone is enough to get all our asses canceled and you fuckin' know it. We're here because we're your girls and as *your* girl I'm telling you: This. Shit. Is. Fucked. Up."

"WHAAAH. WHAAAAH."

"No. I'm paying back a debt. LeShelle murked her own for me and in return I dusted off this bitch. But if the crooked ho even thinks about doing me dirty, *this* lil muthafucka is insurance. No doubt Python will cancel that bitch in order to get his flesh and blood back. Fuck. I might have his ass do the shit regardless. There needs to be payback for the trick shooting my boo full of holes."

"*Your boo?*" Adaryl swipes a hand over mouth. "Did my ass miss some shit?"

I shoot my gaze back over to her ass.

Adaryl tosses up her hands. "Cool. Whatever, bitch."

Lil Bit shakes her head as the sky opens up and pelts us with rain.

"WHAAAAH! WHAAAAH!"

"Shit." Now I have to worry about the baby freezing to death. "I'll finish this shit myself." I shove past them and march to my old black Ford Exploder. In the back, I find my duffle bag and dig through it until I find a pair of old sweat clothes and gym towel. The shit is going to have to do in a pinch. I deposit my knife and gloves in the bag and clean off the baby.

"WHAAAAH! WHAAAAH!"

"Hold on, lil man." I double-check to make sure that was a small dick I saw and not some gigantic clit dangling in between its legs. "Damn. You already rocking more pipe than some of the niggas I done fucked with." I smile, but the baby sucks in another deep breath and really lets me have it.

"WHAAAAAAAH! WHAAAAAAH! WHAAAAAAH!"

"Okay. I have a stupid question," Tyneshia says, stepping up behind me. "Who's gonna take care of that muthafucka? You don't know shit about takin' care of no fuckin' baby."

"How fuckin' hard can it be? Your ass has one." I wrap the baby up and attempt to bounce him, but that shit irritates him even more. "Here. You hold him. We got to hurry and get out of here."

Tyneshia jumps back. "Me? Why the fuck do I have to hold him?"

"Because I said so." I attempt to shove the baby into her arms, but the bitch jumps back.

"Nah. Nah. I ain't in this mess with you. No way."

"Are you kiddin' me? You're up to your eyeballs in this shit." I shoot my gaze from her to Lil Bit and Adaryl. "All of you. You feel me? I go down. We all go down. So remember that shit before any of y'all start thinking about droppin' dime on this hit."

The three of them blink back at me while the driving rain drenches our asses. I'm sure that they get where I'm coming from, but Tyneshia looks unmoved. "Fine. You want out?"

Feeling herself, Tyneshia thrusts up her chin. "Damn right."

"Then you're out." I whip out my Glock from the back of my jeans and blow her ass away. When she hits the rocky gravel, a thin wisp of smoke curls out of the center of her fore-head.

"Holy shit!" Lil Bit screams. "Are you crazy?"

"What the fuck did you do that shit for?" Adaryl roars.

"Does anybody else want out?"

The girls stare wide-eyed at me.

"I didn't hear y'all. Do either one of you bitches got some-thing else to say about this hit?"

Lil Bit and Adaryl share one last look before shaking their heads.

"Good. Now move your asses and let's get the fuck out of here."

4

Alice

Rain shatters like white diamonds across the van's windshield as my new nigga pulls our black van off the main road. My heart pounds like a fuckin' racehorse, anticipating seeing my Nana Maybelle's old house. It's been so long and there's so many memories—good and bad.

"Are you sure that you can see where you're going?"

He cocks a lopsided grin. "Don't worry, baby. I got this."

I hate to tell him that I don't trust any nigga. After we travel a half a mile down a gravelly road, the house finally comes into view. Gone is its former regal beauty. The place has seen better days, but that's a'ight, it will suit my purposes. To be honest, I feared that this day would never come. Don't get me wrong, I've dreamed of this moment for years, but it was too much to believe that I could ever pull it off.

Now I have.

Look. I've done a lot of fucked-up shit in my life. I know that—but a lot of times, the shit wasn't my fault. The cards have always been stacked against me. From my being born to a momma who pumped out babies until her insides fell out to my being shipped out of the cotton fields of Mississippi to my Nana Maybelle in Memphis. At first, I remember being excited. Back in the day, Memphis was the shit. The music scene was jumpin' and niggas was making big money hustlin' everything from numbers to smack. No one hustled harder than Nana Maybelle.

When I arrived, I thought Nana was rich. None of our asses went without a muthafuckin' thing. We wore the best clothes and lived in a big-ass house. People respected Nana's gangsta like she had balls saggin' between her legs. One thing she made sure of was no one fucked with her people or her paper—and not in that order.

But nobody stayed under her roof for free either. If we expected to keep that roof over our heads then we were expected to pull our weight. So I was taught how to run numbers, do drops, and collect taxes within days of my ass moving in. As far as protection, my sister, Maybelline, taught me how to wield a blade. I got real good at the shit, too. We lived like fuckin' kings and queens and there was no bigger queen gangster than Maybelline. She had a line of niggas callin' her Peaches and ready to lick the crack of her ass despite her having a big monkey on her back. Everyone pretended like they didn't see it.

I did, too—for a while.

Shit jumped the tracks when I turned twelve and I made the mistake of waking up in the middle of the night. . . .

"Alice, what the fuck are you doing in here?" Maybelline barked.

My eyes bugged at the sight of a man's yellow behind pumpin' in between Maybelline's legs.

"Get the fuck out of here," she snapped again. "Go back to bed." She dropped her head onto the pillow and started moaning and groaning.

I couldn't tell if she was enjoying what was happening or not. The sounds confused me. I stood there, not sure of what to do. Yet, at the same time, I was fascinated.

SQUEAK. BANG. SQUEAK. BANG.

It was the bed making all that noise.

SQUEAK. BANG. SQUEAK. BANG.

"I said get the fuck out of here!"

The yellow man chuckled. "Let the girl be. Maybe she's learning a thing or two." He wrapped an arm around Maybelline and flipped her over. "You see how much your sister like this good dick I'm throwing at her?" he asked me.

Was she?

"Leroy, stop playing . . . OH . . . shit. That's my spot, baby."

"Hell, yeah. Big Daddy knows how you like it," he bragged. He spread open my sister's booty and I twisted up my face in disgust. "Shit is good, ain't it, baby?"

"Fuck yeah." Then Maybelline spotted me again. "A-Alice . . . oh . . . shit. Dammit. Don't make me tell you again. NOW GO!"

Turning, I ran out and slammed the door behind me. Back in my own room, I slammed my own door and then covered my mouth with my free hand. Then, I laughed. Hard. I simply couldn't believe what I'd just seen. It wasn't like I never heard of sex. I had heard things and even seen some nasty pictures, but I'd never seen the shit raw like that. I set Nana's gun down on top of the chest of drawers next to the door and giggled my way back to bed.

SQUEAK. BANG. SQUEAK. BANG. SQUEAK. BANG.

I shook my head. I couldn't wait to tell Nana Maybelle about this shit. Maybelline was gonna get it. Nana done told us plenty of times not to bring niggas up in her house when she wasn't home.

The squeaking and banging went on forever. In order to get some sleep, I ended up burying my head underneath the pillows. No sooner than when I dozed off, I felt something slide up my leg. Groggily, I kicked it away, but it became rougher and more persistent. Alarmed, I tossed off the pillow and tried to sit up, but I didn't get an inch up off the bed before I was pinned back down with a huge hand shoved across my mouth. Who in the fuck?

"Shhhh," the man said, peeling back my bedsheets. "We don't want to wake Peaches up, do we?"

My eyes bulged as I realized who it was. I screamed and shoved him off me, but my voice was muted behind his hand and he was far too strong.

"Now. Now. You want to be nice to your Uncle Leroy, don't you?"

I screamed again, but he laughed and shoved a hand between my legs.

"Ah. Yeah. This is what I'm talkin' about. Your shit is tight as fuck." He crammed in two more fingers and wiggled them around. "Has another nigga been up this shit before?"

I didn't understand what he was asking me. Tears rolled from the corners of my eyes.

"Nah. This is some fresh pussy here." He chuckled his beer breath into my face. "Shit. It must be my muthafuckin' birthday." He yanked my panties off of my hips and then snapped my legs open like a wishbone.

"Aaaaargh!" Leroy backhanded me so hard, cartoon stars rotated around my head.

"Shut the fuck up!" His hand crammed back over my mouth. "Are you tryna get my ass in trouble? Huh? I just came in here to give you what you wanted, baby girl."

Hot tears blanketed my face. I didn't want this. He was hurting me.

"I saw how you were looking when I was doing Peaches. You wanted a taste of Leroy for yourself, didn't you?"

"Noooo!"

Leroy's backhand rocked my head in the opposite direction. A second later, blood oozed into my mouth.

"You're a muthafuckin' liar." Leroy grabbed my hand and then forced it around his dick. "You like that, baby girl? It's all for you."

My heart raced around my chest. His shit was hard and thick. Surely he didn't think that he could fit all of that inside of me.

"You like that, baby girl? Hmm? You feel how hard you got me, *thinking about your tight pussy? Fuck. I bet your shit is sweeter than Peaches's."*

"Please," I mumbled under his hand. "Don't."

"It's gonna hurt for a second, but after that you're gonna be begin' my ass not to stop."

His hand pressed harder against my mouth—to the point that I thought my teeth were gonna collapse. Where the fuck was Peaches?

"Be happy, baby. Uncle Leroy is about to make a woman out of you." Before he even finished the sentence, he thrust up his hips and split me wide open.

I screamed, cried, and bucked like hell; but he remained on top of me, ripping me apart.

"Aw, shit," Leroy panted. "This is some good shit. Oooh." He huffed and puffed and drilled his hips. He seemed unaware I was suffocating—that or he didn't give a shit. My chest hurt, my head swelled, and the demon on top of me kept drilling his dick.

Suddenly, the door burst open and Maybelline bolted inside.

"Peaches, you come in here to join us?" Leroy asked, still stroking between my legs.

"Muthafucka, get off my sister!" Peaches ran toward the bed, leapt onto Leroy's back, and pounded him on the head. "You sick, muthafucka. She's just a kid."

"Wh-what the fuck! Get off me." With one powerful swing back, Leroy sent Maybelline careening back toward the wall.

She hit it headfirst and then dropped down on top of the nightstand below. However, she didn't stay down long. She bounced up, grabbed my brass lamp, and swung it at Leroy's head.

Thunk!

At last Leroy was lifted off of me.

I shot up, wheezing for oxygen, and then scrambled off the bed.

"I'm going to fuckin' kill you!" Maybelline sprang back onto the bed, fists flying.

Leroy acted as if he felt no pain. He grabbed my sister by the throat and then whaled on her like a punching bag.

I rushed for Nana's gun on the chest of drawers and swung back around.

"Have you lost your muthafuckin' mind, bitch?" Leroy's fist crashed against Maybelline's jaw. "Do I look like some punk mutha-fucka to you? Huh?" He switched up and hit her with a right hook.

Maybelline dragged her nails straight down his face, fuckin' up his shit forever.

He howled, but then delivered two more punches.

The gun shook in my hands. I felt like a human earthquake. What if I missed and he came after me?

"You just wanted all this good dick to yourself, didn't you, Peaches? You ain't got to worry about a damn thing. There's plenty of this good dick to go around." He snatched open Maybelline's legs.

I couldn't take it anymore. I drew a deep breath, closed my eyes, and fired.

POP! POP!

"What the fuck?" Leroy roared.

POP! POP!

I peeled open my eyes to see Leroy jerk around as my bullets slammed into him. It looked so good that I couldn't stop firing.

POP! POP!

"Aaaaargh," Maybelline yelled. "You shot me!"

I eased off the trigger. Leroy slumped over on the bed. His big golden eyes stared up at nothing while his dick remained rock hard.

It's that look that haunts me to this day. . . .

My man parks the van in front of the house and kills the engine. Instead of us jumping out and getting to work, we just sit there—listening to the sounds in the surrounding woods. My nerves are humming so bad that I dive for the glove compartment for a cigarette.

"Are you all right?" he asks.

I ignore the question until I put fire to the tip and suck in my nicotine fix. "Let's do this shit," I say. I open the door and hop out of the van before he can ask me any more dumb-ass questions. The rain drenches me from head to toe. I stomp over leaves and broken tree branches. A tiny voice in the back of my head shouts that it's not too late for me to back out of this shit, but I laugh at that. Grabbing Maybelline was messier than I intended.

At the back of the van, my boo opens the door and reveals the rolled bloody carpet inside. I smile and puff out a long stream of smoke.

"Feel better?" he asks.

"I'm having an orgasm just standing here," I tell him.

Smirking, he tosses the carpet over his shoulder as if the body tucked in it doesn't weigh shit. Strong niggas makes my clit hard. Who knows—I might keep his ass around.

Maybe.

Relationships aren't exactly my strong suit.

Drawing in another deep drag, I follow my man's steady march to the front door. I'm turned on by the young brothah, but I'm watching his ass. Like I said: I don't trust nobody. I toss the cigarette and smash it into the wet ground with my heel before entering the house.

We get through the front door and edge our way to the stairs leading to the full basement. The place is a mess, but who really gives a shit? It will serve its purpose. I hit the switch and watch the light flicker while it decides whether to stay on. A whiff of mildew-funk assaults us as we descend the creaking stairs. At the bottom, we fight our way through a maze of spider-webs to the spare room with a warped wooden door.

The room is as big as a matchbox. Inside there's a single rollaway, a nightstand, and a wooden chair with one leg shorter than the others. There's also a window with iron bars.

"Where do you want me to put this?"

My head swings back to my man at the stupid question. "On the floor. Where else?"

"All right." He tilts the carpet off his shoulders and then eases it onto the floor. "There you go."

I walk up to it and kick it until it rolls open and reveals the body within. "Maybelline, Maybelline, Maybelline." A smile stretches across my lips. "Welcome to your new home."

5

Lucifer

"This shit is fucked up," Bishop swears, pounding his fist on the back door of this banged-up Escalade. Unlike me, my brother has never had a problem showing his emotions. He's a tough soldier, but Fat Ace has been like a brother to him since we were kids. They rose up the ranks together. There was mad love and respect between them. I feel all that he's feeling and more.

"I hear you, cuz," Cutty says, tightening his grip on the steering wheel. Memphis's city light passes by in a long blur.

Normally, I'm the one that's behind the wheel, handling business and getting it done, but there ain't shit normal about tonight.

"I hate to even think about what those sick GD fucks will do with our man's body," Novell adds, shaking his head. "Fat Ace deserves better, cuz."

More tears sting my eyes, but with no rain inside the vehicle to cover them up, I fight those muthafuckas back with everything I got.

Stupid. Stupid. Stupid.

A large sob grows in my throat, but I choke on that muthafucka instead of letting it out. Now that my body has been untwisted and I'm not pinned inside that wrecked SUV, I can breathe a little better—and think clearer.

"We gotta get over there," Bishop announces. "No way we let them keep Mason's body."

Hope springs up in my chest. I reach for a gun that I no longer have at my side. "Let's do it."

Cutty lifts his head and stares at us through the rearview mirror. "Say what?"

"Nigga, I didn't stutter. Let's do this."

Cutty glances at Novell in the front passenger seat only to see cuz hang his head.

"Strap me," I tell Bishop, ignoring the incredible amount of pain ricocheting throughout my body.

He twists his face. "Hell naw. We're dropping you off at Dr. Cleveland's so he can patch you up. We'll handle this shit."

"Don't you dare treat me like a bitch."

Bishop tosses up his hands. "But, heifer—"

"Ain't no buts to this shit. I'm a muthafuckin' gangsta, nigga. All life long, baby. Now what?"

Bishop clams his jaw tight though I can see he wants to come hard at me. I can't let that shit happen—especially in front of our people. If he clowns me, my authority goes out the window. I mush the side of his head. "Fall back and play your muthafuckin' position."

Bishop glares.

"Now strap me," I order him again.

Swearing under his breath, Bishop reaches down to his pants leg and retrieves his backup.

I eyeball it and then his TEC-9. He knows what's up before my ass even has to ask. We exchange guns. "The only reason I ain't goin' upside your head right now is because we're blood."

"Are you two fuckin' crazy? We're not going to get any closer than we did last time."

"The fuck we won't," I tell him. "They would never expect our ass to hit them twice in one night."

"That whole area should be swarming with cops by now," Cutty shouts.

"Fuck them. I ain't worried about the fuckin' police," I yell back, heated.

"You need to be," Cutty shoots back. "We may have the captain in our back pocket, but that nigga don't do miracles. We need to scrap these rides and lie low."

"But—"

"But nothing," Cutty barks.

I blink. Who this muthafucka thinks he's talking to?

He adjusts his tone. "All I'm sayin' is that we need to think this shit through. Unless that nigga Python is dumb as shit, he ain't gonna be rollin' over to Shotgun Row neither. It's too hot over there right now. *If* he's got our boy—"

"There's no *if* to this shit," I snap. "I watched the nigga take Fat Ace with my own eyes."

"A'ight. A'ight," Cutty gives in. "I ain't doubting your word, ma."

"Ma?" I snatch up the TEC-9 and plant that shit to the back of his head. "Who the fuck are you callin' *ma?* Do I look like one of those fuckin' chicken heads you get slobbin' on your shit? Huh?"

Cutty throws his hands up. "Whoa. Whoa. Whoa."

"Show the proper respect, nigga."

"My bad." He flinches. "I didn't mean to step out of line, Lucifer."

Novell dives over from the passenger seat to grab the steering wheel while Cutty and I play out our drama.

After a long, tense silence, Bishop leans over.

"C'mon, Willow. He didn't mean nothin' by that shit."

"Fuck that," I growl. "Muthafucka talkin' like his ass been promoted. You think because our leader is down that you can talk to me any kind of way?" I jam the barrel harder at the back of his head. "Huh?"

"Nah. Nah." Cutty shook his head. "That's not what's up."

"You sure?"

"Hell yeah. You got your stripes. I wouldn't dare come out of pocket, cuz."

"I *used* to think that shit—but you were bumping those gums mighty hard a few seconds ago."

"I apologize, Lucifer. It's all good."

The car heats with tension while we eyeball each other through the rearview mirror. While I waver whether to pull the trigger, Bishop leans over again.

"He's a good soldier, Willow."

I grind my teeth and then lower the gun.

Cutty's shoulders slack as his hands return to the steering wheel. His ass dodged a bullet.

For the next mile, nobody says shit, but all eyes keep darting back toward me. Only Bishop has the balls to speak.

"So what do you want to do?"

It burns my ass to admit Cutty is right. Hell, I hear sirens all over the place now. "Nah. That nigga wouldn't go back to Shotgun Row. He'd be hiding out somewhere." I cut my gaze toward Bishop. "Where are some of the other places you tagged his ass?"

"Just to this one place out in West Memphis—an old warehouse that looks as if it's been converted into a crib. He was only there for a hot minute. He could be laying his head there or maybe one of his jump-offs."

"Shit. He got plenty of those stashed everywhere." I roll my eyes at that long shot.

Bishop bobs his head.

"Fuck it. Let's roll," I say.

"You got it, cuz." Cutty says, cheesing and flooring the accelerator.

I shake my head, knowing that he's tryna get back on my good side. From the corner of my eyes, I see worry lines stretch across Bishop's forehead. "What?"

He hesitates for a second.

"C'mon. Spit the shit out," I tell him, agitated.

"I ain't too sure about the lay of the land, nahwhatImean? I don't know how many niggas he got stashed over there. Could be none, could be a whole lot. Like I said, he only dipped over there for a few minutes when I tagged him."

"Fuck it. Call in backup." I pat my pockets and realize I lost my burner inside the crash. "Give me your phone."

Bishop reaches into his pocket and hands me his burner. I hit Tombstone and he picks up on the second ring.

"Holla at your boy," he answers.

"Hey, man. This is death calling. What's the damage over your way?"

"Far as I can tell we're down eight. Minimum damage. What's the head count in your neck of the woods?"

A boulder rolls into the center of my throat. I can't get into this shit about Mason with him right now. I clear my throat. "Status report due later. Right now, we gonna need some backup."

"You know I got you. Where you rollin'?"

"Hold up. Here's Bishop. He'll fill you in." I hand the phone back to Bishop. While he gives directions, I tune out and pull my shit together. Every fucking muscle, tendon, and nerve feels like they're rubbing over broken glass while my lungs threaten to collapse with each breath I take. I should go to the hospital—but I'm determined to see this shit through.

Twenty minutes later we creep down on a few row houses off Jackson Avenue in West Memphis. At first glance they ain't much to look at, but that's probably the fuckin' point. I spot a few flagless hustlers and chubby hoes squeezed into clothes three sizes too small and hugging empty corners in the rain. So far nobody makes a move or sends out a warning. No surprise, really. It's long been rumored that West Memphis gangs were disorganized with a every-nigga-for-themselves mentality.

It's a fucking disgrace.

"Which one?" Cutty asks.

"Ease up, man. It's the last crib at the end of this drive," Bishop says.

Cutty hits the lights and pulls his foot up off the accelerator until we roll to a stop against a curb.

We scope the perimeter to see if any roaches run out, but the rain has chased them all inside. *Figures.*

Novell removes his shades. "You think he's in there?"

"It looks like the perfect place for a snake to slither and hide," I say, eyeballing the peeling paint and overgrown hedges.

The boys chuckle among themselves as Tombstone rolls up behind us. Everyone checks their weapons and slaps in new magazines.

"Y'all niggas ready?" Bishops asks.

I look down at my fucked-up legs, concerned that I can't feel them. How in the hell am I going to pull off this miracle?

"Why don't we hit the back and you and Dougie stay out here in case the nigga tries to blast his way out of the front?"

Bishop is playing big brother, looking out to save me from making a fool out of myself. "Sounds like a plan," I say, grabbing hold of the lifeline.

Cutty, Novell, and Bishop climb out of the car and then huddle up with Tombstone, Dougie, and Red.

Bishop explains the situation and I can hear them cursing about the loss of the big man. My eyes feel like they're sitting in battery acid.

"Fuck yeah. Let's do this shit," Red says, pounding his chest. "It's waaaay past time we murk this nigga Python."

Tombstone throws down what is left of a cigarette. "I'm in."

Dougie strolls up to the SUV that I'm sitting in and hops

behind the wheel. The other soldiers follow Bishop to the house at the end of the drive.

I hit the power button to the back window and prop the TEC-9 up on the frame. I feel like a punk-bitch sitting up in this muthafucka. I reach up to soothe a sudden irritating tic against my temple only to be surprised about the amount of sweat beading my brow. I need a doctor.

My gaze shoots up to the rearview mirror to see Dougie watching me.

"Are you all right?" he asks.

"I'm fine," I lie. *Is that my breathing sounding so choppy?* I shift my attention back to the house, hoping that it's enough to discourage him from asking any more questions. However, the longer I sit there, the more intense the pain.

C'mon, you ugly muthafucka. Bring your ass on out here.

Unfortunately, the seconds feel like hours and the minutes feel like eternity. So far, the only thing that's happening is that the rain is picking up speed. Sweat drips into my eyes and it burns as much as the tears I'm fighting back.

Two minutes.

Three minutes.

"What the fuck is taking them so long?" I snap.

Tombstone's mountainous shoulders shrug.

Four minutes.

Five minutes.

A light clicks on in the house and I perk up, halfway expecting gunfire to clash with the rumbling sky.

Nothing happens. There's just the steady pounding of the rain on the roof.

Six minutes.

Seven minutes.

I'm pissed now and can barely sit still. The house lights click off and at long last our people creep back out the way they came. Instead of five people racing back, there's six. The addition is a small boy who looked no more than seven or eight.

"Now who do we have here?" Dougie says.

"I don't know."

"Nah. I'm talkin' about at six o'clock." I frown and jerk my head toward the back of the car. I know that '77 black Monte Carlo anywhere. "Python." I open the back door but spill out onto the concrete. Despite the pain exploding inside me, I'm able to roll over and aim the TEC-9.

RAT-A-TAT-TAT-TAT!

Windows explode on the Monte Carlo as Python swings his big-ass car around while simultaneously sending a burst of fire our way.

POW! POW! POW!

My people join in on the fight and the whole street lights up.

RAT-A-TAT-TAT-TAT!

POW! POW! POW!

Python guns the accelerator.

"Get him," I shout at Dougie. "GO! GO! GO!"

On command, Dougie shifts into drive and peels off from the curb. It's one time I don't mind having to eat exhaust fumes.

"Oh, fuck," Bishop swears.

I turn and see Red pulling himself off the ground and Bishop, Novell, and Tombstone kneeling over the little boy. "Just grab him and c'mon." We still had the other SUV. But then my gaze sweeps over the little boy's face. "Christopher?"

6

LeShelle

The wail of the ambulance ricochets through my brain and then rattles the back of my teeth. I've known pain in my lifetime, but nothing like this. This shit is on a whole other level. It's both intense and . . . *orgasmic*. It's sick, I know, but it's the way I'm wired. I've been through so much fucked up shit in my life that I've learned a long time ago how to turn pain into pleasure.

"Hang in there, Miss. We're almost at the hospital," a bulky paramedic tells me, leaning over the gurney. "Blink if you understand me," he says.

I close my eyes but then struggle to open them again.

"That's a good girl. Hang in there." The man winks and then disappears from my line of vision.

I find a spot on the ceiling of the ambulance and concentrate all my anger and rage on it. If Ta'Shara thinks that she got the best of me then she has another thing coming. Blood be damned—this shit is war now. That bitch has only had a small taste of what the fuck I can do.

I clench my jaw and struggle to breathe into the mask strapped across my face. I've done everything and given everything to protect Ta'Shara.

It was my name that shielded Ta'Shara in the streets and

that fucked up school she goes to, but did she appreciate that shit? Fuck no. She hooks up with a Vice Lord—and not just any VL soldier, but the head nigga, Fat Ace's younger brother. What the fuck was she thinking? Where was the fucking respect?

I warned her ass once, but she played me stupid by taking that nigga, Profit, to the prom. So I treated her like any other bitch that crossed me. Had to. Python was looking at me sideways and dangled what I've always wanted in front of me: to take me from wifey to wife. Why the fuck should I jeopardize my position for Ta'Shara? She made it clear that she didn't give a fuck about me. It's every bitch for themselves out here.

Yeah so, I ordered her to be sexed into the Queen Gs and I had her ass branded so that she would never forget who owned her ass. To make sure that she never strayed again, I dumped a full clip into her man. But the nigga took those bullets like a soldier and was still standing after my last round slammed into him. Just when I thought I was staring at some ghetto Superman, his knees finally buckled and he hit the ground.

Problem solved.

Until the muthafucka rose from the dead. I still don't understand how the fuck he survived that night. With him laid up in the hospital and Ta'Shara's ass lost in space at the mental hospital, I thought my problems were solved. It wasn't my goal to put her up in there, but it got her out of my hair while the war on the streets between GD and VL heated up.

For months I've avoided rollin' by to check on her ass. What for? I was told that the bitch had mentally checked out. But then I got my ring. Python is gonna come through on his promise and give me his last name. I couldn't help it, but I wanted to rub it in Ta'Shara's face that I didn't need her anymore. Python and I are going to start our own family.

Fuck her.

My eyes burn as hot tears slide down my face. Instinctively,

I want to wipe them away, but my arms feel as if they weigh a ton. What the fuck? Queen Gs don't cry.

I try to blink the tears away and man up, but my eyes aren't cooperating and the tears start flowing faster.

"Her pulse is dropping," a voice says around me.

I hear the words, but I don't understand them. It feels like I'm struggling to stay in my own body.

"Don't worry. We're here," the voice tells me.

My lashes flutter, but my eyes barely open. Feet shuffle around me and then the ambulance door bangs open. Next, my gurney bounces and wobbles around as they roll and then lift me out.

"You're going to make it," the voice keeps promising. "We're going to take care of you and fix you like new."

I cling to that promise as strong as I do to my vow of revenge.

7

Qiana

I don't know what it is about murder that gives you the best sleep of your life. But it's true. Murder is the best high dollar for dollar, pound for pound—period. Like a sugar high, the crash is like taking a bottle of sleeping pills. This morning, I'm forced out of the serene bliss by a long, growing wail of a crying baby. Irritated, I squeeze my eyes shut and bury my head beneath a stack of pillows. But the cries won't go away. If anything, they get louder. What the fuck? Somebody shut that kid up. On and on it goes until my nerves are grated thin and I bolt up in bed, ready to take someone's head off. That's when it hits me that the cries are coming from inside my room.

Bang! Bang! Bang!

My closed door rattles.

"Hey! Keep it down in there! Niggas are tryna sleep," my father, Nookie, barks through the door. A second later, I hear the electronic hum of his wheelchair as he drives away. No doubt he's on his way back to his room where his latest and greatest Social-Security-check-diggin' girlfriend is waiting for him to eat her ass out. It's the only thing he can do since his dick works as good as his legs. His ass got caught slipping ten years back fuckin' with a sideline bitch. Her nigga rolled through unexpectedly, caught them in bed together and sprayed Daddy as he tried to dive out of the window. He survived, but his ass is still addicted to pussy.

WHAAAAH! WHAAAH!

Groaning, I glance at the dresser where the baby is nestled in the top drawer in a makeshift baby bed. As the screams grow louder I contemplate closing the muthafucka.

My door rattles again. "Goddamn! What the hell is going on in there?" My older brother, Charlie a.k.a. Tombstone, rattles my shit. "What the fuck? You got a kid in there?"

"Mind your own muthafuckin' business."

"Who in the fuck would trust you with a kid?"

"Your baby mommas!"

My door bursts open and Charlie strolls his big ass through my door. "Hey!"

"Hey nothing! Your ass ain't got nothing I want to see." He marches over to the wailing baby. "What in the hell?" He leans over. "Who's this lil nigga?"

"None of your business, Charlie. Get out of here." I jump out of bed and shove him away. I'm not in the mood to take any of his bullshit. "My room is off-limits." I push and shove, but he doesn't move.

"Why the fuck do you have him in the drawer?"

"Because I don't have anywhere else to put him."

He frowns. "What the fuck is wrong with the bed?"

"Get the fuck out of my room," I bark.

Charlie tosses up his hands. "Fine. Don't get your panties twisted. I'm leaving." He wrinkles his nose. "You might want to change that muthafucka's diaper, though. Lil nigga is foul as hell."

"And what's your excuse? You're sour as fuck, too."

"I was out puttin' in work all night. Real work. Something your ass don't know shit about."

If only you knew. I grab his huge muscled arm and drag him away from the screaming baby. Truth be known, its high-pitch wailing is working a number on my nerves, but I can deal with that shit.

"Is he sick?" Charlie asks.

"Why? Are you a doctor?"

"If I was I'd fix your face," he says chuckling.

The jab hurts. A year ago I was the dime piece of Ruby Cove. Sexy frame and a beautiful face, niggas lined up outside my door and blazed up my phone 24/7, but the only nigga that caught my eye was Profit. Since the day his ass arrived from Atlanta, I'd been counting down until I branded his fine ass as mine. Shit. I believed that it was just a matter of time before his ass ascended the throne and I wanted to be the Flower on his arm.

Sure there were a lot of Flowers jockeying for the position, but I wasn't sweating that shit. I knew Profit would want a real dime instead of a knockoff. I dreamed about carrying his seeds and playing wifey with his fine ass—then fate dealt me a harsh hand, and Ta'Shara turned my future baby daddy's head. I don't get it. She ain't all that cute and she ain't as smart as she thinks she is or she would have known better than to cross the color lines. Regardless, I still didn't think the shit would get serious. Ta'Shara was GD by blood. At most, I hoped Profit would splash off on the chicken head and then move on.

That shit didn't happen.

Ta'Shara had Profit's nose so wide open that if he walked outside on a rainy night his ass would drown. I couldn't have that shit. Bitches in my own crew clowned and gave me grief because I had bragged about locking his ass down—so I stepped to Ta'Shara, told her to back down. She and her pip-squeak friend, Essence, bucked—so the next time there wasn't no fucking talking. I came hard at the bitch, figuring that shit would settle it, but I got the surprise of my life. Ta'Shara's blade game ain't no joke. I didn't expect that shit from a straight-A bougie bitch. Hell, I didn't even see her ass spit that razor out, but I sure as hell felt it when it split my cheeks wide open, fucking up my mug shot. Now I'll never win Profit's heart.

Lesson: *any* bitch can be a gangsta nowadays.

Charlie stops at the door and glances back again.

"All right. I'll change him," I say in order to get him on the other side of the door so I can shut it in his face.

He nods, but doesn't move.

"Charl—"

"Look. There's no other or better way to tell you this," he says, cutting me off. "Fat Ace fell off the throne last night."

"WHAT?" I shout above the baby's wail. There's no way that I heard him right.

His head drops. "We thought we had a solid lead on Python's whereabouts last night, but shit got messy and now most of the city looks like a fuckin' war zone. Seriously, today is not the day to be flagging colors. We're expecting some heavy artillery for payback."

"But how . . . where—?"

"Short version, there was a car chase and our nigga lost control of the wheel and . . ." Charlie shakes his head. "Lucifer is banged up pretty bad, too. Dougie gave chase, but ain't nobody heard back from him. It ain't looking too good."

"Damn." I absorb it all in and have to say it again. "Damn."

The news plus this hollering baby got me shook. Fat Ace—*gone?* That shit can't be possible. For as far back as I can remember our leader has been larger than life. He has survived more bullets than most could keep count.

Dead?

"It gets worse. That muthafucka also took Fat Ace's body."

I'm confused. "What muthafucka?"

"Python."

"Get the fuck out of here!" I *know* I heard that shit wrong. "He *took* the body? What the fuck for?"

"Who knows what's in that sick nigga's head? He thinks he's a fuckin' snake for Christ's sake. He's liable to do anything."

The possibilities are endless. "Fuck."

"Tell me about it."

For a moment, our usual sibling bickering is put on the back burner as we stare at the floor, reflecting on Fat Ace. He kept the Peoples Nation a unit after his father Smokestack got shipped off to the Big House. He'd been a great leader: hard, ruthless, but also loyal and fair. Niggas respected his gangsta and he was the main reason our people didn't disintegrate to a bunch of reckless muthafuckas in for self like so many gangs around Memphis.

"So . . . who steps up?" I ask.

"By all rights Lucifer . . . but . . ."

"Niggas bucking," I fill in for him.

"I ain't saying that her gangsta ain't tight. She has stepped up plenty of times when Fat Ace was on the mend or out of town on business—but it's a whole 'nother thing for niggas to accept her as a supreme chief. If you ask me, the throne should go to Bishop. Fat Ace put just as much trust in him as Lucifer."

"Plus he has a dick." I shake my head. "That's some fucked up shit." I feel sorry for Lucifer. She has more balls than any nigga I know but, in the end, it's not enough. "What about Profit?"

Charlie shakes his head. "Ain't ready. Man got heart, he'd done proved that shit going toe to toe with me and then takin' that full clip to the chest, but he's still a rookie who ain't put in no work."

"Lucifer ain't gonna step off that throne without a fight," I say. "A bitch don't need a crystal ball to see that shit."

Charlie nods. "I think that's what everyone is afraid of—but that's gonna be Bishop's fight."

"Fam against fam. It ain't right."

"It be that way sometimes," he reminds me. "Anyway, me and Red are heading out to the hospital to pick up Profit. Bishop wants our people close, you feel me?"

"Profit is coming home?" I ask.

Charlie's lips spread wide at my eagerness. "Figured that shit would cheer you up."

"Nah. Nah. I was just asking." I shrug, tryna play it off.

"Uh-huh. There's something else, too," he adds.

I eyeball him. "Good news or bad?"

"Bad. We found Cousin Skeet's grandson, Christopher."

"Goddamn, y'all really were busy last night."

Charlie bobs his head. "Problem is we found him alive, but he took a bullet during a battle. I think he's going to be all right."

"What?"

"Nigga Python showed up and the kid got caught up in the middle."

"Fuuuuuuck. You know Skeet is gonna go on a warpath over that shit."

"Long as it's directed at those GD roaches, I don't give a shit."

Charlie walks back over to the baby. "Hey, lil man. What are you fussin' about, huh?" He grins and then tweaks the baby's nose.

To my shock and surprise, the volume of the baby's cries dials down.

"I gotta tell you," Charlie whispers. "If I had my sister for a babysitter, I'd be hollering, too." He glances around. "Where are the diapers?"

Hell, if he wants to change him, I ain't gonna stop him. "By the closet," I tell him, nodding toward the grocery store bags I picked up coming home last night.

Charlie snatches up the bags and then spots the pile of bloody clothes I took off last night. "What the fuck?"

I rush over to kick them out of the way, but it's too late.

He picks up my blood-soaked shirt and then stabs me with a hard look. "What the fuck were you doing last night?" His gaze slices back over to the drawer. "And whose baby is that?"

8

Lucifer

Drugs are a wonderful thing.

Back at my crib, I don't know what the fuck Dr. Cleveland gave me, but it has my ass high as hell. The best part is that I don't feel a thing. Not a damn thing. Frankly, that's exactly how I like it. Now if he just had something in his magic bag that would help me forget. It feels like I've been propped up in the bed forever, the memory of that car accident playing over and over in my head.

"How she doin', doc?" Bishop's gravelly voice floats above me.

"Remarkably well." The doc sighs. "She's a lucky girl."

"Humph. Better hope that she doesn't hear you calling her that."

"Lucky?"

"No—a girl."

I attempt to push up a smile at my brother's bad joke, but can't. I doubt if I'll ever be able to smile again.

"A broken leg, a broken arm, and a couple of cracked ribs . . ." The doctor sighs. ". . . but she'll live." He snaps his bag closed.

"Good deal." Relief floods Bishop's voice.

"As for you," the doctor adds. "You look like hell. When was the last time you slept?"

"Sleep is not an option right now."

"I can give you a sleeping aid if you're having trouble."

"Nah. That legal shit is worse than what we sling on the streets. I'm a'ight."

"You may be right about that." Cleveland chuckles. "But uh—"

"Yeah. Yeah. My man Tyrese got that brick for you in the other room," Bishop tells him. "You know we're always gonna hook you up."

The doctor laughs as he drifts toward the door. "It's good doin' business with you."

"Same here." Bishop follows, slapping a hand across Cleveland's back for a job well done. "I'll be in touch." He ushers him out and then shuts the door.

"All right. You can stop pretending that you're asleep," he tells me, reaching inside his jacket and removing a pre-rolled blunt and lighting up.

"How did you know?" I ask, opening my eyes.

"'Cuz nobody knows you better than I do." He draws in a deep drag and then holds the shit in his lungs.

With Mason gone, he's right. I drop my gaze.

Bishop releases his toke and shakes his head. "Yo, man. All this shit feels fuckin' surreal. Big man gone . . . I just . . . fuck!" He runs a hand through his low-shaved head. "It ain't supposed to be like this."

"It is what it is," I say, tryna hide behind a brave face.

"Don't do that shit," Bishop warns. "Not now. Not about our boy."

My gaze cuts back up at him. "Let me guess. You rather we sit around in this muthafucka and throw ourselves a pity party while Python and his roaches are out there preparing Armageddon. C'mon, Juvon. We ain't got time for tears."

Bishop's gaze rakes me. I probably look a sight with two casts and my chest wrapped like a fuckin' mummy.

"You're cold, Willow. Always have been." He takes another long drag.

"I'ma gangsta bitch."

"So you keep reminding me," he says, looking disappointed. "I thought that after you and Mason hooked up—"

"Don't." I want to shut this shit down now. "My business is my business. I thought that was something you understood a long time ago."

"What the hell is that supposed to mean?"

"Mason told me about your cock-blockin'."

"Sheeeeiiit." Bishop exhales another long stream of smoke. "You're going to blame all that shit on me? Hell, I tried to stop your ass from doing a whole lot of shit. I don't recall none of that stopping you from doing whatever fucked up shit that crosses your mind. Don't put that bullshit on me."

"Whatever."

"Yeah. Whatever." He takes a couple of more tokes. "Since you want to discuss business, I sent Tombstone and Red to the hospital to pick up Profit. We need everybody close to home. NahwhatImean?"

"What—you're giving out orders now?" I force myself to sit up in the bed, grateful that the drugs continue to dull my pain.

Bishop tosses up his hands. "Here we go."

"What? I'm just asking a question."

"No. You're ego trippin'. Ain't nobody tryna cross your toes. You weren't up to making decisions at the time and the shit needed to be done. End of story."

I stare him down.

"What?"

I shake my head. "You forget. Just like you claim to know me, I know you." That shuts him up while we engage in another staring contest.

KNOCK. KNOCK.

"Come in," I bark.

Red opens the door and pokes his head inside. "Yo, man. We're back."

"You got Profit with you?"

Red nods.

Despite my gangster act, my heart drops clear down to my knees. Am I ready to deal with this emotional shit with Mason's little brother? *No.*

"Bring him in," Bishop says.

I cut him another look.

"If that's all right with you," he adds.

"We'll continue this conversation later," I promise Bishop and then shift my attention back to Red who was waiting for *my* say-so. "Bring him in."

Red disappears behind the door and then, a second later, he rolls Profit and his wheelchair into the room.

The tension in the room vanishes and is replaced with a sad awkwardness. I have a hard time meeting Profit's large, caramel-brown eyes, but when I do, I see that he already heard the news.

"Bishop, give us a few minutes."

Instead of moving, my brother twists up his face.

This shit is confirmation that my ass ain't paranoid. Bishop is calculating how he's going to make a play for the throne. Fuck. I can hear the wheels squeaking in his head. "Are you waiting for me to ask you again?"

Clamping his jaw tight, Bishop shuffles toward the door but stops for a few seconds to squeeze one of Profit's large shoulders in solidarity.

My brows stretch while I wonder whether he has a hearing problem.

"I'll be outside," he says, and then takes his time strolling toward the door.

I nearly gnaw my tongue off waiting for my brother to complete his long walk out of the room. When the door closes behind him, my gaze shifts to Profit. It's been a minute since

I've seen him. The last time, he was laid up in the hospital after surviving sixteen rounds. He and Mason had that Superman shit down pat.

"You look like hell," Profit croaks, looking me over.

"You're one to talk," I tell him, since it looks like he's lost thirty pounds on what was already a lean six-three frame. It's easy to see why he's turned all the Flowers' heads. He's a pretty boy, complete with a butterscotch complexion, silky-wavy hair, and dimples.

He looks nothing like Mason.

Most know that the two weren't really brothers, since the junkie who'd raised them was as white as the fresh driven snow and Mason was one shade lighter than crude oil. But the two were raised together and that made them brothers—and the love between them was stronger than blood.

During my own investigation, I'd learned Mason's real mother was an even worse junkie who'd put Mason in an oven when he was a baby. Her dealer, Cousin Smokestack, found him there and took him away from her while she was wasted on the couch. He and his girlfriend, Dribbles, laid claim and raised him as their own. But I have strong reason to believe that Mason's *real* father is Smokestack's brother, Cousin Skeet, who is none other than the Captain of the Memphis Police Department. That big secret complicates shit because it means that prior to falling into my bed, Mason had been fucking his own sister. I hope I'm wrong about that shit.

"I want Python dead," Profit says.

I nod. "He's a dead man walking and don't even know it. Trust and believe."

"Y'all keep talking that fat shit and nothing ever fuckin' happens," Profit snaps back.

"Look, Profit—"

"Nah. You look. Y'all been gunning for this nigga for years and every fuckin' time, he slithers away. We look like a joke to that pussy muthafucka! Hell. Him and his bitch has come at me TWICE and they're still walking the streets. Now they done stole my brother's body and you want to spit more promises," he roars. "I ain't tryna hear that shit. I want him— NOW. Don't tell me what the fuck you're gonna do, do the shit."

The more he barks, the more heated I get. "Check your tone," I warn.

"How about you go fuck yourself?" he charges back, and then wheels his chair around with his long arms.

"Profit . . ."

He ignores me and snatches open the door.

"Profit, we need to finish talking."

"I'm finished talking," he growls. "Since y'all muthafuckas can't do shit, I'll handle this nigga myself." He rolls out of the door.

"That went well," I mumble under my breath.

Tyrese knocks on the open door and rushes in before I answer. "Yo, man. You need to check this shit out." He rushes to the television set in the corner and turns it on to the news.

"What's going on?" Bishop asks, returning to the room.

Seeking to calm the citizens of Memphis rattled by a wave of crime last night, Mayor Wharton and his new police chief, Yvette Brown, ramped up the tough talk saying that they are going to flood the streets with police during a full-court press to combat crime.

The city's leaders gathered at City Hall in the wake of a violent and chaotic twenty-four-hour period in which an unprecedented fifty-two people were killed by gunfire.

"We want to make it clear that we are taking to the streets. We are going after these criminals with an intensity that has not been seen in some time. This violence will not be tolerated."

The footage on the screen switches to a nighttime recording of a car chase on the old Memphis–Arkansas Bridge.

Caught on camera is a car chase turned deadly. One of the vehicles seen here is believed to belong to FBI-wanted felon, Terrell Carver. He is most recently wanted in connection with the shooting death of police officer Melanie Johnson and the kidnapping of her son, Christopher. The son was found last night in West Memphis through an anonymous tip.

I block out the rest of what the reporter is saying and stare in shock at the shaky footage. Python's Monte Carlo is being chased by Dougie's SUV. Sparks of gunfire are even seen on the tape. They both zoom over the bridge when suddenly Dougie clips the tail, spinning Python around. Then footage gets confusing and there's a lot of flipping. A third car is hit, and then an explosion and all three cars tumble off the bridge into the Mississippi River below.

"Oh. Fuck!" *Mason.*

"Holy shit!" Bishop says from behind me.

"Turn it off," I order, feeling myself getting sick.

Tyrese shuts it off and then we all stare at each other.

Mason and now Dougie.

"Get out."

Tyrese and Bishop stare at me.

"I *said* GET THE FUCK OUT!" I grab the water pitcher next to the bed with my good arm and throw it at them.

They duck and then scramble out, closing the door behind them. A second later, a tear skips down my face.

9

Alice

"Yes! Yes! Fuck me, you nasty muthafucka. Oh, fuuuuck meeeeee!" My eyes roll around in my head. This nigga's dick got my pussy creaming. The last thing my old ass needs is a young buck that wants to lay up in some pussy all day, but after this muthafucka proved his ass wasn't all talk and helped me with the job last night, I'm going to feed his ass all the pussy he can handle.

"Aw. Sheeeiiit, baby. I'm comin'," he announces, rotating his hips.

My pussy squirts while I start talking in tongues—which tickles me because I've never been inside nobody's church.

"You love this dick, baby? Hmmm?"

"You know it." I throw everything I got back at him. I watch as his handsome face twists in ecstasy. A second later, he pulls out his glazed dick and candy-coats my pink pussy.

Afterwards, he crawls down the bed and laps all that good shit up. Turns out, the nigga's dick action ain't got shit on his head game. *Oh. My. God.* "Oooh, sheeeiiit." I cream and squirt. But my new man gobbles it up until we get stuck on an endless cycle. Exhausted, I beg him to stop so I can catch my breath.

At long last, he takes pity on me and climbs back up my body.

"Kiss me," he orders, and then shares our essence with me. I ain't gonna lie. We're sweet as hell.

After a nap and a shower, I make my way to the living room to see if there's anything on television about the job we pulled last night. I click the TV on and a blast from the past, Captain Melvin Johnson, fills the screen with a reporter trying to shove a microphone under his mouth. How this crooked muthafucka still got a job is beyond me. It's no secret that he's a stick-up nigga with a badge and a VL through and through. He gets his people the best shit because he robs all the good connects.

Supercop my ass.

Caught on camera is a car chase turned deadly. One of the vehicles seen here is believed to belong to FBI-wanted felon, Terrell Carver. He is most recently wanted in connection with the shooting death of police officer Melanie Johnson and the kidnapping of her son, Christopher. The son was found last night in West Memphis through an anonymous tip. He suffered a bullet to the shoulder and is expected to pull through.

"What the fuck?"

The cameras cut to the image of an older black woman sitting out on her porch with a head full of hair rollers.

"Everybody knows the truth of what's goin' on out here—and it's time somebody put a stop to it. People can't even step out of their front door no more in fear of these kids out here shootin' all the time. I'm sick of it. We got buildings blowing up, car chases and bullets flying into people's house. Somebody got to do somethin' about this." She shakes her head as her mouth curls in disgust. *"You can't tell me we ain't living in the last days. People have just gone damn crazy."*

The camera returns to the news reporter and Captain Johnson's picture is replaced with a face I know very well. My son, Terrell. I turn up the volume.

We have yet to confirm that Terrell Carver is the driver of this '77

Monte Carlo. The Federal Bureau of Investigation remains on a city-wide manhunt for him. If you have information about Mr. Carver's whereabouts, please call . . .

I shut off the television and try to make sense of what I'd just heard. Now don't get me wrong, I ain't one of those clueless mommas who think her baby is some kind of angel—but kidnapping and shooting some little boy? What the fuck did Maybelline teach his ass? I block out my own failings as a mother to my other little boy, Mason. They say I sold him for a few rocks, but I don't buy that. I would never be that fucked up to do something like that. Never. Maybelline was behind that shit, I know it. Her trifling ass couldn't stand the fact that I could have babies and she couldn't. That's why all her niggas found their way to my bed.

I shut off the television and try to digest the news, but it's all too much. I got questions—a lot of questions, but after escaping the crazy house, I can't just stroll my ass into a police station for a one-on-one with Melvin's crooked ass.

"The FBI," my boo says, coming up behind me and shaking his head. "I hate to say it, but Python is always in the middle of some shit."

I give him the shut-the-fuck-up look.

"What?" He shrugs. "What did I say?"

"That's my baby you're talking about." I mean-mug his ass and mush his face. "Have some fuckin' respect." Just because this nigga can throw some good dick around don't mean that he can talk out the side of his neck.

He smirks but tosses up his hands. "A'ight. Whatever."

I catch an attitude. "What are you trying to say?"

"I didn't say shit. I just came out here to see what you were cooking for breakfast."

"Cooking?" I look him up and down. "Is there something wrong with your hands? I don't fuck *and* feed niggas. If you're hungry then go and fix you something to eat."

He stares at me like I'd slapped the shit out of him. When

he sees that my shit is for real, he backs up. "Damn. It's like that?"

My expression doesn't change. What the fuck do I look like?

Shaking his head, he turns and walks away, but not without adding, "That shit's foul. You could at least make a nigga a sandwich . . . or some flapjacks."

Flapjacks? "What the fuck did you just say?"

He keeps marching toward the kitchen.

"Nigga, you hear me." I rush after him into the kitchen and get in his face. "WHAT THE FUCK DID YOU JUST SAY?" Boo stares at me, looking stupid. "All right then, roll your mute ass up out of here."

"What?"

"Oh, now your ass can speak?" I rock my head and then jab a finger in the center of his chest. "Then tell me this: how the fuck do you know Maybelline?"

He blinks.

"And think *real* hard before you spit out a lie. My ass ain't stupid."

He blinks faster.

"You've fucked her," I answer for him.

"What?" He tries to laugh the shit off. "Don't be ridiculous."

"Maybelline fixes flapjacks for niggas after she finishes fuckin' them. Now here you are, asking me for *flapjacks?*"

"All right. All right. My bad. I didn't mean to upset you."

I stare him down.

"A'ight," he gives in. "Peaches and I had a little thing a while back—and then she dumped me for that nigga we murked last night at her crib. Bet they asses ain't laughing now. Payback is a bitch."

I don't fuckin' believe what the fuck I'm hearing.

"What's the big deal? The shit is over with." He steps closer and pinches my titties. "I'm with you now."

"So you left my sister's bed to crawl up in mine?" *Fuckin'
story of my life.*

"Well, it wasn't exactly like that."

"Uh, huh. And now you want me to fix you flapjacks like
Maybelline used to do for you," I shoot back to make sure I
got the shit straight. "Were you comparing me to her when
you were eating my pussy, too?" I reach over to the ten-slot
butcher block and whip out the biggest knife. "Go ahead and
lie. I dare your ass."

"Whoa. Whoa." He backs up.

"Don't fuckin' 'whoa' me, *Arzell.* Go ahead and speak your
mind. You done already told me that I was a lousy muthafickin'
parent a few minutes ago. What else do you got to say? I want
to fuckin' hear it."

"I didn't say no such a thing." His face twists harder as he
backs up.

"Oh. So I'm fuckin' crazy now? I'm just hearing shit, is
that it? Is that what you're saying?" I feel the muscles in my
face twitching.

Arzell eyeballs the knife in my hand and I read in his face
that he's going to make a move for it a full second before he
launches.

Big fuckin' mistake. I wield a blade second to none. He
moves and in the next second, the butcher knife is sticking out
the center of his chest. He looks at me all shocked and shit.

"Tell the devil to fix your ass some flapjacks."

10

Ta'Shara

"**P**lease, let me go. She's not dead yet. She's not dead," I warn, tossing and jerking against my restraints. In fact, I can't stop moving. The muscles in my body feel as if they are wired to a battery completely separate from my mind. After a night of this, I'm exhausted.

Every once in a while I manage to close my eyes. In those few precious seconds my soul would float above my body and I could see the sweaty mess that I was: jabbering nonsense and practically foaming at the mouth.

I could even see outside the door where Tracee wept in the nook of her husband's arms while he hugged her tight and whispered words of comfort. I bet that he really regrets ever bringing me and LeShelle into their lives.

I don't blame him.

Once LeShelle tried to prove to me that Reggie was just another closeted pedophile and set out to seduce him. That shit backfired and she ran away before the Douglases had the chance to send her back to Children's Services. She wanted me to leave with her, but the Douglases had been good to me. I wanted to believe their bullshit about how I could be anything I set my mind to.

It was the first time I chose someone over LeShelle.

Profit had been the second time—and apparently the last time.

The medical staff recanted their versions of what had happened to the police. None of them understood a damn thing. And every time I try to explain it to them, my words get jumbled up. It's all the damn drugs they've pumped into me.

"Please, please," I sob. *"I have to kill her."* Those are the words I'm trying to say, but I mentally know that's not matching the gibberish flowing out my mouth. I have to keep trying to warn them. LeShelle isn't going to go away. She's evil. Pure and simple. I didn't understand that before, but I do now. Just like I understand that I have to be the one to bring her down.

I have no choice.

I am twitching and sweating like a junkie, and my brain is begging for sleep. Maybe after I get some sleep I'll be able to get my mouth to work and explain everything to these dumb people.

"Please. Please. If I don't kill her, she's going to kill me. Why don't you people understand that?"

The door to my room bursts open and three men in long white coats stroll in with their noses high in the air. Maybe they have been able to understand me after all and they're coming to set me free. Another voice inside my head cackles at that thought. Nothing about these dudes reads understanding, freedom, or compassion.

If anything, they are as dangerous to me as LeShelle.

"Get away from me," I warn, but again the words tumbling out of my mouth don't match those that are in my head.

"Calm down, Ms. Murphy," the one white doctor with pale blue eyes says. "No one here is going to hurt you."

"Bullshit!"

He jumps back as if I tried to bite him. Wait. Maybe I did. Fuck it. It serves his ass right. I don't want to be up in this bitch anyway.

The good doctor's face flushes with embarrassment as he

shares an awkward laugh with his white-coat friends. "All right. All right. Let's take it down a notch," he says, trying again. This time, when his hands come toward me, I jerk my face away.

"A little help here," he barks at his sidekicks.

The next thing I know, multiple hands come at me. I bite at a couple of them, but in the end, they manage to hold my head straight while Mr. Blue Eyes flashes light into my eyes. The shit triggers a memory of LeShelle's gun flashing. . . .

"NOOOOOOOOOOOOOOOOOOOOO!"

Profit jumped and wiggled around as bullet after bullet slammed into him. His face was filled with rage as he glared at LeShelle. If he could have reached her, he would have torn her apart limb by limb with his bare hands. At long last, there was an audible click when the evil bitch ran out of bullets. However, to everyone's disbelief, Profit re-mained standing— but barely.

"What the fuck?" one nigga marveled.

The shit spooked the small crowd as they stared open-mouthed at Profit. Hope blossomed in my chest, but then died when Profit wob-bled on his weakening legs. Blood streamed from his mouth.

"Profit." I took advantage of my shocked captors and scrambled out of their grasp. But by that time, my man dropped to his knees like a stone and his eyes slowly rolled toward mine.

The doctor removes the light from my eyes and the mem-ory fades, but not before fresh tears roll from my eyes.

"Let's get her one more shot of Cogentin," Dr. Blue Eyes says, pulling out a syringe from nowhere. The size of the nee-dle gets my ass twitching even harder.

The door bursts open again and Tracee rushes in looking like I felt. "What the fuck are you doin'?"

Even in my state of mind, I am shocked to hear her use such language.

"Mrs. Douglas, we're going to have to ask you step out of the room."

"No! You told me that you wouldn't give her any more drugs," she shouts.

"This is for her own good," he says, leveling her with a look of superiority.

"No!" Tracee wedges herself between him and the bed. "No more drugs! REGGIE!"

Reggie walks into the room. His expression reads that he'd rather not be dragged into a dispute between the doctor and his wife.

"Reggie, tell him to put that damn thing away. They will not continue to dope her up."

The doctors shift their attention to Reggie.

He hesitates.

Tracee's confidence fades. "*Honey,* tell them!"

After another beat of silence, her face collapses into disbelief. "*Reggie?*" Her voice is edged with a final warning.

Reggie licks his lips and slides his hands into his pants pockets. "Tracee, baby. Maybe the doctors know what's best for her."

"What?"

His lip-licking becomes a nervous tic. "All I'm saying, *baby,* is that . . . she isn't herself right now."

"No shit, Sherlock," she snaps back. "That's because they're pumping her full of God knows what."

"Tracee, she tried to kill her own sister. God knows what else she's capable of. She's dangerous right now. It could have been you instead of LeShelle. Have you thought about that?" he asks, thinking he's found the right argument. "It could've been you lying in the hospital on life support."

She looks at him as if she doesn't recognize him. "Ta'Shara would have *never* attacked me."

Reggie steps forward. "You don't know that."

"Yes, I do!"

"Mrs. Douglas," Dr. Blue Eyes tries again. "We really are trying to give her the best care." He pats her on the shoulder, but she knocks his hand away.

"Don't touch me," she barks. "And you're not giving my *daughter* any more fucking drugs. Do you hear me?" She cuts her narrowed gaze toward her husband.

The doctor glances at Reggie for help.

"Don't look at him. *I'm* speaking. No drugs. DO I MAKE MYSELF CLEAR?"

Lying here and listening to this exchange, I feel my heart swell with both pride and love. She called me *her daughter*. Watching her fight so hard for me causes more tears to speed down my face.

"No more drugs," Reggie agrees. No doubt he finally realizes his marriage depends on him backing his wife's position.

Tracee's shoulders droop with relief, but her upturned chin swivels toward the doctors.

Sighing, Dr. Blue Eyes caps his syringe and then gives her a disappointed glower. "As you wish." He glances at his companions and signals for them to follow him back out of the room.

When the three of us are left alone, Tracee tears into Reggie. "Thanks for having my back, *honey.*"

At least he has the decency to look contrite. "C'mon, baby—"

"Don't fuckin' 'baby' me," she snaps, giving him her back to stare down at me.

I wish I could smile instead of twitch my appreciation for what she's done. When she reaches to brush my sweat-drenched hair away from my face, I do manage not to bite her hand off.

"It's going to be all right," Tracee tells me with a smile. "No one is going to hurt you as long as I'm around."

I believe her.

Behind her, Reggie huffs out a frustrated breath, which

pulls Tracee's attention back to him. "And *you*. I've never been more disappointed in all my life."

"Baby—"

Tracee shoves him back. "I swear to God if you call me baby one more time, I'm going to scream." She cocks her head. "Then again, maybe you'd like that."

"What?"

"Yeah. Then maybe you'll have them rush in here and restrain me and pump *me* full of drugs so you won't have to deal with me, either."

"Okay. Now you're talking crazy."

"See? There you go. I'm crazy." She twirls her fingers around the side of her head.

Reggie doesn't have a response to that—or maybe he is too scared to say what he's really thinking.

"Let me ask you, Reggie. Do you think that children are disposable?"

His face twists in outrage. "That's cr—" He clears his throat. "Of course not."

"Then why are you acting like we should run away from Ta'Shara because she's having problems right now?"

"I never *said* that. I just said that maybe the doctors know what's best for her right now. I'm not a doctor. Are you a doctor?"

"Doctors don't know every fuckin' thing."

"No. But they may know more about how to deal with someone suddenly coming out of a damn near comatose state to try and kill someone."

"Yeah. Someone who probably has something to do with her even being here."

"Oh, please." Reggie tosses up his hands. "We don't know that. It's more likely it has something to do with that Raymond kid that took her to prom. You've seen the news. His brother is some big-time gangbanger and he's likely one as well. That would explain what really happened at that shoot-out at the hospital last year. Face it. He's every bit the gangster his brother is . . . and I let you talk me into letting him take Ta'Shara to the prom." He's on a roll and starts pacing.

"So now this is all *my* fault?"

He doesn't answer.

"Ohmigod,"Tracee exclaims, flabbergasted.

"I didn't say that it's your fault," Reggie relents.

"You're definitely insinuating it."

"No. No. I'm just saying that . . . we're waaaay over our heads in this situation. Suddenly it's like we're surrounded by gangsters. First the hospital shoot-out, then Ta'Shara is raped, and then her best friend is blown up at a gas station and now this shit? We're waaaay over our heads and I resent your standing there holier than thou and casting judgment on me. Have you given one thought to what we're going to do when we take her home? That Raymond kid has been calling ever since he came out of his coma. You have any idea how we're going to keep those two apart?"

My heart stops. *Profit is alive?*

11

Qiana

"**W**hat the fuck did you tell him?" Lil Bit asks wide-eyed in the middle of my kitchen. "You didn't tell him the truth, did you?"

"Do I have stupid stamped on the center of my forehead?" I hand her the screaming baby. "Please do something about him."

Her face twists in horror. "Like what?"

"Like shut him up. I can't get him to stop hollering." I rub at my temples because they feel like they are just seconds from exploding. What in the fuck did I get myself into?

"Maybe he's just hungry," Lil Bit suggests. "Have you tried to feed him?"

"Of course I've tried." I gesture to the mess I've made on the counter with the baby formula we picked up last night. "He wouldn't drink the shit."

"Did you heat it up?"

"What?"

"Ohmigod, Qiana. Do you know *nothing* about taking care of a baby?" Lil Bit laughs.

"You mean do I know *anything* about taking care of a baby. Jeez." I roll my eyes.

"Whatever," she barks back. "If you spent more time thinking through your harebrained schemes as much as you do correcting my English, you'll be ahead of the curve."

"Fuck you," I snap, defensively. "And the answer to your question is no. Why in the hell would I know about babies? I ain't out here tryna raise a bunch of seeds."

"But you're out there, cutting them out of bitches' stomachs?" She laughs. "I'm glad you set me straight on that shit." She turns her attention to the baby. "Here you go," Lil Bit says, pulling out a tit and rubbing the nipple in the baby's face. "Go ahead, l'il man. It's all right," she coos.

I watch this shit with a fried brain. I always heard these little fuckers can be a pain in the ass, but goddamn! How do bitches do it? This loud muthafucka hasn't stopped screaming since I opened my eyes two hours ago.

At long last the baby quiets down and latches onto Lil Bit's limp tit and starts sucking with everything he got.

"Thank God," I moan.

Lil Bit thrusts up her chin. "I told you he was hungry."

"What the fuck ever. Your ass is hired. You take care of him."

Lil Bit shakes her head. "Fuck that. I got three of my own at my granny's house. She done told me if I brought another crumb-snatcher in her house she was putting me out. Sorry, girl. I can't help you on this one."

"Fuck. I need to get better friends." I push myself up out of the chair and shuffle to the refrigerator and pull out the grape Kool-Aid. Some niggas need coffee or a cold beer to start their day. For me, this is the shit that gets me gassed up in the morning. This . . . and a Hot Pocket. "You want one?" I ask Lil Bit, holding up the box.

She shakes her head. "Nah. I'm good."

"Suit yourself." I pour a glass and then throw my breakfast into the microwave.

"So what did you tell your brother this morning?" Lil Bit

presses. "After he spotted the clothes, you had to tell him something."

I lean against the counter and cross my arms. "I ain't got to do shit. He ain't my fuckin' daddy."

The second I say that shit, Nookie's new bitch screams out with another throaty orgasm.

My face heats. The crippled muthafucka never cared about embarrassing me in front of my friends. For most of my life, they were subjected to listening to the sex moans coming from his bedroom as much as Charlie and I were.

"Speaking of daddy, I'm not telling his ass shit, either," I amend my comment.

Lil Bit shakes her head. "You know, I'm always amazed that your father never suffers from lockjaw. I've never heard of anyone eating as much pussy as he does."

"At least we know how he got his name."

Lil Bit laughs and I can't help but join her on that shit. *KNOCK. KNOCK. KNOCK.*

"Be back," I tell Lil Bit and go answer the door. Now that the baby has stopped screaming, my nerves are settling down. I open the front door to see Tombstone's current flame and baby momma GG standing on the other side.

She flashes me a quick smile. "Hey, Qiana, girl. Is your brother home?"

"Nah. He's out handlin' some business for Bishop," I tell her.

"Business for Bishop or Lucifer?" she asks, unable to keep her jealousy in check.

We all know that my brother has been feeling Lucifer for a long time. "He said Bishop."

"Humph." GG settles a hand on her thick hips and glances down Ruby Cove. "I saw one missed call from him on my cell phone, but now when I call him he's not pickin' up. Do you know if he's comin' right back?"

I shrug. "Anything is possible, I guess."

"Mind if I come in and wait for him?"

Sighing, I step back from the door. "Come on in."

"Thanks, girl." GG pulls open the screen door and enters the house.

Now I don't have a problem with GG. She's cool people. And she turns plenty of niggas' heads despite carrying more than two hundred pounds on her frame. The weight is where it counts: tits and ass. Compared to all the trifling hoes Charlie used to deal with, GG is my favorite. She has never said anything out of pocket to me and checks my brother when his brotherly teasing goes too far.

"Hey, Lil Bit. Y'all girls just hanging out?" she asks, walking into the kitchen.

"Oh, hey." Lil Bit glances up from the baby and smiles.

"Aww. You brought over . . ." She stops and frowns at the baby. Undoubtedly she doesn't recognize the child as one of Lil Bit's kids.

"Oh. He's not mine," Lil Bit answers.

"Ah. Thank goodness. I thought my mind was playing tricks on me," GG laughs.

I, on the other hand, want to slap the taste out my girl's mouth. How many times have I told her to never answer a question that hasn't been asked?

GG bounces her head and grins at the suckling baby. "You two are babysitting?"

"Something like that," I tell her and then shuffle over to the microwave just as the timer beeps. "Want a Hot Pocket?"

"Pass." GG shakes her head. "I don't know how you can eat that shit."

"What the fuck you talkin' about? This is the breakfast of champions."

GG laughs. "Y'all petals heard about our niggas puttin' in work last night?" she asks. "The shit made national news. We may have lost Fat Ace, but Python got his; roasted and flipped off the old Memphis-Arkansas Bridge."

"Fo real?" I ask, only mildly interested.

"Yup." GG tosses up our gang signs. "Our people blew up that eyesore, the Pink Monkey, too. 'Bout muthafuckin' time. Those bitch-ass hoes working on those poles spread more shit than the Center of Disease Control can keep up with."

Since GG's a nurse at one of the free clinics, I guess she would know.

"It just too bad the murder train didn't make it all the way to Shotgun Row, those roaches need to be exterminated. You feel me?"

Lil Bit and I nod.

"Fuck. Bishop is ordering a blackout on that nigga. He wants anyone even remotely related to that slithering muthafucka wiped out—given how many babies and baby mommas that nigga got, it could take a while."

Me and Lil Bit look at each other.

"Shit. It ain't gonna be too hard getting at his main bitch, LeShelle. Her ass is up in the hospital fighting for her life."

"What?"

GG smirks. "Yeah. Word is that the bitch's sister finally snapped out of it and tried to kill her. Poetic justice, huh?"

My mind reels. Did I do all that bullshit last night for nothing?

"Bishop ordered it? Don't you mean Lucifer?" Lil Bit asks.

GG pauses, but then ends up shrugging her shoulders. "Yo, I don't know how all this gonna shake out. The throne is hers by right, but . . ."

"She has a pussy," I fill in for her.

GG looks sheepish. "I ain't got a dog in this fight. I'm a Flower through and through. I let our niggas handle the soldiering shit."

"I hear you on that," I say, but I still think the politics are pretty fucked up. Why should it matter whether she has a dick or a pussy in between her legs? Lucifer has put in more work than Bishop—and people fear her name more than her brother. Fuck, it don't take much to put a finger to a trigger nowadays. The measure of a true gangster is the ability to put in *wet* work—and Lucifer is a fuckin' artist with a knife. *Kinda like how I was on that yellow bitch last night.*

A smile ghosts around my lips as my gaze shifts to the now-sleeping baby in Lil Bit's arms.

"Anyway," GG continues. "Somebody gonna have to step up because the Crips smell blood in the water."

"What do you mean?"

GG shrugs again. "I'm telling you what I heard."

One thing about GG, her ass hears everything. Just as I think that shit, I catch her sneaking another peek at the baby. Is it possible that she already knows? *Where the fuck is Adaryl?*

Lil Bit struggles to keep up with the conversation. "So what you saying? Those niggas are thinking about doubling up on us?"

"Get the fuck out of here."

"That or take over the game," GG says. "Think about it. With Python and Fat Ace wiped off the map and Lucifer and Bishop potentially fighting for the throne—the city is primed for a fuckin' Crip hostile takeover."

12

Shariffa

CRIP RIDDA.

Standing before the floor-to-ceiling mirror, I smile at my new tat inked across my lower back. This shit is gonna put a smile on Lynch's face when I'm riding his shit tonight. I tend to get all extra tryna erase my new set's memory that my ass ain't always been flagged for the Grape Street Crips. Five years ago, my ass was the HBIC of the Queen Gs—that is until a Crip nigga by the name of King Loc got my ass in a twist. Next thing I know, I was creeping on my nigga, Python, thinking my ass was too muthafuckin' slick.

But shit done in the dark always comes to light. Python rolled up on King Loc and riddled him with so many bullets his ass had to be identified by dental records. After making my ass watch, Python turned his wrath on me. I only remember the first couple punches before I blacked out. When I woke up, I was laid up in the hospital and sucking on a tube for months.

For a long time, I hated that I even woke up. I was dead to the Gangster Disciples and I knew when I crawled out of the hospital that any member from my old family was going to blast my ass on sight for the disrespect. To add insult to injury,

Python wasted no time putting another bitch in his bed and crowning her head bitch.

I know my ass was wrong, but it didn't mean that I didn't love Python. If anything, I loved him too hard. But why was it okay for him to drop seeds all over the place? I was tired of being played. The straw that broke the camel's back was when I learned that Python was still dealing with some cop's daughter who he had feelings for back in high school. His ass was still in love with the bitch and thought my ass didn't know.

Shit. Every bitch gets tired of being played.

I looked for a nigga that was gonna make *me* feel special.

In the end, that shit almost got me killed.

Fuck that ugly muthafucka. Him and them nasty-ass snakes he always had slithering in the bed. That shit was demonic as fuck. The muthafucka could only bust a nut when he was drilling a bitch's ass and choking her out. I didn't need to get that fuckin' close to death in order to bust a nut. Besides, that nigga never loved me—he was still hung up on that bitch-ass cop whose daddy ran the ultimate street gang: the police.

Still, I felt some kind of way when I was replaced so fast.

Python's new bitch has made a rep for herself. Word spread quickly that her ass wasn't the bitch to fuck with. She made a lot of bitches across all sets step up their game. Now it's common knowledge that Queen Gs, Flowers, and Crippettes put in more work than the average foot soldier.

Starting over in a new set wasn't easy. In fact, it was damn near impossible. I lived with the constant threat of sucking on a nigga's 9's. Nobody trusted my ass. I went through some humiliating shit to climb up the ranks. But what else was a bitch gonna do, roll over and die?

Naw. Muthafuckas got me twisted if they thought that shit. I'm a fuckin' survivor. You can drop my ass in the middle of a deserted island and my ass would munch on seafood and coconut milk like a muthafucka.

Shit started looking up for me with the Grape Street Crips when I cliqued up on a bank robbery. My ass rocked a Kel-Tec KSG Shotgun like I birthed that muthafucka. The Fat Albert security guard tried me and I deflated that gut like a flat tire. The score took less than two minutes, but it was a score that changed my rep and my life.

Sure. Every now and then a bitch looks at me sideways, but I always make sure that it's the last time.

Lynch, a chief enforcer, peeked my gangster and liked that I kept my shit tight with my fitness. Bitches always kill me how they let they shit go sometimes. You can go hard, but you ain't gotta look hard. Anyways, Lynch caught my eye, too. Not only is his gangster on point, but he's a cute muthafucka. Six feet, Hershey's-Bar-brown and built like a football quarterback—complete with a tight ass—I couldn't wait to eat his chocolaty ass.

I'm not sayin' my new man ain't got his own fetishes, he does. But it's shit that I can deal with.

Two years after we hooked up, I birthed our twin boys and took his last name: Rodgers.

My ass is official—sky's the limit. I make sure that my nigga knows that there's nothing that I won't do for him. Now, looking back on all the shit I've been through, I have to say I wouldn't change a muthafuckin' thing.

Karma is a bitch.

The Gangster Disciple and Vice Lord drama is playing in the streets and all over the news like a bad hood soap opera. Ain't nobody been able to confirm shit about Python's status, but shit is a hot mess on Shotgun Row. Ain't no telling how those niggas over there are feeding themselves. Things a little different over on Ruby Cove with the Vice Lords—them muthafuckas have too many chiefs and not enough Indians. That don't mean we ain't trying they asses though. We play this shit right and we can rule the whole damn city. I smirk while an image of Python's car flipping off that bridge plays in my head.

Yeah. Karma is a muthafuckin' bitch.

"You like it?" Crunk asks, shutting off the needle and admiring his work.

"Yeah, nigga. You did your thang." Instead of cash, I pass his ass a care package. "Go ahead and rock it up. You earned that shit."

Crunk pockets his shit. "Stay skeemin, diva."

"Watch me push on all they asses."

He chokes on a couple of staccato chuckles as I look around for my bitch, Trigger.

I spot her ass in the back rubbing her titties on some underage corner boy. Muthfucka is probably skeeting in his pants with her titties in his face. I'm gonna hand it to my girl, bitch is a quarter piece in a jar of dimes. Men loved her Heinz-57 ass. Her Asian momma gave her silky black hair and half-moon eyes and her mulatto daddy gave her his green eyes. Niggas fall into a trance wherever she goes.

"Bitch, you ready?" I ask, glancing down at the time on my smartphone. "We gotta roll out."

"I'm always ready, bitch," Trigger says, turning with a smile. "I was getting tired of playing with this nigga anyway."

Young buck glares at me the second Trigger steps back.

I laugh in his face and then roll out of Crunk's Ink. At seven sharp, we hook up with our girls Shacardi, Brika, and Jaqorya, and gear up. I ain't talking about no regular combat shit. We got our flyest shit on, causing a scene. By the time we get our stroll on, laughing and acting silly, every nigga we pass on Orange Mound try to push up on us. We flirt with a couple, but keep it moving. When our target is in sight, we slow down, making sure the lookout boys get an eyeful.

"Yo, shawty. Let me holler at you," says this lanky-ass nigga with dreads hanging to the center of his back, flashing his yellow teeth.

We look around, tryna figure out who the hell he's talking to.

"You, China doll," he says, pointing to Trigger. "What yo name is?"

Trigger puts on her shy act and creeps on up to the duplex to hear his game. But the second she pushes her titties up on him, muthafucka also gets a .45 pressed against his temple. "The name is Trigger, Rasta—as in I have an itchy one. Now make the wrong fuckin' move."

Rasta freezes up as me and the girls rush up the stairs. We pull hardware out from our titties and panties and force the dude out front to be a human shield.

"Open the door," I hiss.

"A'ight. Chill," he says in a squeaky-ass voice.

"Shut the fuck up," I snap, grinding my .357 in his back. He gets the point and opens the door of the VL trap house. Quiet as a mouse we creep through the door. Ain't shit on the first floor—no furniture, no TV—nothing. The only option is to head up the staircase. Shacardi and Jaqorya hang back and hug the front door. Trigger and I force our hostage to another door on the top floor.

"Open it," I order, feeling a surge of adrenaline.

"Y'all bitches don't want to do this," he argues back.

"Fuck this," Trigger says, then blasts the lock and kicks the door down.

We shove Rasta through first.

He screams as his boys on the other side blast his ass full of holes. We break out Charlie's Angels-style from behind our human shield, picking these niggas off left and right.

We keep our shit tight and in less than three seconds we got seven dead niggas at our feet, a table stacked with money, bricks, and weapons. *Ka-ching!*

"Move it! Move it! Move it," I shout. We take another thirty seconds to grab as much shit as we can and then run our asses back out of the door. As we race downstairs, the back door bursts open.

Shacardi and Jaqorya start blasting holding back those black and gold niggas. The five naked bitches are lying face down on the floor, screaming and shit as the place turns into a complete war zone. We get to the front door, only for more bullets to whiz by our heads. In the distance, wheels squeal and the beautiful sound of Brika's TEC-9, mowing niggas down, fills the air as she jets her Denali to our rescue.

Heels be damned, we get our G.I. Jane on, taking niggas out like a fuckin' video game. In a blink of an eye, we all jump in with our stash and then peel off the block, laughing our asses off.

"C'Z UP, NIGGAS!"

Three trap houses in three days—this shit is like taking candy from a baby.

13

Lucifer

Propped up in my bed looking half-mummified for two weeks, I can't stop myself from watching the YouTube news clip of Dougie and Python crashing on the old Memphis-Arkansas Bridge. The force with which the SUV hits what has to be the gas line of the Monte Carlo takes my breath away each and every time because I know Mason was in there and was probably burned to a crisp by the time the car hit the Mississippi River below.

Oh God, Mason.

When I'm not playing this clip, I'm playing the clip of the city's search-and-rescue team extracting the vehicles out of the river. So far, they've only recovered Dougie's body, halfway to Louisiana. Any day, they'll find Mason.

Any day.

"That can't be healthy."

Startled, I jerk my head up to see Cousin Skeet, our resident dirty police captain, standing in my doorway out of uniform. "What are you doing here?"

"What the hell do you think? You guys got a little carried away and turned the whole fuckin' city into a damn war zone."

"Don't play stupid. You know how we get down. You supplied the fuckin' weapons."

"I always supply the weapons, but I didn't expect y'all to get sloppy. I got the whole fuckin' city breathing down my neck. The body count is so high Homeland Security is looking at us sideways."

"You got your grandson back."

"Yeah. That's the one good thing you guys got right." Skeet sucks in a deep breath. "Thank you."

I would say he was welcome, but since I lost Mason, I didn't think it was a fair exchange.

"So. How are you holding up?"

I frown. *Are we supposed to be friends now?* "How does it look like I'm holding up?"

Skeet's gaze sweeps over the cast on both my arm and leg. "It looks like all the king's horses and all the king's men put you back together again."

I smile without having meant to.

"As for . . . Mason," he clears his throat. "I'm sorry for your loss."

My heart clenches like a mild heart attack. "Thanks." I study him to see if there's any trace of him grieving for the son he never claimed or knew was his. In the end, I couldn't tell. "I'm sorry for your loss as well."

He looks confused. "Melanie," I say. "I never gave you my condolence for the loss of your daughter."

He nods. "Thanks."

We fall silent for a few awkward seconds before he remembers some more news. "By the way, LeShelle Murphy is laid up in the hospital."

"I heard."

Skeet chuckles. "Apparently, her younger sister snapped out of her psychosis out at the mental hospital and damn near stabbed her to death with a pair of sewing needles. She's listed in critical condition at Baptist Memorial."

"I'll send—"

"No. No. No." Skeet shakes his head.

"I wasn't asking for permission," I tell him.

"Hands off. I can't have or afford for you guys to go shooting up the hospital again. And as much as I want to strangle the bitch myself for what she's put Christopher through, she's going through the system. That's *if* she survives."

"You gotta be shitting me. What the hell am I supposed to tell Profit?"

"I don't care what you tell him. Keep his ass out of that fuckin' hospital. I gotta start closing cases before my new boss tosses words like 'early retirement' around. Matter-of-fact, I'd appreciate it if the Vice Lords eased up on the body count for the rest of the year."

I laugh. "We're in the middle of two wars and you want me to call a cease-fire?" *That's the last thing my soldiers wanna hear from their first female chief.*

"Look. It is what it is. I'm cutting you off on any more weapons until the first of the year. If you gotta eighty-six somebody, please do me the courtesy of dropping the body over the state line."

"Oh. You're cutting *me* off?" *Muthafuckas are already testing me.*

"Shit, Willow. Don't take it personally. It's just for a couple of months."

Pissed, I glare at him until he starts backpedaling out of my room.

"I'm glad that we are able to come to an understanding." Skeet winks at me. "I'll see my way out."

"You do that." It takes everything I have not to throw something. A few minutes later, I hear my mother giggling downstairs. No doubt he's turned on the charm. I swear I don't know what the fuck she's see in that man. A few minutes later, I hear Bishop coming into the house.

Round two.

I get less than a minute to prepare myself before Bishop fills my doorway. "Got your summons," he starts in on my bad side. "What's up?"

"C'mon in. Sit down." I gesture to the foot of my bed.

He hesitates and then finally drifts inside.

"I wanted to give you a heads-up that I'm gonna call a meeting with our high-ranking members sometime next week. I'm going to lay out some new plans and directions for our set going forward."

Bishop's brows clash in the center of his forehead.

"What?"

"Nothing." He shrugs and does a slow drag over my two casts. "Just . . . do you really think that you're up for something like that?"

"What do you mean? We have chairs, I've certainly mastered the art of sitting on my ass these past couple of weeks."

"I know. It's just . . . nobody's going to blame you if you take a little more time for yourself. I mean, I can handle things until you're back on your feet." He reaches over and squeezes the knee on my good leg. "You should be focusing on getting better."

The used car salesman's smile creeps me out. "I appreciate the offer, but I'm fine."

"C'mon, Willow. You're pushing yourself too hard. Clearly, you're still having a hard time dealing with . . ." He glances at the laptop. ". . . Mason's passing. You're not eating. You're not sleeping. I didn't want to say this, but you look like hell."

"Yeah. It looks like you were struggling to tell me that."

"I'm going through it, too. You know how much Mason meant to me. He was like the brother I never had."

That part of his story is true. "I know."

"Then let me do this for you. I want to."

"You mean that you want to take over permanently," I correct him.

"Sure. I mean,…uhm…."

Unable to hold it in any longer, I laugh. "Juvon, who in the hell do you think you're fooling?"

"What?"

"This whole concerned bullshit. You can't possibly believe that I'm falling for it."

"What?" He stands up from the bed. "You think I'm faking this?"

"I don't think, I *know.* You might want to get those wheels in your head greased because I can hear them turning a mile away. I'm not even in the mood to pretend that I don't know what you're up to."

Bishop's face performs all kinds of acrobatics while he tries to think of something to say. "I don't know what the fuck you're talking about."

"You don't know what I'm talking about?" I'm heated.

"No," he says, stubbornly sticking to his lie.

"All right then. When were you going to tell me that you've already called a meeting with the leaders for *tomorrow?*"

Blood drains from his face while it does that whole acrobatic shit again.

"See. You're showing me all kinds of disrespect right now. You know that, don't you? If you were *any* other nigga I'd be going upside your head."

Our gazes crash.

I decide to give him one more warning. "Don't come at me sideways."

Bishop rolls his eyes and backs up just in case I go for the cane next to my bed and carry out my threat. "A'ight. So I called a meeting—but it wasn't because I was tryna sneak behind your back. I was tryna to help—like you always did for Mason. Didn't you always have his back? Didn't you step in whenever he was locked down or laid up? I don't remember you always asking for permission to step in or step up. What's the problem?"

"The problem is people are already whispering about you plotting to come at me for the throne. Seems some disloyal and gossiping soldiers are swoll about having a woman running the game. Now here you come cock-blocking—again. What the hell am I supposed to think?"

"That's not what's up," he insists, looking guilty as hell. "Besides, since when do you listen to gossip?"

"Every time my name comes up."

"Fine. You see it how you see it. I didn't come here to argue with you."

"That's because you don't have an argument. I told you once, now I'm going to tell you again. Fall back and play your position. If I have to tell you a third time, it's gonna be a fuckin' problem."

Bishop clearly got something to say so I wait for his ass to say it, but then he punks out. "Anything else?"

"I canceled your meeting," I tell him.

He grinds his teeth together. "Anything else?"

"Nope. We're good."

He nods and then storms out of the room. *This is not going to be the end of this.*

14

LeShelle

There's an endless stream of voices floating around my head. I try to concentrate on what they're saying, but it's too hard and I just give up and drift among the memories swirling around. . . .

The room was pitch black. Not even the moon bothered to shine through the open window. I hated that house. It smelled like old cat piss and Newport Menthol cigarettes. The tiny twin-size beds we had to sleep on were as hard as rocks and the pillows were as flat as pancakes. It was our fourth foster home in three months and the drill was pretty much the same. The woman of the house, Ms. Ruthie, didn't want us to be seen or heard and she damn sure didn't want our asses eating too much.

In the first two weeks of our moving in, soap and water never hit her ass. She was planted in a La-Z-Boy in front of the television and would only get up to eat and shit—and she did a whole lot of both. Her face reminded me of Aunt Esther from Sanford and Son *and she kept her hair in braids except in patches of bald spots.*

Her man was a white nigga who insisted that his name was Abdul and he was at least ten years older. He didn't smell no better. But he would get up every fucking morning like he had a W-2 to get to, but in reality, that muthafucka never went farther than the front porch. He sat out there and talked a lot of shit about how niggas was ruinin' the neighborhood.

I wasn't in that house two seconds before figuring his ass out. Hell, I knew a pedophile when I saw one. When he got the right amount of alcohol in him, he didn't even hide the lust in his eyes and would do it in front of his bitch, too.

"Get me a beer," he'd always say when he wanted a close inspection.

I wanted to bark that I wasn't nobody's trained dog, but a few foster homes back I got busted in the mouth for that smart remark so I knew better than popping off. Each time I handed him a beer, he'd make me stand there with the bottle held out while his gaze dragged over me.

"You sure are a pretty lil thing," he'd say. "I betcha your pussy is just as pretty."

I never responded.

"How old did you say you were again?"

Silence.

"What's the matter? Cat's got your tongue?"

Silence.

"That's all right." He'd reached for the bottle. "I like a bitch who knows how to keep her mouth shut."

It was a matter of time. I knew it—and he knew it. Which was why on the night shit went down I was laying there in that eerie darkness with my ears strained for the slightest sound. For a long time, all I could hear was Ta'Shara slow-breathing in the bed next to me.

"T?"

There was a long silence and then, "Yeah?"

"Let's run away," I blurted out, sitting up. We'd done that before but this time I was determined we wouldn't get caught.

"Where would we go?"

"I don't care. Anywhere."

She didn't say anything.

"Don't tell me that you rather stay here."

"God, no. It's just . . . it's so dark and scary outside."

I huffed out a breath, remembering that during the last escape, Ta'Shara cried every time she saw a crackhead shaking down the sidewalk.

"I don't know, LeShelle."

My hands balled at my sides. Why did she always make things difficult? Five minutes passed before I tried it again.

"T? Are you still awake?"

She hesitated. "Yeah."

"Well, do you want to?"

"I—"

SQUEEEAAK.

My head whipped around to the door. There was somebody coming up the hallway. Not wanting to take any chances, I grabbed the blanket and pulled it up over my head. I don't remember ever praying so hard in my life. "Please, God. Not this shit again."

SQUEEEAAK.

The sound grew closer, so close that I knew that whoever was out there in the hallway had already walked past the half-bathroom. My stomach knotted up when the doorknob turned.

"Don't worry, Shelle," T whispered. "I locked it."

I released a sigh of relief, but then a key slipped into the lock and rattled around.

SQUEEEAAK.

The door hinges sounded far worse than the loose floorboards in the hallway. The moment Abdul edged into the room, I smelled him.

SQUEEEAAK.

He closed the door behind him and then called himself tiptoeing his way toward my bed. The bed was so hard that when he sat down it didn't even dip.

Squeezing my eyes tight, I prayed: God, make him go away. God, make him go away.

"Hey, lil girl." He felt around and then snatched down the blanket. "Whatchu doing hiding under there?"

"What do you want?" I hissed, angry that God hadn't answered my prayers.

Abdul's funky breath singed my nose hairs. "C'mon, girl. You've played this game before. Anyone can take one look at you and know that your cherry was popped a long time ago." He jammed his hands between my legs and squeezed. "Ain't that right?"

I bolted up, but before I could jump out of the bed, he'd grabbed and pinned me back down.

"Where are you going, you lil cock tease? I'm not finished with you."

The thought of that muthafucka putting his pasty-ass dick anywhere near me had that undercooked chicken Ms. Ruthie fixed for dinner rolling around in my stomach.

"Get off of me!" I twisted, kicked, and tried to buck him off.

"Aww. You're a feisty bitch, huh?" He wrestled with me, but after a while he got tired of the game and slammed his fist across my jaw. Stars exploded and circled around my head like a cartoon. In case my ass was about to say something else, he sent another blow in the opposite direction. Blood gushed out of my mouth and I was too stunned to say anything. While I tried to clear my head, Adbul snatched my cotton nightgown off.

His rough, calloused hands roamed over my body like he didn't know where to start playing first.

If there was anything to be grateful for, it was that I couldn't see him. Light continued to avoid the room. All I could do was close my eyes and hope that he would nut fast and get the fuck on.

Something sharp trailed up my leg. He had a knife.

"You better be nice to me or I'll cut this hot lil pussy up." Proving he meant business, he slid the tip of the blade across my clit.

I flinched at a sharp sting of pain.

His ass was crazy.

"You know in some parts in Africa men cut the girls' pussies out to stop them from becoming whores." He chuckled. "Maybe I'll do the same thing to you."

The blade glided down the other side of my clit. I jerked, tryna get away, but he locked me down with one hand and emitted another wave of stank-ass funk in my face.

"That's it. I love it when you lil bitches fight back." He shifted around until I felt his dick hit my leg.

I froze. The shit was about go down no matter what I did. Something snapped inside of me and I gave up. The sooner I let him do whatever he was gonna do, the faster the shit was gonna be over with. I took one deep breath, closed my eyes, and then let my arms and legs go limp.

To my surprise, Abdul went from excited to confused to pissed. *"What the fuck?"*

To get another rise out of me, the blade returned and made another slice. I forced myself not to react.

Abdul grew angrier. *"Oh, I know what you need."* He rammed his dick between my legs. He huffed and puffed but my pussy remained dry as a desert.

"Ah, Shit. Ah, shit," Adbul kept moaning. That, and, *"I love fuckin' black pussy."*

On and on it went. What this rapist lacked in size, he made up in stamina. Every time I thought that his ass was about to come, he would just flip me over into a new position and go back at it.

Throughout his bullshit sex talk, I could hear T whimpering and crying in her bed. During a few dry thrusts, I wondered what the hell she was crying about. It wasn't like he was stretching out her pussy. My resentment melted away and I reminded myself that it was better that I endured this shit because I was stronger. I was the protector.

Hell. Most of the time Ta'Shara was scared of her own shadow. She couldn't take it when other kids picked on her or looked at her sideways. It had become a habit of mine to step up and fight her battles. That's how it's supposed to be. We're family. We only have each other.

SQUEEEAAK. SQUEEEAAK. SQUEEAAK.

My heart leapt. Ms. Ruthie was up. She's gonna catch this muthafucka and get him off me. Our bedroom door burst open.

"Ain't you through yet?" Ms. Ruthie snapped.

Adbul kept deep stroking. *"Does it look like I'm through? Aw. Shit. I'm about to cum."*

"It's about time. You've been in here almost an hour."

"Ah, shit. Ah, shit. This bitch got some tight shit, Ruthie. You just don't know. Ah, shit."

"What? That fast bitch? Please. Tell that shit to somebody else." I spotted the glowing tip of her cigarette at the door before she responded.

"Ah, shit." He kept pounding.

"What about that other one?" she asked. *"You test her out yet?"*

"FUUUUUUCCCK," Abdul blew out my eardrum. By the way he convulsed, I guessed it meant his ass came. He didn't even bother to pull out.

"Shit. It's about time," Ms. Ruthie huffed. *"Now c'mon. You done played long enough."*

Abdul grunted. *"Damn. You ain't gonna let me catch my breath?"*

"If you're talkin', you're breathin'. Now c'mon."

He sat up and whined, *"I haven't played with the other one yet."*

"It's late. Now bring your ass on."

"Dammit, Ruthie." He stood from the bed and shuffled to the door. *"You said I can do both of them."*

"Don't get mad at me because you spent all your time with the slutty one," she argued back. *"Do her tomorrow."*

"Fine. Tomorrow then." They walked out of the room and closed the door.

SQUEEEAAK. SQUEEEAAK.

Ta'Shara and I listened as they headed back to their bedroom. Neither of us moved or said a word until we were sure Abdul and Ruthie were back in their bedroom.

At last, Ta'Shara popped up and raced to turn on the light. We expected to see my sheets drenched with blood, but they weren't. Like I said, Adbul was hardly my first rapist foster dad, but I could still feel those three cuts on my clit.

"Shelle, are you okay?" Ta'Shara asked, rushing over to me.

I wanted to scream, *"Does it look like I'm fuckin' okay?"* But T was too young to understand.

"Shelle?"

"Yeah. I'm all right." Those four words hurt like hell to get out of my mouth.

"I'll go get you a washcloth."

She turned to run off, but I grabbed her wrist. *"Wait until they're asleep. We don't know if he'll creep back out."*

"And grab me?" she asked with fear blanketing her face.

I wanted to reassure her. She didn't have a single curve on her young body yet. What would he want with her? Then I remembered that some dudes like young boys—or anything with a hole—and Ta'Shara had as many as I did.

"He's gonna beat me and stick his weenie in me, ain't he?"

I shook my head.

"But he said—"

"Don't worry about what he said. I'm going to take care of it."

"But—"

"Hey." I grabbed her chin and forced her to look at me. *"Don't I always take care of you?"*

Ta'Shara nodded.

"Then leave it to me." I sucked in a deep breath. *"Go back to bed."*

"Don't you want me to help you clean up?"

"No. I can take care of it myself. Go!"

She hesitated.

"Go," I hissed.

Ta'Shara slunk back over to her bed and crawled beneath the sheet.

I felt guilty for yelling at her, but damn she could be hardheaded sometimes. I sat up in that bed for another hour with no clue on what the fuck I was going to do. I kept thinking it was best for us to pack up our shit and go. I was a smart girl. We could survive the streets. I'd seen plenty of abandoned and boarded-up houses on the way to school. Why couldn't we stay in one until we could get some real money flowing?

That shit sounded real good to me and I was convinced that we could do it. When I was sure that Abdul wasn't coming back, I climbed *out of bed and walked like a zombie toward the door. On my way out, I turned off the bedroom light. I told myself to go straight to the bathroom to clean myself up, but I ended up in the kitchen without thinking about it and pulling out a butcher knife.*

The floorboards didn't squeak when I eased my way back down the hall. I evened out my breathing so that I wouldn't make a sound. The only time that my heart tripped up in my chest was when I turned the doorknob to Adbul and Ruthie's bedroom. I waited to see whether the old hinges would announce my presence. When they didn't, a sinister smile curled up the corners of my lips and my grip on the knife tightened.

Meow.

Curled up at the bottom of the bed sat Ruthie's fat orange cat, Milly. It stared at me with glowing yellow eyes before meowing some more. I hated that cat, but I couldn't waste my element of surprise by trying to chase it around the room. The only other light in the room came from the red digital numbers glowing from the nightstand table. I knew Ruthie slept on that side of the bed and instead headed to the opposite side, where Abdul snored like a bulldozer. With each step, more heat rushed through my body and my grip tightened on the knife. Yet, for some reason, I didn't feel the small stab wounds I made into my own legs. I focused my attention on my target like a laser beam.

Once I reached the side of the bed, I wasted no time raising the knife high over my head. An incredible power surged through me.

Meow!

Milly's warning cry failed to wake her owners.

"Fuck you, muthafucka!" With each ounce of strength I had, I plunged the knife downward. The blade sliced through Abdul like he was made of warm butter.

Abdul sat up with a roar, waking his fat bitch.

"WHAT? WHAT'S GOING ON?"

I yanked the knife out, but Abdul's arm shot out and blindly grabbed my wrist.

Ruthie jumped out of bed and turned on the light.

Shock colored their faces when they saw me standing there with the bloody knife.

"You little bitch." Ruthie dove across the bed, tryna reach me. With renewed strength, I snatched my arm free and then slashed anything that came near me. For a full minute I tore their asses up, but then Ruthie tackled my ass to the floor and knocked the knife out of my hand. From there she wailed on my ass like a heavyweight fighter.

I didn't even remember blacking out. . . .

15

Alice

Niggas keep dropping like flies around me. That shit is just a fact of life. I'm long past the days of when I gave a fuck. Clearly, Arzell thought the dick was so good that he could spit out the side of his neck at me. What the fuck? Comparing me to that no-good grimy bitch in the basement. He must've lost his fuckin' mind.

I lean over Arzell's permanently shocked face and smirk. "You let the gray hairs fool you, didn't you?" When I realize that I'm actually waiting for an answer, I straighten up and head to the refrigerator for a cold one. I need my morning buzz so I can think.

After I pop the top, I take a couple of swigs to clear my mind up. It's fair to say that my situation out here has gotten worse. "You just had to pop off at the mouth, didn't you?"

Disgusted, I march out of the kitchen and head back to the living room to turn on the television. Terrell's face is on every channel. My ears perk when reporters are unable to confirm reports of someone escaping the Monte Carlo as it splashed down into the Mississippi. All I can do is hope.

Why couldn't I pull my shit together to be a better mom to my children? Could'ves, should'ves, and would'ves fill my head while I drain the beer bottle. The truth is that back in the day that crack rock had my ass shook. There was no better lover, mother, or friend in the whole world. When I had that shit in me, nothing and no one else mattered. Hell. It's been ages since I've had a taste and I'm still jonesing for that bullshit.

Still, I should've never left Terrell with Maybelline. The bitch was the reason for my downfall—is it no wonder that my older baby is now the Most Wanted Nigga in Memphis? *My firstborn.* I close my eyes and place a hand over my empty belly.

But what about Mason?

Guilt crashes through me, causing my eyes to burn and my throat to tighten. That whole Mason shit wasn't my fault. I didn't sell my baby for no crack rock. I mean, I know that I've done some pretty fucked up shit—but I wouldn't do that. I wouldn't.

I feel a prick of doubt at the back of my head. The same one I've had since that horrible day . . .

In the early nineties my ass was a full-blown crackhead. Muthafuckas acted like I should've been ashamed of that shit or something, but I wasn't. Those fuckin' rocks were the only things in my life that made me feel good. One puff and it felt like every strand of hair on my body was having an orgasm. So what if I had to rob, blast, fuck, or blow muthafuckas in order to get down? The shit was worth it for no other reason than that I'd stop seeing Leroy's raping ass when I blazed up—stop feeling the pain of my legs being snapped open for the very first time and him telling me how much I wanted him before ramming into my dry pussy and ripping my young world apart.

No one understood that shit, least of all Maybelline. Sure, she would toss me a "sorry" every once in a while, but "sorry" didn't stop the nightmares. Frankly, she had a way of looking at me like I should be apologizing to her for the loss of one of her legs.

Selfish bitch.

Anyway, me and Jerome didn't work out. It was pretty much a rap when his ass left me to deliver my own baby in the middle of a check-

cashing place that we had robbed. If the muthafuckin' security cameras had been working in that place, my ass would've been hauled into jail for the dead bitch Jerome took out behind the counter. In the end, it didn't matter. It wasn't like Terrell was his kid no ways. That honor went to Supercop himself, Melvin Johnson.

Sure, when the dust cleared, Jerome tried to holler at me again, but I wasn't tryna hear all that noise he was spitting. I was on patrol for a real nigga, doing real thangs.

With Jerome out of the picture and Maybelline banning my ass from Nana's crib just because we stole a brick of coke from her, that meant my ass had to hustle hard. That shit was damn near impossible with a baby. Terrell was a good baby. He didn't cry, even on the days when I'd blaze and forget to feed him. He would look at me with those big ole eyes as if he understood my pain better than I did.

Dribbles, one of the bitches that would patrol some of the same corners with me, took one look at Terrell and said that he had an old soul—like he'd been here before.

That shit freaked me out a bit. Like . . . what if it was Leroy's trifling ass, coming back from the dead to fuck with me some more? From that day on, I couldn't look at Terrell the same. I knew that shit was foul, but it was the truth. I mean, what kind of baby don't cry? Ever?

Unable to deal with Leroy fuckin' with my mind from beyond the grave, I decided that a boy child was probably best off with his damn daddy. So that's where I took him.

It took more than a couple of bus transfers and an additional two-mile walk to get to the suburban home. Hell, I didn't know that Memphis still had nice little nooks of postcard-perfect homes. I had never seen grass so green or so many flowers perfuming the air. I kept looking down at the address Dribbles got for me and thinking that the bitch had just pulled a fast one on my ass. Still, I marched on up to the front door and rang that doorbell.

I stood there for what felt like forever, peeking out at a few neighbors who wandered out onto their front porch to get a good look at me. Suddenly, I was aware of every tear, hole, or food stain on my clothes.

It probably wouldn't have hurt to run a brush through my hair a couple of more times before I'd gone out there. As the time stretched, I warred with myself on whether to press the doorbell again. I started to walk away, but another look at Terrell's dark, watchful eyes and I pushed the button again. Almost immediately, the door opened and I was staring at a woman who looked like she was cut out of a magazine. Perfect hair. Perfect clothes and a smile so white, her teeth didn't look real.

"May I help you?" she asked sweetly.

"Yeah. Uhm . . . is Sk—I mean, is Lieutenant Johnson here?"

Though the woman's smile remained in place, her gaze performed a quick, suspicious drag over my entire body. "And whom shall I tell him is calling?"

Calling? My ass wasn't on no phone. "Uhm, Alice." I adjusted Terrell on my hip. "He'll know who I am."

After staring at me and then Terrell for a long while, she glanced over my shoulder and noticed the number of neighbors out on their porches before putting the smile back on her face.

"Won't you come in?"

I pushed up my own smile and stepped inside. The entire house smelled like peach cobbler and it quickly had both me and Terrell's stomachs rumbling.

"Can I get you anything to drink?" she asked. "Coffee, tea, or some water?"

"You wouldn't happen to have something a little stronger, would you?"

Her brows shot up at that. "How about a gin and tonic?"

"That will work," I told her, disappointed she didn't offer something with vodka or rum, but beggars couldn't be choosey. She led me to a room filled with books and a computer and then told me to take a seat.

Terrell cooed softly.

"How old?" she asked.

"Two months."

"Boy or girl?"

"Boy," I answered and watched sadness touch her face.

"Melvin and I have been trying to have a baby." Her gaze returned to Terrell.

I instinctively gathered him close. Could she see her man in Terrell's face? My eyes fell to her free hand that kept knotting up into a fist.

"You know what?" I said, springing to my feet. "This was a mistake. I shouldn't have come here."

Her silence told me that she agreed and she said nothing as I raced toward the door. But it was Skeet's voice thundering from above that stopped me in my tracks.

"WHAT THE FUCK ARE YOU DOIN' HERE?"

Turning, I glanced up the stairs to see fury blanketing his face.

Fuck. It wasn't like my ass rolled up in there, tryna rob the place.

"I-I . . ." I looked at his wife for help.

"She was just leaving," his wife said. "Weren't you?"

Terrell picked that moment to utter his first words. "Daa-Daa."

Melvin's wife gasped and then slapped a hand across her mouth.

Melvin flew down the stairs.

I turned for the door, but he caught up to me and grabbed my hair and yanked me back. "You dirty bitch, you have the nerve to bring your ass to my house?" He yanked my hair again and Terrell fell out of my arms and hit the floor.

"My baby!"

"You must be out of your muthafuckin' mind!" He shoved past his wife and dragged me into a study room.

"I'm sorry. I'm sorry," I yelled.

"Oh, you are about to be sorry."

Next thing I knew, he was beating me so bad that I never took my ass back there again. The next week, word got to me that Nana had passed away. I swallowed my pride and rolled over to see Maybelline. If she was happy to see me, she didn't say, but she took to Terrell like fish to water.

And Terrell liked her, too. I could tell.

I stayed clean for about three days. Long enough to kinda help *with the funeral arrangements. Not too much later, the monkey hopped onto my back again. Being in that house, sleeping in that bed . . . it was all too much. Leroy's ghost was everywhere. I didn't understand how Maybelline never saw him. Soon, I needed a little taste to take off the edge. I snuck two hundred dollars out of Maybelline's purse, promising myself that I would pay her back.*

"Where are you going?" Maybelline asked the minute my hand touched the front doorknob.

"Out."

"Out? Ain't you forgetting somebody?" she asked, jabbing her hand on her hip.

"Fuck, Maybelline. I'm just running to the store real quick. Can't you watch him?"

She gave me a look like I'd just slapped her with a handful of shit.

"Ten minutes," I lied. "He's sleeping any damn way. You want me to wake him up just to take him to the store?"

Terrell started cooing through the baby monitor Maybelline bought. That boy and his timing was killing me.

"Looks like he's up now," Maybelline said, smugly.

"Fuck, Maybelline. I said I will be back." I went ahead and threw open the door, daring her ass to stop me.

She didn't.

I cursed her name all during my soldier march out of the neighborhood, past the store and all the way to my favorite corner boy. I spotted Dribbles unzipping one nigga's jeans to suck him off for a hit and hollered out. "Girl, I got you!"

She turned and saw the money I was waving in my hand.

"What the fuck?" the nigga with his dick in his hand whined.

"Put that dick on ice, baby boy. Me and my girl are about to par-rrrtay!" Dribbles said expectantly.

And that was just what the fuck we did. We stayed blazed for days. When the rocks got low, I thought about going back to get Terrell, but I knew that I'd have to hear Maybelline's fat mouth. So I put it off.

For five years . . .

★ ★ ★

I click off the television and head over to the stairs leading to the basement. The second I open it I hear a loud banging.

"ALICE! I KNOW YOU'RE OUT THERE. LET ME OUT OF HERE!"

Looks like Sleeping Beauty has finally woken up. I smile and hit the light switch. Slowly, I descend the stairs while the lightbulb goes through its flickering routine.

"ALICE! ALICE! DO YOU HEAR ME?" Maybelline pounds her fist on the door. "YOU CAN'T KEEP ME DOWN HERE FOREVER!"

"I don't know about that," I answer calmly during a small break in her banging and screaming.

"ALICE? IS THAT YOU?"

Crossing my arms, I lean against the locked door. "Were you expecting someone else?"

She calms down. "What are you doing, Alice? Why the fuck am I in here?"

"C'mon, Maybelline. Don't play stupid. It doesn't suit you."

"Fuuuuuck," she groans. "Leroy? Still? Damn, Alice. How long are you going to keep punishing me for that shit? You know I've never meant that shit to happen. I lost a leg, I've supported you, I raised your child—"

"Ha! Kill yourself with that Mother Teresa shit."

She sighs. "So what do you want?"

"Why, I want us to spend some time together," I tell her. "That's not so wrong, is it?"

Maybelline doesn't answer.

"How about this—are you hungry?"

Silence.

"I bet you are. Tell you what. Why don't I go back upstairs and fix you something to eat? Then we can have a long sisterly talk. Sound good?"

Silence.

"I'll be right back. Don't you go anywhere." I rush back upstairs and into the kitchen. I step over Arzell's body and head over to the stove. "You know what? Maybe I will fix some flapjacks." I rummage around until I find an old bottle of Pine-Sol underneath the sink. "I'm going to fix the best damn pancakes this bitch has ever had."

Resurrection

16

Lucifer

October . . .

Mason "Fat Ace" Lewis
September 13, 1990–August 24, 2011

Two months after Mason's death a decision within the Lewis family is reached, and a funeral is scheduled. The prospect puts the city on edge. Even media outlets express their concerns about potential violence between rival gangs breaking out during the services. As it stands now, chaos reigns in the streets and as long as a majority of them are GD roaches, I have no desire to end the war—not until I have Python's grimy ass sucking on my 9mm.

Cousin Skeet uses the citywide concern as an excuse to pack the funeral with cops. Rumors ran rampant in the streets about what really went down that night on the bridge. Some insist that someone was seen coming out the river that night. Despite the odds and common sense, too many times I find myself hoping that the rumors are true and Mason is laid up somewhere lost and with amnesia. Hell, it works on those soap operas I was forced to watch while I was on the mend.

The city spent a lot of money pulling vehicles out the mighty Mississippi and, so far, only Dougie's bloated body has been found. If Python had been the one to survive that shit, then I'd be convinced that the muthafucka made a deal with the devil.

Every once in a while, I remember him clutching Mason and weeping like a little child. That shit still has me stuck. No matter how I turn the shit around in my mind, I can't explain it and I damn sure haven't told anybody about it.

Profit's mother, Barbara, flew up from Atlanta. I have to admit that I don't recognize her as the same white, dirty crackhead that used to patrol our corners and parade on Smokestack's arm. She claims to be clean now and has made a new life for herself. Smokestack made big moves and was released from prison in order to attend the funeral, but he has to go right back to prison when it's over.

A nineties OG, he is still pretty-boy fine with a mean-ass swagger. Like the old days, women still clock his ass whenever he's around. The soldiers give him nothing but mad respect and each make a point to make their way over to shake his hand and flood his head with praise.

However, Smokestack only has eyes for Dribbles, but she's sending out signals that she's shut the door on that part of her life and refuses to make eye contact.

I watch everything feeling like a widow without the ring. Cloaked in my Grim Reaper black, I stand between Bishop and Smokestack as Profit strolls forward. After two months of intensive rehabilitation, Profit has packed back on his thirty pounds of muscle and has developed a swagger that commands attention. As he thrusts up his chin to speak to our people, the resemblance between him and Smokestack is stunning.

"First, let me start off by saying, I want to thank each and every one of you for coming out here today," Profit begins. "Seeing so many of you out here brings home that we are more than just soldiers on a battlefield—we're family. Blood be damned." He pauses a beat while he works his jaw muscles to control his emotions. "We might not have shared the same blood"—he glances over at his mother and father and tosses them a smile—"but he was my brother . . . no matter what anybody says . . . and I loved him."

While mother and son share a tender moment, I choke down a knot in my throat and mentally beg myself to keep it together.

"We *all* loved him." Profit turns back toward our street family. "And because of that, his death will be avenged. The war against the Gangster Disciples niggas is far from over. This murkin' season has just begun. SIX POPPIN', FIVE DROP-PIN'!"

Our soldiers pop off a few shots and cheer.

At last, Profit's brown eyes shift to me. "I'm not choosing any sides or even saying that I speak for anybody else but, for me, this war won't be over until we murk every last one of those pitchfork muthafuckas."

More gunfire and cheers, but I zero in on his comments about choosing sides. Only one person would have asked him that. I cut my gaze over to Bishop. That knot in my throat now tastes like acidic bile.

Bishop glances away first, mainly because he knows that I never would.

I tune back in to Profit's speech just as he removes his own piece from his waist, kisses it, and then holds it up to the sky. "All is well until we see our brothah in the sky." With that he fires off his pistol.

In solidarity, I remove my gat and then empty it into the clouds. Seconds later, Mason's gold casket lowers into the ground while one of our soulful Flowers sings "His Eye Is on the Sparrow."

The feelings tripping inside my chest paralyze me. I feel like a coward for not saying a few words during the ceremony. Truth is that I can't. I don't trust myself not to get up there and submit to my inner bitch and start balling my eyes out. I can risk muthafuckas looking at me sideways. I've never been no weak, crying bitch and I'm not starting now.

I never aimed to be on top. I rocked my flag to prove that I was as good as my brother and Mason. Now that I wear the crown, I'm not about to let any muthafucka knock me off.

Mason would be disappointed if I did.

For a brief moment I close my eyes and allow the words of the song to tear up my heart. A memory of my and Mason's first kiss plays behind my closed lids and I experience that same rush of heat sweep through my soul. I remember dropping my towel and then pressing my wet body against him. The wonderful feeling only lasts for a moment before it's replaced by a bottomless ache that keeps threatening to drag me down. My knees are seconds from buckling, when a strong arm wraps around my shoulders and holds me up. When I open my eyes, it isn't Bishop's arm, but Smokestack's. He even breaks me off an encouraging smile, but it does very little to lift my spirits.

The song ends, and then a processional line of VL soldiers march by the casket to toss in their gold flags before leaving the grave. Though my casts are off, I'm pimping a black-and-gold cane as I leave the gravesite. Smokestack doesn't let me get too far.

"What? You don't have no love for your cousin Smokestack no more?"

"All day, every day. You know that shit," I spit out our usual routine and then push up what I hope is a smile. "I'm sorry for your loss," I tell him.

"Thanks, Willow. The same back at ya. How you holding up?"

"I'm still standing."

"True dat," he says, looking me over. "But how are you feeling? You look as if you could use some sleep."

"Me and sleep aren't exactly seeing eye to eye these days,"

I acknowledge. "There will be plenty of time for that on the flipside of the grave."

"Don't talk like that." His attention shifts over to the golden casket.

"Sorry," I say. "That was insensitive."

"It's all right." He pauses for a moment. "I don't know if you two ever had that talk, but given this new situation, I don't think that I'd be considered a snitch now if I tell you that my boy had serious feelings for you."

That damn knot in my throat grows as heat rushes up my neck.

"Aw, shit." Smokestack cocks his head. "Are you blushing?"

"Nah. Nah." I shake my head and look around to make sure no one is ear hustling on our convo. From across the way, Bishop and his new crew are hugged up tight and whispering.

"Anyway," Smokestack says, producing a cigarette and lighting up. "I always thought that in the end, you and Mason would put the guns down long enough to do the right thing."

The memory of Mason fucking me against the bathroom door flashes through my mind. It was the first time I truly felt like a woman. Already I miss the way our bodies snapped together as if we were one.

"Wait." Smokestack cocks his head the other way. "Y'all hooked up, didn't you?"

The heat on my face becomes an inferno and all I can do is stare and wordlessly bump my gums.

"I'll be goddamn." Smokestack's chest gets all swoll as he brags, "My boy closed the deal." We share a beat of silence. "I'm glad. I'm sure that you made him really happy."

For two hours. That was the total time of our intimate relationship. I press my lips together, determined to keep the details of my and Mason's short relationship to myself. It's the only real treasure that I have.

Smokestack's gaze jumps over my shoulder toward Barbara. Judging by the longing in his eyes, he really wants to talk to her, but even I'm getting a little frostbite from her cold-shoulder. "Love is a bitch," he says, sucking in another drag of his cigarette. "We all learn that shit the hard way."

I bob my head as he shifts his attention back to me and tries to catch my gaze. I hate to deny him this bonding moment, but the game is watching me and I can't fuck up now.

Smokestack checks out where my gaze is swinging and comments, "Feeling the weight of that crown, I see."

"Something like that."

"Heavy, ain't it?"

"Nah. I'm just finding enemies where I least expect it, that's all."

"That's what it means to be king or queen of the jungle." He pauses for a second and then asks, "Bishop?" Smokestack blows out a long stream of smoke and then offers it to me for a puff.

The question hangs while I accept the cigarette and drag on it gladly.

Smokestack bobs his head as if he understands my silence. "Brother or not, it ain't easy for a man to be answering to a woman. That's keeping the shit one hundred."

Anger flares through me as I lean forward and hiss, "I'm so fuckin' sick of hearing about niggas' paper egos and glass dicks, I don't know what the fuck to do."

"I hear what you're saying, but let me ask you this: Why the hell do you want this shit anyway?"

"Oh give me a fuckin' break." I roll my neck away.

"What? The question is legit."

"The fuck it is. Are you going to walk over there and ask Bishop that shit—or any other nigga that's dreaming and conspiring to blast me off the throne? You're standing there saying that I gotta prove myself to you, too?"

"A'ight. Toss a little water on that fire, baby girl. I ain't tryna get on your enemies list. I'm in your corner on this," he assures me.

Now I hold his gaze tryna evaluate whether that's true.

"What? You don't trust *me* now?" He looks amused and of-fended.

"Sorry, Smokestack, but if my own damn momma walks over here right now, I'm gonna be lookin' at her sideways, too."

He smiles. "Smart girl. No wonder my boy was crazy about you." He winks and then meanders off toward Profit.

Jealous, I stand there and watch as father and son huddle together for their shared time of grief. As if to stab more knives into my heart, Bishop struts his ass over to the family to pay his respects. Clearly, Profit isn't giving him as much grief as he's giving me over the loss of his big brother. Soldiers are clocking this shit and whispering. Lines are being drawn and sides are being picked.

I'm not sure if I'm hearing my name fall off everyone's lips or I'm just imagining it. Either way, I'm ready to bounce. While waiting inside the limo, I make myself a drink. Minutes later, Dribbles climbs into the caddy. Her large blue eyes are drowning in an ocean of tears. However, when our gazes meet, she pushes up a smile.

"Hello, Willow."

"Hey," I croak through my tightening throat. I shift in my seat and watch as she closes the door behind her.

"I've been meaning to talk to you, but you're a hard woman to nail down," she says.

"Yeah. Well, I'm sorry about that, I have a lot on my plate lately."

She nods and then struggles to continue the conversation. "Look, I've heard that you and Mason—"

"From who?" I snap, defensive.

"From Profit," she answers. "He tells me that . . . well, that Mason had some strong feelings for you—"

Damn. Did everybody know but me?

"—and I sort of remember you always hanging out with

him and your brother . . . well, I guess, what I'm tryna say is that . . . I really appreciate you always being there for my son. After I got myself cleaned up, I tried to talk him into leaving this crazy life out here, but the street has always been a part of him. It was all he ever knew—all most of us knows." She blots her eyes with a kerchief. "When I left here, I thought I was at least saving Raymond from this madness, but the struggles of a woman tryna raise a man—a *black* man at that—isn't any easier in the streets of Atlanta. Now—" She looks out of the tinted windows of the limo toward her son. "Profit has the fever and I'm afraid that one day I'm going to get another phone call." Her hands fall so that her tears roll freely down her face.

Though I feel her pain, I can't help but be annoyed with all the waterworks. Tears ain't never brought anybody back—then again, neither have bullets.

"But you can get out," Dribbles whispers softly before turning her gaze back toward me. "It's not too late for you."

My annoyance quickly flows to anger and suspicion. "So who sent you—Bishop or Profit?"

"Baby girl, nobody sent me. I'm talking to you woman-to-woman. Take this shit from someone who has been in your shoes." She glances back out of the window and this time, I know she's staring at Smokestack. "Love can't survive out here. The streets don't have a retirement plan. You either end up like my son Mason or his father Smokestack—dead or in prison."

I let that public service announcement hang in the air for a moment, but then decide to come at her direct. "But Mason's father isn't in prison—is he?"

Stunned, Dribbles stares and blinks at me.

"Cousin Skeet was his father, wasn't he?"

"Who told you that? Mason?"

"I doubt that Mason had a clue. So . . . was he the father?" I watch her shift in her seat for a while before answering.

"No."

I blink. "But Smokestack said that Mason's mother used to deal with Cousin Skeet."

"She did—and she did have a kid by him, but it wasn't Mason. It was his older brother."

Now my world is spinning. "Mason had an older brother? Who is he?"

17

Momma Peaches

I'm going to die in this hellhole. The shit is hard to accept, but I wish death would come the hell on. I'm an old woman . . . and I used to think that I'd done seen about all there was to see out here in these streets. I was wrong. I ain't never been in no bullshit like this. Sure, I've been behind bars plenty of times for big shit as well as small shit. But this right here? It's blowing my mind. I've been reduced to pissing and shitting in a bedpan, sipping on one glass of water a day and eating food that tastes like sawdust. I don't know what day it is and I've lost track of how long I've been down here. When it's hot outside, it's an oven in this bitch and when it's cold, the room turns into an icebox. I've been sick for so long, I done forgot how to be any other way. Painful stomach cramps and violent vomiting, I can't take my body aching and my head throbbing like this too much longer.

I can't.

I don't know if anybody is out there looking for me or if my ass is S.O.L. All I know is that I wish my crazy-ass sister would either let me go or put a bullet in my dome. I'm tired of being haunted by images of Cedric lying in a pool of his own blood. His handsome face so much like his father's, and my first love, Manny. He's dead because of me—because of my shit. Whatever this shit is.

I've always known that Alice and I hadn't ended things on a good note. I had deliberately cut her out of my and Terrell's life. Yes, she was his biological mother, but after that bullshit with Mason, I had to cut her off. But what else could I have done? I had put up with so much shit. Enough was enough. . . .

For weeks after Alice's second son, Mason, disappeared while she was high off crack, Alice's face was splashed all over the news. Majority of the city's opinion was that she'd sold her six-month-old baby for a couple of rocks. After all, her precious rocks were on the table with her passed out on the sofa when I walked in and the baby was gone. I never liked jumping to conclusions, but one plus one will always equal two.

Not to mention, I had to deal with my own soap-opera drama back at my own crib. I came home straight from that bullshit to find my husband digging out my so-called best friend and neighbor, Josie. It wasn't like I had shit twisted and thought that my man was faithful. I learned the hard way that a dog is always going to roam—but to stick his dick in bitches that close to home. Nah, I wasn't having that shit. His ass had to go. Fuck all the money and bullshit that he was slinging in the streets. A bitch gotta stand for something or she'd always fall for anything.

Josie was lucky that all she got was a bullet in the ass. Fo' real. She gave everyone on Shotgun Row a real thrill when she ran naked out my front door, hollering, screaming, and bleeding. Isaac wrestled me to the floor because he knew that when I finished with Josie's ass, he was next.

"Peaches, Peaches, calm the fuck down," he barked.

"Fuck you, muthafucka! I hate your grimy ass!" Under normal circumstances, Isaac's big muscly ass could've had my ass in a choke hold in two seconds, but my rage had my one-legged ass on equal footing. This nigga was sweating and putting in work to pin my ass down.

Finally seizing my shooting hand, he lifted it up and banged it against the door frame, crushing my fingers and damn near breaking my wrist.

"*Aaargh, fuck nigga. That shit hurts.*"

"*What the fuck, Peaches? You know that bitch don't mean shit to me.*"

Disgusted with his lying ass, I hock up a loogie from the back of my throat and spit that shit dead in his face. "*Punk-nigga!*"

Muthafucka backhanded my ass so hard, I swore I saw my own momma giving birth to me. "*You done lost your fuckin' mind,*" *Issac roared.*

I was pretty sure that his ass was about to haul off and hit my ass again, but at that very moment, a shot rang out.

We froze and glanced up.

Terrell stood in the doorway with my .38 firmly gripped in his hand. Behind my nephew stood his best friend, Kyjuan, holding another piece that he must've gotten from the front room. Both aimed at Isaac.

"*Get the fuck off her,*" *Terrell said in a menacing voice that defied his age.*

If Isaac was surprised by the change in events, it didn't show in his face. In fact, he eyeballed the two boys hard while he calculated his odds on the situation.

Fuck. I struggled on whether to give the command for them to blast his ass or intervene. That's how pissed my ass was.

Isaac must've come to the calculation that Terrell wasn't playing because suddenly his hands came up and he eased his big ass off of me. "*All right, Terrell. You're right. Shit got a little out of control in here. I wasn't tryna hurt your Aunt Peaches.*"

Terrell's aim and gaze didn't waiver. "*Momma P, you want us to shoot his ass?*"

I sat up and then scooted the hell out the way.

Isaac tossed me a curious look, concerned that my ass hadn't told the boys to put the guns down.

I took my time, feeling on my busted lip while weighing my deci-

sion. Finally, my senses came back to me. I couldn't have these little boys commit their first homicide before they finished the first grade. "Nah. Don't shoot him."

Though he didn't show it, I knew Isaac's ass was relieved.

"Y'all go on back outside and play," I told them. "Put the guns back in the table drawer in the living room."

They didn't move.

"Go on now," I shouted, agitated.

They lowered their weapons, but took their time creeping from the door.

"Took your damn time with that shit, didn't you?" Isaac growled.

"Don't start. It ain't too late for me to call them back and tell them to shoot your cheating ass." I sat there and glared at his ass while my heart ripped its way out of my chest.

Isaac heaved out a deep breath while he figured out a different way to come at me. "You're right. My shit was foul. I don't know what the fuck I was thinking. That shit is squashed. Word is bond on that shit."

Lie. Lie. Lie.

I shook my head and fought my emotions. Before I knew it, Isaac had squat down next to me and tried to pull me into his arms. "Get off me." I shrugged him off. "You really picked a bad day for this shit," I told him as my troubled thoughts circled back to Alice and Mason. Before I knew it, tears were rolling down my face.

"Fuck," Isaac said, stunned. He had never seen my ass cry before. Hell, even I couldn't remember the last time I did that shit.

"What's really up with you, ma?" Isaac gathered me back into his arms, but that time, I didn't have the strength to fight him off. I unburdened myself onto those strong shoulders. It was a good thing, too, because the phone started ringing off the hook from reporters. Frankly, it looked like those nosy muthafuckas were more interested in tearing up my family than actually helping us find Mason. Alice's and my long-ass record had police—people who didn't even know us—concluding that Alice more than likely sold her baby for crack.

After reading Alice's account of the last time she'd seen her son—

I believed that shit, too. She claimed some chick she blazed with, Dribbles, could back her up, but reporters hadn't been able to locate anyone by that name. Clearly, Alice was just pulling shit out her ass.

For the days that followed, I squashed the shit between me and Isaac . . . temporarily. I told myself that we would pick up that bullshit after we found my nephew, but after two weeks, the media no longer cared about a crackhead's missing black baby. The phone calls stopped, the media vans disappeared, and the police moved on. Shotgun Row was happy to see the attention leave because their presence was affecting niggas' pockets, but my thirst for justice and answers had only gotten stronger.

That meant I had to see Alice.

The second I planted my ass in the chair in the visiting room, I wanted to bounce back up and waltz out of that muthafucka. I couldn't get the image of Mason lying in a ditch somewhere or maybe even tossed in the bottom of some garbage dump out of my mind. If Alice didn't want the baby, she could've left him with me. Sure, I would've bitched, but I would've taken care of him. I had always picked up the broken pieces.

The metal door opened and a line of women in prison uniforms marched out to take their seats before the Plexiglas and their visitors.

When Alice strolled out, she looked rough as hell. Her once beautiful, black hair was long and stringy, her eyes were hollow and shifty, and her full lips were pale and dry. For a second, my heart softened and all I could see was that twelve-year-old with tears rolling down her face and blood oozing down her leg. I had a feeling that she was always going to be that girl to me.

Alice took one look at me, pivoted, and started to march out.

I leapt to my feet and pounded on the Plexiglas. "Alice!"

The guards jumped to attention and one even came up behind me to pull me back. "Alice!" I shrugged off the guard. "If I leave I'm never coming back."

That didn't seem to bother her.

"And you'll never see Terrell again," I threatened.

She stopped.

The guard's hand landed back on my shoulder and I tossed up my hands. "Okay. Okay. I'm going," I told him. If the bitch didn't want to talk to me then fuck it.

"Wait," Alice yelled.

I almost didn't stop, but I did. By the time I turned around, Alice was sitting in her chair and picking up the black phone. Grudgingly, I returned to my chair, but I waited before picking up. For a few seconds we listened to each other breathe.

"Well?" she asked, twitching in her seat. "What the fuck do you want?"

"What do you think? I want to know where Mason is."

Alice's face hardened. "Why don't you tell me?"

I dropped the phone and rolled my eyes to the sky. "Lord, give me strength." When I looked at her again, her eyes were brimming with contempt. I knew then that she was going to stick to her bullshit story. "I don't have time for this."

"Please. I'm not stupid," she said, twitching in her seat. "I know that you took Mason. It couldn't have been anybody but you."

It was too big of a bait for me to ignore so I snatched the phone up again. "And why in the hell would I do that?"

"Because your dried-up pussy can't make any babies," she shot back and then leaned toward the Plexiglas. "You can't stand that I'm more of a woman than you'll ever be. Face it. That's why all your niggas creep they way into my bed. They want to be with a real woman. That loose shit between your legs never could keep a man. In the end they all come to me wanting a taste of the real thing. Ask Isaac."

The bottom fell out of my stomach. The evil bitch just shot me in my heart. I didn't even have time to beat back the tears. "You're lying," I whispered.

Alice watched the water roll down my face and thrust up her chin with pride. "Am I?"

Our gazes crashed in what felt like a duel to the death, but my ass came up short. "You hate me that much?"

"If you were me, wouldn't you hate you, too?"

What the fuck could I say to that shit? She was never gonna see *things from my side. What was the point of wasting more time and words on the issue? "All right. I'm glad that you got all that shit off your chest. Now that I know how the fuck you feel, we can squash the make-believe sisterly bullshit between us once and for all. I'm tired. You and your bullshit make me so fuckin' tired. But it's over. You hear me? You're dead to me."*

"Is this what the fuck you came down here for—to make me watch you climb up on that cross again? Squash that shit. I'm dead to you?" she shouts. "You're dead to me, bitch. I should've killed you when I took out your nigga Leroy!"

The image of twelve-year-old Alice firing our Nana's gun flashed in my head again. Two bullets slammed into Leroy's chest and two blazed holes into my left leg.

"Trust and believe that the world would've been a better place without your ass in it," she spat.

I slammed the phone back down and stood up.

"YOU HEAR ME? I SHOULD HAVE KILLED YOU!"

"Fuck you. I hope your ass rots in here," I mumbled under my breath as more tears rolled down my face.

Alice ranted as I headed out the door. "I want my sons back, bitch! GIMME ME BACK MY SONS!"

As the memory drifts away, I squeeze my eyes tighter and beg a God that I no longer believe in to end this shit. Apparently, He doesn't believe in my ass either because the only answer I get is the familiar squeak from the basement stairs.

She's back.

Groaning, I struggle to uncurl from one corner in the room, but when I move an inch my body mutinies and I ball up even tighter. A key rattles in the lock and then a second later, Alice strolls into the room wearing a bright smile.

"Good morning," she sings, after spotting me in a corner. "I see you're up early." Alice walks over to the rickety wooden chair at the foot of the bed and sets the food down.

The smell of bacon and eggs has my stomach twisting into double knots and a new sheen of sweat beads my hairline.

"I figured that you should be sick of flapjacks by now so I switched it up."

"Alice, please. I need . . . to get to a doctor."

"Oh. You're fine. You probably just have a stomach flu. You'll shake it off in a couple of days." Her smile thins out as our eyes connect.

She's changed since I've been down here. Her long gray hair has been dyed back to it once youthful color of a warm chestnut, except for a strip in the front—exactly how I used to wear my shit. She's wearing makeup and if I'm not mistaken that's my blue dress, hugging her slim body. *What the fuck is wrong with this girl?*

"I see you staring." Alice spins around so that the dress's skirt fans around her. "You like?"

My stomach does another painful lurch. "Alice, please."

What's left of my sister's smile fades. "Humph." She cocks her head and inches her way toward me. "You know . . . maybe you're right. You don't look so good. In fact . . . you look kind of green." Alice stops at our invisible line. She knows how far the chain shackled around my one good leg and arm will allow me to reach—if I wasn't doubled over in pain. It doesn't matter. The chains stopped being necessary a while ago. Pain is my shackle now.

"It doesn't feel so good when someone tosses you in a cage and then throws away the key, does it?" Alice asks, looking philosophical. "The feeling of abandonment is so profound, isn't it? The absence of love, caring, and understanding. It's downright inhuman."

My answer is a long, winding groan. I can't help it. It feels like I've swallowed a box of nails. The simple task of breathing is a bitch. "Get me to a doctor," I plead in between trying to process small sips of air, but I think my lungs are shutting down. "Please."

Alice sighs and shakes her head. "Sorry. No can do. Seeing how I've escaped the hospital myself, I'm sure you can understand why it's best that I avoid them."

"You can . . . just drop me off in the emergency room," I reason. "I promise . . . I won't tell anyone about this."

"There you go again—treating me like I'm stupid." She tsks under her breath as if scolding a child. "I've always hated it when you did that shit. Just like I've always hated how you thought your ass was always better than me. We came from the same place. At one point, we both had monkeys on our backs." She closes her eyes as if just mentioning them brought her to ecstasy.

When she opens them again, I see something that makes my heart skip a few beats.

"You're never going to see a doctor." Boldly, she crosses over the imaginary line and hunches down next to me so that she can take a long whiff of my hair.

I can feel her shutter as another wave of ecstasy washes over her.

"Face it, Maybelline. This room is your coffin . . . and the only time you're coming out of this basement is when I bury you by the big oak tree in the yard."

18

Lucifer

Dribbles draws a deep breath and rakes her hands through her hair like she doesn't know where to begin. I try to wait her out, but my curiosity is all over the place.

"You gotta tell me something. I'm freaking out over here. Mason had an older brother?"

"It was all so long ago and . . . it doesn't matter now anyway. Sometimes it's best to let sleeping dogs lie." She turns and looks out the limousine's window.

She has a point, but that's not satisfying me at the moment. "Do you have a name? Maybe . . . this *brother* would like to know what has happened to Mason. I could go and . . . what is it?" I'm freaked out about the number of tears falling over Dribble's lashes.

"Let it go. Trust me, going down that road will only lead to more trouble. He's gone now. Just let it go."

"Gone? You mean Mason or the brother? What about Alice? Is she still alive?"

Dribbles flinches. "How did you know her name was Alice?"

I hesitate for a moment and decide that the best way to get her confidence is to give her some of mine. "Smokestack."

"Oh, he did, did he?" She searches for his face by the gravesite. "Funny. I don't remember him being so chatty. Did he also tell you that *he* was the one who decided to take Mason from Alice that day?"

"Well, he did find him in the oven. Imagine if she had turned the damn thing on."

Dribbles looks agitated. "She was high. I give you that— and she made a mistake, but what happened to her afterwards, she didn't deserve that—prison and then the crazy house. We shouldn't have taken her baby."

"You wanted to give him back?" I ask, shocked.

"Everybody deserves a second chance. I'm living proof of that." She crosses her arms and hugs herself. "Don't get me wrong. I loved Mason. Lord knows I did, but I wasn't any better than Alice. You remember. I was a hot mess roaming up and down these streets, robbing, stealing, and fucking anything just to get to high. You're lucky. You don't know what it's like. You deal that poison, but you've never fucked up and got a monkey on your back.

"If nothing else, I understood Alice. We may have come from different backgrounds, but we were fucked up together. What Alice did could've easily happened to me. We were friends. She used to confide in me. Let me tell you that girl went through some shit that really messed her up. I'm the last person who should judge her."

I'm trying hard to understand where Dribbles is coming from. "If you felt that way about it, why didn't you take Mason back?"

"The way shit blew up, taking him back would've landed me in jail. There was a nationwide search for him for about a year. I was convinced that no matter what I said, they would've thrown the book at me."

"But Cousin Skeet knew that you had him."

"C'mon. Skeet wasn't going to turn in his own brother. Besides, he thought Smokestack would do a better job with the kid than Alice anyway. After all, she'd already abandoned Mason's older brother with one of her family members. He thought it would be just a matter of time before she did the same with Mason."

I let that hang in the air between us for a few minutes. Before, when Smokestack had told me the story, I was glad that Smokestack and Dribbles came to Mason's rescue. If they hadn't, I would have never met him. I can't imagine where I'd be if Mason had never been a part of my life. Now, Dribbles has made Alice sound more human.

"One year turned into two and then three and then pretty soon, Smokestack and I were the only parents Mason knew. I loved him as if he were my own." She wrings her hands. "Still, it doesn't make it right though."

"No. But if you ask me, you made the right decision."

Dribbles' watery gaze shifts back to me. "Yeah?"

"I've learned that life is filled with a lot that's hard and unfair. We do what we do and hope that it all comes out in the wash at the end. You and Smokestack saved a life that day and then you provided and loved him the best you could. You have to believe that it was enough."

She smiles. "You're very wise."

"I don't know about that," I laugh.

"I do. You're very smart . . . and beautiful. You could do anything that you set your mind to. Why would you want . . ."

My smile melts away. "What? Say it."

"Why would you want to go down this violent and dangerous path as the supreme chief of the Vice Lords? You're smart enough to know that there's only two ways on how this is going to end."

"Actually, there's only one way *all* our stories are going to end. Nobody gets out of life alive."

Dribbles throws back her head and laughs. "I guess you got me there."

The conversation draws to an end and my curiosity is still

getting the best of me. "I still think that we should at least send his other family something . . . even if it's anonymously."

She shakes her head again.

I'm at the end of my patience. "All right. What's up? Why all the roadblocks?"

"Why can't you let go?" she pushes back. "Nothing good will come out of it. If anything, it will just cause more problems."

"Fine. I guess I'll just go online and find the information out for myself. It shouldn't be too hard to search the newspapers' archives for the story."

Dribbles' shoulders deflate in defeat. "Why are you doing this? Is it that important?"

"It is now." We engage in a stare-down that I win easily.

"Fine." Dribbles tosses up her hands. "What do you want to know?"

19

LeShelle

November . . .

"DIE, BITCH! DIE!"

Ta'Shara flies toward me with a pair of knitting needles and my eyes suddenly spring open. I blink, then glance around, confused by my surroundings. A loud, steady beep catches my attention and I swing my head to the left and recognize a heart monitor.

What the fuck?

I try to move, but my body mutinies until I give up. That's when I notice the tubes and needles sprouting out of my arms and hands, as well as—handcuffs?

"Well, well, well. Look who rose from the dead."

Startled, I jerk my head to the right and toward the last muthafucka I want to see: Captain Johnson. "What the hell do you want?" The second the question clears my dry throat, I erupt into a spasm of coughs.

Captain Johnson strolls from the door and bears down on me. "You have the right to remain silent. Anything you say can and will be used against you in a court of law. You have the right to an attorney. If you can't afford one then one will be appointed to you. Blah, blah, blah." He stops at the bed's railing and leans down. "I've been waiting three months for you to wake up."

Three months? That shit can't be true.

"Where is he?" Johnson hisses.

The alcohol on his breath singes my nose hairs. "Who?"

A wide, sinister smile slithers over the corners of Johnson's mouth while he plucks one of the pillows from behind my head and starts fluffing it. "Don't play. My patience is real thin. It wouldn't take much for it to snap."

This crazy muthafucka places the pillow against my mouth and nose and glares into my eyes. "You feel me?"

I clamp my mouth shut.

"Now I'm going to ask you again: Where is Python? I *know* that he survived that car crash. Only you know all the little places that snake likes to hide. SO TALK!"

What the fuck is he talking about? I don't even know where the hell I am.

Johnson adds pressure to the pillow.

I twist my head in an attempt to steal some air, but Johnson locks my head between his hands. Air traps itself in my chest. My eyes bulge while the beeping on the heart monitor speeds up.

"Your fuckin' life don't mean shit to me," he growls. "I'd be doing the world a favor by erasing you off the face of the earth. He killed my daughter and you're the sick fuck who tortured my grandson."

The pressure mounts, causing my temples to hammer my skull. My survival instincts kick in and my weak limbs fight back. Next thing I know, I'm dragging my nails down the side of his face.

"Aaaarggh!"

Johnson's grip on the pillow loosens and I'm able to push him and the pillow off my face. The instant stream of oxygen sends me into another spasm of coughs.

Johnson touches his face and then gazes down at his blood-painted fingers. "You fuckin' bitch!" He comes at me again with his fist cocked.

"What the hell is going on in here?" a woman's voice snaps from the doorway.

Johnson and I jerk our heads to the door where a plus-size woman in a pair of floral hospital scrubs glares at us like a disappointed parent. By the time Johnson finds his tongue, the nurse charges toward him and shoves him out of the way.

"She's fine," the captain barks. "We were just talking and she got a little excited."

The nurse frowns and then scolds him for his answer. "You should have called the nurses' station." When she turns to me, her frown morphs into a smile. "As for you, Ms. Murphy, we're glad to have you back." She picks up the discarded pillow, fluffs and then places it behind my head.

"You could have fooled me," I croak through my dry throat. "You guys have one hell of a welcoming committee." I lift and refer to my shackled wrist.

The nurse's frown returns. "Let's not focus on that right now. You need to concentrate on getting better. My name is Maureen and I'm going to be your nurse on duty today. I've already paged Dr. Berg and he is on his way."

"Fine. Fine." The captain shoves Maureen. "I need to finish interrogating my prisoner."

Maureen snatches her arm back and stands her ground. "This is not the time or place for that. Under the circumstances, I doubt whatever this young lady says will stand up in a court of law anyway. We don't even know whether she's lucid enough to understand what's happening."

"Mind your own damn business."

Maureen jabs a hand onto her hip. "*This* is my business. You can either step out or get knocked out. Your choice." She tilts her head side to side, cracking a few bones in her neck.

I don't doubt for a second that she can take Johnson. Her *I-don't give-a-fuck*-attitude reminds me of Momma Peaches.

Johnson gives the nurse a nasty look while his face purples, but whatever bullshit he's about to blast is cut off when a man in a white coat strolls into the room.

"Ahh. So it's true. Our sleeping beauty has awakened." The doctor with snow-white hair flashes a smile and reaches for a pen-sized flashlight in his front pocket. He's completely oblivious to the war he's interrupted. "I'm Dr. Berg—and I've been taking care of you these few months."

In the next second, I'm blind.

"Look to your left. Uh, huh. To your right. That's a good girl." He clicks off the light and then gets busy jotting shit into my chart. "How are we feeling today, Ms. Murphy?"

Captain Johnson backs away from the bed.

"Much better now that you guys are here," I croak.

"That's good. That's good." The doctor starts unsnapping the buttons in the front of my gown. "Let's me just take a peek at how some of your wounds are healing."

It takes a second before my brain catches up to what he's saying, but by that time, my gown is open and I glance down at a minefield of multicolored stabs wounds across my chest. Fuck. I don't even recognize my shit.

"You're one lucky girl," Dr. Berg says, smiling and writing again. "Do you remember anything that led to your being here?"

"I don't know where here is," I tell him.

"You're at Baptist Memorial. Do you remember what happened?"

DIE, BITCH! DIE! Ta'Shara's demonic face flashes before my eyes and my hands ball at my sides and I nod my head.

The doctor smiles again and then buries his head into my chart. For the next thirty minutes, I suffer through a flurry of activity and a battery of questions. To my horror, this dirty cop hadn't lied. My ass has been knocked out for three whole months. *Where are my people at?* I glance around the room.

Ain't nobody here to hold me down? They ain't got *no* love for the throne?

Johnson steps back into the room.

The monitor besides me beeps like crazy.

"Her blood pressure is skyrocketing," Nurse Maureen announces. Her gaze follows mine to the captain. "Maybe it's best that you step back out of the room."

"Fuck that," he barks. "I'm not going anywhere until I get some answers out of that . . ." He chews on the word that he wanted to say. ". . . your patient."

The nurse and doctor exchange annoyed looks, but Johnson ignores them.

Another nurse enters the room, rolling a cart of some kind. She looks stunned to see that I'm awake.

"If you've come to draw her blood come on now," Nurse Maureen says, pulling out a small vial.

The new nurse scrambles around Johnson and comes up on the left side of the bed. While she preps to draw blood, Nurse Maureen injects something into my IV.

The doctor smiles. "This is just something to calm you down."

Instantly, the shit puts me on ice.

Dr. Berg spits out a laundry list of tests that he wants to perform. I try to concentrate on what he's saying but it goes in one ear and out the other.

I jump at a sudden sharp pinch. "What the fuck?"

"Sorry," the nervous nurse says after stabbing me with a needle. "You moved your hand."

Does everybody think my ass is a pin cushion? I keep an eye on her, wondering if this is the first time that she has done this.

"All right," the doctor says, flipping my folder closed. "If you don't have any questions for me, I'll leave you to get some rest. If you need anything, press the button next to you. It'll connect you to the nurses' station. Okay?" He flashes me a smile and pats me on my leg. "We're going to get you fixed up and out of here as soon as we can."

Barely able to keep my eyes open, I nod and then track him as he heads for the door. My attention zooms back toward the silent nurse when I feel something being crammed into my hand. Frowning, I look down at a folded piece of paper.

The nurse gives me a look, telling me to keep this shit on the down-low before she scrambles to catch up with Dr. Berg at the door.

Captain Johnson steps up to the bed's rail, ready for round two.

"Doctor," I call out despite my burning throat.

Dr. Berg turns and the nervous nurse tenses up.

Fighting the drugs, I continue, "I just need a witness of me telling this dirty muthafucka here that I don't have shit to say until I talk to my lawyer."

Rage seizes Johnson's face as he swings his heated gaze between me and the doctor.

"Any further interrogation or attempted murder on his part will be brought up before a judge as a breach of my civil rights." I glare back at Johnson. *That's right, muthafucka. I know how to play this game.*

Dr. Berg clears his throat. "I'm sorry, Captain. But I'm going to have to ask you to leave."

"She is under my custody," Johnson seethes.

"First and foremost, she is my patient—that takes precedence." The doctor puffs up his chest. "Ms. Murphy has sustained quite a bit of trauma. I can't have you adding to her stress. Besides, she requested to speak with an attorney, I don't see why you or your man can't just wait outside the door until one arrives or she's released from our care. I assure you, she's not going anywhere."

Johnson plants himself in the doctor's face. "I don't give a fuck about that shit. The bitch is going to talk!"

"Captain Johnson," the doctor gasps. "The young lady has just awoken from a three-month coma and has requested to speak with an attorney. Now, I'm going to have to ask you to leave—or you'll leave me no choice but to place a call to your superiors."

Checkmate, muthafucka.

Johnson struggles with his temper until he jabs a finger toward me and snarls. "This isn't over, Ms. Murphy."

"Captain Johnson," the doctor warns impatiently.

"Fuck off," Johnson barks.

The doctor jumps back.

"And as for you," Johnson hisses as he leans back over the bed. "I'll be back—maybe even with a certain young man soldier who wants to talk to you about a certain prom date you crashed."

My heart stops.

His smile returns. "Think it over."

Instead of cussing his ass out, I clamp my jaw tight and glare at everyone as they clear out of my room.

Once alone, I remember the folded piece of paper in my hand and read:

I got you—
Python.

20

Lucifer

Pregnant.

After spending a full hour pissing on a dozen home-pregnancy tests, it's time for me to accept the truth—but I can't. In fact, I don't even want to leave this bathroom, let alone hop off this toilet until one of these sticks stops turning blue.

What am I gonna do?

I can't be that bitch that wobbles into combat, hoping my water doesn't break.

"Jeez." I toss the stick over into the sink and then drop my head into my hands. *This can't be happening.* Mason flashes behind my closed eyes and I'm ashamed of the way that I'm reacting.

My mind has been spinning for the past month from all the information Dribbles unloaded on me. The moment she said the name Carver, pieces of the puzzle started snapping together. Memories of how Python wept when he clutched Mason in the rain. *How did he put two and two together?*

I should have drilled Dribbles for more information, but I was too busy tryna reject what she was saying. *Brothers.* How the fuck could that be? And what the hell would happen if that shit ever got out? Would it change anything or would it change everything?

I wish that I could talk to Bishop about this shit, but things between us are getting worse with each passing day. At every meeting, Bishop feels way too comfortable challenging and confronting every decision I make. It's not clear that he's winning anyone over, but I can tell they are all waiting to see how I'm going to check my own brother.

The alarm on my watch sounds and I reach over to the bathroom sink and check the results of yet another test.

Still pregnant.

Who gives a fuck what niggas think? I'm having this baby.

The second the declaration thunders in my head my shoulders get lighter and a sad smile twitches at the corners of my lips. My cell phone rings and I have to reach down and retrieve it from my pants pooled around my feet.

"Yeah."

"We need to meet," Cousin Skeet says

Just like that, the weight returns to my shoulders. "Whassup?"

"In person. Make it over to Hemp's for a one-on-one."

"Time?"

"Fifteen minutes."

I draw a deep breath. I don't feel like dealing with Cousin Skeet right now—especially since he's been throwing up roadblocks like a muthafucka, preventing me and Profit from getting at LeShelle's tube-sucking ass lying in the hospital. Skeet's taking a lot of heat from the city for the escalating wars on the street—says it's his ass if we turn the Baptist Memorial into another war zone tryna get that bitch.

"A'ight." I end the call and roll my eyes.

The shit is on ice but I'll get that bitch, either in the hospital or a jail cell. I don't give a fuck which.

Exactly fifteen minutes later, my boy Tombstone rolls us up

to Hemp's Liquor Store. I peek behind the bulletproof windows to see if anybody's mobbing too deep. There are two cars in this busted-ass parking lot and one crackhead couple stumbling down the sidewalk and beating on each other.

"Why the fuck am I out here?" I mumble before climbing out of the car. "Stay here," I order Tombstone.

"You got it, boss."

On full alert, I march through the front door. A loud cowbell announces me, getting the fat chick with a red Ronald McDonald-colored wig on to look up from her magazine.

"Go on back. He's expecting you," she says, hitting a buzzer that unlocks a metal door off to her left.

I erase all emotions from my face and march through the second door.

Off the bat, Cousin Skeet stops pacing to look up.

"I'm here. Speak your mind," I tell him.

"Have a seat," Skeet says, gesturing to an unfolded iron chair.

"I'll stand."

He gives me a look, and then must realize that he needs to change up the attitude. "All right, look. I know that we have never really gotten along in the past, but I'm hoping that we can try to let bygones be bygones—especially if we're going to continue being business partners."

"Humph. *If* being the key word."

The smile melts off Skeet's face. "So it's true. You have reached out to the Angels of Mercy to run guns for the Vice Lords."

Shit. Bishop sold me out.

Skeet storms up to me.

"You really want to deal with those racist fucks?"

"Don't take it personal. It's just business. Supply and demand. I have a demand and they can get me my supply. You cut me off. Remember?" I hold my ground while he breathes fire into my face.

"Nah. Nah. You're tryna cut me."

"You sound a little paranoid."

"Don't fucking play me. Do you know who the fuck you're dealing with?"

I clamp my mouth shut and indulge him his temper tantrum.

"You think those white muthafuckas are going to do right by the VLs? All they give a fuck about is the money. They don't give a fuck about the cause."

I remain silent.

Skeet's face purples. "Listen here, you bitch. You have another thing coming if you think you can just cut me out. I've been the backbone of this organization since before you were swimming around in your daddy's nut sack. You and half the damn set would be pumped with a bunch of lethal injections if it weren't for me. Who the fuck do you think you are?"

Silence.

I don't know what color to call his face now, but I can tell he's itching to go for that gun on his hip.

"Mason and Bishop fucked up with you," he says, waving a finger in my face. "I always said 'let a bitch play with men's toys and suddenly she thinks her ass got balls.' Well, let me tell you something, little girl. You *do not* want to fuck with me. Our arrangement stands and for this latest insult an extra fifteen percent has been tacked onto my not-putting-your-ass-in-prison fee."

"That's not going to happen," I tell him.

"Excuuuuuse me?" Cousin Skeet moves in so close that our noses touch.

"You heard me. The arrangement stays as it is—until I decide to change it," I say evenly. "If you think that you want to go to war with *me*, then that's your choice; but I guaran-damn-tee you that the shit ain't going to end the way that you think it is. And as far as trying to replace me on the throne with Bishop, that shit ain't going to happen, either. Now, I'm going to walk out of here and pretend that this conversation never happened. For your sake, it's best."

We fall into a glaring contest and, about thirty seconds later, Skeet backs the hell out of it.

"All right. We'll play this shit your way—for now."

"For now." I give him my back and head toward the door. "Oh, by the way, how is that bitch holding up in the hospital?"

Skeet pauses. "Still out of commission."

"You can't protect her forever."

"The last damn thing I'm doing is protecting that bitch. Don't forget that I have a score to settle with her myself for the trauma she and her nigga put my grandson through. He's seriously fucked up, trembling and pissing on himself all the time. I'm going to be stuck with therapy bills for the rest of my damn life."

I struggle to hold my tongue. After all, Cousin Skeet's family issues aren't my problem or business—not anymore.

"She's in the system. I gotta give the city something, my neck is still on the line."

A smile twitches at the corners of my lips.

Cousin Skeet's eyes narrow. "I wouldn't be too happy about it if I were you. If I go down, so does VL."

"You threatening me again?" I square around on him. "You really believe that shit, don't you?" I laugh. "Nigga, you ain't nobody. You ain't putting in no serious work or moving no fuckin' cause. You want to know why I don't like you? It's because I can't stand muthafuckas who wear two faces. I'm straight up about who I am and what the fuck I do. And in case you done forgot, I'm your worst muthafuckin' nightmare." I jab my finger against his chest. "I won't think twice about slicing your ass like the fucking pig you are and bathe in your goddamn blood. I dream about that shit. So remember that the next time you're throwing threats around. I. AM. KING. And *nobody* has bigger balls than I do."

Cousin Skeet steps back with stunned disbelief.

Now that I've gotten that shit off my chest, I relax and flash him a fake smile. "You have a nice night." I turn and stroll out of the door. Once I'm out of Hemp's, I stop and suck in the night's cool air to lower my blood pressure. *Bishop. Bishop. Bishop.*

I don't know why I don't immediately hop into the car. Maybe I just need a few more minutes to think—but as I do, I get the distinct feeling that someone else is watching me. I glance around, see a few niggas scattered about, but no one that's paying me any particular attention . . . and yet, the feeling doesn't go away.

Tombstone rolls his window down and sticks his head out. "Everything all right, boss?"

I doubt anything will ever be all right again. "Yeah. I'm cool." I take one last look around and then hop into the SUV. "Swing by the grocery store. I'm craving some ice cream . . . and pickles."

Chaos

21

Qiana

December…

Profit's fine ass is a god. His name stays on the lips of every Flower in a thirty-mile radius. We all have caught glimpses of his ass working out in Fat Ace's old gym. Sweat pours down and glistens all over his body, getting every bitch hot. I have the perfect view from my bedroom window and more than a few times I've laid across my bed and stroked my clit while he did his thing. It's been some of the most powerful orgasms I've ever had. I wish there was some way that I could make him mine, but with my fucked-up mug that shit ain't in the cards for my ass right now.

My dream boo's dedication has been so strong that other soldiers are now tryna step up their game. Some of them doin' all right, but all eyes fall on Profit—and it's causing ripples with the power players. At the moment, Lucifer still has the most juice. Bishop is a close second but is growing bolder every day by openly politicking to dethrone his own sister. There's no doubt that Bishop has a reputation of being a strong soldier and leader, but the truth of the matter is that niggas ain't scared of him like they are of his sister. In war mode, Lucifer is just that: the devil with breasts. The few times that we exchanged words, I've damn near pissed in my panties. The bitch is that intense. I only question how much more rope she is going to give Bishop before he hangs himself. Some don't think that she has the balls to smoke her own brother over the shit. I say Bishop is the one who don't have the balls.

For my money, the real threat to her throne is Profit. Though my boo ain't been a soldier long or put in a catalog of work like a lot of niggas, there's just something about his swagger that has our people thinking his ass is a natural-born leader. Fuck. I recognized that shit a while back. While there's a potential war within our ranks, GG kept it 100 on her prediction with the Crips. Those niggas are all the way foul. Plus, they're hittin' the streets with a new product that got the crackheads and drug fiends buzzing. I've tasted the product and I ain't gonna lie, the shit is tight enough to change the game.

With Fat Ace murked and Python M.I.A., those slob niggas are hustlin' corner boys off their spot and upping the number of drive-bys. Purple flags are flying everywhere. The shit forced Lucifer to pull some soldiers from the hunt for Python to deal with the new threat, but the next thing we knew we were engaged in *two* wars. The dead bodies stacking on the news is like reading the roll call of who's who of the gang royalty.

You'd think that niggas would wall up and stay the fuck out of the streets with so many bullets flying, but danger has a way of drawing people out. Vice Lords mob deep in the streets and we all have itchy fingers—my ass included.

Almost everywhere I go I keep Jayson—that's what I named that high yellow bitch's baby boy—strapped to my chest. I gotta say that despite having an ugly-ass daddy, Jayson is turning out to be a pretty cute kid. I ain't claiming to be domesticated or no shit like that, but I'm getting better at taking care of him. At least he's stopped hollering all the time and sleeps though the night. I'm just wondering if there's something wrong with him since his head is bigger than the rest of him.

Today, I catch word that a few soldiers have talked Profit's ass into hanging out at Da Club. I hit GG up and talk her into watching the kid for a few hours so me and my girls can be in the spot. I'm lucky that GG has also taken a liking to the kid and agrees.

Me, Lil Bit, and Adaryl ain't old enough to be at the spot, but being Tombstone's sister does have it privileges.

Adaryl discovered some flesh-colored bandages and lined three on each side of my face. The shit isn't perfect, but it stops me from looking like Frankenstein and sort of like my former self—especially when the hem of my black-and-gold dress barely covers the bottom curve of my round ass and the V in the front dips two inches above my belly button, but I keep my titties protected by using that special dress tape so I can avoid wardrobe malfunctions. It don't matter because without a bra, my nipples are saying hello to every nigga when I step into the club.

My wing girls look equally fly. Adaryl's young, Coke-bottle curves are encased in a black catsuit while Lil Bit's short ass is flossing a gold Gucci dress she snatched off the rack in one of the malls. We're three teenagers tryna look grown and doing a damn good job.

"You two be on your best behavior tonight," Cutty warns from the door. "The last thing I want is for Tombstone to be putting his foot on my neck if something happens to his kid sister."

"Whatever." I roll my eyes at all that noise Cutty is bumping and strut my ass inside. Even though I put on a hard front, inside my nerves are twisted into knots.

"Damn. Your brother be cock-blockin' even when he ain't here," Lil Bit complains.

"Fuck that." I wave her and Cutty off and then cut my way

through the crowd. A few slick niggas call themselves being funny and grab my ass. When I turn to cuss them out, everyone puts on they innocent face. "Uh, huh. Scary-ass muthafuckas." I turn and switch my hips through the crowd. Bodies are bumping and grinding to Juicy J's latest track. Hell, I don't even have to pull out my own shit to get the party started, there's a thick weed cloud hovering over everybody. There's everything from Kush, AK-47, and White Widow rolling up in here.

"Goddamn. This shit is strong." Adaryl waves her hand in front of her face. I sneak a peek over my shoulder to see her eyes droop. She's about as fucked up as I am.

Lil Bit already has some nigga in her face, flashing his platinum grillz and rubbing his chest on her titties for a cheap thrill. Jealousy ain't an easy monster to try and control. There was a time not too long ago when I was the first bitch in my clique to pull niggas.

"What can I get you ladies?" the bartender asks once we make it to the counter.

"Two Blue Muthafuckas," I order and then glance around the club.

"What time you think Profit and them showing up?" Lil Bit asks, peeping at her cell phone for the time.

"I don't know. They'll get here when they get here." Irritated, I eyeball the door.

The bartender sets down our drinks. "Here you go, ladies. Compliments of the house."

"Well, all right now!" Lil Bit shrieks, slapping high-fives and reaching for her glass at the same time. My girl may be small, but the bitch drinks like a fish. I already know that I'm going to have to keep one eye on her while checking for my boo to arrive.

Off the bat, I see chicken heads grinding on a whole lotta bustas who ain't gonna do nuthin' but pour liquor down they throats, bust 'em out, and then call it a night. "These niggas are whack as hell," I complain.

"You want to go somewhere else?" Lil Bit asks, bouncing in her chair to the beat.

I shrug and try not to sulk that ain't no nigga approached me to dance yet. An hour later, Lil Bit and Adaryl return from burning up the dance floor while I'm sucking on my third drink and holding up the bar counter. *Where the fuck is Profit's ass at?* I'm feeling like a real busta right now.

"Hey. You don't think Profit is already here and is hugged up with some tricks back there?" I ask.

My girls bob their shoulders.

"Anything is possible," Adaryl says, signaling the bartender for another drink. "I hear they have private parties back there."

"Shiiit." I'm out here for a party that I can't get at?

My girls laugh as I stretch my neck as far as possible to see if I can catch a glimpse of Profit in VIP. "C'mon." I hop off my stool and adjust my skirt.

"Where are we going?" Lil Bit asks, frowning up as another nigga eases up on her.

"To VIP." I grab her by the wrist and drag her ass with me.

"Oooh. You finally gonna make a move?" she asks, grabbing Adaryl's wrist so that we form a train.

I don't answer because I ain't sure of what I'm going to do. All I know is that I want to see Profit. When we approach the all-important gateway to VIP, Hennessey, with his big bulky ass, blocks our entrance.

"Where do you think you girls are going?"

"Where does it look like?" I cop as much attitude as he dishes out—but he ain't having it. "Naw, shawty. You're not on the list."

"I'm on *all* the lists," I correct him.

"Not until you have a couple of more birthdays," he says, crossing his arms.

"C'mon, Qiana." Adaryl grabs my elbow. "Let's go."

Annoyed, I jerk free with embarrassment scorching my face. "Do you know who my brother is?"

"Of course I do. That's why I ain't letting your ass up in here. This here section is for grown niggas 'bout to do grown-ass thangs. You and your girls can go back and hold up the bar or shake your ass on the floor, but what goes on in here ain't for you."

"What the fuck? Are you serious?"

"Don't I look serious?" he asks, tilting down his shades so I can see his ink-black eyes.

"I'm the same age as Profit and you let his ass in."

"Shawty, you're seventeen and who said he was here yet?"

"Ain't he?"

Hennessey shrugs. "Maybe—maybe not. Who's to say?" He stretches his big baboon lips into a smile.

"Why, you big, greasy—"

"Qiana, let's just go." Lil Bit snatches my arm back.

"Listen to your little girlfriend there cause you ain't gettin' up here tonight, Qiana."

Me and this Godzilla muthafucka engage in a stare-off, while I fight the urge to fuck him up. In the end, I have to walk away with my tail tucked between my legs. To make shit worse, the niggas let the giggling bitches that was standing behind us switch they asses on through. I give Hennessey a *What the fuck?* look only for him to smirk at me. I toss him my middle finger and make a mental promise that the next time I see his big ass, I'm fuckin' him up on sight.

Bottom lip sagging, I let Lil Bit drag me back toward the bar. Halfway through, one bold muthafucka steps in my path and causes me to slam into his chest and break the hand connection with my girl.

"Whoa, sexy," his deep baritone rumbles above me. "Where's the fire?"

Twisting a frown before I glance up, I'm ready to take my

anger out on this dude, but my venom evaporates the minute my eyes fall on this sexy muthafucka. He's six four, green eyes, honey-baked, and built like a heavyweight champion. My ass blinks a couple of times to make sure that those four drinks I had ain't fucking with me. But this nigga gets finer with every blink I make. Dressed head-to-toe in white, the brothah stands out like a diamond in a pile of coal—with the name DIESEL tatted around his neck. That shit alone causes an extra gallon of honey to drip out of my honeypot.

When I don't answer, his sexy, plump lips spread out into a smile. "What? Cat got your tongue, Scar?"

My anger blazes back. "Fuck you!"

That shit tickles his balls because the next thing I know his muscular arm wraps around my waist and pulls me up to his frame. Any other complaint I have dies when I feel this nigga's anaconda rub against my wet panties.

"If fuckin' is what you got in mind we can make that shit happen right here."

Watching his green eyes twinkle, I realize this muthafucka is serious. Despite the desire rolling through me, I push at his chest, but the nigga's hold doesn't allow an inch to separate us.

"What? Don't tell me you're scared."

As much as my horny ass wants to jump him, my spidey sense is going haywire. "Ha. Ha, muthafucka. Who the fuck put you up to this?"

With his other hand, he puts a fat blunt up to his lips. His light green gaze turns pale blue while he studies me. Once he pulls the blunt away, he leans forward and tells me, "Open your mouth."

Under a trance, I obey and cum instantly when he blows that sweet skunk into my mouth. That shit takes my ass to another level.

"You feeling that, baby?" His lips hitch up to one side because he already knows the answer.

"Who the fuck is you?"

"The man of your dreams, thought you knew." This time he puts the blunt to my lips and tells me to "suck."

Again, my ass follows his orders. In no time at all I'm so high I can't feel my feet. Something in my belly starts fluttering when I watch him lower his head and open his mouth. Puckering my lips, I blow a steady stream of smoke back into his mouth. Before I'm done, he catches me off-guard and closes his mouth over mine. I've never tasted anything so sweet. Everything around me disappears.

When our lips part, I open my eyes and I am horrified to see that I got my arms wrapped around his thick neck and I'm grinding on him like I'm tryna to get *his* ass pregnant. Embarrassed, I spring back, but his hold remains firm.

"Where are you going, Scar?"

"Stop calling me that." I mush the front of his head.

"What?" His lips stretch wider. "I like a roughneck bitch with battle scars. What's your government name, shawty?"

I stare while I weigh whether I'm really mad. Cocky muthafucka is probably used to bitches falling all over his ass. "It's Nonya. As in 'none of your business.'"

"What if I made it my business?" His arm loosens.

I'm speechless on that shit.

"You got a man, Nonya?"

"What if I do?"

"I might take him out back so I can holler at him for a minute." He puffs on his blunt again while he stares me down. "How old are you, ma?"

"Old a damn 'nuff. Why?"

"Why you think? I'm feelin' you, but I ain't interested in going back in the joint for bustin' out no Girl Scout."

"I'm definitely no Girl Scout."

No lie, his blue eyes are now green again. Is his ass a human lie detector?

"Besides, I don't know you and I only fucks with my people. You feel me?"

"Your peoples, huh?" His lips hitch higher. "So you *are* a gangsta bitch."

"A gangsta diva, nigga." I toss up my VL signs and wait to see what the fuck he's gonna do next.

"Whatever, ma. Do you. I don't play that follow-the-leader bullshit. I'm my own nigga. I look out for number one. You feel me?"

He releases me and I try to squash my disappointment as he turns and walks away. For some reason, I follow his ass all the way to a booth on the opposite side of the club where another brothah is whispering in another chick's ear. When she looks up, my heart sinks.

"What the hell are you doin' up in here?" Amira, a Flower that lives a couple of doors down from me, asks.

"I'm minding my damn business, tryna set an example for your ass," I spit back at her. I know she ain't dumb enough to drop dime on my game.

Diesel snickers.

"Whatever." Amira shifts her glassy gaze between me and this new nigga before scooting out of the booth. "C'mon. Let's dance."

The nigga she's with climbs out behind her. Diesel cocks his head up with another smile. "You know how to clear a table."

I fight back a cocky smile.

He reaches for the Cîroc bottle on the table and refreshes one of the empty glasses. "So what's up, ma? You wanna holler at an independent nigga now?"

"I hate to tell you but every nigga up in here is VL. Where you from?"

"ATL, baby. All day." He pops his collar.

"You a long way from home. What—you get lost?"

"Just moved to town."

"You chose to *move* to this muthafuckin' city? What—you got a thing for graveyards or some shit?"

He shrugs. "I don't know. It ain't so bad here."

"You have pretty eyes, but clearly you're blind."

"I don't know about that. I certainly like what I see in front of me. Who knows, you might even get around to telling me your real name."

Nibbling on my bottom lip, I waver on what I wanna do about this nigga. Maybe I tease him for too long because suddenly his mood changes up.

"A'ight. Look. Let me help you out, ma. You can go ahead and step. I'm a grown man. I don't play games." He tilts up his drink.

My time has run out. I have to piss or get off the pot. "My name is Qiana."

He nods and then repeats my name with his sexy baritone pouring over each letter. "Qiana."

My ass is in love.

22

Trigger

This shit is like taking candy from a baby.

Things are falling into place just like my girl planned. The minute I spot Bishop in Da Club, I know just how to play his punk-ass. It don't hurt that he ain't that hard to look at neither. He's a cross between pretty-boy and handsome, his swag is a little off point. He's trying too hard to impress and exude power. If the rumors in the streets are to be believed, his pouting ass can't handle the fact that his sister, Lucifer, is the one with the balls sagging to the ground. If he had a bitch like me, it would help knock that insecurity chip off his shoulder.

I've seen Lucifer a time or two. I wouldn't mind getting a taste of her ass myself. Everything about her screams money, power, and respect. A few months back, she was slicing mutha-fuckas' dicks off and jamming them down they throats. Shit like that gets my clit hard.

Yeah. I fuck bitches and niggas. I don't give a fuck as long as I nut.

When Bishop finally spots me, I have an image of sexing him and his sister at the same time—that would be a nice VL sandwich.

The smile on my face is huge by the time Bishop pushes up on me.

"Damn, shawty. If you tell me that you got a nigga, I'ma have to put a bullet to his head on general principle."

Whack. Holding my smile like a professional, I slide my hands down the front of his pants and grip his shit. *Holy fuck!* "I'm feeling you now, daddy." From my other hand, I take a sip of my apple martini.

Bishop's lips stretch wider. "Now this is what I'm talking about—a woman who goes straight for what she wants. What's your name?"

"Sweet Pussy."

He laughs. "Is that right?"

I nod. "You wanna sample?"

"Don't mind if I do."

I release the pipe in his pants and dip my finger into my drink. "Open up."

On some zombie shit, he does exactly what I say and then I tip my finger into his mouth. He closes his thick lips around it. Instead of sucking, I feel his tongue rotate around it and then beat the tip like it was a clit.

Yeah. I gonna break this nigga off a piece.

Bishop releases my finger and eases his hand around my waist for a good grip of my round ass. "How would you like to go to a private party?"

"I looooove parties."

His smile matches the size of mine as I allow him to lead me toward the back of the club. I spot my girls Shariffa and Jaqorya in the crowd and wink. Guarding the entranceway to the VIP is this big mountain of a dude who is in some kind of private competition to see how far he can stretch his belly. Bishop nods and the human blob steps aside.

"Ooooh, a baby boy with power," I purr.

"All day, every day."

We enter the VIP, but then stroll to the back of it where there's another door that leads to a huge backroom. In the center is a large poker table and a cluster of slobs flagging gold and black.

Heads snap our way while Bishop escorts me through more thick clouds of weed.

"My nigga. My nigga. Where did you find that dime piece?" one slob with orange-red hair asks, checking me out like a CT scan.

"Roll your tongue back up into your mouth, son. I got this," Bishop brags.

By the way these niggas are eye-raping me, I've upgraded Bishop in their eyes. It's cool. That's the way it is no matter whose arm I'm hanging on.

"C'mon, cuz. You gonna bet or what?" one huffing nigga barks across the table.

"My bad," the nigga says, still peeping me as Bishop leads me through the room. "Y'all save a seat for me. I gotta handle some business before I jump in the game and take y'all's loot."

I lift a brow at the mountain of Benjamins on the table. Muthafuckas are balling out of control back here.

"I hear you talkin'," Red says, checking out my ass as we walk past the table.

As we go, I do a body count and check all entrance points. "Where we going, baby?"

"A spot where I can get a better taste of that pie." He pulls me in close so that he can suck on my ear.

I have to admit, I'm feeling anxious about this hit. Bishop's dick is already riding up the back of my ass while he's pinching on my titties. He leads me to another door. When he opens it, I see it's a small bathroom with one sink, a toilet, and a floor littered with paper towels and toilet paper. A few inches melt off my smile.

"Over here and sit down," he tells me.

What—on the toilet?

To help me out, Bishop hikes up my dress and tugs on my panties.

All right, freak. Whatever you say. I remove my clutch tucked under my arm and place it on the sink. Once I'm squat on the toilet, Bishop rushes to unzip and peel his pants off his hips. Immediately afterwards, the prettiest brown dick I've ever seen springs up and taps me on the chin.

"Say hello to my *big* friend," Bishops chuckles.

"Well, hello." I lick my lips and wrap my hand around his thick dick. For starters, I press a feather kiss over its one eye and then slowly roll my tongue around the tip. "You are a sweet muthafucka, too."

"Hmm, huh." Greedily, he thrusts his hips one time, and I open my mouth and slide his shit in real slow.

"Awwwww. Fuuuucck. Yeah. That's what I'm talking about." Bishop gathers my silky black hair up into one hand and then wraps it into his fist so that he can have a better view of my skills. To let him know he ain't dealing with an amateur, I take the shit to the balls, squeeze my throat muscles and let him grind for a full twenty seconds.

"Awwww. You sweet bitch, you. Yeah." His face twists and, if I'm not mistaken, a tear rolls down the side of his face.

The second I spring off the dick, I lift it and T-bag his balls while sneaking a finger into his back door. Most niggas don't let chicks know how much they like that shit, but I know that even the hardest muthafucka got a little bitch in them. Bishop's ass ain't no different, because I watch his eyes roll to the back of his head.

"You like that, big daddy?"

"Yeeeeesss. Yeeeesss. Do that shit."

With pleasure. I roll back onto the dick and go down deep until his salty precum dribbles down my throat. "Uhmmmm. Delicious."

"Yeah? You like that shit?" he asks me.

"Uhm. Hmmm," I moan.

Bishop dips his knees and slides a middle finger in between

my legs. My entire clit is honey-coated. "Look at you. You're ready for a nigga."

"Uhm. Hmm," is all I can manage 'cause, no lie, the dick is good.

A second finger goes in.

A third.

Fourth.

His dick springs out of my mouth so that he can squat down further. "Lean back and spread your legs.

He doesn't have to tell me twice. I ease back on the seat and point my legs east and west.

"Scoot down."

Like a good soldier, I follow directions—accidently flushing the toilet as I go.

Bishop plants his chin in between the U of the toilet and starts eating my pussy like a starving child from a third-world country. "Fuck, nigga. Fuck." I grab the back of his head and hold on for dear life. I didn't know these fucking slobs got down like this shit. My toes curl up out of my red-bottom pumps while I simultaneously grease his face up real good. In no time, I'm nutting all over the fucking place and can't catch my breath.

"Stand your fine ass up," he commands, climbing back onto his feet and stroking his shit.

My fuckin' legs don't seem to be working right and it takes me a few seconds to do what he says.

"Turn around," he says, but then spins me before I have a chance to do it on my own. "Hands on the wall—wait, naw. Let's move over here." Bishop drags me over in front of the mirror. "Grab the sink."

I give him a sexy smile in the mirror as I follow his direction.

"Aw. Shit. Look at this fine ass right here." He whips his hand down and gives my shit a hard *SMACK!* "Damn, the man upstairs was on some good shit when he made your fine ass." He makes another *SMACK* on the opposite cheek before spreading them open in opposite directions. "Oh, yeah."

Bishop sandwiches his cock between my ass and rubs it up and down so that it probably looks like a fat-ass sausage in a toasted bun. "Where have you been all my life, Sweet Pussy?"

"All that matters is that I'm here now," I tell him, wiggling my ass. I ain't one for being teased.

Bishop meets my gaze in the mirror while one side of his lips curls. "Let me see if you can handle all this good dick."

"You gonna wrap it, baby?"

"Why? You dirty?"

"No, but—"

"Fuck that. I wanna feel every inch of that good pussy." He grabs his shit and eases his fat mushroom head in so exquisitely I have to clamp my damn teeth together. "Aw. There it goes," he brags, watching my expression.

I try to keep it cool, but that shit is hard to do when a nigga is stretching you this good. He keeps taking his time with it too: inch by slow-ass inch. By the time he fills me up, I swear his dick is laying on my tonsils.

"Ride," he commands, and then gives each of my ass cheeks a hard slap. *SMACK! SMACK!*

Bishop remains still as I glide up and then push back. He leans forward and nibbles on my shoulder. "That's it, Sweet Pussy. Take your time."

Humph. He don't know that I got something for his ass.

He has no muthafuckin' idea. Slow jamming is only good for so long. Before long, I'm riding like a cowgirl from the Old West. This slob got some good shit. I forget myself and damn near rip the sink out of the wall.

SMACK! SMACK! SMACK! SMACK! SMACK! SMACK! SMACK!

Any minute Bishop is gonna holler, "Yippy-Ki-Yay." I'm sure of it.

Two nuts shoot up from my right toe and explode in my clit, back to back. Instead of his ass, I'm the bitch screaming in this muthafucka.

"Yeah. Yeah. Give it all to daddy." He fists my hair again and yanks until I'm staring up at the ceiling. I explode again and start hollering out jibberish.

Bishop springs out of my pussy and fires off white bullets down the crack my ass. "Ooooh, yeah." He glazes his dick up with his own cum while he goes back to rubbing his sausage dick between my buns. "Oh, fuck. I think I'm in love, Sweet Pussy."

While I'm struggling to catch my breath, I twist around and smile down at his chocolate éclair-looking dick. "That makes two of us."

BANG! BANG! BANG!

"Y'all gonna be fuckin' in there all day?" someone shouts from the other side. "Some niggas gotta shit."

Instantly, Bishop is hot "Muthafucka, if you don't back away from that door, I'ma bust a cap in your ass!"

"Whatever, B. Ain't no reason to get all swoll. You sharing or what?"

No this nigga didn't!

Bishop jerks toward the door and snatches it open, dick swinging. "Nigga, I ain't playing with you. Get the fuck on."

"A'ight." That red-headed nigga holds his hands up, but sneaks a peek around Bishop's shoulder to smile at me. "Goddamn, nigga. Is she still alive? We thought you killed her."

"Get the hell on with that shit."

Behind Red, the niggas around the poker table crack up. "Y'all niggas need to grow the fuck up," Bishop snaps and then slams the door in his boy's face. "Sorry about that," he says, still pissed.

"Don't be." I wink and slide my arms around his shoulder.

His frown flips upside down and he grins at me like a puppy. "What's your real name, Sweet Pussy?"

I hesitate.

"Oh. It's like that?" He chuckles and turns the water on in the sink. "Must mean you got a man."

"Nah. I'm a free agent, baby."

"Is that right?" He washes his dick in the sink. "Then maybe I can be your man."

I laugh. "You just met me."

"You just fucked me."

"That's because you're cute . . . and you have a big dick."

"And you're fine . . . and have the sweetest pussy I've ever tasted. You never know when I might have another sweet tooth."

We grin at each other and something passes between us— something unexpected. "Ja'nay," I confess like a dumb bitch.

Bishop nods. "Ja'nay, pleased to meet you. I'm Juvon—but you can call me 'your new man.'"

I grin like a fool.

My man tucks himself back into his pants and then reaches for my arm. "Come on. Let me properly introduce you to my niggas out here."

"Uhm. Give me a couple of minutes to clean myself up," I say.

Bishop's face splits with a smile as he walks over to me and peppers my neck with kisses. "Take your time, Ja'nay."

A warm rush races over me while he walks out the door. *Pull yourself together.* I lock the door behind him, grab my clutch off the floor, pull out my cell phone, and text my girl, Shariffa.

23

Shariffa

"**S**o how long do you think that Qiana's going to keep that baby she cut out of Python's Baby's Momma?" a drunken voice floats over to me from the other booth. My ears immediately perk up.

"Girl, I don't know," the second girl says. "Every day I wait for them to find that dead bitch she cut that kid out of and splash it all over the news. It ain't gonna be hard for niggas round our way to put two and two together and start eyeballin' us sideways."

"We should have stopped her."

"Yeah, and we would be lying right next to that high yellow bitch just like Tyneshia's ass, too."

"Well if she gets caught, she better not snitch our names. She gets what she gets for dealing with that LeShelle bitch. We're only catching a break because that crazy bitch is laid up in the hospital."

"Shhh. Keep your voice down."

LeShelle? I frown and try to put the pieces of the conversation together but can't get them to fit. Something about LeShelle and a baby being cut out of one of Python's baby mommas? Why the fuck would Leshelle be fucking with a couple of young Flowers? I can't even see that shit happening.

My phone vibrates against my lap, pulling me back to what the fuck I'm supposed to be doing. "It's about time," I mutter when my cell phone vibrates in my left hand. I turn my back from the crowded bar inside Da Club and peek down at the text from Trigger.

"I bet her ass broke him off a piece first," Brika gripes from over my shoulder. "Did you see them grabbing each other's shit off the jump?"

I roll my eyes. Brika needs to squash this jealousy bullshit. I don't have the time for it. "She counts five niggas. One door with a Remington bolt lock and four windows." I shake my head. "She also says there's a mountain of cash stacked back there, too."

"That's what I'm talking about. Cash moves everything around me," Brika says.

From my right, Shacardi cuts in, "Money makes my clit hard."

I slip my phone back into my purse, and then loop the strap so that it hangs diagonally across my body. "Let's do this shit. Brika, you come with me. Shacardi, y'all know what to do."

Jaqorya bobs her head. "Hurry up. I'm cooking up in here under this wig. I don't know how some of these fake bitches do it." To prove her point, she scratches the side of her head and her blond hair wiggles on top of her head.

I *feel* her pain. My shit is tryna squeeze my brain out, too. "C'mon." I grab Brika by the arm as she slips into the character of a drunk bitch who can barely hold herself up. "I got you, girl. Let's get you home." We stumble through the crowd on our way out the door. A few bitches catch an attitude as we bump and stomp on a few toes.

"Oh, God. I think I'm going to be sick," Brika moans. Her toned legs wiggle like Jell-O.

"Sloppy bitches," a muthafucka snickers as we slip past the bouncers.

"Fuck you," I snap, giving him the bird.

"Oooh." Brika moans and hikes up her skirt like she's about to piss right there on the sidewalk.

"Whoa. Yo!" A bouncer thunders toward us. "Y'all chickens need to get the fuck on with that bullshit."

"We're going. We're going. Fuck, nigga. You ain't got to get all swoll." I wrap my arm around Brika, pull her back up and then help her move on down the sidewalk. I take a quick peek to my left and spot Crunk still slumped down low in the getaway car and tapping his fingers on the steering wheel. Our eyes connect for a split moment, long enough for me to mentally telepath for his ass to calm the fuck down.

I don't know why we signed him up for this job. He doesn't have any experience doing this shit. At the same time, Lynch would have shit a brick if I told him what I was up to tonight. I'm tired of pussy-footing. I want to prove that we can strike at the heart of these muthafuckas.

Brika and I turn the corner toward the back and spot one more mountain-size soldier standing guard at the back door.

My girl ups her game, moaning louder and tripping out of one of her shoes.

The guard dog spots us and glares wearily. As we draw nearer, he shakes his head. "Nah. Nah. You bitches are gonna have to back the fuck up," he barks, settling his hand onto the cannon he got at his hip.

Shit.

Brika plunges on. "Oh. I'm going to be sick."

"You're going to be dead if you don't back on up away from this door."

Committed to the role, Brika throw up chunks all over this nigga's Air Jordans Limited Editions.

"What the fuck?" His hand comes away from his hip as he

jumps back. "Bitch, do you know how much I paid for these shoes?"

Without missing a beat, I come up with my gat drawn. "Here's your fuckin' refund." I tap the trigger once and then watch the side of his face split open after the muffled shot. Muthafucka drops like a stone—but in front of the door.

"Fuck!" I want to kick my own ass. Now we got to try and move this big nigga. "Grab his feet. I'll get his arms."

Brika frowns. "You sure? He's like four hundred pounds— eight hundred now that he's *dead* weight."

"Unless you got a fucking crane parked out here some-where, we gotta do what we gotta do. Now come the fuck on!"

Brika spares me the rest of her bullshit and grabs Black-zilla's legs. The first couple of tries, the muthafucka doesn't move.

"I don't believe this shit." If we don't get moving, we're gonna fuck this hit up.

"Roll his ass," Brika says, rushing over to get into position behind his hips.

The shit sounds good to me so I drop his arms and slide my hands beneath his back. "One . . . two . . . three—push," I hiss.

Muthafucka nearly throws my back out. It's like tryna push a Mack truck up a steep hill. After a couple heaves and a heel snapping off my right shoe, the muthafucka rolls forward and flops on his face. "Again," I order. Huffing and puffing, I lose the other heel, but once we get another good roll, I'm willing to charge this shit to the game.

"That right there is ridiculous," Brika says, looking down at the fat man in disgust.

I agree with her, but it's not the rolls of fat that catches my attention. It's the man's cannon strapped on his hip. "Oooh, baby. Come to momma." I tuck my own shit back to my thigh holster and reach for the sexy gat that has my ass hypnotized.

Brika looks green as shit for not having spotted it first.

"You through shopping? We got to do this shit before we leave our girls twisting in the wind."

She's right. I turn and level my new best friend at the door. When I pull the trigger, there's a loud explosion and I'm nearly knocked off my broken heels.

Brika charges through the room a second before me. "C'Z UP, NIGGAS!" She fires off warning shots to let them know that we mean business.

POW! POW! POW!

I flow right behind her, firing the cannon at a redheaded nigga with a listening problem. He goes for his weapon. I unload the cannon. This time I handle the kickback, but watch in amazement at the size of the hole in the center of his chest. Hell, it even takes him a second to realize that his ass is dead before keeling over on the poker table piled with money.

"What the fuck? Have you bitches lost your mind?" Bishop bolts to his feet, but then gets the shock of his life when our girl Trigger presses her .38 to the side of his head.

"Slow your roll, big daddy. Me and my cousins here are just gonna relieve you of some of these Benjamins.

POP! POP! POP!

Jaqorya and Shacardi are setting it off in the club to get the chaos going.

Bishop's narrowed gaze shifts to Trigger. "You set me up?"

She smiles. "It's just business, boo. Money over everything."

Brika's jealousy surges. "Y'all fucked?"

I don't have time for no soap-opera bullshit. "Grab the money and let's roll," I tell them.

Brika and Trigger get to work. Each pull a garbage bag out of their purses while keeping their gats trained on different targets.

Every nigga in here looks hot to death.

"You bitches don't know who the fuck you're messing with." Bishop's rage makes his face ten shades darker.

"Of course we do. You're Lucifer's lil brother, ain't you?" I ask, knowing that the shit is the other way around. Mutha-fucka's face looks like an eggplant now.

"This shit ain't over," he swears. "You can believe that shit."

"It never is," I tell him. The war in the streets will continue on long after all our asses are dead and gone.

Brika tugs the dead nigga off the pile of money so she can finish filling the bags with the bloody Benjamins.

"It's been a pleasure," Trigger says, clearly with a double meaning.

They share a look—and I can't tell whether he wants to kill her or fuck her. If it's the latter, I might pull up a chair and watch.

"Let's go!"

Brika throws the bag over her shoulder and races to join me at the door.

Trigger starts to creep around Bishop with her gun still trained on him. She only manages three steps before his anger gets the best of him and he lunges for her.

"You fuckin' bitch!"

When he moves, the other niggas jump into action and then everyone starts shooting.

24

Qiana

POP! *POP! POP!*

Belatedly, I register the pops of gunfire. But by that time, Diesel is out of his seat, gat in hand and tackling me.

"Get down!"

People scream and rush the exit.

I reach for my dropped clutch bag because my piece is in the bitch, but the minute I do, several red-bottom heels stab my hand for the effort. "Shiiit."

Diesel snatches my shit up and then drags me along with the herd. Ain't nobody stopping to see why or which niggas are shooting. We're tryna get the fuck out. It isn't until after I've been rushed into an iced-out Range Rover that I even think about Lil Bit and Adaryl's asses. "Yo, what about my girls?"

"It's every nigga for theyselves," Diesel says, peeling his whip out of the parking lot. Another smile hits his lips after he corners the next street. "Don't worry, Scar. I ain't gonna rape you."

I look him up and down and then return his smile. "I ain't the one that needs to be concerned about being raped."

He laughs. "You talk a lot of shit for a little girl," Diesel says, shaking his head.

"Who the fuck you calling a little girl?" I challenge, biting my lower lip and easing my way across the center console. "Trust me. I'm more woman than you can handle." I rub my titties against his muscled arm to try to get him to forget any possible statutory rape charges, but my shit backfires and I end up getting myself horny as hell.

Diesel flashes his crooked grin. "Everything ain't a game. Everyone you meet ain't meant to be played."

My hackles rise at his playful warning. I ease back a bit and glance around his whip. His shit is tight to def. I peep his outfit again and calculate shit in my head. "What is it that you said that you did again?"

"Why? Are you wired?"

I relax again. "I don't know. Why don't you frisk me and find out?"

His green eyes caress my frame, but then linger on the cosmetic bandages on my face. He still doesn't look repulsed by it. If anything there's a flicker of desire.

"Take those off."

I could play dumb, but what's the point? I reach up and remove the strips, keeping my eyes locked on him the entire time. When they're off, Diesel's lips inch higher. "Nice."

He cups my chin and pulls me closer for a kiss. My mind is blown.

Diesel sneaks a look at the road and brings the car to a stop as he approaches a light. "Sit in my lap."

The order surprises me, but he doesn't have to ask my ass twice. I hike up my skirt and climb over, my knees folded on either side of his hips. When I settle over his cock, a thrill sweeps throughout my body at the sheer size of him bumping against my wet panties.

"You think that you can handle all of that, lil girl?"

Oh shit. This nigga is going to turn my shit into a crime scene. Instead of being scared, I get hotter than ever. I pull my bottom lip in between my teeth and nod.

A horn blares behind us.

The light is green. Diesel eases off the brake and drives through the intersection. "All right, Scarface. I'm putting you on. Show me what you can do."

Confused, I blink like a deer caught in headlights.

He hikes up a brow as if asking what I'm waiting for.

I feel the car drift off to the right and peek over my shoulder to see that he's turning on the highway.

"What's wrong? You scared?" he asks.

A challenge. Embracing the danger, I reach in between our bodies and unzip his jeans. When I wrap my hand around his cock, my heart trips up in my chest and the muscles in my belly quiver.

"And what are you going to do with that, hmm?"

"I'm gonna ride it," I answer.

"Is that right?"

Diesel's baritone grows husky as I slide my hands up and down his dick. I can't stop because his shit feels like velvet.

"Well, don't talk about it, be about it." He sneaks a quick peek over my shoulder at the road but then returns his attention to me.

A thrill-seeker. The challenge has been made and it's now up to me whether I'm going to be down. My gaze sweeps over his fine ass once more and a sense of recklessness washes over me. "Watch the road," I tell him, pushing up on my knees and reaching back in between my legs to push my damp panties to the side.

"Don't worry. I got this. You just do you, ma."

I don't know what it is about him, but I grow bolder by the second. I want to please him in the worst way. I want to prove that age ain't nothing but a number and I'm down for anything. My limited experience in car play involves giving a soldier a blowjob while he coasted down the highway and one backseat quickie in the parking lot of the Horseshoe Casino. This shit here is on a whole 'nother level.

I ease my shaved pussy down over the fat head of his cock and suck in a sharp breath as my shit stretches open to accommodate his hard, silky pole.

"Fuuuuck," Diesel exhales in a low, winding hiss.

The vehicle picks up speed.

Another injection of adrenaline rushes through me as Diesel's dick fills me from wall to wall. By the time I make it to his balls, I'm convinced I'm stretched to capacity.

"Damn, girl. You're gangster." He slaps me on the ass. "Fuck me."

"You mean like this?" I ask, grabbing the headrest behind his head and getting my deep grind on.

His sly smile grows devious. "That's it, Scarface. Work that shit."

The vehicle speeds up again.

A car horn blares and I look to my right and see a group of niggas laughing and pointing. One muthafucka whips out his cell phone and starts filming our asses. I smile back and then reach down and get my titties to bounce in Diesel's face.

"Put one in my mouth," he orders.

I comply and experience another thrill when instead of sucking, this nigga bites and chews on my hard nipples. It doesn't take long for a familiar sensation to flutter in my belly.

Diesel growls.

More horns blare as more cars peep us out. For the moment, I'm the hottest porno star on the planet and I want to make sure that I give them all something that they'll never forget.

I grind harder.

Diesel growls louder.

The vehicle flies faster.

The very thought that our asses could die at any moment is like a wild aphrodisiac that gets me higher than any drug I've ever tried. My nut launches up from my toes. I plant my hands up on the ceiling. Our gazes lock. I don't care if he can't see shit. I want his attention on what our bodies are doing—feeling. I want us to be on the same vibe. He's here with me. I know it. I can feel it. In one nuclear orgasmic explosion, I cry out and then shatter into a million pieces. My white honey gushes like a geyser over his dick. In response to my quivering honeyed walls, Diesel's growl turns into a roar as he splashes his hot seed deep in my belly.

I collapse and rest my head on the crook of his neck.

Diesel glances over my shoulder at the road. "Oh shiiiit." He wraps his arm around me and hits the brakes. His tires scream in protest and the unmistakable smell of burning rubber fills the vehicle. When I think I'm about to go sailing through the window, Diesel pops off the brake and swerves into the left lane, causing another series of horns to blare. To my right, I see the eighteen-wheeler we float by and realize how dangerously close we came to crashing into that muthafucka.

Now that the moment of danger has passed, I can still feel Diesel's heart thrumming in his neck. I don't know why, but I laugh.

He shakes his head. "You're a bad bitch," he says, sounding impressed. "You really ain't scared of a muthafuckin' thing, are you?"

"Not when a sweet dick like yours is at stake." I suck on his neck while he slaps me on the ass again.

"Scar knows how to work a muthafuckin' dick." His laughter rumbles deeper than the joke warrants and I get suspicious. "What's so funny?"

"Honestly? I didn't think your ass would really do it. What the hell were you thinking? We could've been killed."

"What?" I jerk my head up, blocking his view of the road again.

"I ain't never done no sick shit like that before. You're wild lil girl."

Shocked, I shift off his lap and plop back into the passenger seat. "I *ain't* a lil girl."

"Well, you don't fuck like no lil girl, I'll give you that," he says, tucking his wet dick back into his pants. "Do you always do what people tell you to do?"

I blink. Is this muthafucka trying to do a Jedi mind trick on me? I'm tryna decide if I should be embarrassed or pissed.

Suddenly, another smile breaks out across his face. "Own your shit. I asked you to fuck me and you wanted to fuck me—and well, too." He stretches his hand out and sinks his fingers into my pussy. "Now how about I take you over to my crib so I can return the favor?"

Hell. I hadn't even asked him where we are going—or if he had a destination in mind. Either way, my brief annoyance is already ebbing away with his finger pumping in and out of my pussy.

"Would you like that, Scaface?"

Funny. That name is growing on me. "Mmmm." I ease back against the door and spread my legs so that he has better access. I watch as his green eyes light up while he finger-fucks me.

"You're a nasty bitch. Look at you. You want to be grown. Your nigga Diesel is gonna make a real woman out of you tonight."

I moan and squeeze my titties. In no time at all, I'm popping off another orgasm. Yeah. I'll roll with this muthafucka anywhere.

25

LeShelle

Despite drifting on a cocktail of drugs in the middle of the night, a bitch can't get any sleep in this hospital. I'm grateful for the drugs because after a month of physical therapy, I constantly ache everywhere. Every hour on the hour, a nurse floats into my room to prick my hands and arms for more blood. I've gotten so used to it that I don't even flinch when the door swishes open.

"LeShelle."

Confused, I battle to open my heavy eyelids. I get about half an inch, but then have a hard time making out the fuzzy image in front of me.

"Hey, bitch. Wake your ass up."

"Kookie?"

"The one and only." Kookie cocks a smile. "Your vacation is over. We're busting your ass out of here."

"Music to my ears." I roll my head around. "What about the guard?"

"You mean that muthafucka over there?" Kookie steps back so that I can see the tall cop slumped over on the floor with a huge hypodermic needle jammed into the side of his neck. "Nigga never saw what hit him."

"Cop killer?"

"Nah. He's just knocked out," Kookie says.

"We got to hurry and get her out of here," a voice says.

Groggily, I roll my head to the other side to spot the silent nurse from earlier.

"Maureen is going to be back soon."

Kookie rolls her eyes and dismisses the girl. "Girl, ain't nobody stuttin' your boss." She produces a key and unlocks the handcuffs.

"Where's Python?" I ask. "I thought he was comin' to get me. A month ago"

"Don't worry. You'll see him in a few."

"What—so just you?"

Kookie removes the bracelet from my wrist and then lowers the guardrail while the nurse rushes around the bed with a wheelchair.

"C'mon. C'mon. C'mon," the nurse chants. She looks and sounds about as scared as a deer running in front of a den of lions.

Kookie brushes my legs over the side of the bed and then leans over to help me sit up. "Can you stand?"

What kind of fuckin' question is that shit? I shove myself off the bed, but one second I'm up, and in the next, my ass drops like a stone.

"Whoa." Kookie and the nurse catch me before I eat linoleum. "That first step is always a bitch."

I try harder to shake off the drugs.

"Push yourself up," the nurse coaches. "Yeah. There you go."

Back on my feet, I sigh in relief. Kookie rolls a wheelchair up to the bed and together they help put my legs in the metal footrests.

"All right. Let's get the fuck out of here."

"We out this bitch." Kookie grabs the handlebars and we take off.

The nurse pokes her head out of the door first and then waves for us to hurry and come on out.

The intensive care unit looks like an abandoned graveyard. There's not a soul in sight.

"This shit don't look right," Kookie mumbles.

At least we agree on something.

We take off like a bat out of hell toward the elevator bay. I have to admit that I'm still stunned at this low-key operation. After Python's note, I'd envisioned him blazing through this muthafucka like the Terminator to rescue me. He did that much when he thought Mason's ass was walled up in the hospital.

Kookie jabs the down button about a dozen times in quick succession.

"Is Python waiting out in the car?" I ask.

"Huh? What?" Kookie jabs the button twelve more times. "Goddamn. What's takin' this muthafucka so long?"

Something's not right. I shake my head to clear the drug fog. The elevator doors slide open.

Kookie grabs the handlebars again and we sprint into the small compartment and nearly take out the woman that's about to step out.

"Hey. Look where you're going."

"Fuck you, bitch," Kookie snaps.

"What?" The woman slaps out her hand and stops the elevator's doors from closing.

I jerk my head up, and my drugged gaze meets Nurse Maureen's angry one.

"Where in the hell do you think you're taking this patient?" She glances around. "And where is her police detail?"

"Shit." Kookie fumbles at her waist for her gat. "I'm her security detail."

Nurse Maureen gasps and removes her hand from the door. When I think that she's about to rip out a scream, that silent-as-a-mouse nurse creeps up behind her and jabs another big-ass needle in her neck. The woman's eyes roll up and she hits the floor and cracks her head.

"Fuck. Fuck. Fuck." The little girl hops around like she can't believe what she just did.

Kookie hands me the gun and then rushes to try and move Nurse Maureen's feet from keeping the door open.

I tuck the gun in the side of the wheelchair and hope that she forgets about it.

The panicked nurse presses her hands up against Maureen's neck. "Oh my God. She's dead. I'm really going to get fired now."

"Fuck that bitch. Help me move her legs," Kookie barks.

"Who in the hell planned this shit—Bozo?"

"I got this shit," Kookie grumbles, kicking the dead woman's feet. "Fiona, help."

Fiona snaps out of her self-pity and hustles to move Nurse Maureen. "I'm coming with you," she announces and hops onto the elevator with us. When the doors close, we all look at each other—relieved for getting off the floor. Kookie and Fiona are huffing and puffing like they're in a 100-yard dash.

"I don't know what the fuck I'm going to do now," Fiona mumbles while eating her nails. "My momma got me this job."

"Shut the fuck up, Fiona," Kookie snaps.

The elevator doors slide open and my girl Pit Bull is standing there, looking mean as ever. "Well, it's about muthafuckin' time," she growls. "What the hell were y'all doin' up there?" Her gaze falls on me. "Yo, bitch. Welcome back."

"I stay ten toes down and ready for the world to blow up." I smile. I'm feeling a little more loved.

"That's my bitch." Pit Bull tosses up our gang signs as Kookie rolls me out the elevator.

"We good?" Kookie asks, peeking around the corner.

"All good in the hood."

"I wish I can say the same shit. Fiona took one bitch out that was givin' us trouble. We gotta roll."

Pit Bull glances at Fiona. "You're shittin' me."

"I'm going with y'all," Fiona's scary ass says.

We corner one hallway and see the hospital entrance's glass double doors. But then I'm sucked into a horror movie as Captain Johnson marches into the hospital.

I go for the Glock tucked at my side.

"FUCK," Pit Bull cosigns, grabbing her shit like a gunslinger.

"HOLY SHIT," Kookie says and makes a sharp left that nearly tips me out of my seat.

"Ohmigod," Fiona squeals, struggling to keep up.

"Shut up," Pit Bull barks at a full run.

Fiona either doesn't hear her or is unable to shut off her mouth. "Did he see us? Do you think he saw us? What is he doing here?"

"Fuck, Fiona. I can't even hear myself think," Kookie snaps.

"This fuckin' escape plan is so fuckin' booty," I complain.

"If you don't like it, we can always take your ass back upstairs," Pit Bull tosses out as we hustle for our lives down yet another hallway.

I roll my eyes, expecting bullets to start flying behind us at any second.

Pit Bull pulls out her cell. "Ayo, Avonte. Change of plans. Superpig is in the building. Meet our ass out back."

Pit Bull lowers the phone. "Fiona, what's the shortest way out this bitch?"

Until that moment, it hadn't occurred to her to lead instead of follow. "Uh. Uh."

"C'mon, bitch. Don't make me punch you in your throat."

That shit makes her stammer harder.

Is this the way I'm gonna be taken out of the game, surrounded by stupid bitches?

Fiona's brain kicks in. "This way!"

Three short hallways later, we bust out an exit door by several tall garbage bins.

"Now what?" I ask. At this point, I won't be surprised if these bitches break out bus passes.

"Avonte, where your ass at?" Pit Bull growls into her phone.

Two bright beams of light slice through the inky night a second before a loud car engine catches my ear. In no time at all, I'm able to make out a black, beat-up Oldsmobile as it screeches around the corner.

"There her ass go," Kookie huffs in relief.

My wheelchair takes off again and we meet the car halfway across the lot.

"Let's go! Let's go! Let's go!"

More Queen Gs jump out of the car to help.

My heart bubbles over at finally seeing my fam working to get my ass up out of here. This is my real family. Ride or die. It's the game that binds us. I still have a place in this world.

I. Am. Queen.

My eyes burn with rare tears as everyone fusses to help get me into the car. I'm weak but I do most of it on my own. Once I'm tucked in, everyone scrambles back in and we float our ass out of there.

"Where to?" I ask.

Avonte glances up and meets my gaze in the rearview mirror. "It's a surprise."

26

Ta'Shara

Home. The word sounds foreign to my ears and I have a hard time untangling my emotions so I can process how I feel about being released from the hospital. My attempt to kill LeShelle had been treated like a temporary psychotic break and the state attorney elected not to press charges. It was one of the few times in my life that I'd gotten lucky. However, I would have to be blind not to notice the tension my release is causing between Reggie and Tracee. In fact, Reggie doesn't even look at me.

Tracee, on the other hand, is ecstatic when they arrive at the hospital to pick me up. Her smile is twice its normal size and every move she makes is overly animated. It's too bad that she never had any kids of her own. She really would have been a great mom.

"Heeeey, Ta'Shara," she sings, wrapping her arms around me and squeezing me tight. "Are you ready to go home?"

There's no point in trying to match her enthusiasm so I don't bother—but I do manage to push up a smile. I want to get out of this place. If you're not crazy when they bring you in here, you will be when you leave. For me, I'm hoping that my nightmares will end once I leave this place—and certainly when I finally get to see Profit again.

Ever since I learned that he had survived, I've been begging to see him. But Tracee sided with Reggie and refused to add his name to the visitors list. She also spent hours telling me that I needed to forget about Profit. He was no good for me. They also told me about Essence and I couldn't shake the feeling that LeShelle was behind her death, too. Their impassioned rant went on and on—until I dropped the subject and didn't bring up his name again.

From that moment on, I focused on getting out. I resisted taking the medicine they gave by tucking the pills in my cheek, much like how I would a blade. The doctors wanted to talk about the night of my rape, but I lied and said that I didn't remember anything about that night. No matter how hard they pressed, I stuck to that story. Once they realized that they couldn't break me, the doctors recommended my release.

The drive home is a long one with the tension nearly choking all three of us to death. It's so bad that I doubt that things can ever go back to being the way it used to be. This is just one more thing that LeShelle destroyed.

"What do you say I run you a nice, warm bubble bath?" Tracee asks, as she helps me out of my coat.

"Thanks. That'll be nice," I tell her.

"Great." She kisses my forehead. "I'll go run it for you right now." Then she is off, leaving me alone with Reggie.

After looking around skittishly, he tosses his keys on top of the bombé cabinet in the foyer, shoves his hands in pockets, and rocks on his feet.

"I guess I should go up to my room," I suggest and head toward the stairs.

He nods, and then waits until my foot lands onto the first stair before he speaks. "I'm glad you're back home."

Stunned, I turn back around and meet his direct gaze.

"I mean it," he says with his eyes wetting up. "That night. When we opened the front door and saw you lying there . . ." Reggie shakes his head while his Adam's apple bobs in his throat. "I've never been so terrified in my life. I . . . I blamed myself for that night because I didn't want you going to that prom with that boy. I knew that after the hospital shooting he was nothing but trouble. I went against my better judgment. Then . . . I blamed my wife for talking me into letting you go. Then . . . I blamed you." He stops while his last sentence hangs in the air.

I should say something, but I have no idea what. Should I thank him for being honest or tell him to kiss my ass and that I don't give a damn about what he thinks?

"I was wrong," Reggie confesses.

Stunned, I stare at him dumbfounded.

"It wasn't your fault. It wasn't Tracee's fault . . . and I said things during that time that I'm not proud of . . . and I can only hope that one day you will forgive me."

I must have been staring at him for too long because his nervousness showed—and I was touched. "I forgive you," I tell him, letting him off the hook.

At that moment, tears leap over his lashes and roll down his face like twin rivers. He closes the distance between us with two confident strides and then wraps me in his strong, powerful arms. When his body starts to quake, I feel my own face flood with tears.

Ten minutes later, I ease my aching body into a tub of lavender-scented bubbles and try to relax—but can't. In my mind I'm counting the minutes until Reggie and Tracee go to bed so that I can try and reach out to Profit. I could sneak out and steal Reggie's car again, but I'm not all that confident that Ruby Cove will welcome me with open arms. I have no idea where my cell phone is so I'll have to call Profit on the house line. That's not going to be easy. Tracee and Reggie are going to be watching me like a hawk. I decide on 3:30 A.M. Unless they are going to monitor the phone in shifts, I figure it's later than Tracee can manage to stay awake.

I remain in the tub until the last bubble pops before climbing out and making it to my old bedroom. It feels strange to see the stuffed animals and the princess-like décor. It's the room of a child—but what little innocence I once had is long gone.

There's a knock on the door behind me and, when I turn, Tracee pokes her head through and smiles.

"Are you getting settled in?" she asks, grinning.

"Yeah. Everything looks exactly how I left it."

"If you want, I can brush out your hair before you go to bed," she offers, entering the room.

"Actually . . . I'm really tired. I'm going to go ahead and go to bed."

Her smile falls. "Oh. Okay then. Well, good night." She backs out of the door, but hesitates in closing it. "If you need anything, me and Reggie are right down the hall."

"Okay," I answer. I want to tell her that there's no need to crowd me so much, but I don't want to hurt her feelings.

Tracee slowly closes the door as if hoping that I'd call out for her to come back in. When I hear the soft click, I sigh in relief and then turn toward the bed. The door springs back open and Tracee pokes her head back inside. "What was that? Did you say something?"

It's all I can do not to laugh at her endearing eagerness. "No. I didn't say anything."

"Oh." She smiles. "Good night."

"Night."

We do the whole door dance again, but this time, I'm too afraid to make any noise as I inch my way over to the bed. When I climb under the sheets, the clock on the nightstand reads 11:00. After clicking off the lamp, I stare up at the ceiling and listen as the clock ticks off the minutes.

At 11:15 a pebble of anxiety rolls around in my chest.

11:30—it's a rock.

11:45—it's a boulder.

I don't know how in the hell I'm going to make it to 3:30

A.M. Plus, what am I going to do if he doesn't answer his phone? What if he's changed his cell phone number? How would I find him? How would I get in contact with him? I wish Essence was here—not just to help me with this shit, but because I miss her sass and her way of trying to talk sense into me.

11:55—a mountain sits on my chest.

At the stroke of midnight, I hear a strange pecking. Suspicious, I hold my breath to see whether I hear the sound again. I do—and it's coming from the window. I bolt up and reach for the light, but then think better of it in fear that Tracee will run back in here.

PECK. PECK. PECK.

I climb out of bed with my anxiety dissolving into hope.

PECK. PECK. PECK.

I tiptoe over to the window, praying and begging God for a miracle. "Profit."

27

Lucifer

The moon throws an eerie glow over the cemetery. The only thing that's missing is a howling wolf and a black crow to complete the tragic scene. I lose track of time whenever I come out here to Mason's empty grave. People say that it's cathartic to talk to these cold slabs of granite, but each time I come, it feels as if my lips glue together. I can't figure out what to say and I sure as hell don't know what do with all this guilt.

If only I had been able to strike that spark.

It's not the first time that thought has raced across my head. Hell, it's been known to just skip around for hours. Had I blown the SUV up that night, not only would I have saved myself from this empty misery called life, but I would've dragged that muthafucka Python down to hell with me.

Mason "Fat Ace" Lewis
September 13, 1990–August 24, 2011

I have to be strong for the baby. I purse my lips together while sliding my hand over the barely-there baby bump. "You're going to have some very big shoes to fill." A small part of me worries about my lack of maternal instincts but I'm sure I'll be better at the whole mommy gig than Mason's real mother. *I wonder if she's still alive?* Maybe I should check into it. *And maybe not.*

Squatting, I remove twigs and debris tangled in the flowers. This is the kind of shit I'm gonna be doing until they plant my ass in the ground: creeping out here in the middle of the night to keep this grave clean.

Pathetic.

I press two fingers to my lips and then transfer the kiss to the engraved name across the tombstone. "Forever, my nigga." Feeling the burn at the back of my eyes, I stand and march off into the darkness.

Snap!

I whip around and am unable to make anything out. However, I get that weird sensation that someone is watching again. My hand drifts from my belly to the back of my hip for my gat. After a full minute of straining my ears for the slightest sound I convince myself that I must be hearing things. I trek back toward the car where Tombstone is waiting for me.

Halfway there, I almost miss another lone figure, standing in the dark.

You're slipping, Willow.

I dismiss that thought as I reach for the gat tucked at my lower back—but then I notice the woman gazing down at another grave—oblivious to everything around her.

Pathetic—just like me.

I should keep it moving, but my owl-like night vision detects something familiar about her so, instead, I head in her direction. When I get five feet out I peep the name on the tombstone in front of her:

Essence Blackwell
November 23, 1994–August 22, 2011

"I wondered whatever happened to her."

At the sound of my voice, the woman whips around and reaches for her own weapon.

"Ah. Ah. Ah." I shake my head and I level my shit at her chest. Instant recognition registers in her face and I get a comedic view of her eyes widening.

"You have me at a disadvantage. You know who I am."

"I have *you* at a disadvantage?" she asks, incredulous.

"A figure of speech," I answer with a careless shrug and then wait for her to introduce herself.

"Cleo," she spits out, reluctantly. Her eyes deflate to their normal size.

The name bounces around in my head, but I come up with nothing. "Sister?" I ask, taking in the resemblance to the little girl I tortured out behind the hospital months ago. The girl had heart.

Cleo throws up her chin in defiance. "What's it to you?"

I stretch one brow out of formation.

"Yes," she answers, having second thoughts about catching an attitude.

"Guess that means that you're a Queen G, too."

The muscles in her jaw twitch while her teeth grind together.

"Don't mistake me for a bitch who repeats herself," I warn.

"Yes."

I nod and weigh what I want to do about this situation. Killing a QG might be the sleep aid I need to have a peaceful night.

"Well?" she prods.

I stare at her, prolonging her anxiety.

"Shoot if you're going to shoot," Cleo snaps. "You already killed my sister, you evil bitch! Go ahead and pull the fucking trigger. Get the shit over with."

"Anybody tell you that you bitches need to change your

name to *Drama Queens?* If I wanted to shoot you, I would've done it already." That shit throws a monkey wrench into her performance. After my words sink in, her entire body visibly relaxes.

"Then what do you want?"

"What—a bitch can't hang out at a cemetery if she wants?" I stump her ass again. She's as much fun to fuck with as her sister was. "What the fuck did you mean by that shit that *I* had already killed your sister? Where did you get that shit?"

"Don't play me stupid," she hisses. "I know it was you who doused my sister with gasoline and then tossed a match into the car when she tried to get away from you."

"Fuck. That sounds like an awful way to go."

Cleo goes for her gun.

POW!

Her shit goes flying out of her hand.

"Fuuucck!" Cleo flaps her hand around.

"I warned you."

Cleo glances at her shit and marvels at how my shot didn't put a hole through her hand.

"You're welcome." She fixes her mouth to thank me, but then stops herself at the last second.

"What the fuck do you want?"

"Though I'm not sorry that there's one less Queen G in the world, I didn't kill your sister."

"Liar!"

"And I would lie because . . .?"

She opens her mouth, I guess, to air it out because she doesn't say shit to that.

My attention shifts to the lonely tombstone behind her. "Without using too much brain power, I'm willing to bet that your snake-fucking head bitch told you that I was the one flame-broiled your sister."

The bitch blinks at me like a deer in headlights. *Why am I bothering with this silly bitch?* "Fine. Believe what you want to believe. I really don't give a fuck." I tuck my gun back into place. "Have a good night." I turn to leave.

"LeShelle wouldn't lie about something like that," Cleo shouts.

I stop and glance over my shoulder. "Really. Where the fuck do they recruit you dumb bitches, off a yellow bus?"

Cleo shakes her head as tears gloss her eyes. "*Why* would she kill her? Essence was working . . ." She clamps her mouth shut.

I cock my head with a half smile. "She was working for who—LeShelle? Or was she working for me?"

"What?"

Annoyed, I march back over to this simple bitch and jab my finger repeatedly in the center of her forehead. "Think. Damn, girl. You really think that I'd just let a Queen G roll up in my kingdom and hang the fuck out? Your girl LeShelle dumped a full clip into Mas"—I catch myself and lower my hand— "our leader's brother after his prom. The only reason I *allowed* your sister visitation with Profit is because we struck a deal."

"Essence was no snitch."

"Essence wanted revenge." I wait for her next stupid remark, but when it doesn't come, I suspect sense is finally sinking in. "LeShelle ordered her best friend's brutal rape that landed her in the crazy house—are you connecting the dots?"

Cleo nods as she loses color beneath the silvery moonlight. "You killed all the guys who raped her."

"Because I got their names through Essence." I step back. "I'm a heartless bitch, but I'm an honest gangster. LeShelle had her own sister raped—and you don't think that she would lie to you? Bitch, wake up."

"She found out," Cleo concludes. "Somehow LeShelle found out that Essence was double-crossing her."

I give her a small applause. "Congratulations. You did it."

"That bitch," Cleo swears under her breath, her dumb-founded look transforming into a mask of anger. "I'm going to kill her."

"Humph. You mean if she ever wakes up in the hospital."

Cleo's face jerks back up.

"What?"

"You haven't heard?"

I tense up. "Heard what?"

"LeShelle is awake. She has been for a month."

28

Ta'Shara

Every part of me melts at the sight of Profit's smile on the other side of the window. I try to take him in, but he's changed so much. It's the same handsome face, but fuller . . . more distinguished. His shoulders are huge, his chest wide, and his arms bulging with muscles.

Profit winks and then cocks his head. "Are you going to let me in?"

I rush to unlock the window. I'm so excited that I can barely get my fingers to work. He's here. I can't believe how good he looks. "What are you doing here? How did you know I was home? How—?"

Profit silences me with a kiss. Every question and thought flies out of my head. It's been so long and he feels so good. It isn't long before the salt of my tears blends with the sweetness of his lips. I'm on sensory overload as we cling together and devour each other's lips. I don't even remember how or when we moved from the window to the bed. All I know is how much I want him—how much I need him. I sense that he needs me, too. He's the most beautiful thing I've seen in a long while, but there's a troubling sadness dulling his brown eyes. "What is it?" I ask, wanting to take his pain away.

He shakes his head as if he's unable to speak on whatever is troubling him.

I try to wait him out, but he doesn't budge. "I know about Fat Ace," I tell him, reaching for his hand. "I'm so sorry."

"Thanks. I appreciate that."

An hour later, we're lying side by side, holding each other's hand staring into each other's eyes. I want to make love to him . . . but I'm not ready yet—too many bad memories of that horrible night.

"Do you remember me coming to visit you in the hospital?"

"You came?" I ask, surprised.

"Once. You were still out of it, but I kind of hoped . . ."

More tears leak from my eyes. "I'm sorry—but thank you for coming. It means so much . . . but how did you get in? I thought Reggie and Tracee—"

"Essence. She got me in."

"Oh." My gaze falls "Do you know what happ—"

Profit presses his fingers back against my lips. "No. Not tonight. There's plenty of time to . . . talk on heavier things later. A lot has happened while you were away. Right now I need to hold you—to make sure that you're real."

He kisses me again and for a while I feed off his peppermint-flavored lips, but then his hand touches my thigh and I tense.

Profit pulls back and frowns. "Did I hurt you?" Fear and concern ripple across his face.

"No," I whisper, reaching up to caress the side of his cheek. "You could never hurt me."

His gaze sweeps my face as if memorizing every detail. "I knew that you would come back to me."

Shaking my head, I whisper back, "I still don't understand how it's possible that you're here. I held you in my arms that night. I thought that you were . . ."

"Shhh . . ." Profit presses a finger to my lips because I'm on the verge of breaking down. "I'm here because we belong together. We always have and always will." He peppers kisses across my face before zeroing in on my lips. Profit was my first lover and we have made love at least a hundred times since that night at the drive-in, but tonight it is different. It is our first time all over again. He's so delicate with me as he pulls my nightgown up my body and then over my head. Seconds later his clothes follow mine, discarded on the floor.

I gasp at the sight of his broad, muscular chest in the silvery moonlight. "My God. Look at you." I reach out and run my hands over his new incredible body. "You're so hard." My hands drift over his washboard abs. "What did you do, move into a gym?"

"You like?"

"No. I love." I draw his head down for another kiss. "But I love you no matter what you look like. You're my heart and soul. I didn't know how to live without you. Maybe that's why I was so lost."

A sad smile hugs his lips as he caresses my face. "That makes two of us."

Gazing into Profit's handsome face is like staring into my destiny. Him being here is already erasing the nightmares of LeShelle and her gang of rapists from my mind.

Although the black-and-blue bruises are gone, he touches me as though he can still see the scars. "I should've been able to protect you that night." He brushes his hand down the center of my ribcage. "I let you down."

"Oh, baby, no." I cup his chin and force him to look at me. "Don't blame yourself for that night. You fought for me and that means more than you'll ever know. There's only one person responsible for that night and I will deal with her."

"Not if I get my hands on her first," he hisses with his jaw clenched. "Cousin Skeet has been blocking my ass on getting my hands on her. He says he's under pressure to get the city's violence under control. He has a cop posted outside her door for the past few months."

Surprisingly, conflicting emotions war within me before I vow, "I won't fail the next time."

"Don't tell me that my good girl has gone gangsta on me," Profit chuckles.

"Shhh. Keep it down. We don't want to wake up Tracee and Reggie."

He kisses my finger. "Well? Have you?"

"I don't know what I am anymore," I confess. "I just want her dead."

"Then you'll have it." When his lips return to mine, it's as if we're the only two people who exist.

"We're together now," Profit whispers. "Nothing is ever going to come between us again. I promise."

A phone rings and Profit and I jump up.

"Get it before you wake Tracee and Reggie," I hiss urgently.

Profit falls over the side of the bed, sounding like a red oak crashing on the house. I slap my hand over my mouth to stop my bark of laughter.

It seems like forever but Profit finally pulls his phone out of his pocket. "It's Lucifer," he says and then answers the call. "Hello."

Lucifer must've got to the point because in the next second, Profit tenses.

"I'm on my way," he says gravely and then disconnects the call.

I don't like the look on his face. "What is it?"

"I have to go," he tells me, jumping up from the floor and snatching up his clothes.

"Why? What's going on?"

"Your sister—she's awake."

29

LeShelle

Never let bitches see you sweat.

I learned that shit the hard way—even now when I'm surrounded by my family but they're all acting strange. These bitches haven't turned on me, have they? My mind races through a catalog of bad deeds and at the top of the list is my fear of Python finding out I struck a deal with a Flower to murk one of his baby mommas. I'm sure he didn't give a fuck about her, but he would care about killing the seed that was in her belly.

"Where the fuck is that bag—or are y'all gonna keep me with my ass hanging out in this muthafucka?"

Pit Bull cheeses up as she shoves the black, leather duffle bag my way. "Your nigga picked your shit out," she tells me, envy lacing her voice. "Everything is set."

Kookie shifts her attention to the window.

"What the fuck is wrong with you?" I ask.

She glances back at me to see who I was spitting to. "Who—me?"

"Yeah, you. What's with the long face? I thought you were glad to see me out?"

"Of course. You know that you're my girl." Kookie flashes me a big smile, but the shit doesn't reach her eyes. "We'll talk about it another time," she adds before I can interrogate her further.

Whatever the fuck she gotta tell me everybody else must already know because they all go as silent as the grave.

Avonte ain't playing behind the wheel because she floats our ass out of Memphis in no time flat. In the meantime, I change out of the ugly hospital gown into the packed clothes in the bag: black lacy underwear, short white mini-skirt and a white, crop cami—accompanied by a pair of breathtaking silver Louboutin pumps. If this is an apology for him not personally busting my ass out, apology accepted. I rush through the toiletries and then put my hair in some kind of order. No sense in looking like *Whodunit and what for* when I step out of this bitch.

"How do I look?" I ask, turning to Kookie.

"Like a muthafuckin' queen."

Heads nod in agreement all around me, but that doesn't stop a few butterflies from tickling my belly when the car rolls to a stop. I can't help but twist up my mug shot at seeing where we are. "A church?" I take in the old, red-brick building with paint-chipped columns and wonder whether this shit is some kind of a joke.

"C'mon. We better hurry up," Pit Bull says, hopping out of the car. "Our asses is already late."

Everybody scrambles out like fuckin' roaches, but my ass is still stuck on stupid on why the fuck Python's ass is hanging out at a dilapidated church with a graveyard out back.

"Girl, are you comin'?" Kookie snaps.

Swallowing my list of questions, I climb out of the car. My ass was already wobbly before the fuckin' heels. Now I feel like a toddler tryna walk for the first time.

Kookie and Pit Bull flank my sides.

"It's all right, girl. We got you."

Never let bitches see you sweat.

"That's all right. I got it." I shake them off and they fall back a step. I start to head round back, thinking that's where we need to enter, but once again, Kookie grasps hold of my wrist and leads me toward the front door.

"This way."

I give her a look. The last thing I need right now is for the man upstairs to strike my ass down for rolling up in his house. For most of my life the Lord and I had an understanding: I stay out of his business and he stays out of mine. When I glance at the girls again, my nerves knot in my gut. *These bitches are up to something.*

"Are you going to go, girl, or what?" Pit Bull snaps impatiently. "Python's waiting on you."

This bitch better not be lying. I pat the Glock at my waist before turning and heading up the steep stairs. At the door, I pause, place my hand on the Glock, and then jerk the door open.

Immediately, an organ plays . . . *The Wedding March?*

Shocked as hell, I glance around wide-eyed to see a rather large gathering of jeans-clad, but blue-and-black-flagged niggas in the pews. In the center of the aisle is a grave-looking preacher . . . and Python.

Python.

My nigga, ugly as sin, but physically sexy as hell, looks like he's packed on ten more pounds of muscles on his shoulders and arms. Black jeans hang off his trim waist while a gray-and-white plaid shirt covers his entire tatted body. Upon seeing me, he snatches off his shades and gives a lopsided grin that usually means that he's in the mood for some pussy.

Kookie shoulder-bumps me. "Better get your ass down there, gurl, before that nigga changes his mind."

I blink out of my shock but still manage to bat back the river of tears flooding my eyes. *This shit is really happening.* My hand falls away from my Glock and I begin the slow march down the aisle. My gaze never leaves Python. He's smug because he's pulled off the surprise of the decade. He fidgets and then he rolls his forked tongue over his thick lips, giving them a nice, sexy gloss.

By the time I reach him and the preacher, my heart's pounding its way out of my chest.

"You all may be seated," the preacher announces.

For a second, I think that he means my ass, too, because my knees dip. Python holds. *Shit. It's hot up in this bitch.*

"Welcome back, baby," Python says, winking and taking my hand.

I look down and I'm taken aback by ugly burns covering his hands. *He was in that car accident.*

He smiles and I push all my questions to the back of my head for another time. We turn toward the preacher, who opens his Bible and begins his spiel.

"Dearly beloved, we are gathered here today to join this man and this woman in holy matrimony. . . ."

I sneak a peek to my right and see Python heavily engrossed in what the preacher is saying. I, on the other hand, have a hard time concentrating on the words. *I'm about to be a married woman.* Every fiber in my body explodes with joy. I've wanted this for so long. I fought more bitches than I could name for this moment. No more playing house. No more wifey. No more "ride-or-die chick." The official title will be *wife. Mrs. Terrell Jerome Carver.*

A little boy trots up to us with a pillow and two gold bands.

Python picks up one and slides it next to my diamond ring before repeating after the preacher, "I, Terrell Carver, take you, LeShelle, to be my lawfully wedded wife. Knowing in my heart that you will be my constant friend, lover, and partner in life. I pledge my love and promise to stay by your side in sickness and in health, in good times and bad. I will protect you from harm, comfort you in times of distress, and cherish you for as long as we both shall live."

There's no fighting back the tears after that. I've waited all my life for someone to say these words to me—for someone to want me. With blurry eyes, I reach for the other gold ring and repeat the same vows.

The preacher turns toward me. "Do you, LeShelle, take this man to be your lawfully wedded husband? To have and to hold from this day forward?"

Oh shit. "I do."

"Do you, Terrell, take this woman to be your lawfully wedded wife?"

Python's beastly face splits open with a smile. "I do."

"Then, by the power vested in me, I pronounce you two man and wife. You may kiss the bride."

Niggas erupt out of their seats as Python sweeps me into his arms and lays a fat-ass kiss on me. Shit. Nothing ever tasted so sweet. I throw my arms around my *husband's* neck and pour every ounce of love into him that I can. It isn't until my lungs beg for oxygen that I break the kiss, but I hold on to him for a long time after.

Later, muthafuckas bum-rush us with congratulations.

"Girl, you should've seen your face," Kookie crows. "You would've thought your ass was about to walk into a shoot-out or some shit."

"I know that's right," Pit Bull cosigns, drawing me into a hug.

I stop trying to hold back these muthafuckin' tears. I'm happy—and I want the whole fucking world to know it. Swinging my big-ass grin around the room, I search for Momma Peaches . . . then for McGriff . . . and there are a few more missing soldiers. I turn my pinched-up face toward Python and I see for the first time just how hard he's struggling to hold up his plastic smile.

"Are you ready to roll, *Mrs. Carver?*" he asks before I can get my interrogation on. "There is a little matter of a honeymoon night."

I hesitate for a beat and my joy is too great to let a few missing gray clouds ruin my wedding day. "I'm rolling with you until my last breath."

A rare, genuine smile stretches across my *husband's* lips before he wraps a muscular arm around my waist, plants another kiss on me, and then directs me toward the church's front door.

Everyone cheers and waves as we make it down the aisle then burst through the doors. The celebration follows us outside. Python's beloved black Monte Carlo pulls to the bottom of the stairs. The word "Newlyweds" is written across it with silver cans tied to the bumper. We race forward beneath a shower of rice and confetti.

Halfway down the stairs, the unmistakable sound of tires squealing catches my attention.

RAT-A-TAT-TAT-TAT!

POW! POW! POW!

There's no time for me to react before something burns me and Python lunges his large body in front of me. The next thing I know I'm swept off my feet and then a second later, hitting the hard, concrete stairs with the wind knocked out of me.

"FIVE POPPIN', SIX DROPPIN', NIGGAS!"

30

Lucifer

R*AT-A-TAT-TAT-TAT!*
POW! POW! POW!
I watch as Python pulls his bitch back and then throws himself in front of our spray of bullets. His big un–dead ass is lifted about three feet in the air before crashing back on the white concrete steps on top of his new bride.

"FIVE POPPIN', SIX DROPPIN', NIGGAS!"

For a few seconds it feels like shooting fish in a barrel. They fall one after another. *He's Mason's brother.* That shit loops around in my head. My finger eases off the trigger as Tombstone floats our asses off into the distance. I pay no attention to the bullets whizzing by my head as the Gangster Disciples' army spills out of the church to return fire.

Suddenly, I'm uncomfortable about the emotions whirling inside me. On the one hand, I'm thrilled see to his big, ugly ass go down and on the other, I'm attacked by the image of Python clutching his brother and weeping from his soul.

RAT-A-TAT-TAT-TAT!
POW! POW! POW!

Through the exchange of gunfire, I catch sight of Cleo, standing boldly at the church door. For a brief second our eyes connect, a transmission of an understanding passes between us and if I'm not mistaken, a ghost of a smile haunts the corners of her lips.

"Yes, goddamn it! Yes!" Profit punches his fist into the air. "We got that muthafucka. Did you see his face?"

"Guess his ass wasn't dead," Tombstone says.

"He's dead now," Profit declares.

My chest swells with pride. I'm happy to give him this moment. Calling him was the right thing to do. Who knows—maybe we can even begin to repair the bridge between us? At least I can hope.

"Pussy-ass punk niggas," Profit spits, slapping in a second clip. "We ought to back up and shoot his ass again. The muthafucka got nine lives."

The back window explodes and Novell spits out a stream of curses. "Fuck! Those roaches got me!"

I drop back in from the car's window, spin around, and hit the interior light. "Let me see."

Novell moans and groans like a bitch about to drop a baby.

Stretching back over the seat, I snatch the sleeve on his T-shirt up and examine the damage. "Get the fuck out of here. It's nothing but a scratch. The way you're carrying on I thought your ass was really hurt."

Profit and Tombstone laugh.

Novell's face twists up. "Yeah. Whatever. That nigga, Python, got more than a scratch. We cut his ass in half. That shit was for our man Fat Ace. May he rest in peace."

I shut off the light and flop around in my seat.

"Fuck yeah," Tombstone cosigns, nodding and checking the rearview mirror to make sure that the coast was still clear.

Wedding. I can't fucking believe it. When Cleo dropped dime about that shit I thought I was going to pop a blood vessel. Like how dare that freak of nature go on about his shit while my man is rotting at the bottom of the Mississippi River. *Maybe we should go back and shoot his ass again.*

I close my eyes and savor the taste of revenge, but it's already bitter on my tongue. My elation fades into the black hole where my heart used to be.

"After taking out that muthafucka, our name is going to ring out in the streets," Novell boasts. "The throne is yours, Lucifer. Ain't nobody gonna doubt that shit after tonight."

"The throne is already mine," I say, irritated.

Profit's smile vanishes like a poof of smoke.

What is he thinking? Is he still thinking about forming an alliance with Bishop? That shit pricks my pride more than I care to admit.

Novell doesn't know when to shut the fuck up and continues blabbering, "I know. I know. I'm just saying that all that side noise Bishop has been—"

"Squash that shit," I bark. "I don't want to speak on that bullshit." Tombstone glances at me sideways. I grind my teeth together, determined not to get into any discussion about Bishop. Novell is right. This shit tonight squashes any planned mutiny.

Tombstone changes the subject. "Why didn't Cousin Skeet tell us that bitch, LeShelle, woke up?"

A *good question.* "No clue."

"Think Bishop knew?" he asks.

Another damn good question. "No clue."

Tombstone's gaze sneaks back over to me. He's probably wondering what the hell *do* I know.

"Watch the road," I tell him, my emotions safely tucked behind a stone mask. In the backseat, Novell rehashes the night's events, tryna convince himself and Profit how much their street fame is about to put them on.

None of it interests Profit. He's lost inside his own head, probably realizing the same thing I am. Revenge can't bring Mason back. I know this, but in the back of my head, I still hoped.

"We need to muthafuckin' celebrate," Novell says. He's the

only one in the car still high off our hit. "Let's hit Da Club. That shit should be bumping right about now."

It will be just the place for him to blow his shit up.

When none of us say shit, Novell glances around and notices our long faces for the first time. "What the fuck is wrong with y'all?"

Silence.

"I don't believe this," Novell thunders. "This shit is the end of an era. We're the new kings on the street. Now that we settled this shit with those paper gangsters we can focus on stomping those cripple-walking Crips back down into the ground and rule the whole muthafuckin' city. All is well, my people." He slaps me on the back and gets a sharp look from me.

His smile wobbles at the corners until he removes his hands and holds them high into the air. "My bad."

I cut my eyes away from him, knowing in the back of my head that I overreacted. "A'ight," I say, nodding. *Either we're going to sulk or we're going to celebrate—and I'm tired of sulking.* "Let's head out to Da Club." *I'll deal with Cousin Skeet's ass later.*

Forever the faithful soldier, Tombstone bobs his head. "You got it, boss."

A half hour later, we roll up toward a sea of flashing blue lights surrounding Da Club. Dread creeps up my spine. "What the fuck is it now?"

Novell pulls up the backseat floorboards and starts gathering up everyone's gats and cramming them down into the secret compartment. "All clear," he announces before climbing back up into his seat.

Tombstone turns into the parking lot, but is immediately barked at by a cop.

"Sorry but you're going to have to pull out, sir. This is a crime scene."

I ignore his ass and hop out of the car. "What's going on?"

Profit and Novell follow suit.

"Ma'am, sirs, I'm gonna need you all to get back into the vehicle. You can't be here right now."

"The fuck we can't," I snap. "This is my shit. What the fuck happened?"

"Are you the owner?" the young cops asks.

At the front door of the club, I see them break out the yellow tape. "I asked you what the fuck happened?"

The cop looks like he's 'bout ready to check my ass when Hennessey and Cutty shout across the lot. I know the shit is serious when I see my two big boys break away from the crowd and jog to get at me.

Tombstone shuts off the engine and climbs out of the car, too.

"Ma'am!" the cop shouts again. When he lunges for my hand, Tombstone steps up and shakes his head at the rookie.

"You don't want to do that, son."

The police officer looks confused, but then decides fuckin' with us ain't worth the headache.

Meanwhile that flush of dread feels like a tsunami crashing around inside my soul as Henessey and Cutty draw near.

"Lucifer, thank God you're here," Hennessy says, already sweating from the short run.

"Whassup?" My gaze swings between him and Cutty. If I'm not mistaken, Cutty looks like he's been crying. Now that they have my attention, they act as if they've forgotten how to speak. "Whatever it is just spit it out."

"It's . . . Bishop," Hennessy says.

The hairs on the back of my neck stand at attention. Tombstone and Profit step up behind me. "What about him?"

Hennessey and Cutty shoot another look at each other before Cutty tosses a hand grenade into my world. "I'm sorry . . . but Bishop is dead."

31

LeShelle

Muthafuckas keep walking across my grave.

That's the only explanation I have for my ass surviving yet another attempt on my life. The shit has me shook. After the Vice Lord slobs peel off, a few of our niggas who survive the assault pour out into the street, blasting at the fading backlights of a black SUV.

"Muthafuckas slashed all of our shit," one brothah curses, staring at row after row of flat tires.

My chest threatens to collapse. I attempt to push Python off of me, but it's like lifting a brick building. Around me, people are crying, wailing, and cursing. I can't see what's all going on. At long last, I hear a small stampede of sneakers rushing back up the church stairs.

"Python, man. Are you all right?"

Like the rest of them, I wait with bated breath for an answer. The seconds feel like minutes before Python groans and rolls off of me. Relief sweeps through me for the oxygen as well as my having avoided having the shortest marriage in history. "I'm fine," he grumbles, sounding anything but fine. "Shell? Baby, are you all right?"

I can't recall the last time Python has spoken to me with such tenderness and concern—if the shit has ever happened.

We've always talked so much shit to each other that I'm thrown for a moment. When I glance up, I see something that I've never seen before in his face: fear.

He really does love me. "I'm good."

Python helps me up into a seated position. I do a quick body-check, but I'm stunned that there isn't a drop of blood on me anywhere. "What the fuck?"

Smiling, Python rips open his shirt and reveals a bullet-proof vest. That explains the extra bulk on his frame. "You were expecting this shit?"

"Nah. But wasn't taking any chances. Enemies all around me with their dicks out ready to piss on my grave." He glances over his shoulder and together we take in the carnage around us.

There are at least ten bodies down, but only one catches my attention. "Oh fuck." I stagger to my feet, ignoring the stinging scrapes on my knees and hands. "Pit Bull."

Beside her, Kookie wails, snotting up like she's lost her soul mate. I take one look at the blood pooled around Pit Bull's body and know that her ass is gone.

"Shit." My girl was a good soldier. I hang my head for a few seconds and wish her luck on the other side, before I take another look around.

Python is huddled up with our people, no doubt plotting and planning revenge. Rage floods my veins. *Those muthafuckas ruined my wedding.* When I replay the scene over in my mind, that bitch Lucifer sticks out like a sore thumb. There's no mis-taking that evil bitch, but I'm certain that one of the other gunmen I saw spraying bullets was Ta'Shara's nigga, Profit.

"Looks like the children want to play." My lips curl into a smile as my mind races with evil possibilities, but my fantasies are interrupted when I feel the heavy weight of someone's stare. I search around and can't find the source of my uneasi-ness. *Maybe I'm imagining things.*

"Shell," Python hollers.

My attention whips back to my man, who is waving me

over. I tense when I see another car cruise up the street. I don't relax until it rolls to a stop and Dutchboy pops out and rushes around to open the back door.

"Let's roll," Python roars.

Nodding, I rush to his side. The whole time, I can't shake the feeling of someone watching me.

"Let's get you out of here, baby." Python presses a possessive kiss against my lips that takes my breath away. This new version of Python continues to surprise me. "C'mon. Get in."

I climb into the SUV and scoot across the leather seats. A chill races down my spine. *Some muthafucka is walking across my grave.* Python climbs in after me and shuts the door. I do another desperate sweep of the scene from the backseat window. That's when I spot her—staring a hole in the center of my head.

Cleo.

32

Qiana

I can't move.

Lying on silk sheets across Diesel's California king bed, every inch of my body is sore—but in a good way. Diesel has fucked me in so many different positions that I can barely remember them all. I've never been with no real nigga like this before and I definitely have never been in no big crib like his, either. Muthfuckas out here on St. Andrew know how to fuckin' live. Everywhere I look oozes money. Big money.

Smiling, I open my eyes and instantly drown in Diesel's beautiful green eyes.

"Morning," I whisper, hoping my morning breath ain't too fucked up.

"You mean afternoon," he corrects, his shit all minty-fresh.

"What?" I pop my head up off the pillow and look around, tryna spot a clock. The glowing red numbers on the nightstand back up his claim. It's 2 P.M.

GG is gonna kill me.

I rush off the bed with a reserve of strength that didn't exist a moment ago.

"Problem?"

"I gotta get home." Frantic, I search around the floor for my clothes.

"Why? Your man looking for you?" Diesel asks, lazily folding his arms behind his head.

It's in that position that I notice his dick standing straight up beneath the bed's black sheets. Instantly, my pussy throbs. "I told you. I don't have a man." I swallow and lick my lips. I remember what that fat muthafucka feels like gliding between my lips.

"You sure about that?" Diesel slides his free hand beneath the sheet to massage his hard-on.

"Positive." I drop my clothes back onto the floor.

"Then get your fine ass back in here and take care of this shit." He pulls the sheet down so I can watch his chocolaty dick stretch up a few more inches.

GG is gonna have to understand. I fly back into the bed and ride that fat dick until I black out. Time slips away and the next thing I know, I'm waking up again and the glowing red numbers on the clock read 3:00 and Diesel is nowhere in sight.

Groggy and still saddle-sore, I peel off the sticky sheets and go in search of my new fuck toy. The minute I step out of the bedroom, I hear Diesel talking downstairs. I creep over to the banister and peek over the rail.

Diesel grins at a curvaceous amazon of a woman who looks as if she's stepped out of the pages of a glossy magazine. The blood in my veins heats up.

He leans in and whispers something in the bitch's ear. She giggles and wiggles her breasts in his face. Bitch.

Diesel cocks his head and checks her out from head to toe. His gaze lingers on her thick ass.

Pissed, I clear my throat.

Both heads snap up in my direction.

"Oh. I didn't know that you had company." She smiles but she doesn't bother stepping back from *my* man.

Diesel doesn't react to my standing naked above them. In

fact, he dismisses me, and then inches closer to the bitch to whisper something else in her ear.

The woman laughs and then tries to downplay the shit by slapping her hand over her mouth as if that's gonna soften the blow.

No this muthafucka didn't just disrespect me like that!

Enraged, I bolt back into the bedroom and search for my clutch purse on the floor. I whip out my gat and storm back out of the room.

"Yo, bitch. I got something for you to laugh at."

I reach the top of the staircase and take aim.

"WHAT THE FUCK?" Diesel's reflexes kick in and he jerks his giggling girlfriend out of the way at the moment I fire.

POW!

Ms. Ha-Ha screams as they hit the floor.

The bullet slams into the wall above them.

"QIANA, PUT THE DAMN GUN DOWN," Diesel roars.

"Why don't you suck my dick?"

POW!

They split up. Diesel bolts toward the staircase while his bitch scrambles toward the front door.

"WHERE ARE YOU GOING, MS. GIGGLES?"

POW!

The third bullet tears a chunk of the door frame as my prey flees the house. I take off down the stairs in hot pursuit.

I'm so focused on getting at this bitch that I forgot about Diesel until he tackles me in the center of the stairs and knocks the gun from my hand.

"Get the fuck off me!" I swing at him, but he pins my hands down over my head and mean-mugs me hard.

"Have you lost your mind?"

"Fuck you—you and your silly ho!" I fight harder to get loose, but he's like one large wall of muscle and my energy drains in no time flat. When I stop struggling, I'm left panting like a dog in heat.

Diesel's lips slope into that sexy grin again. "Are you through?"

I refuse to answer him. I'm waiting for him to release me so that I can beat his ass.

"Thinking about whipping my ass?"

I blink. Can he read minds?

"Since you can't speak then maybe I'll keep you pinned down like this. The shit makes my dick hard anyway."

"Fuck you." I smirk. "You're gonna have to get up sooner or later."

Diesel's smile grows wider. "Damn, Scar. You'd think that I was your man or some shit."

I cut my eyes away as my anger flips the script to embarrassment.

He laughs. "You want me to be your man?" he asks me point blank. "Is that why you're running around shooting at women? I done sprung that ass already?"

"Nigga, please."

He laughs. "Look at me."

I don't want to.

"C'mon, Scar. Look at your man. You were just fighting for him."

Ignoring the voice in my head, I peek up at him and see amusement dancing in his green-blue eyes.

"I see right now that I'm going to have to train your ass if I'm gonna keep you around."

"Who said that I want to stick around?" I challenge.

"Then it sounds like I have some more fucking to do." He leans down and bites me on my lower lip. "Because you belong to me now."

That shit makes me hot as fuck. Next thing I know we're back in bed having angry sex and clawing up the sheets. At 4:00, I wake to see Diesel watching me again. I smile lazily when something on his neck catches my attention. "What's that?"

Diesel frowns. "What?"

"On your neck." I squint. "It almost looks like a horseshoe. It's kind of cute."

"Oh. That." He shrugs. "It's a birthmark."

Wiz Khalifa's "Black and Yellow" blasts from my phone. *GG!*

I groan. I don't want to talk to her ass. All she's gonna do is cuss me the fuck out for leaving Jayson with her for so long.

"Let it go to voice mail," Diesel says, pinching on my titty. My eyes bulge—but it feels . . . nice.

The song cuts off, signaling the call going to voice mail. In the next second, it plays again.

Damn, bitch. Go away.

The phone cuts off.

It plays again.

Diesel chuckles. "Better answer that shit before your man sends the whole Peoples Nation after you. You gangbangers stick together, don't you?"

"I done told you that I don't have a man."

Diesel laughs. "You ain't got to be scared to call him back," he says, nuzzling my neck. "I'll be quiet."

He's being so cute right now that I don't even know what to do. These past few hours have been like a dream and I don't want it to end.

"Go ahead. Call," he says but there's an underlying dare and suspicion in his voice.

I crawl out of bed to get my purse and dig out my phone. I sigh at seeing Charlie's name printed across the screen. "It's my brother."

Diesel leans back, folds his hands behind his head, and watches me.

"Hello."

"WHERE IN THE FUCK ARE YOU?" Charlie thunders.

I pull the phone away from my ear to save my eardrums.

"I'VE BEEN CALLING EVERY-FUCKING-WHERE LOOKING FOR YOU!"

"Charlie, calm down. I'm fine." I glance up at Diesel. "I'm with a new friend."

"I don't fucking believe this shit. Da Club gets shot up last night. Lil Bit and Adaryl say you were there, but no one has seen you since. You leave GG with this baby and you have the nerve not to answer your phone? This kind of shit, I expect your ass to be lying in a gutter somewhere. You feel me? We're in the middle of two damn wars right now—and Bishop dropped last night."

"What?" I couldn't have heard him right. "Bishop is dead?"

"Ain't that what the fuck I just said? He was killed last night. Lucifer is . . ." His sentence hangs for a second before he changes the subject. "Get home."

His bossiness sparks my anger. "You're my brother not my father. I'll get there when I get there."

"COME HOME!"

Instead of answering, I disconnect the call.

"Problem?"

"I gotta go." I check out his sexy poise lying in that bed and I poke out my bottom lip. *I don't want to go home.*

Wiz Khalifa starts up again.

Without looking at the caller ID, I yell into the phone: "Dammit, Charlie. I'll be there when I get there. Get off my ass!"

"Gurl, it's me, Lil Bit. Where the fuck are you? Your brother has been blowing up my shit up all day."

Thrown, I exhale and calm down. "I'm still hanging out with a friend."

Lil Bit gasps. "Don't tell me that you're still out with that fine muthafucka you were hugged up on last night."

"Fine. I won't tell you. What happened last night? Charlie just told me that Bishop is dead."

"Yeah. Everybody's tryna find out who was poppin' off at Da Club. Some people are saying it was GD, some say it was the Crips or rather those pussy-puck Crippettes that's been hitting our trap houses and shit. But there's a couple of crazy fucks spitting that Lucifer set the shit up."

"That's crazy!"

"Is it? Everybody knows that power struggle was going to get bloody one way or another."

"But to erase her own blood? Nah. That's not Lucifer's style."

"Cain killed Abel. I remember that shit from Bible school."

"Bitch, your ass ain't never been up in nobody's church. You done forgot who you're talking to."

"Whatever, ho."

"Well, I don't believe that Lucifer shit. The bitch is cold, but—"

"Yeah. Yeah. I don't believe it, either. But that ain't all. That nigga Python was still alive, girl."

"What?" Shit, the whole damn world has flipped upside down while I'm out here screwing this nigga's brains out. "But I thought—how?"

"Muthafucka must've made like a fish and swam his ass out of the Mississippi. Doesn't matter because Lucifer and Profit found his ass and guess what."

"I'm almost too afraid to ask."

"The nigga was getting married at some old-ass church out in West Memphis."

"Get the fuck out of here. Who was he marrying? Ain't his girl still laid up in the hospital?"

"She was. Cousin Skeet going crazy all over the news because she busted out that muthafucka."

"What?"

Lil Bit clicks her tongue. "Yeah, girl, but they're dead though now. Lucifer and Profit handled they asses when they came out of the church."

"Y'all sure? Sounds like death don't want to have shit to do with their asses."

I glance up at Diesel, who's watching me like a hawk.

"Well, you better get your ass back over here. Enemies are all around—and you need to get rid of this baby."

33

Ta'Shara

*L*eShelle *is awake.*

The very idea fills me with terror and anger. What's worse is that it's been more than twelve hours since Profit flew out my window with murder in his eyes. I begged to go with him. I wanted to be the one to actually put a bullet in LeShelle's skull, but he insisted that this was something that he had to do. Profit didn't stick around to argue. He was gone in a blink of an eye.

Sleep eludes me as I lay watching the clock next to my nightstand. I keep telling myself that Profit will return any moment with the news of LeShelle's death. Any guilt about that also eludes me. The love I had for my sister died on that awful prom night. Now all I can do is wait.

Tracee takes one look at me and then shifts into panic mode. She doesn't like my color, my temperature, or the large bags under my eyes. Reggie is dragged in to take a look at me and he's concerned as well.

"I'm fine. I'm fine," I keep telling them, but even to my own ears it sounds like a lie.

Doctors are called, prescriptions are phoned to our local pharmacy and, before I know it, sleep claims me, whether I like it or not.

I don't.

Only nightmares wait for me on the other side. From the second I close my eyes, a kaleidoscope of laughing faces and grunting niggas assault me—and the pain. I will never forget the pain of battering fists against my rib cage or the dull switchblade that carved *GD* on the side of my ass.

My screams ring inside my head, but those damn pills won't let me wake up. I *can't* wake up. *Please, God. Let me wake up.*

"TA'SHARA! TA'SHARA, HONEY. WAKE UP! WAKE UP!"

At last, I'm snatched out of the nightmare. I emerge from my tangled sheets like a drowning woman, breaking through the ocean's surface.

"It's okay. It's okay." Tracee throws her arms around me and squeezes out what little breath I have left. "I'm here now. Everything is going to be all right."

She means well, but I'm suffocating. I push her away and tumble back off the bed to scramble for the bathroom.

"Ta'Shara, honey. Are you all right?" Tracee rushes after me, committed to her new role as my shadow.

In the bathroom, I barely get the lid up on the toilet seat before I throw up everything but my lungs into the porcelain bowl.

"I'm so sorry, honey. I'm so sorry." Tracee grabs a face cloth and runs it beneath the cold water in the sink. "They told me that those pills wouldn't be that strong," she rambles, wringing out the towel and rushing over to slap it across my forehead.

I don't have the strength to shove off her smothering again. I can barely handle the dry heaves that are wracking my body and twisting my belly into a huge knot. I admit the cold compress feels good against my face, but my screams and LeShelle's gunshots are still ringing in my ears.

Is she dead yet? She can't be—or my nightmare would end—wouldn't it? Yes. I'm sure of it. But as long as the bitch is alive . . .

I force my thoughts away from LeShelle and wedge myself between the toilet and the bathtub. I don't know how long I remain curled there before Tracee calls on Reggie to help get me back to my bedroom.

Reggie is a lot stronger than he looks. The studious professor is able to lift and carry me as if I weigh nothing. But when he plants me back into my bed, I beg him, "Don't let me go back to sleep."

They glance at each other with worried lines tunneling across their foreheads.

"I'll fix you something to eat," Tracee volunteers. "Some soup. That should help settle your stomach." She races out the room before I tell her that food is the last thing on my mind.

Once she's gone, Reggie and I stare at each other like survivors on top of a roof after a bad hurricane. What do we say? What do we do?

Reggie is the first to try and communicate. He clears his throat and rasps, "She means well."

"I know." I sit back up in bed and hug my knees to my chest. "You mean well, too."

His brown eyes wet up. "None of this would have happened if I—"

"Don't do this again. I told you that Profit tried to save me that night. It wasn't his fault."

Reggie shakes his head. He doesn't want to accept anything other than his version of events. "You're trying to protect him."

"Yes," I admit. "Just like he tried to protect me."

Again with the head shaking. "You're not to see him again. Ever."

"I'm sorry. But I can . . . and I will. I love him." I thrust up my chin in defiance.

Reggie's head jerks back as if I'd spat in his face. Then he looks at me with such compassion and heartbreak. "It always happens. No matter how good the parents or how much promise and potential you girls have—the moment some nappy-head thug flashes a smile—you young girls throw everything away to go chasing after some ghetto fantasy."

"It—it's not like that. You don't know Profit."

"Yes. It is—and yes, I do." Reggie's chin rises as well. "I've seen this too many times to count. Little girls like you drift in and out of my classrooms every year. Bright-eyed, bushy-tailed and despite all the good-looking, intelligent brothers sitting right next to you in class, deep down you all want a thug: some nigga that can't keep their pants pulled up, body's tatted and brags about the fat knot of cash in his pants. Those guys think that the money in their pockets make them men and the guns they have tucked at their backs make them even bigger men.

"Big men like your boyfriend, Profit, are always being zipped up in a body bag on the nightly news. If a few bullets don't get him, then he's thrown in the back of one of the tax-payers' fine patrol cars where he'll spend his youth behind bars. Of course, he'll ask you to wait for him on the outside—you and God knows how many babies he'll put on you and his other women. And you'll try—but it gets hard being a single mother without a high school diploma or a college degree. You won't be able to find anyone who'll pay you more than minimum wage. So you turn to the game, too—get your own knot of cash and a gun and then suddenly you're a gangsta diva until a bullet or jail claims you, too."

A long silence hangs in the air before I realize that I'm supposed to say something. "It's . . . not . . . like . . . that. That's not us. That will never be us," I tell him even though doubt creeps around the back of my mind.

"No. Of course not. Your love is going to turn your gang-ster into Prince Charming and you'll ride off into the sunset and live happily ever after. Ain't that the fairy-tale bullshit that you keep telling yourself?"

During the next silence, I can't think of anything *else* to say.

"I should have *never* let you go to that prom with him. I

knew better." With a final shake of his head, he turns and walks out of my room.

I sit, hugging my knees and shaking my head. "It's . . . not . . . like . . . that. It's not."

But it is.

34

Shariffa

It's a fuckin' miracle that me and my girls got our ass out of Da Club alive. None of us are a stranger to war, but that shit last night cut *way* too fuckin' close. Looking back on it with 20/20 vision, I'm thinking that hit bordered on stupid more than brass balls.

My nigga, Lynch, ain't stopped bitching since we rolled our asses back home. Instead of a good dicking down for a job well done, I'm sitting on the edge of our bed wired and sleepy as hell from his bitching all night. In the light of day, I think he, like the rest of the niggas on our block, is jealous and mad that they weren't the one that rocked the VLs' second-in-command to a permanent sleep. Those bullets are gonna put me and my girls in the streets for years to come. All I can say is that muthafucka got caught slipping. Grape Street Crips are true players in this game for real.

Lynch stops pacing and mushes me in the head. "Are you even listening to me?"

I can't even take his mean-muggin' seriously no more and start rolling my eyes.

"No. The. Fuck. You. Didn't." His fists ball at his sides like he wants to get something jumping.

My twin babies start whining from the back room. I stand

up only for Lynch to shove me back down at the foot of our bed. "Lynch, I'm tired of this shit. I know you hear them boys." Knowing my boo, my twin boys are probably still sitting in the same diapers I put on them before I left out of the house yesterday.

"Let Momma take care of them. I ain't through hollering at you. We still have a few muthafuckin' things to get settled."

"Like what?" I yell. "What's done is done. Me and my girls got paid, we squashed another roach and everything is everything. What's the big deal?"

"The big deal is that you're busting way too many moves without my sanctioning the shit. Niggas are talking. You need to know your place. I'm the muthafucka swinging the big dick up in here. I ain't down for feasting off a bitch who thinks she has bigger balls than me."

Outside our door, I spot Lynch's cranky-ass mother shuffling extra slow tryna ear-hustle on our conversation.

Lynch follows my gaze and spins around. Seeing his nosy-ass momma, he strolls to the door and slams the shit in her face.

I smile because I know that shit pisses her off.

My nigga sees me grinning and gets more irritated. "See. Your ass is worried about the wrong damn thing."

"I hear you talkin'," I tell him. *You just ain't saying shit.*

"Dammit, Shariffa. What the fuck are you and your five-dollar crew tryna prove? Hitting a Vice Lord club for that bullshit take?"

"Ha!" I bounce up from the bed and dodge his ass in case he's thinking about pushing my ass back down. "My *five-dollar crew*, as you put it, is putting in work. Mad work—and we getting shit done. I fail to see what the muthafuckin' problem is. Did you declare war on these muthafuckin' slobs or not?"

"Yeah. *I* declared war. This shit is for real soldiers. Grape Street ain't blasting behind no iron skirt like those black-and-gold, faggoty flag heads. You wanna hit some trap houses for some pocket change? Fine. Do you. But a real battlefield? What the fuck was you thinking?"

"You know what? We better squash this because I can't believe half the shit that's coming out of your mouth right now." I turn toward the door, but Lynch grabs my wrist and jerks me back.

"The shit is squashed when *I* say shit is squashed, dammit."

This nigga's face is so fuckin' close, his nose is bumping mine and I swear to God that I see steam rolling out of his ears. But I can take a beating and keep on ticking, if it comes down to that. In the meantime, I'm not gonna let anybody punk me, not even my man. I rock my neck and rake my gaze up and down his shit before snatching my arm back. "Let's get some shit clear," I tell him. "I love you, but you don't *own* me. Gone are the days when I let a muthafucka put hands on me. You do that shit one more time and you're gonna be pulling back a nub. Try me if you want to. I didn't do none of that shit last night to stomp on egos—so if any of your soldiers got their balls twisted in they panties over that shit, they ain't no real soldiers anyway. All that matters is that Grape Street Crips come out on top. The fact that we even pulled that shit off last night goes to show just how weak those slobs are now that Fat Ace is out the picture. The time to crush those muthafuckas is now."

The muscles in Lynch's jaw twitch like they're plugged into an electrical outlet. But after a long, hard minute, he backs up a step, even though his voice remains deadly. "They were weak as long as their loyalty was split three ways," Lynch says. "With Bishop out the picture, those niggas are just going to fall in line behind that he-bitch, Lucifer. If you really wanted to impress my ass, that's the roach you should've handled last night. She's more of a threat than her brother ever dreamed of being. Now you done gone and pissed her off."

"What about Profit?"

"Fuck. You got more work put in than that young gun. Lucifer is the bitch we got to watch out for. L-U-C-I-F-E-R," he emphasizes like my ass is stuck on stupid. After another minute of reflecting on it, I see his point, but I can't swallow my pride and admit that he's right. "If that's the case then we'll handle that shit when the time comes. I ain't scared of no muthafucka that pisses sitting down."

"I ain't too sure that she does," Lynch grunts. "The plan works as long as we divide and conquer. We don't have the Vice Lords' numbers. You knock one of them down and ten more are standing there to take his place before you go home and rest your head."

I wave that shit off. "As long as they're selling bullets, we can blast all day every day. And as far as those Gangster Disciples, they asses are on life support. Our territory is only gonna grow and so will our number of soldiers. Win-win, baby. I'm telling you. It's a new era. We got this shit."

"I'll believe that when someone brings me that ugly snake head on a silver platter. Him and his crazy bitch LeShelle."

"So you think he's still alive?"

"Fuck yeah. That nigga don't die—only multiply."

The idea of Python's severed head gets my tits tingling. How I would love to squat over that muthafucka and take a good, long piss. However, seeing the worry lines knit across Lynch's brow, I ease off of him.

"LeShelle's ass is out of the picture. The bitch's sister took care of that shit."

"I thought so, too, but word on the news last night was that the bitch woke up and broke out the hospital, dropping more bodies."

Fuck. These roaches don't die. My mind zooms back to that convo I overheard at the club—something about LeShelle and some baby being cut out of some chick. I shake it off and focus on the problems at hand. "Baby, you worry too much." I slide my hands up around his neck and pull his head down for a reassuring kiss. I take my time, sucking on his tongue and rubbing my horny ass against his muscular frame. "One day, *we're* gonna rule it all. I'm going to make damn sure of it." Feeling like some of the heat has cooled between us, I slide my arms around Lynch's neck and give him my best puppy-dog look. "I'm sorry if I stepped a toe over the line, baby. It's just that I want what's best for you. I see you locking Memphis down under *one* throne—but I can't want this shit more than you. We gotta be partners in this shit." For an extra ten points, I rub up on him.

"One throne." He shakes his head. "You dream big, baby."

"But I thought that was what you loved about me?"

Lynch's hands slide down my backside to squeeze my ass. "There's a whole lot of shit that I love about you, baby. But we got to play this shit right. No more flying off half-cocked and off script. You run everything by me. And I mean, *everything.*"

"Yes, *daddy.*" That shit gets me a firm smack on the ass.

Smack.

"I really should throw your ass across my knee for that stunt," he threatens.

Smack.

"Even if I promise not to do it no more?" I bite my lower lip to tease him some more. Clearly the storm has passed and it's time for us to play.

"It's the only way that your ass is going to learn."

Smack.

"In that case, I'll go get the baby oil." I wink and then slide out of his arms so that we can begin my *punishment.* There's no end to what a bitch got to do in order to get some dick around here.

35

Ta'Shara

1:30 A.M.

"Where in the hell is he?"

The sun has long set and I'm completely going out of my mind. Profit should have called or rolled by here by now. During the slow torturous event called dinner tonight, my gaze kept drifting toward Reggie's car keys setting on the foyer's bombé with the urge to snatch them and make a run for it. Hours later, I'm lying in bed, staring at the red, glowing numbers on the clock and thinking about those damn keys again.

It's not like I don't have any experience of sneaking out of the house and stealing his car. The last time I did it, I fucked up his shit and got myself involved in a hospital shoot-out. I thought the blowback would land my ass back into foster care.

It didn't—which is why my ass is weighing whether it's worth the risk to float out to Ruby Cove to find out what's up. All I want to know is whether my baby survived whatever the fuck went down last night. The main hiccup in that plan is whether niggas over that way is gonna shoot first and ask questions later. With all that's gone down, I can't imagine that I would be welcome in the Vice Lords' neck of the woods.

What about Tracee and Reggie? How much more am I going to put them through before they finally give up?

2:00 A.M.

Wide-eyed, I can't stop twitching beneath the sheets. Unless I pop another one of those pills, sleep is going to pass me by. *Profit, where are you?* I close my eyes and suck in a deep breath. The image of Profit's bullet-riddled body flashes in my mind and fear puts my heart in a death grip and refuses to let go.

I rake the sheets off of me and bolt out of bed. At the window, I stare up at the full moon. "If LeShelle has harmed a strand on my man's head, I'll hunt her down and kill her with my bare hands." A tear trickles down my face. "I'll do it. I swear, I'll do it." My throat tightens to the point that I can't breathe. I open the window for some fresh air and then catch sight of Profit's new muscular frame jogging across the front yard.

I gasp as if a shot of adrenaline has been jabbed into my chest while more tears rush over my lashes. Like a black Spiderman, he climbs up the trellis and onto the roof. He grins up at me like a big, goofy kid and once he's in reach, I grab him by his black T-shirt and drag him into the house.

He laughs as we tumble onto the floor. If I hadn't spent most of the day scared out of my mind I'd beat him senseless. As it is, I keep washing his face with tears and kisses.

"Oh, thank God you're all right." I kiss his eyes, his nose—his ears. I don't give a shit. I'm just thankful to have him back in my arms again.

"Damn, baby. I love how you welcome your man back." He relaxes in my arms and basks in the shower of my love. Once the reality of him being safe sinks in, I punch him on the shoulder.

"Oww," he whines, but flashes me with his beautiful dimples. "What was that for?"

"Why didn't you call me?" I punch him again. "Do you know how worried I've been? I thought you were hurt or dead." I'm crying so hard that I can't see.

Profit's broad smile collapses into a genuine mask of concern. "Oh, baby. Don't cry. I don't like it when you cry." He pulls me into his arms before I can take another swing at his shoulder.

I melt against his chest and inhale his scent like a cokehead. "I love you so much. Don't you ever scare me like that again."

"I won't. I promise," he says, brushing kisses atop my head.

Did you do it? Is she dead? I don't know why I can't get the question from my head to my mouth all of a sudden, but I can't. Maybe there's a part of me that's ashamed of the hope blossoming in my heart. Once I hear the words will it change things? Will shame and regret haunt me for the rest of my life? After all, once upon a time, LeShelle was my protector. *Then she became your worst nightmare.*

Profit tilts up my chin and stares into my eyes. "I love you, Shara. It was never my intention to scare you. Believe that, ma. From this day on nothing and no one will ever harm you again as long as I'm around."

And there it is. She's dead.

One last tear trickles down my face.

"You believe me, don't you?" Profit asks.

Sniffing, I wipe away the tear tracks from my face and nod. "Yes." I wait for the shame and guilt, but it doesn't come.

Profit's beautiful dimples wink at me again as his smile eases back across his lips. "From now on, I only want to see you smile." Profit tilts my head higher so that he can plant his soft lips against mine. "It's me and you from now on. You cool with that?"

I nod and answer at the same time. "Yes."

"Then come with me."

"What?"

"Tonight. Right now." He traps my head between his hands. "Come with me."

My heart stops.

"I mean it. I'm tired of this sneaking through the window bullshit. We're not kids anymore. We belong together . . . on Ruby Cove."

I open my mouth but no words come.

"I love you . . . and I want to marry you." His smile inches higher as if his words are a revelation to him. "I don't have a ring for you or anything right now but . . . say yes."

My tears flow again like a broken faucet. I can't believe what I'm hearing. "You . . . want to marry me?"

"I want to be your man."

"You *are* my man," I choke over the huge lump in my throat.

"Then say yes," Profit urges.

"Your love is going to turn your gangster into Prince Charming and you'll ride off into the sunset and live happily ever after. Ain't that the fairy-tale bullshit that you keep telling yourself?"

"Y-yes." My answer is rewarded with a sudden deep, sensual kiss. I throw my arms around his neck and pour all the love that I am feeling into him. What choice do I have? He's my world now.

I moan before I'm able to stop myself and in just a couple of heartbeats we tear off our clothes. The need to be with him is so strong. Gone is the sadistic vision of that awful rape that has terrified me for months. I *need* Profit. Right here. Right now.

We fall to the bed, a tangle of arms and legs, each tugging at the other's clothes until we're lying exposed to one another. Slowly his hands roam my body. I quiver with anticipation.

I didn't think that I would ever be able to have this reaction to a man's touch again—even my man. Profit knows my body. His gentle strokes leave me breathless, and yearning for more.

His soft lips abandon mine to sweep toward my ear while his hand slides up my thigh. By the time his strong fingers glide into me, I'm melting like liquid candy. "Oh, baby. You're so wet." He pulls my lower lip between his teeth. "I've missed you so much."

"I've missed you, too." My back arches in a way that allows his fingers to slip in deeper. My body feels like one large G-spot and my first orgasm detonates in less than one minute—then the second one, just thirty seconds later.

"Oh. Look at you. You're so beautiful when you come, baby." He sucks on my ears during a few more strokes and then he begins to inch down my body.

I toss and turn and then his mouth drifts south across my bellybutton. Before I know it he's gently peeling open my legs. I come up off the bed when his tongue caresses my clit.

"Profit, baaaaaabby." I slide my hand over his bobbing head with the intent to slow him down, but instead I press his face in deeper. I can't breathe, but I don't give a damn.

The next orgasm begins to build in my toes and then rumbles up toward the back of my knees and then the wave reaches tsunami levels as it zooms toward my clit.

"Ahhhhhhhh." With my hands still locked on the sides of Profit's head, I twist and then bite into my pillow in an effort to quiet my cries. The last thing I want is for Reggie or Tracee to walk in and disturb this groove. Finally the wave hits at precisely a delicious moment when Profit's tongue tunnels in deeper. As a result, every cell in my body implodes. By the time I return to earth, Profit is still mopping up my juices from every nook and cranny of my pussy.

"How do you feel now, baby?" Profit asks, climbing back up my body.

"I feel . . . loved." I loop my arms around his neck.

Profit's wide smile is breathtaking in the moonlight. "You *are* loved—to my last breath and even beyond. I love you so much, Ta'Shara."

Our lips lock with my essence still on his tongue and it's a taste that gets us high on our own love. At the same time, I can feel him positioning himself between my legs. His cock is as hard as steel yet satiny smooth as it pokes the corner of my thighs and then rubs against my creaming pussy. I arch my back as a growing ache begins to throb at my core.

I need him inside me more than I need air to breathe—but he's in no hurry to ease the ache. I can only take his dick see-sawing over my clit for so long before I start begging for him to put me out of my misery. "Profit . . . please."

"Are you sure you're ready for this?" he asks, sounding like he can hardly stand his own resistance. "I don't want to stir any bad . . . memories."

The sweet sincerity in his voice tugs at my heart. I cradle his head between my hands, forcing our eyes to connect. "What bad memories?"

For a few heartbeats, he searches my face—then he moves his hips just so and enters me in one long, fluid stroke. What makes it even more special is that we never lose eye contact, even when the strokes go deeper.

And deeper.

And deeper.

My legs tighten around Profit's waist while the arch in my back inches higher.

"You feel good," he praises, through gritted teeth. "So fuckin' good."

Beads of sweat roll down from his hairline. At the same time, my skin becomes dewy, my belly flutters with butterflies, and I start to burn with an orgasmic fever.

"I love you," Profit repeats over and over again as his thrust quickens. Soon we're both on that magical ride that leaves us oblivious to our surroundings.

My mouth stretches into a wordless scream and Profit buries his head into the crook of my neck while his own release fires off inside me.

"WHAT THE FUCK IS GOING ON IN HERE?"

Profit and I jump up as Reggie storms into the room with Tracee meekly creeping behind him, clutching her satin house robe. Her quarter-sized eyes are now half dollars.

Horrified, I reach over to the bed and snatch off the top sheet in order to cover myself. When my gaze returns to my foster parents, I wither beneath their looks of hurt and disappointment.

Profit jumps between me and the Douglases. "Mr. Douglas—"

"COVER YOUR DAMN SELF. DON'T YOU SEE MY WIFE STANDING HERE?" Reggie's nostrils flare while his hands ball at his sides. "You have some nerve showing your face here."

Profit's face twists from being barked at. A couple of muscles twitch along his jaw and biceps.

I grab his arm as a preemptive move. "Baby, please," I urge softly. The last thing I want is to make this situation worse between the people I care about the most.

Understanding my plea, Profit forces himself to relax and then snatches up his boxers from the floor. Once he's covered, Profit tries again. "Look, Mr. Douglas, I know you're angry right now—and I understand that—but you gotta understand that I love Ta'Shara. It ain't right how you two been tryna keep us apart."

As each word floats out of Profit's mouth, Reggie's face turns a deeper shade of purple. When he takes a step forward, it's Tracee who grabs Reggie's hand and tries to pull him back. "*You* are going to preach to *me*? Where the fuck do you get off?"

Profit licks his lips and rolls his eyes skyward. His patience is thin. "Look, man. I ain't tryna get in it with you. You got it in your head on what you *think* went down and there's not a damn thing I can do to change your mind on that shit. But one thing that *you* can't change is how me and Ta'Shara feel about each other. We're going to be together whether you like it or not."

"Oh. Is that right?" Reggie snatches his arm out of Tracee's grip.

"Yeah. That right." Profit snatches his arm out of my grip to square off.

"Profit, please," I beg.

"Reggie, don't do this," Tracee pleads.

Reggie ain't tryna hear none of this shit. "The way I see this, son, is you crawling back out that window or I'm gonna toss you out of it." He chest-bumps Profit.

Profit takes a step back and chuckles. "Look, old man. I ain't tryna hurt you in your own crib."

"Old man, huh?" Reggie challenges and before Profit can respond again, Reggie swings.

Quick as lightning, Profit ducks but then tackles Reggie on his right flank. The men tumble to the floor and then crash into my dresser.

"Profit!"

"Reggie!"

Tracee and I dive into the scuffle and try to pull the men apart. Instead of exchanging body blows, the men are locked in a violent wrestling match. It seems that no matter how long we scream or how hard we struggle to tug them apart, we get nowhere with them.

At last, Tracee jumps up and races out of the room.

I'm sure that she's gone to call the police and I get more desperate with my pleas—that is until she returns with a gun and shoots that muthafucka straight into the ceiling. "ENOUGH!"

The men spring apart, huffing and puffing while chips of plaster rain on them.

I blink at the odd image of her mean-muggin' us with a gat pointed up to the ceiling. Has the whole damn world gone crazy?

After chugging in deep, angry breaths, Tracee lowers the weapon. "Now if we can all calm down, I'm sure that we can talk about this."

"Fuck that." Reggie climbs off the floor and deftly takes the gun out of Tracee's hand. "I want you out of this house right now."

My heart drops but then I realize that he's not talking to me.

Profit jumps up and wraps an arm around my waist. "Sorry, Mr. Douglas, but I'm not leaving here without Ta'Shara."

Reggie takes a threatening step forward and my eyes fall to the gun he's clutching at his side. To prevent the worst, I move to stand in front of Profit. However, he drags me back to his side, determined to show that he's not afraid of a damn thing.

"Ta'Shara is not going anywhere," Reggie growls.

"Is that right?" Profit grins. "Why don't you ask her about that?"

Everyone's eyes shift to me and I step back from Reggie and Tracee's expectant gazes. *This isn't how I wanted this to go down.* After all they've done, they deserve better than this.

"Ta'Shara," Tracee rasps with her large eyes begging me to make the right choice. "Tell your friend to leave."

"I—I—can't." I swallow and then lick my dry lips. "I'm sorry." Anger, betrayal, and humiliation ripple across their faces. I've seen it before—only on LeShelle's face when I chose the Douglases over her. I need to explain my decision better, but are there really any words that can fix this situation?

The silence stretches for forever in my small, pink, princess room until Reggie finally backs up, nodding his head. "All right then. I want both of you out of this house. *Now!*"

Tracee gasps. "Reggie!" She grabs for his arm, but he snatches it out of her reach, turns, and storms out of the room.

I watch him go with his broad shoulders still stiff with anger. I turn my pleading gaze toward Tracee's tear-streaked face, but her gaze drifts to the floor. "Better grab your things and go." Without looking back, she follows Reggie out.

Tears rush my eyes. "Oh, God. What did I do?"

"It's going to be all right," Profit says, pulling me into his arms so that I can wash the crook of his neck with my tears. "*We're* going to be all right. I promise."

36

LeShelle

"**G**ood morning, Mrs. Terrell Carver."

A huge smile spreads across my face as Python's thick lips brush across the back of my neck. I let my new last name loop inside my head and I feel something that I've rarely felt my entire life: joy. Rolling over onto my back, I beam up at him. "Good morning yourself, *Mr.* Carver."

Python chisels a smile onto his face, but it doesn't reach his eyes. *What the fuck? Didn't he want to marry me?*

I stamp back a surge of panic and remember all the shit he'd been through. After catching me up on Momma Peaches' disappearance, the massacre at the Pink Monkey and the construction site, and his own near death, there's really no wonder his shoulders are weighed down.

Pushing him onto his back, I climb up and straddle his hips. "Let me help you relax."

"I am relaxed, Mrs. Carver."

I can't help but smile. "We really did it."

"We sure did. I'm a man of my word." He folds his arms behind his head and sweeps his gaze over ugly gashes and keloids scattered across my chest. The new battle scars Ta'Shara left behind. Watching him, I try to gauge what he's thinking.

The silence between us stretches for so long that my eyes burn like they're sitting in battery acid. When I can't hold the tears back any longer, Python sits up and starts kissing each one of my scars. "I love you so much, girl."

I throw my arms around him as the dam finally breaks and that battery acid pours down my face. "I fuckin' love you, nigga. Don't ever forget it." I cling to him as if my life depends on it. Now that we're back together, shit is going to be all right. We're going to get the streets back in order and get our asses back onto our throne on Shotgun Row. I'll make sure of it.

But first there are a few debts to pay. Ta'Shara flashes in my head, and then her boyfriend, too. Fantasy images of those two lying dead in a joint grave get my clit thumping so hard that I reach back for Python's cock and position it so I can ease back onto it. It's never easy easing his fat, mushroom head into my back door.

"Ssssssssssssss." Python's hands lock onto my waist as he tosses his head back. Ecstasy ripples across his face. He knows his shit is home now.

I take his hands off my waist and plant them on my neck. I know what he wants and I know what he likes. One night of that slow lovemaking bullshit is enough for me. I need a good pounding out to relieve some major frustrations.

"Squeeze," I order, gritting my teeth. "Enough of this wife shit. I'm your bitch now."

Python's forked tongue slithers out of his mouth as I feel the pressure of his large hands pressing against my larynx.

"That's it, baby," I hiss. "Harder."

The corners of his lips inch higher as he tightens his grip and cuts off my air supply.

Yes! I slam my eyes shut and throw my ass back as fast and as hard as I can. In my mind, I imagine cramming a 9mm into Ta'Shara's mouth as she snots up and cries like a bitch. It's going to feel so good to spit in her face and shows her who's the real head bitch in charge. I'm gonna make her beg and suck the end of that barrel like a ho tryna make the mutha-fuckin' rent.

My clit thrums harder as white stars dance along the edges of my fantasies. My rhythm slows, frustrating Python. In a flash, he tosses me off top and throws me onto my back. He snatches the wide leather belt from off the floor and wraps the shit around my neck. The buckle bites into my windpipe, caus-ing my nut to rise.

"Sssssssss. Time to ride this shit right. On your knees." *Smack!*

Eager as shit, I pop my ass up high in the air and scream when his fat dick violates me again. The pain feels so good.

Smack! "Shut the fuck up and take this muthafucka." He yanks the belt back so fast and hard that it's a wonder that my neck doesn't snap off. I fire off my first orgasm of the morning. The shit is so strong that my hands and knees wobble while the rest of my body trembles like an earthquake.

"You comin', baby?" Python asks, chuckling from behind. He loosens the belt a fraction so I can drag in a sliver of oxygen.

Despite the pain in my chest and lungs, I beg. "More."

"That my girl. You missed this shit, didn't you?" *Smack!* "Your man got something for you." The bed shifts, letting me know that he's reaching over for something else inside the nightstand drawer.

I peek over my shoulder to see him opening a package with silver cucumber-shaped probes. "What are those?"

"You'll see." He smiles as he works the package.

I open my mouth to ask a question when he touches the two probes together and a zap of electricity crackles between the probes. *What the fuck?*

"Your nigga is gonna hook you up," he promises, fisting the belt and snapping my head back again.

Fear slices through me at the sound of crackling and a humming electricity. We ain't never done no play like this before. "Py—"

Smack! "Shut the fuck up. You're my bitch right now, right?" Python hunches over me. His dick bounces off the crack of my ass as he palms my right tit and sends a small shock to my nipples. *BUZZ!*

"Aaaargh!" I bounce up out of shock, while a delicious tingle ricochets down to my clit. *Do I like that shit?* I ease down, pressing my tit back into his hand.

Python's rumbling laughter vibrates off my back. "I knew that you'd like this shit." *ZAP!*

The next scream is out of my mouth before I can stop it. My bruised chest is aching, my nipples are on fire, and my pussy is dripping all over these nice-ass sheets.

"Spread your legs," he orders, pulling the belt back farther.

I obey, greedy for that next shock of pain.

Python palms my clit and at the same moment he rams through my back door.

BUZZ!

No shit my eyes roll to the back of my head and it feels like I'm flying. Soaring above so much fuckin' bullshit. Those baby-raping foster daddies, those evil child-beating bitches who'd locked me in rooms and starved me for days on end, and that back-stabbing, selfish bitch of a sister. *I'm above all their bullshit.*

Python drills into me—every few thrusts, I'm jolted with that wonderful zap that has me clenching the back of my teeth and soaring through those clouds in my mind. After the fourth time, I realize that Python loves the shit because it makes me clench my ass muscles tighter.

"Sssssssss. That's it, baby. That's it."

ZAP! BUZZ! ZAP!

I don't know what happens next. My brain shuts down or

I black out for a few seconds. All I know is that I wake to the feel of Python glazing my ass with his hot nut.

"Sssssssssssss." He collapses on top of me. "I really missed your wild ass."

I laugh because I don't know if he means literally or figuratively. We curl up into a spoon where I can enjoy the feel of his softening dick against my ass while he peppers my back with kisses. "How do you feel?"

"Satisfied."

He chuckles, nibbling on my shoulder. "No doubt."

I'm eased onto my back again and smile into that ugly face that I love so much. I'm on the verge of spitting that saccharine-sweet bullshit at him when I see that damn sadness again. *Honeymoon's over.* "So when are you going to tell me what's on your mind?"

Our gazes lock.

"I've never been good at hiding shit from you."

"No. And if you tell me that there's another bitch about to have your baby, I'm going to cut your fucking dick off . . . *honey.*"

The entire bed shakes with his next rumble of laughter. But when I don't crack a smile his shit peters out until there's dead silence between us.

He rolls away and falls onto his back. "I'm not in the mood to be dealing with no jealousy shit." He covers his face with one hand and uses his thumb and middle finger to massage his temples.

"You ain't in the mood?" I jet up on the bed. "When the fuck are you *ever* in the mood to hear this shit? Now that I have your last name, I ain't having a bunch of miscellaneous bitches disrespecting my ass. You can try me if you want to and you'll be like the rest of these muthafuckas and find out how I get down. Believe that."

He doesn't say shit.

"Python!" I shake his meaty arm. "Nigga, I know you hear me talking to you."

"Is that what you're doing? Sounds like you're nagging the shit out of me."

Pissed, I slap the taste out of his mouth.

Out of reflex, Python swings his muscled arm toward me but stops short from making contact. A new smile breaks across his face. "Look at my little gangsta bitch." He chuckles and lowers his hand.

"Ha. Ha. Muthafucka. I'm not playing. There's going to be some changes," I tell him. "If I'm your Queen—your Boss Bitch, then, dammit, I want you to start treating me like it. Look around. Ain't nobody rolling harder with you than I am. We in this shit together—to the grave, baby."

He studies my ass like I'm a new nigga on the block. "I hear what you're sayin' but—"

"Nah. Fuck that." I grab his hand and place it over my heart. "I want you to *feel* what I'm saying. I'm your bitch. To-gether, we're gonna rule it all."

He rolls his eyes.

"Listen." I drop his hand so I can brace his head and force him to look at me. "We're going to fix this shit. You'll see. We're going to be back on top. We're going to settle old vendettas and remind everyone who really rules the streets—but I'm your partner. I never have and never will deal you dirty. I'm not like Shariffa . . . or Melanie. I'm your true rib—'til I die. Recognize and give me the respect I deserve."

A long silence stretches between us before a slow smile hooks the corner of his thick lips.

"A'ight. I'm putting you on, baby girl. Me and you—ride or die." He reaches for the belt still wrapped around my neck and jerks me forward. "I warn you. If you *ever* cross me or do me dirty, I'll have no fuckin' remorse on your ass."

I return his smile. "Ditto, muthafucka."

37

Lucifer

The mortician snatches the white sheet from Bishop's head. At my side, Momma releases a gut-wrenching wail that twists my gut into knots. I force steel into my back while I clamp my jaw tight, all in a desperate attempt to stop the unthinkable.

Don't cry. Don't. You. Fuckin'. Do. It.

I can't believe that I even have to say this shit to myself—but life is dealing me too many body blows and I'm seconds from giving in.

My mother, on the other hand, loses it. She jets from my side and throws herself across Bishop's cold, dead body. I should pull her back, but I know that she'll fight me off so I let her have her moment. In my absence, the mortician steps forward and before he can even touch my mother, I pull him back and shake my head.

"I'll give you two a few minutes," he says.

I keep my glare leveled on him until he exits the room. Even then, I cling onto my anger as if it's going to save me from drowning in an ocean of unwanted emotions.

Too many emotions.

"My baby. My baby. Whhhhyyyy?" Momma's sobs grow so loud that my ears ring. How long should I let her do this to herself—five minutes—ten minutes? Momma had changed a lot over the years. Her once-fit frame is now ringed with love handles and breasts giving in to the pressure of gravity. And though her beautiful caramel skin is still wrinkle-free, there's a permanent sadness in her eyes. Momma has never been anybody's fool, she knew Bishop and I followed our father's path into the street.

Of course, she preferred I'd taken my place among the Flowers instead of getting involved with the wet work. But she was old-school, when women just married the game—not played it. Momma and I never saw eye to eye on much, especially after she crawled into bed with Cousin Skeet so soon after Daddy's death. And with my own situation after Mason's death, I understand it even less now.

Unless there was something going on between them before Daddy was killed.

I shake my head to erase the thought, but it's not like my head is an Etch A Sketch. This thought has been circling for more than a decade and each time it does, I hate her even more for it.

Closing my eyes, I hang my head. Today is not the day for this shit. *Juvon is dead.* I flinch from the stabbing pain in my heart. As a line of defense, I shift my gaze to the floor and pretend to be fascinated by how clean the white linoleum looks. Slowly, my eyes crawl upward.

Don't look him. Don't. Do. It.

I can keep it together if I don't look at him. But my eyes have a mind of their own and they keep traveling his body until they land on Juvon's sunken gray-black face and the huge hole in his right temple. *Dammit, Bishop. Why did you have to go and get yourself killed?*

My hands ball at my sides. Maybe if I'd been at Da Club that night then none of this would have happened.

I don't know if that shit is true, but the thought keeps creeping around in my mind. With new rumors swirling around that Python and LeShelle had somehow survived that hit outside the church, it's just one more hard blow that I have to deal with. It's hard to believe that twenty-four hours ago, I was worried about a tag-team alliance between him and Profit. Now, if I could turn back time, I would gladly step down and give him the damn throne.

But I've been wishing for a fucking time machine for the past few months.

Fifteen minutes pass and Momma's wails grow louder. Finally, I step forward and settle my hands on her shoulders. "C'mon, Momma. Let's go."

"No. No. I can't leave him like this," she sobs, fighting me off. "I can't leave him alone."

I close my eyes and step back and watch her do what she has to do. An hour later, Momma finally releases him, weak and exhausted. When I start to lead her out of the room, she grabs my arm and forces me to look at her.

"You find out who did this shit to your brother." Her fingers dig into my skin. "I know that you have ways of finding out. You do it. You hear me?" Momma's jaw trembles with renewed anger. "You kill those muthafuckas who did this shit to my baby."

I swallow the boulder in the center of my throat as I nod. "I will."

"Promise me," she insists, her nails damn near hitting bone. "I want them dead—every last one of those muthafuckas."

At long last, something we see eye to eye on. "You have my word, Momma."

38

Alice

Arzell smells bad. I keep telling myself that I need to clean up what came out of his dead body and drag him out to one of the freshly dug graves I have prepared by the big oak tree, but so far I keep putting it off. Maybe it's because it feels like a form of punishment to deny him his final resting place. Maybe I'll leave Maybelline to rot in the basement, too, once she croaks.

I know she has to be begging God by now for me to just put a bullet through her head. So far, I do just enough to keep her alive. I'll never get over losing my baby *or* his daddy. . . .

It had been almost five years since I'd left Terrell at Maybelline's to run to the store and there hadn't been a day that passed that I didn't contemplate going back, but I had a list as long as my arm on why that shit was a bad idea. Every year on his birthday I sent him a birthday card to let him know that I was thinking about him. It was probably stupid. It wasn't like Terrell could read.

"Just go and visit him," Dribbles said in between shoving hand-fuls of catfish into her mouth. It was one of those rare days when we'd hustled a few extra dollars to put some actual food in our bellies. "You know that you want to. I'm sure that your sister will let you see him."

"Not without giving me a hard time or . . ."

Dribbles frowned and licked her fingers. "Or what?"

I shrugged. "I don't know. You don't know Maybelline. She got this whole holier than thou thing down pat. I'm surprised that no one has nailed her to a cross already."

"Hell, there's one of those in every family," Dribbles laughed. "All I'm saying is it's clear that you want to see Terrell so . . . go see him."

I grabbed my cola and wished that it had something stronger in it so I could handle this conversation.

"You scared she's gonna pack Terrell's things and make you take him with you?"

"No," I lied. "And even if she did, it's not like I couldn't take care of him. I mean . . . it would be a little adjustment, but I could do it. If I had to."

Dribbles nodded and let me bump my gums. She wasn't buying a word I was saying. When I finished, she had one response: "Go."

Two days after Terrell's fifth birthday I knocked on Maybelline's doors. After I did, I was suddenly hit with the feeling that I was making a terrible mistake. I turned to jet off the porch when the front door was opened.

"What can I do you for?"

I whipped back around at the rough baritone voice and was taken aback by the thuggishly fine, bold, chocolate brother filling up the door. To make things worse, he was bare-chested with a tapestry of tats, a gold rope chain and wore jeans that sagged off his hips.

Black Gangster Disciple Isaac Goodson was a mean muthafucka by the way of Chicago—at least that was the word on the streets. When he rolled into town and opened his own auto shop off Airways, bitches streamed in and out of that place tryna lock his fine ass down. I had heard that Maybelline had been the lucky bitch to drag him down to the courthouse but until that moment I hadn't realize just how lucky she was.

"Are you going to stand here with your mouth open all day or are you going to tell me what you want?"

Licking my dry lips, I straightened my clothes and hand-ironed my hair. "Is . . . is Maybelline and Terrell in?"

"Nah. She took lil man down South to visit family." Isaac propped his weight against the door frame and took his time checking me over. "You're Alice, aren't you?"

Surprised, I blinked up at him. I couldn't imagine Maybelline having had anything nice to say about me. "Yeah. I just came by to, uhm, wish Terrell a happy birthday."

"For the past five birthdays?"

"Hey! You don't know me." The brothah jumped from my fantasy list to shit list with a quickness.

"No—but I know your son. And I know that he would like to see his mother every once and a while."

"I'm here, ain't I?"

"And he's not. That's what some would call a logistical problem." He toked on a fat blunt and stared at me. Despite my addiction and homeless situation, I still had quite an effect on the opposite sex and I knew when a man was interested in me. Flipping the script, I checked his ass out, too. My jealousy mounted when my gaze rested on the growing dick imprint in the front of his jeans.

"Soooo how long are they gonna be gone?" I asked, pushing up a smile.

"They'll be back on Monday." He blew out a long stream of smoke. "Wanna come in and wait?"

"For three days?"

"You got something else to do?"

I smiled. "As a matter of fact, I don't."

Isaac stepped back and allowed me to enter.

The next three days had to be the best sex that I've ever had. When we weren't screwing, we were blazing it up and vice versa. It was wrong to be fuckin' Maybelline's husband in her bed but it was even worse to fall in love with him. I couldn't help myself. Isaac was as addictive as the best rocks on the street. When the time drew nearer for Maybelline and Terrell to return, I had a new reason to not want to face her.

So I left.

Isaac and I fucked a few more times in his office at his shop, but *then he just cut me off. It wasn't because he suddenly had a conscience. He had simply moved on to the next bitch. I know because I stalked his ass.*

"Fuck him. I don't give a fuck about that muthafucka." I flicked on my lighter and rotated it beneath the spoon of cocaine and baking soda. "I hope his ass catches something and his dick falls off."

"You keep saying that," Dribbles said, twitching and rubbing her arms. "Hurry up with that."

"I mean it. Who the fuck does he think he is? Humph. I like his nerve. He ain't the only nigga out here. I can get any muthafucka I want, if I put my mind to it. Sheeiiiiit." I put the lighter down and then worked the oil with a knife.

"Yeah. Well, whatever you do, don't go crawling back to Skeet's crazy self. He don't do nothing but beat your ass anyway."

"He ain't beating nobody's ass. I don't know where you get that shit from."

"From Smokestack. Plus, I got two eyes. He beats on all us street bitches but then puts his wife on a fuckin' pedestal."

"Smokestack needs to get out of my business. He's always talking that black militant shit while tryna crawl up your ass. No offense."

"None taken. But just because I'm white doesn't mean that I can't be down for the black cause."

I laughed. "That's exactly what it means."

"Whatever, girl. What about Terrell? When are you going to try and see him again?"

The question dropped a mountain of guilt on my shoulder. "I'ma see him." One day.

Dribbles shook her head. "Whatever, girl. I gotta piss." She stood up and went into the bathroom. By the time she returned, I'd already thrown a couple of rocks into the pipe and was coasting through the clouds.

"Alice, what the hell is this?"

I heard her, but I couldn't open my eyes.

"Alice!"

"Whaaaat?"

"Whose pregnancy test is this?" she demanded.

"Fuck. Who do you think? It's my room."

"You're pregnant?"

"Shit, naw. That muthafucka gotta be wrong. I'll pick up another one tomorrow."

"Girl, these things are pretty accurate. Why the fuck are you smoking if you're pregnant?"

"Ah, shit. Don't you start in on me." I blindly reached over and snatched the test out of her hands. "If I wanted a sermon I'd take my ass to church."

"Well, whose it? Isaac's or Skeet's?"

"Why? What difference does it make? We already know that Melvin ain't gonna lay claim to nothing that doesn't come out of his bougie wife's pussy. Besides, I ain't messed with him in a minute."

"So it's Isaac's?"

"Fuck him," I blurted out again. "Maybelline deserves his cheating ass," I said, pretending that I was more mad than hurt.

Dribbles plopped down next to me and grabbed the pipe. While I drifted among the clouds, Isaac's fine ass kept interrupting my thoughts. I knew that he wasn't mine, but I couldn't stand the thought of Maybelline having him. I snuck over to Maybelline's a few times and even watched Terrell play with the neighborhood kids, but I was more interested in Isaac as he worked the shop, hustled his corners, and inducted brothas into the Folks Nation. I never once drew up enough courage to ring Maybelline's doorbell again.

What did it say about me that I wanted my sister's man more than I wanted Terrell back?

I thought about going to the clinic and getting rid of his baby. I feared Isaac's response would be like Melvin's when I told him about the pregnancy. Eventually, I caved and went to see him at Goodson's Auto Shop soon after entering my second trimester and handed him the four-month-old pregnancy test.

"What the fuck are you giving me this shit for?" he asked, waving the stick around.

"Why do you think?"

Isaac's expression remained stony as he closed his office door and walked around me to take a seat behind the desk. "You need some money and a ride to the clinic?"

I flinched. He didn't even blink on that shit. "I'm keeping it."

His head rocked back with his burst of laughter. "And then do what? Drop it off at my crib for me and Maybelline to raise like your other boy?"

"No. I can raise this baby. We can raise the baby."

"We?" He laughs. "That ain't my baby."

"Muthafucka, you know how babies are made. I ain't been messing with nobody but you since we first hooked up."

"Sheeeiiit. You need to get the hell on with that. That can be anybody's baby. I've heard all about how you hustle for them rocks—and we ain't fucked in months."

"I know. I'm four months pregnant," I barked.

"So? You're a ho and you were a ho four months ago. That doesn't make that seed mine."

"Fuck you! I know that this is your baby and I'm keeping it!" Silly me, I held a small nugget of hope that he'd want this child. After all, he had no problem raising Terrell as his own. Shit. I could take Terrell back and we could raise both kids together. I was probably a better mother than Maybelline.

Isaac sucked in a deep breath and took a moment to calm down. "Okay. Let's slow this down. I can't do this with you. You gonna have to handle that."

"Why not?"

"I'm married—to your sister."

"Did you forget that while you were fucking me in her bed?" I snapped. "Maybe I should go over there and have a little talk with Sister Dearest and let her know that she has been sleeping in my wet spot."

Isaac bolted out of the chair. I went for the door, but before I knew it I was jacked up against the wall with his hands wrapped around my throat.

Scared shitless, I clawed at his hand, trying to get air.

"You're not going to tell Peaches a damn thing. You hear me? I'm not about to let you fuck that shit up. Hear me?"

He rammed my head back against the wall. Stars exploded behind my eyes while I fought for oxygen.

"If you ever even fix your mouth to tell Peaches anything about this right here, I'll personally give you a muthafuckin' abortion. You feel me?"

I tried to answer but I couldn't get anything out. Isaac slammed my head one last time and then released me. I collapsed to the floor, gasping. Once I dragged in enough air, I grabbed his leg. "I'm sorry. I'm sorry. I didn't mean it. I just wanted us to be together." I clawed my way up and tried to unzip his pants. "Here, baby. Let me make you feel good. You know I can make you feel good again." I unzipped him and tried to whip out his dick.

"Stop it. Stop." He wrestled with my hands, but I was determined to prove to him that I could fuck him the way he liked.

"Please! Let me show you," I begged and then eventually won the war. We fucked on the floor, on the desk, and even up against the wall. I was sure that I was back in good with him. But the next day he was back to acting like he didn't know me. Any time I tried to get at him at the shop, he had corner boys on the lookout to make sure I stayed away. Once or twice, I thought about following through on my threat and drop dime to Maybelline, but each time, I remembered Isaac's threat and believed that he was a man of his word so I stayed away.

That October, Mason Carver came into the world, kicking and screaming.

Isaac never even came to the hospital to see him.

39

Trigger

"We fucked up," I tell the girls during our private party at my crib. "We should have never made that hit at Da Club. I liked Bishop. That short time we were together was fun. Why couldn't he just sit still and let us take the money? Now we got to worry about the wrath of his sister. I won't be surprised if she pulls a one-eighty and focuses her army on us. We were good as long as GD were getting the brunt of their attacks—but killing the bitch's brother?" I shake my head and lean over the glass table to inhale a line of coke. The shit hits my brain like a locomotive and leaves my mind blown.

Behind me, Jaqorya and Sharcardi are already passed out.

"Goddamn, Trigger," Shariffa complains. "Don't you start on me with that shit, too. Lynch is already riding my last nerve. We did what we had to do. Ain't nobody's fault that nigga Bishop got all swoll over a couple of Benjamins. That shit is on him. If he had checked his fuckin' ego, and not try to test bitches, his ass would still be sucking air right now."

"Damn straight," Brika cosigns before pushing me aside so that she can snort a line.

I hear what they're saying, but I can't help but feel that this is no ordinary fuckup. Not when it comes to dealing with Lucifer. Muthafuckas say that you will never see her ass coming.

Brika pulls her head up and wipes her nose. "If you ask me, if anybody fucked up, it was your ass, Trig."

"Me?"

"Yeah, you. You didn't have to break that slob off no pussy. That was why he was so hot. He didn't give a fuck about that chump change on the table. That nigga was wide open because he got played in front of his boys. Niggas don't like it when bitches pimp their asses. All you had to do was just tease his ass like we said. He would've been pissed but he would've kept the right side of his head."

True. "Whatever."

Brika cocks her head. "You're just mad because your ass got sprung on that nigga."

"And you're mad because I got your ass sprung." I flash her my titties.

"Don't start nothing your ass can't finish," Brika warns.

Shariffa reaches over and splashes Patrón into her glass and then downs the shit as if it was water.

"Bottom line: we've been poking a stick in the Vice Lords' eyes for a while now. If they come with it, then we'll come harder. Like I told Lynch, we can't win the war for the streets without fighting a battle. Think about how easy that shit was the other night. I'm telling you, without Fat Ace holding them niggas down, the sky is the muthafuckin' limit. The same goes for the Gangster Disciples. Python got everybody from the FBI to Homeland Security checking for his ass, so it don't matter whether he's dead or not, he can't run shit, his niggas McGriff and KyJuan are both six feet under and sucking on the devil's dick. Their whole shit is on life support. Now it's our time to be on."

"I bet you're liking that shit."

"Damn straight. Karma is a bitch. The Gangster Disciples can sit back and watch me ascend the throne with the Grape Street Crips."

Brika laughs. "Girl, you're ambitious as hell."

"But you're ridin' with me though, right?"

"All day, every day—but I don't think this shit is gonna stay easy."

"Why you say?"

Brika hesitates.

Shariffa jumps on her. "Look, bitch. I'm too fuckin' drunk right now to try to read your mind."

"All right. I didn't want to say nothing, but I thought I saw someone in Da Club the other night."

"Who?"

"It was this raw dawg I met in Atlanta a ways back. A green-eyed gangsta that goes by the name of Diesel."

The color drains from Shariffa's face. "Diesel?"

"What? Do you know him?" I ask.

"I don't know if we're talking about the same person, but Python has a cousin named Diesel in Atlanta."

"Well, the nigga I'm talking about has the ATL on lock. No weight moves and no fuckin' bodies drop without his say-so."

"Shit." Shariffa looks sick.

"I take it we're talking about the same nigga then?"

Shariffa nods. "But what the fuck is *he* doing here?"

"Reinforcement," I chime in. "Your ex ain't going down without a fight. If he got mean connects like this Diesel muthafucka, then you're gonna have to put your plans of a city takeover on pause."

Our private party now feels like a wake. The idea that we have to deal with Lucifer *and* Diesel, I keep coming to the same conclusion. "We fucked up."

This time, Shariffa and Brika nod in agreement.

40

LeShelle

The honeymoon is over. Two days of being walled up in this tiny-ass house in Covington. We can't go anywhere. We can't do anything and I'm about to go out of my mind. Python spends most of his time either on the phone or having small meetings with newly promoted soldiers within the set. New connects, new gunrunners, and new money men drift in and out the house while I twiddle my damn thumbs. This is what it must've truly been like for Bonnie and Clyde on the run.

I miss Shotgun Row. I miss Momma Peaches and I even miss those damn snakes that slithered around the house. How much longer am I going to have to put up with this shit? I keep hitting Kookie on her cell, but she never picks up. I wonder if they're arranging Pit Bull's funeral.

After hours of watching morning talk shows and bad soap operas, I decide to take a long bubble bath. I go to the bag where Python had my things packed and start pulling out toiletries. But then I find a worn men's wallet. Curious, I flip it open and am startled to see a photo of Fat Ace.

What the hell? Turning, I head to the living room where Python is still on the phone with God knows who. I clear my throat. When he looks up, I wave the wallet at him. "What's this?"

To my surprise, the color drains from his face.

"Yo, man. Let me call you back." He disconnects the phone, climbs to his feet, and comes and takes the wallet from my hand.

I stand there and wait for an explanation. After a few seconds, I prompt him. "Well?"

Python sucks in a deep breath. "There's, uh, something I haven't told you about the night of my accidents."

The fact that he can't even look at me lets me know that I'm not going to like what he's about to say.

"Okaaaay." I roll my hands along for him to speed up and spit it out.

"I know it's crazy, but . . . I believe that I may have found my long-lost brother."

I flinch. That was not what I was expecting him to say. "Mason?"

Python nods.

"Where?"

He holds up the wallet. "Fat Ace."

My ears can't be working. "What in the hell are you talking about?" I back away from Python and look at him like he sprouted a second head. "You're fucking serious."

"Afraid so."

I blink, waiting for him to say more, but he's looking at me about as hard as I'm looking at him. After a while, I figure it's best that I pick my mouth off the floor. "Okay. Let's slow this train down and you tell me where in the hell you got this crazy idea in your head."

"All right. But maybe you should sit down."

Irritated, I open my mouth to argue, but then think better of it. I'm not sure whether I can handle another bombshell. I plant my butt down in a nearby chair and this time listen to an unedited version of what happened the night the Vice Lords tried to run a murder train to Shotgun Row. As I listen I find myself wishing I'd been there in the heat of the battle.

My heart skips a few beats during the parts where the chase between him and Fat Ace extends down the wrong way on I-240, when he clipped an eighteen-wheeler and spun off the shoulder, and when Fat Ace and his demon bitch Lucifer flipped into the air.

"Then I dragged his body out that wreckage hoping that he was alive just so I could kill him." Python holds up his hands, balls them into fists, and then just stares at them as if he was amazed at their large size.

"Python?"

He snaps out of his strange trance to look at me, but I'm not sure that he sees me. "The minute I saw Fat Ace was still breathing, I thought, 'Finally, I have him.' I was going to put an end to all this clash of the street kings and all that rah-rah bull-shit."

I frown. "A lot of soldiers have laid down their lives for this 'bullshit.' Bitches like me have risked everything to marry into the game."

"Makes us all fools, doesn't it?"

Okay. He's scaring me. "What in the hell has gotten into you? You've lived this street life since your momma squeezed you out while tryna rob a check-cashing place over off Lamar. Now you're shitting on everybody? What the fuck is that about?"

"That's just it! I don't fuckin' know! This whole Mason shit has my mind blown. What was up is now down and down is up. I feel like I'm in a *Twilight Zone* or something."

"How did you leapfrog from beating Fat Ace's ass to concluding that he's your long-lost brother? I don't get it."

"He has the birthmark."

"The . . . what?" I shake my head, still tryna clear it. "A birthmark? What the fuck? I can toss a quarter out the window right now and I guarantee you that I'll hit *two* muthafuckas with a birthmark." I laugh. "Damn, Python. You really had me scared there for a moment." Relieved, I stand and wrap my arms around his neck. "That big gorilla was *not* your brother."

Python's expression remains hard as he shakes his head and unhooks my arms. "It's the *Carver* birthmark. A small horse-shoe on the left side of his neck."

He twists his head so I get a better view of his own birth-mark hidden in the six-pointed star tattoo. I've seen the birth-mark before and even noted that Momma Peaches had the same one once. I remember noting that it was cute. I never thought it was hereditary.

"That doesn't prove anything," I insist, stubbornly, but not as forceful as before.

"Every Carver in my family has one—in the same place. What? You think it's just a coincidence?"

"They do happen from time to time." I'm grasping for straws, but what else can I do?

"All right." Python flips open the wallet. "Then how do you explain this?"

"What?"

"Read the name on the driver's license."

"Python—"

"Read it."

"Fine." I scan the name and have a chill race down my spine. "M-Mason Lewis." I swallow. "There's got to be hun-dreds or thousands named Mason in the phone book. This . . . doesn't prove—"

"Read the date of birth," Python says, his voice softening.

I suck in a deep breath. "September 13, 1990."

"My brother's birthday."

The room explodes into silence while my knees threaten to drop me on my ass. "I need to sit down."

"You have no idea what kind of hell I've been through these last few months. I've been tryna deal with this alone, I lost Momma Peaches, two sons . . . you." His gaze locks on me. "I really thought that I was going to lose you." He kneels between my legs. "You can't scare me like that again."

I'm taken aback by Python's naked vulnerability. My heart expands in my throat. "I—I won't."

A weak smile wobbles across Python's lips as he eases his muscled arms around my waist and buries his head in between my breasts.

Loving the warmth that's surrounding me, I pepper the top of his head with kisses. "I'm going to be with you always. I promise you. You're all I got. We're in this shit together."

Python squeezes me tight as his words chase themselves inside my head. "Two sons?"

His arms tighten to the point I can barely slip air into my lungs.

"Christopher is back with his grandparents and Yo-Yo—"

I shove him away from me. "Don't you dare mention that bitch's name to me."

Python throws up his hands. "I know how you feel about Yo-Yo. Believe me that bitch don't mean shit to me—not like that. I just want my fuckin' seed, you feel me? She probably has given birth to him by now—somewhere."

I look away guiltily.

"Look. I won't mention the bitch's name again. A'ight?" Python cocks his head and lowers his hands. "I just want my son. You feel me? I've had too many people taken away from me. Blood is blood. There's nothing in this world more important than family. Momma Peaches taught me that much." He hangs his head. "I should've listened to her a lot more than I did."

I feel my man's pain right now. He must be going through hell because I've never seen him torn up like this before. But at the same time, I'm grateful as fuck for this one silver lining in all of this. *Lemonhead is dead—and so is that bastard that she was carrying.* I wrap my arms around Python and pepper his head with kisses. *He's all mine now. No Officer Melanie Johnson or Lemonhead crowding my space.*

As I sit next to Python, his words circle around in my head. "Baby?"

"Hmm?"

"You didn't include Mason in that list."

"What?"

I pull his head back so that I can look him in the eye. "You said that you lost two sons, Momma Peaches, and me. You didn't say anything about losing your . . . brother."

Python stares at me.

Dread skips up and down my spine. "You said that Fat Ace was alive when you pulled him out of the wreckage. He *was* dead when you left him?"

Python doesn't answer.

I don't give up. "Fat Ace *is* dead—right?"

41

Qiana

"What the fuck am I gonna do? My head has been scrambling for an excuse for the past hour and I haven't come up with a damn thing despite my ass having months.

"I should have tossed that muthafucka in the trash a long time ago," I mutter underneath my breath. The moment the words are out of my mouth, I regret them.

"Tossed who into the trash?" Diesel asks, interrupting my thoughts from behind the driver's seat.

Cutting a quick glance at him, I see his attention is more on me than on what he should be doing. "Watch the road," I bark.

Diesel cranks up a single brow. "How about I pull over and you walk your ass back to the projects?"

He ain't playing. If it was any other nigga and I didn't already have enough to deal with right now, I might have set it off up in here. Instead, I cross my arms and roll my eyes to emphasize he's riding my last nerve. "Whatever."

Diesel sucks in a deep breath and shakes his head with another warning. "Little girl . . ."

"Dammit. How many times do I have tell you that I ain't no little girl?"

Bam!

Pain explodes across my face a few seconds before I realize that I've been hit. *Hard.*

"I'm tired of you talking to me like I'm one of your nappy-headed stick-up boys," Diesel growls. "I'm a grown man and your ass needs to recognize that shit."

I turn toward him, holding my jaw and staring at him like he's done lost his damn mind. But this muthafucka has completely flipped the script on my ass. There are so many muscles twitching on his face that he looks like a beast spat out of hell.

Muthafucka, do you know who I am? Do you know that I can rock-a-bye your ass for this shit?

Despite these questions racing through my mind and the instant fantasy of my ramming my gat down his throat, the actual words that tumble out of my throat are, "I'm sorry."

Only two muscles stop flexing against his temple. Diesel still looks pissed as shit. I have the distinct feeling that if and when he drops my ass off at my crib that it will be the last time that I see them.

That shit got my heart tripping up in my chest. It ain't like I got a line of niggas that look at me the way he does or tryna get at me. Once he rolls out how long will it be before that curvy bitch be back cheesing in his face? *Fuck him, then.* I shift my attention out of the window and pretend that I don't give a shit, but then I think about how good he straightened out my back and I get to missing his ass before he's even gone.

"Look. Seriously," I say, turning in my seat to try again. "I mean it. I shouldn't have popped off like that. I—it's just I got a lot of shit on my mind right now and it's all fucked up. I shouldn't have tried to take it out on you." Inwardly, I cringe at hearing myself beg this nigga that I haven't known for forty-eight hours to forgive me. Hell, I even hold my breath while waiting for his response.

"Look, little ma. I like a rude mouth from time to time, but I don't like it when females take shit too far."

"Does that mean that you don't forgive me?" I give him my best puppy dog expression while I wait with my heart in my throat.

He shoots another look at me, but I see the muscles in his face have smoothed out before his sexy lips expand into a smile. "Get over here, Scar."

I unlock my seatbelt without hesitation and scramble over into his lap, careful not to hit the gearshift or steering wheel. The second that I'm seated I'm thrilled to feel that his shit is rock hard.

"Don't get any ideas," he warns, but the corners of his lips are still quirked up. Wiggling my romp and winking at him, I realize that I'm fuckin' sprung on this nigga, despite the sore jaw. Before I know it we roll through Ruby Cove with all the corner boys eyeballing Diesel's shit with their hands on their weapons, ready for shit to pop off at any time. This isn't the time or the atmosphere for unknown muthafuckas to come cruising down the wrong road. The second they peep me out, they relax and allow us to float on through.

"You stay out here?" Diesel asks.

"What? You ain't never been to the hood before?" Even though I'm referring to his crib out in the suburbs, everything about him tells me that shit is a stupid question.

"What do you think?"

My goofy smile stretches even wider. "You gotta be hood or my ass wouldn't be fuckin' with you."

He slaps me on my ass. "Smart girl. Now which one of these houses is yours?"

"Turn right here," I tell him and then moan when we whip next to Charlie's ride. "Shit."

"Problem?"

"Nothing that I can't handle." I sigh and climb out of his lap. It's time to face the music.

Diesel parks and shuts off the car.

"What are you doing?"

"What does it look like?" He climbs out of the vehicle before I can get another word out. *Fuck!*

"Yo, Diesel. Wait up." I shoot out of the passenger seat and rush around the SUV not sure what I'm going to say to stop this train wreck from happening. "Uhm, you know, thanks for uh, bringing me home."

"But?"

"But, uhm, I think I got it from here." I attempt to hug him, but he gives me a look that shuts that shit down.

"Shoot straight with me, Scar. What's the problem?"

"There's no problem," I lie—*badly.*

"Good. Then you won't mind inviting me in."

Fuck! I smile, but I'm pissed that I can't think of anything.

"Scared to introduce me to your people?"

"No."

"Then invite me in."

I hesitate.

"You know what? Never mind. You do you, girl. It's been real." He marches back to his ride.

I trip out of my heels tryna beat him back to his car door. "Where're you going?"

Diesel licks his thick lips and rolls his eyes skyward as if praying for patience. "Clearly you think my ass is stupid. You're tryna hide something and I don't like being played." He drops his gaze back on me.

Suddenly, I can't get my mouth to work.

Diesel shrugs as if he's tossing in the towel. "I thought I made it clear that I was feelin' you back at my place. Don't tell me that a nigga fell down on his job?"

I shake my head, still unable to think of the right words to get him to stay.

"Tell me now if there's another nigga."

I lick my dry lips and rasp, "There's no one." I can't tell whether he believes me or not but his hand drops from my chin.

"Then invite me in."

I nod and head back toward the house with Diesel right behind me. The minute I open the door, we're assaulted by Jayson's high-pitched wail.

"It's about muthafuckin' time," Charlie barks, rounding a corner and thundering down the hallway. "You got a lot of fuckin' explainin' to do!" At the last minute, he pulls up when his gaze crashes into the brick wall walking into the house behind me. Instantly, Charlie puffs up his chest and rakes Diesel up and down. "Who is this muthafucka?"

"He's cool. He's with me," I tell him. That shit does nothing to alleviate the tension.

Jayson's screams grow louder and I rush to take him out of a frazzled-looking GG's hands, but the minute the baby sees me, he turns away and starts kicking and punching the air.

"What the hell is wrong with him?"

"Yo, Q," Charlie thunders. "You didn't answer my fucking question. *I* don't know this muthafucka, and any muthafucka I don't know ain't got no business rollin' up in *my* crib."

I physically try to pry the baby out of GG's arms, but he ain't having none of that shit.

"He's been like this all day," GG says. She looks exhausted with bloodshot eyes and rumpled clothes.

"I'll ask again. WHO IS THIS MUTHAFUCKA?"

"Damn, Charlie, give it a rest," I snap, twisting around with my hands on my hips. "You ain't the only nigga that lives up in here."

"I'm the only muthafucka that's payin' the bills up in here. That makes me the man of the house." He eyeballs Diesel harder.

To my man's credit, he looks more amused than threatened by Charlie's chest pounding. As big as Charlie is, Diesel is at least two inches taller and has at least twenty more pounds of muscle.

"The last time I checked, *I* was the man of the house,"

Nookie shouts, rolling down the hallway with the ho-of-the-day planted on his lap.

"I *know* that's right," this old bitch cosigns, giggling and then laying a fat kiss on his lips.

I nearly throw up in my mouth.

WHAAAAAAA! WHAAAAAA!

"Will somebody please shut that kid up?" Nookie whines.

"I'm tryin'. I'm tryin'." I reach for the baby again. I've been in the house for two minutes and my nerves are already shot.

"Here. Let me try." Diesel walks around Charlie's pumped up chest and Nookie's wheelchair to approach the baby.

The lines in GG's tired face iron out while she grins like a fool.

Diesel plucks the baby out of her arms and when he places the kid up against his chest, the crying stops.

My jaw drops in amazement. "What the fuck? Are you the baby whisperer or something?" I ain't never seen no shit like that.

"Something like that." He cocks a half smile that has GG sighing.

"Does the baby whisperer have a fuckin' name?" Charlie barks exasperated.

"Who gives a fuck?" Nookie says. "Nigga is all right by me if he can keep that punk muthafucka quiet."

"The name is Diesel."

"Diesel," GG echoes while twisting a lock of hair around her finger. "I'm GG. Nice to meet you."

Is she shitting me?

Charlie marches over and grabs my arm. "I need to holler at you for a moment."

"Oww." That's all I'm able to get out before I'm dragged down the hallway to my room.

"Where the fuck did you meet that muthafucka at?" he growls, slamming my door.

"That's none of your fuckin' business. Do I ask where you meet all the bitches you and Nookie parade up in this bitch?" I jab my hands onto my hips to prepare for this face-off. "I'm tired of you always acting like you're my fuckin' daddy. I already got one of those, in case you've forgotten."

"Look, Q. Whether you like it or not, what the fuck you do *does* affect me—that includes you bringing niggas you smashing and rollin' up in here on Ruby Cove on my rep. My name is giving the nigga a bullet-free pass on this block."

"*Your* rep? Nigga, I'm just as much V-L family as your ass—probably more so since you got your nose so far up Lucifer's ass that you can tell me what the bitch had for dinner."

Charlie chest-bumps me so hard that I stumble over the corner of my bed and hit the floor with a loud *thump!*

"What the fuck?"

"Lower your damn voice," he hisses.

I laugh. "What? You think that nobody knows?" I climb up from the floor. "Nigga, your nose has been wide-open since the bitch used to wear dresses to Sunday school. You ain't foolin' nobody—let alone GG's ass. She knows if Lucifer ever gave you the fuckin' time of day that your ass would forget she existed."

"You don't know what the fuck you're talking about."

"Yeah. You keep telling yourself that."

"Shut up." He chest-bumps me again, but this time I remain on my feet.

"I'll shut up when you get your fuckin' nose out of my business."

Charlie's heated black gaze turns murderous. "Fine." He turns and storms out of my room. When he slams the door, he busts the rusted door hinges and the whole thing comes crashing down.

I leap out of the way by just a couple of inches. "FUCK YOU, MUTHAFUCKA!" By the time I make my way back up to the living room, Charlie is jerking an apologetic GG out the front door.

I toss him the bird.

"One of these days, you and your brother is going to play nice," Nookie says before planting his face back in between his bitch's titties.

After another eye roll, I turn my attention to Diesel, who is still holding the baby. "Can I get you something to drink?" I ask, hoping he'd let my rude behavior slide this once.

Diesel's green eyes shift to me. "You didn't tell me that you had a kid."

"She don't," Nookie butts in.

"Do you mind? This is an A and B conversation. C your way out of it."

Nookie's head bobs up for air, but I give him the brick wall before he gets started.

"C'mon, baby. Let's go back to your room," his bitch urges to break the tension. "I have some more homemade blackberry pie ready for you."

The mere hint of pussy springs a new smile across Nookie's face and I'm shoved to the back of his mind. "Mmm. I looove pie." He hits the power button on his chair and he's off.

"Interesting family you got," Diesel comments from the peanut gallery once we're alone with the sleeping baby on his chest.

"You like them, then you can have them."

He cracks a smile that doesn't reach his eyes. "So . . . no children, then who does this little man belong to?"

The hackles on the back of my neck stand at attention. *This nigga really does ask a lot of fuckin' questions.* "I'm just baby-sitting for a friend."

Diesel gives me that look again that calls me a liar. "Baby-sitting? Do you always go out clubbing when you're babysitting?"

I buck. "What's with the interrogation? You a cop or some shit?"

Diesel holds up one of his hands and backs away. "Don't even play like that. The last time I checked, niggas ask questions when they're tryna get to know a chick they're feelin' but you know what? Your ass is startin' to be too much damn work." He walks to the sofa and lays the baby down.

"C'mon. Don't be like that," I beg him. "You know niggas get suspect when people ask a whole lot of a questions. I mean, you know more about me than I do about you." I throw my arms around him and push my body up against him. I'm learning that this big nigga stays hard.

Diesel wavers. "What do you want to know?"

"Everything."

He mulls the shit over and then slaps me on my ass. "A'ight—but at another time. I gotta go. I got some business I gotta handle."

"What kind of business?"

"Now who's interrogating who?" He gives me a flat smile and another smack on the ass. "I'll call you later."

I don't believe him. "You promise?"

"Promise. I've already put my number in your phone. Answer when I call." He leans down and lands a long, hard kiss on me. I'm practically on cloud nine as I walk him to the door. From there I watch him climb into his car and even wave when he rolls out of the driveway. But my thoughts turn dark when I return to the living room and stare down Jayson.

What the fuck am I going to do with you? The kid being an insurance policy against LeShelle isn't turning out the way I thought. In fact, getting caught with the kid doesn't guarantee that LeShelle won't flip the script. *Why didn't you listen to Tyneshia that night?*

I plop down on the sofa next to the baby, thinking. Before

long, I'm stroking his soft hair and brushing my finger against his chubby cheek. "Sorry, but you can't stay here no more." I choke up on the words, this shit is affecting me more than it should, especially since Jayson looks so innocent lying here.

My finger drifts down to his cheek and then stops abruptly at a horseshoe-shaped birthmark on his neck.

"What the fuck . . . ?"

42

LeShelle

"Fat Ace is dead, right?" I ask again, trying to ignore the flare of alarm sparking off inside of me.

Python's face twists in agony. "I don't know. I think so."

"You *think* so?" I thunder, incredulous. "What the fuck does that mean?"

"It means that . . . I don't know," he barks, tossing up his hands.

I can't stop staring at him as he paces around in a circle.

"At the scene of the first wreck, it was raining so hard and he wasn't responding. I thought he was dead, I was pretty sure of it—but then on the bridge—a few seconds before that SUV slammed into me, I thought I heard . . ."

"What? You thought you heard what?"

"That's just it. I don't know—maybe a groan or something. Everything happened so fast. Next thing I remember was flames, then the feeling of falling, and then a shitload of water. Had the window not been down, I would have never made it out of that vehicle alive."

My gaze automatically sweeps toward the ugly burns on his hands and arms. "I'm sorry, babe." I go to him and drape my arms around his neck for support. The whole thing sounds terrible. I lean over and pepper his face with kisses. I stop when I realize that he's not kissing me back. One look in his face and I note that he seems more annoyed than comforted. "What is it?"

Python's black gaze bears into me. "You're not really sorry, are you?"

Gritting my teeth, my arms fall back to his sides. *Hell no. I'm not sorry.*

As if hearing my answer, Python stalks around me, shaking his head. "I don't expect you to understand."

"Understand what, Python? That our number-one enemy is dead? Have you forgotten the rampage that they were on *that* night? They blew up the Pink Monkey, destroyed your construction company, they took out half our leaders and a few members of our Columbia connect. They were on their way to running a murder train down Shotgun Row. And you want me to shed a couple of tears because Fat Ace may or may not be your long-lost brother? Sheeiiit. Blood ain't everything." I step back and expose my scarred chest at him. "This is what family does to you when you let down your guard. Hell, you taught me that shit when your cousin Datwon turned snitch."

Python turns his back toward me.

"You're getting tripped up over the wrong damn thing," I tell him, walking around so that he has to face me. "We're at war. Even if what you're saying is true, what does it change? Huh? Do you think that everybody is gonna lay down their guns and sing 'kumbaya' just because you two got the same momma?"

Python's face twists and contorts. "I didn't say all of that."

"Then what are you saying?"

'Shit. I don't know!" He rakes his hands across his head.

"Well, I *do* know! It changes nothing, especially now that his ass is gone. The Vice Lords are still engaged in a hostile takeover and the Crips have flipped the script and are tryna beat the VLs to the punch and you're in here grieving over shit that don't matter. It's time to get your mind right and get back into the game."

KNOCK. KNOCK. KNOCK.

Python books around me and heads toward the front door.

"Where you going?"

"What does it look like? I'm answering the damn door," he says.

"Are you expecting somebody?" I close my robe and tie the belt as I follow him, curious.

Python creeps up to the door, grabbing his gat along the way. "Who is it?"

A deep baritone growls back.

My eyebrows dip because I didn't quite catch the name.

"Ah, shit. My nigga!" Python attacks the locks on the door like a kid tryna let Santa Claus inside. The second he gets it open, he throws his arms around the man on the other side.

Nosy as fuck, I rubberneck to peek out who's getting so much love from my nigga.

"Bring your ass on in here, cuz."

The brothah that strolls into our small space has my ass shook for a moment. The muthafucka is fine as hell.

"LeShelle, I got someone here I want you to meet," Python says, cheesing and directing the man toward me. This is my cousin Diesel from Atlanta," Python boasts, puffing out his chest.

It's been a minute since I've seen Python this happy. But the name Diesel definitely is ringing some bells. I've heard his name as far back to when I first cliqued up into the Queen Gs. Most of the women who had met him were in love and the brothahs who spoke of his reputation did so with mad respect. Some say that his power even reached into the Atlanta city government and there wasn't a nigga that he couldn't reach out and touch—anywhere—any time.

I don't want to come off like no fuckin' groupie so I check

myself and make sure my poker face remains on point. "Hello," I say simply.

Diesel tips his head. His green eyes make my heart beat faster.

"So what brings you here?" I ask.

Python closes the front door. "With things being what they are, we gonna need reinforcements in the streets." He smiles cryptically. "See. My mind in still in the game."

I give him the same smile back.

"Anyway. I need niggas that I can trust to rein in shit and make sure our soldiers are still eating. You feel me?"

"What . . . so . . . he's supposed to be king by proxy or something?" I shake my head, not liking the sound of that shit. "Naw. Hell naw."

"Damn, cuz. Wifey is rude as hell," Diesel interjects, looking me up and down.

Muthafucka just jumped off my fantasy list and onto my shit list. "It's *wife*." I flash the ring so that he doesn't make the mistake again. "And I don't believe I was talking to you."

Diesel smiles. "My bad."

He's apologizing but it sounds like he's laughing.

Python steps in. "Yo, Shelle. Give us a few minutes."

"What?"

"Weren't you about to take a shower or some shit? Me and cuz here needs to chop up some business."

"What business you got that I can't hear about?"

Diesel snickers. "You got a wife or a new damn momma?"

"Excuuuuse you?"

"Damn, Shelle," Python snaps, heated. "Put that shit on pause and go do what the fuck I told you."

"Fine. Fuck. I'll go wash my ass. Happy?" I roll my eyes and stomp toward the bathroom. The idea of Python putting *that* nigga on the throne got my blood boiling. I don't give a fuck how muthafuckin' temporary Python thinks this shit is. Once muthafuckas get a taste of power, their asses get greedy for more. Why rule one city when you can rule two?

I switch my ass with much attitude as I stroll into the house's one bathroom. When I close the door, I press my ear up against it and listen in.

"So, what's up, D? Whatchu got for me?" Python asks.

"Look, cuz. It's been wild out here. No shit. I peeped out that spot Da Club tryna get at that young buck Profit for you, but he was a no-show."

"Fuck!"

"Yeah, I hear that. My ass wasn't in that joint but a hot minute before muthafuckas started poppin' off."

"Niggas, alcohol, and bullets don't mix," Python gripes.

"True dat. But lookie here, I did hook up with this one lil gangsta bitch with loose lips. Name is Qiana. Know her?"

My heart stops. *Oh shit.* I jam my ear up closer, but I can't hear anything.

Bam! Bam! Bam! The door rattles.

I jump back with my heart in my throat.

"Stop ear-hustlin'," Python barks. "I don't hear no fuckin' water."

I smack the door. "Fuck you!"

Python laughs.

I call him all kinds of muthafuckas as I head over to the shower. My imagination runs wild once I get under the hot water. What the fuck did that lil bitch tell Diesel? How much longer will it be before Python storms in here and blasts my ass full of bullets when he learns that I had his baby and her sloppy, slow-ass momma killed? I swear you can't trust bitches for nothing.

Twenty minutes later, I shut off the shower and take my time toweling off. Maybe Python is waiting for me to walk out of the bathroom before letting me have it. Shit. My heart pounds so hard that I can't hear my ass think.

Gathering my courage, I finally walk out.

Diesel and Python are glued in front of the television.

"What are y'all watching?"

Neither responds.

Since Python doesn't bark for me to go back into the bathroom, I join them to see what's up.

On the screen is a picture of Yolanda's SUV. I'd know that vehicle anywhere since the bitch tried to do a drive-by on my ass a while back. I sneak a glance over at Python. He's clearly shocked as shit.

"I knew something had to have happened to her," he whispers under his breath.

I listen intensely to the news reports. . . .

"*Investigators are still gathering forensic evidence from this grue-some homicide scene. We can tell you that the two young women have been dead for some time, but one of the women is believed to have been pregnant and her baby has been crudely cut from her belly.* . . ."

"THEY FUCKIN' TOOK MY SON!"

The bitch kept the baby? My knees dip, but I catch myself before hitting the floor. *Oh, fuck me.*

43

Alice

I love the sound of Maybelline's raspy breathing as she tries to sleep. At any time, I can end her life. There's not an ounce of guilt in my veins for her treacherous ass and I'm going to draw her misery out for as long as possible. I've already spent the last couple of days shoveling two spots for her underneath the oak tree in the yard.

She took my life. Now I'm returning the favor.

Leaning over the bed, I whisper into Maybelline's ear, "You brought this shit onto yourself."

WHEEZE! WHEEZE!

My smile stretches wider as I brush back strands of hair from her sweat-drenched face. "It's not time yet," I whisper. "You'll go when I say you can go."

Maybelline's eyes flutter open, but I don't worry about her attacking because she's too weak to do anything today. "A-Alice."

"Shhh." I place a finger against her lips. "I don't want to hear any more of your lies. We've moved past that."

Tears roll from the corners of her eyes and even that shit doesn't move me. "You know, I've been thinking," I confess. "It doesn't seem fair that I just get revenge on you. Would you like some company down here? There are few people who have screwed me over the years—left me in that hole to rot and then later to lose my mind in that hospital. You all just forgot about me, didn't you?"

Maybelline doesn't respond.

"DIDN'T YOU?"

More tears drip onto her flat pillow as she musters enough energy to shake her head.

"LIAR!" *SLAP!* Pain explodes in my hand after throwing every ounce of strength into that backhand, but it was all worth it to see my handprint darken her face. It feels so good that I do it again.

SLAP!

SLAP!

SLAP!

SLAP!

Before long my hands ball into a fist and I pound on her until I'm exhausted and her pillow is soaked with blood. When I force myself off, I'm huffing and puffing as if I completed twelve rounds with a heavyweight champion. From the bed, I still hear that thin rasping, but it's interrupted by a gurgle of blood periodically. "Now look at what you made me do."

I draw in a deep breath and pull myself together. "You know we'd get along a lot better if you didn't always provoke me." After another deep breath, I push up a smile. "You lay here and think about what I said while I go out and get you a roommate. Would you like that?" This time I don't wait or care whether she responds. I head out of the room and then lock the door behind me. The only question now is who to go after next.

"Eeny, meeny, miny, mo."

44

LeShelle

"Where are you going?" Python asks, after I rush to get dressed and head toward the door.

"Out." I need to get some-damn-where so I can think. I can't believe that Scarface-looking cockroach pulled some fucked-up shit like this.

"LeShelle," Python barks. "That ain't a good idea. The streets are too fuckin' hot, baby."

"I got some business I got to handle," I tell him and reach for the doorknob.

Python flies across the room and blocks my ass before I can even step a foot out the door. "What fuckin' business you got?"

"Didn't you just bump me out your shit a few minutes ago? How you comin' at me like this?"

"Shelle, I ain't in the mood to be arguing," he says barely holding on to his temper.

"If you don't want to argue, then close your mouth. I ain't gonna be trapped up in this small muthafucka like some damn prisoner. I can take care of myself."

Python draws a deep breath and hisses, "Ain't nobody sayin' shit about you not being able to take care of yourself."

"Then go over there and finish handing your crown to your *cousin*." I try for the door again, but he slams it shut.

"Python—"

"LeShelle, you stressing me. Now you know I gotta keep my eyes and ears everywhere or all of this shit is gonna crumble on my watch. I gotta get new weapons and a strong connect going or our folks are going to stop eating or start defecting. I *know* that you don't want that shit happening, do you?"

Crossing my arms, I look away. I worked my ass off to get on this throne and here he go handing the muthafucka over to some nigga that I've just laid eyes on for the first time? *Shiiiiiit.*

Python grabs my chin and forces me to look at him. "Do you?"

"No."

"A'ight then. Lose the attitude." He releases my chin. "I'm gonna do what I gotta do to lock this shit down—while tryna deal with this sticky situation with the Vice Lords."

"What sticky—oh, shit. Not that again." My eyes nearly roll out of the back of my head.

"Look, Shelle. I know what I know and I know what I saw."

"Whatever."

He glares and huffs out a long breath.

In the back of my head, I know I should be more supportive. As a child, the loss of his brother bothered him deeply to the point that he never spoke or reached out to his mother while she was locked up. None of this means that I should board the crazy train with him. Besides, what did it matter?

"All right. You want to go out, then go out," Python says. "But where are you gonna be at?"

Oh. Now he's my damn daddy. Since I don't feel like arguing all damn night, I go ahead and give him something. "At Kookie's—maybe we'll grab drinks at Passions or just hang. I don't know."

Python gives me a weird look.

"What? Now you don't like Kookie?"

"There's just some shit with—nah, you know what? You go on ahead. This conversation is giving me a headache."

"Cool." He doesn't have to tell my ass twice. I shove him out of the way.

"Yo. Hold up."

"What is it now?"

"Take June Bug and Kane with you. They're out there on lookout. I'll feel better if you have more muscle and guns with you."

"Babysitters?"

"Security."

Sounds like the same thing to me. "Fine. Whatever. Can I go now?"

Diesel chuckles.

My gaze slices across the room. This asshole smiles like his ass ain't being rude as hell. I don't like or trust this muthafucka. I'm definitely gonna have to keep my eye on this pretender to the throne.

"Don't stay out too late," Python says, bringing my attention back to him. "Diesel and I should be done talking soon."

I nod, remembering that I have to do something about that loose-lipped Qiana. If she hasn't spilled her guts to Diesel about Yolanda yet, it's probably a matter of time before she does.

The second I climb behind the wheel of my Crown Vic, I hit Kookie on the cell. "I'm comin' to get you, girl. Be ready."

Half an hour later, I cruise onto Shotgun Row. The corner boys bob and toss up deuces when they see me coming. "Home sweet home." It feels like it's been forever since I've been here. Everything looks the same, but it all feels different. *We can't lose this shit now. I've sacrificed too much.* I look over at Momma Peaches's crib. The place looks so dark and foreboding. It's depressing. Shotgun Row will never be the same without her.

I pull up on Kookie's curb and the bitch hops in like she's escaping a bank robbery.

"What's up, bitch? Don't tell me that the honeymoon is already over."

"All good things gotta come to an end, I guess. You want to go to Passions?"

"Fuck, yeah. My momma and those damn babies are working my fuckin' nerves. I did a three-minute cheer when you called."

"Well, all right then. Let's get our party on." I whip away from the curb and head out.

Two minutes down the road, Kookie leans closer to her side mirror and reaches for her gat. "I don't want you to be alarmed, but I think some muthafuckas are tailing us."

"Yeah. I know. Those are my new babysitters: June Bug and Kane. Apparently, I can't leave home without them."

Kookie relaxes. "Huh. Normally niggas buy diamonds."

"What niggas you been dealing with?"

We laugh as I pull into the club's parking lot. There's a little bit of an apprehension, since the last time I was here, Yolanda's non-aiming ass called herself doing a drive-by.

The nigga at the door sees me and smiles. "Congratulations on the wedding, LeShelle."

I flash the ring and wink. "You know how I do."

We stroll in and are shown directly to VIP. Jay-Z and Kanye have me bobbing and rocking my hips. Damn it feels good to be out. I'm treated like the Queen I'm supposed to be in the streets. I can't wait until all this sneaking and hiding shit stops.

"Oh, girl. Thanks for getting me out of the house. You just don't know," Kookie says. "Ever since McGriff passed, it's been a real struggle dealing with those kids and my damn momma. I was about ready to eat a muthafuckin' bullet it you want to know the truth." She snaps open her purse and pulls out a fat blunt.

"Yeah, girl. Python told me about what happened. Sorry for your loss."

"Thanks, girl. The shit has been rough—and now Pit Bull. The streets are changing."

I shake my head, saddened by the number of bodies that been stackin' since I'd been in the hospital.

"Dem dirty Vice Lords, they're gonna get what's coming to them. One good thing though is that nigga Fat Ace fell off his throne. I keep dreaming of popping a cap in that Lucifer bitch's ass."

"Who hasn't had that dream?" I chuckle. "Meanwhile, something also needs to be done about those Grape Street niggas—and fast. They're filling in where we've fell off, ya know?"

"Yeah. Who ever thought that Shariffa's ass would be right back on top."

"What?"

"You didn't know? She married the head nigga in charge over there a while back. Some are saying that she's the brains behind her man, Lynch. Her shit against GD is personal—and I can't say that I blame her. Python did her dirty."

I'm stunned by the shit flowing from my girl's mouth. "Since when are you a Shariffa fan?"

"Look, don't take it personal. All this shit was before your time—but frankly, I never had no problem with the girl. She was cool. She just got caught up and sloppy when she decided to creep with that nigga King Loc. The way she saw it, Python was splashing off on every bitch that would stand still—so why shouldn't she do the same thing?"

I shift around in my seat. "Whatever."

"Yeah. It don't matter now. If she's flagging for those Crips that officially makes her the enemy. It's hard out here. We're battling VL on our right and Crips on our left. The streets are sloppy as shit right now. But I hear Python is bringing some reinforcements soon."

"Oh yeah?" I steal a second toke. "Where did you hear that shit?"

"FabDivas. Where else?"

I roll my eyes. Those bitches at that hair salon never could keep their mouths shut.

"Well?"

"Well what?"

"Is it true?"

I give her a dismissive shrug and then glance around the club.

Kookie laughs as she grabs the blunt back. "Oh, you gonna play me like that? A'ight then."

"Nah. It's not like that—it's just . . . I don't like the idea of new niggas rolling through. You feel me?"

Kookie nods.

"Python wants to hand the reins to his cousin, Diesel, 'temporarily,' but I ain't feeling that shit."

"Diesel? No shit?" Kookie's voice fills with awe.

"Get the stars out of your eyes. I ain't feeling this worth a damn."

"Yeah. I see what you're saying. Your ass has fought too hard to get on the throne."

"See? You know what I'm talking about. I didn't make all these power moves just so I can be some figurehead. Fuck that shit. Python needs to get his mind right—and quickly."

"Well, he's been through a lot. With that FBI and cop shit, Momma Peaches, the loss of the Pink Monkey and his construction site—"

"Damn bitch. I don't need to run a goddamn checklist. I get it." I snatch the blunt back.

"Fuck. Sorry."

I roll my eyes. "Whatever. Pour me a drink."

Kookie grabs the chilled bottled of Dom. "Didn't mean to

get you heated. You know you're my bitch. With Pit Bull gone, you know we gotta hold each other down."

"Yeah. You're right. It's just that, I got my own pile of shit to deal with, too."

"Ta'Shara?" she asks.

I grind my teeth at the damn mention of her name. "Most definitely that bitch. Believe me, I'm gonna reach out and touch her ass real soon."

Kookie snickers. "I wouldn't want to be that girl right now. You know that she's out of the mental hospital, right?"

I choke over my toke of weed. "WHAT?"

Kookie nods as she grabs the blunt. "Yep. She's been out for a few days now. That's what I heard at the salon. Her foster parents took her home the same day we busted you out of the hospital."

"And the same night her man came gunning for me and Python."

Kookie bobs her head while blowing out a long stream of smoke.

This news bumps Qiana out of the number-one spot on my shit list.

"Well," I say, grinning. "What would it look like if I didn't welcome my baby sister back home?"

Vengeance

45

Lucifer

Juvon "Bishop" Washington
April 12, 1990–October 30, 2011

Another day. Another funeral.

I stand dry eyed above Bishop's casket with my 9mm burning a hole in my pocket. Gray clouds hover above the large crowd while a thin sheet of rain sprays against our defiant faces. The preacher rattles off the same sermon that I've memorized over the years. Hell, there's even the same cadence in his voice. This shit is just a gig to his ass. He didn't know my brother. We haven't rolled up in his church since we were kids. Why Momma insisted on using him is beyond me. Does she really think that after the lives we've lived and the hell we've raised that God, if there really is a God, will welcome my brother through the pearly gates? Is Mason up there, too?

Despite my mental state, hope still blooms where my heart is supposed to be. At long last, the preacher stops talking and I can feel every eye shift to me. They're all expecting me to say a few words. I can't back out of the shit like I usually do. I cast a look around and see someone side-eyeing me like they think my ass has something to do with this shit.

Fuck them. I draw a deep breath and force my feet to move

one at a time. Once I'm front and center, I can't help but be grateful for the closed casket. Even then, the words I've spent the last three days practicing in my head vanish in a puff of smoke inside my head. My iron spine and steel stomach morph into Jell-O oozing into my knees.

You can do this. You can do this.

I lift my head and zero in on one of the friendly faces in the crowd: Tombstone. "As most of you know I'm not one for making big speeches. I'm a woman of action and very few words." I lick my dry lips while I suck in another deep breath. "For as far back as I can remember I've always looked up to my brother. I wanted to do what he did, be where he was— mainly because that was usually where all the action was. I can promise you that Bishop didn't always want me to tag along, but what can I say, I can be persistent."

A few chuckles disperse throughout the crowd.

"This doesn't mean that I've always gotten my way with Bishop—just *most* of the time."

More laughter.

A smile eases across my face, but it's time to address the hard shit. "I'm not going to lie, the last couple of months have been the hardest between Bishop and me." I lick my lips again, unable to keep them hydrated. "I've heard every rumor that's been floating around . . . from muthafuckas that should know better. Whatever disagreement was between us, at the end of the day, family meant the world to *both* of us. We always looked out for one another whether the other wanted it or not."

My smile inches wider while my eyes burn.

"Bishop and I may have been different—in a lot of ways— but our love for each other is and will always be strong and the niggas who pulled this hit will soon feel the steel kiss of my blade. That shit is a fuckin' promise."

The guns come out and full clips are emptied into the gray clouds above. I don't know if I've won over any doubters and frankly I don't give a shit. I've lost my brother and with every breath the shit becomes more real than the second before. I step away from the casket for the next soldier to say a few words. By the time all the speeches are through, the light drizzle turns into fat pelts, drenching everyone from head to toe.

As we head to the line of limousines, I lean over and make my excuses to my mother. She clutches my hands and hisses back, "Are you about to go after those assholes that did this to my son?"

"Yes, ma'am."

"Good." She clutches her jaw so tight that the muscles start twitching along its line.

I help her to the backseat and then switch directions.

"You've been avoiding me," Cousin Skeet says, rushing to flank my side.

"That's because I have nothing to say to you." I keep moving without sparing him a look.

"What the fuck? You need me," he hisses, reaching for my hand.

I yank my shit back and round on him. "Let's get something straight. I don't like you. I've never liked you. That stunt you pulled in not telling me that bitch, LeShelle, was awake only proves that I can't trust you."

"What? I was going to tell you."

"Yeah, right."

"Wait. Wait. We're in this shit together."

"Don't try to bullshit a bullshitter. You need me more than I need you."

"What?"

"Look. I heard about your suspension. LeShelle made a fool out of you. You should have let me put her down when I had the chance. Now she's out there playing Bonnie to Python's Clyde."

"What the fuck are you talking about?" Cousin Skeet grabs my hand and whirls me around to face him.

"Oh, yeah. You probably don't know that shit, either.

Python is alive. Maybe it's past time for you snatch that 'S' off your chest, Supercop.

"Your little gang in blue is never going to find Python and his bitch and those FBI fuckers are only going to put in face time and then pack their shit up and go chase after something that's going to get them better headlines other than this gang-on-gang shit. We're your last hope for you to get revenge for your slut daughter and her bastard son—who is probably Python's kid any damn way."

Cousin Skeet's face twists in outrage. "Who in the fuck do you think you're talking to?"

I get up in his face. "Something that crawled out from beneath my fuckin' shoe."

"Little girl, you *don't* want to make me your enemy."

"Actually, I relish the idea." I give him a hard glare and then step around him. I'm tired of fucking with him.

Tombstone opens the back door to the SUV and then slams it shut after I climb in. Inside, Hennessy and Cutty are slamming new clips into multiple guns.

"Lucifer!"

I jerk around at the sound of my name and see Profit jogging his way over to me. At least he had the good sense not to bring Ta'Shara to Bishop's funeral. Ruby Cove has been buzzing ever since he brought her home a couple of nights ago. It's not like it was before when he brought her over and most people on the block didn't know who her people were. I don't know why she's here or how long she's staying but the shit is only going to cause more problems. It's just another headache that I have to deal with.

"I want to come with you," Profit announces when he reaches the door.

"No. This isn't your battle."

"The hell it isn't," Profit barks. "Bishop was my friend."

"Thanks, but I got this." I power up the window. "Let's do this."

Tombstone climbs in behind the wheel and then peels us out of the funeral line and floats out to the other side of town. By then the sky has gone from gray to black.

We step out of the vehicle and blend into the night, not even a gold flag waving from our back pockets. I have no trouble shifting into soldier mode. The small tattoo shop has a single neon sign advertising that they're open. I'm the first one through the door, jingling a gold bell.

"I'll be with you in a minute," a voice shouts out from the back.

Tombstone locks the door behind us and pulls down the shades.

I circle around with my index finger. My soldiers split off to do a body count within the shop.

"I'm looking for a dude name Crunk," I holler out. "Heard he was the best tat-artist in the city. Is this his joint?"

"Sure is," the voice yells over the steady hum of a tattoo machine. "Take a seat and I'll be out in a minute."

I ignore the directive and follow the sound of his voice. I coach my heartbeat to slow down because I want to enjoy the next few minutes. Behind me, I hear a few muffled shots and know that my men are putting down whoever else is in the shop. I don't break my stride until I'm standing in front of a black curtain. Pushing my emotions aside, I swipe the curtain back. Crunk is bent over some big brothah's back, inking on some huge masterpiece.

Huffing out an exasperated breath, Crunk eases off the foot pedal, shutting off the machine. "I told you that I'll be out in a minute," he snaps, whipping around in his chair. When our gazes crash, the color drains from his face.

"I take it that no introduction is needed?" I ask.

Now that the machine is off, I can clearly hear the soft snore coming from the giant in his chair.

"Wh-what are you doing here?" he asks, looking two seconds from pissing in his pants.

I'm disappointed to see this pencil-thin nigga tremble and bitch out like this. I want a fight. The messier, the more therapeutic—for me.

"I-I, uh, don't know anything," he stammers, hitting the dude next to him to wake him up. "I don't know what you've heard."

Pathetic. I take aim and fire a single bullet into the back of the sleeping giant's head to shut up all that snoring. "Do you remember anything now?"

Crunk jumps up out of his chair and backs up into the station behind him, knocking over needles and tubes of ink. "Oh, shit. Please, don't kill me. I'll tell you anything you want to know."

I can't hide my disappointment any longer. "What kind of soldier are you?"

"I'm not," he whines. "I'm just an artist, man. I ain't into none that street banging. I swear." His Adam's apple bobs in his throat.

"So what's a shitty artist like you doing driving the getaway car after that hit on Da Club three nights ago?"

"Oh, shit."

"Yeah, nigga. Oh, shit." I step farther into the room, pocketing my gun and retrieving my knife. I make sure to pull it out real slow so that I can watch his eyes widen like a cartoon.

"Wait. Wait." He makes a T with his hands like that is really going to call a time out. "I know that shit looks bad, but I didn't shoot no-damn-body. You can't put no bodies on me."

"But you can tell me the name of those bitches who pulled the job."

Crunk's entire body collapses, but there's no doubt in my mind that he's going to snitch long before I make my first cut.

"All right. All right. If I tell you their names will you let me go?"

Chuckling, I cock my head at the dude and ask, "What do you think?"

Tears skip down his face. "Fuck. Fuck. Fuck."

"That about sums it up." I take the blade between my thumb and middle finger and then launch it into his right shoulder.

"Aaaaaargh!" Crunk falls onto the floor like a drama queen.

The performance is so bad that I roll my eyes as I walk over to his crying punk-ass and squat down to yank my shit out of his shoulder.

"Aaaargh!"

"Stop all the hollering before I cut your dick off and make you blow yourself."

He shuts up, but the foul stench that follows tells me his Fruit of the Looms are no longer white.

"I'm going to make you a deal," I tell him, already bored with the game before it even starts. "You tell me the names like a good little boy and I'll kill you quick and easy. You won't feel a thing."

Crunk whimpers.

"But if you drag this shit out, I'll gut you in a way that you'll spend the whole damn night watching your guts spill out of you."

More whimpering.

"Sooo . . . what's it going to be?"

46

Alice

Car lights flash across the window at the same time I hear a car's engine pull up into the driveway. Instead of being nervous, I'm extremely calm in what I have to do. A minute later, I hear a key rattle around in the front door before it opens and closes. Next comes the flipping of a light switch that refuses to work.

"What in the fuck?" the voice growls.

A smile touches my lips as I listen as the man's steady, heavy footsteps head toward the downstairs study. I remain still as the door squeaks as it opens, and there's another flipping of a light switch.

"Damn. Does none of the lights in this bitch work?"

On cue, I twirl around in the executive leather chair behind a mahogany desk. "Need a little help?" I lean on over and click on a lamp.

Big, bad police captain Melvin Johnson jumps back and goes for his gun.

"Ah. Ah." I lift up my gun with an extended muzzle. "I wouldn't do that if I were you."

We engage in a staring contest until his hand drifts away from his hip.

"Who in the fuck are you? What are the hell are you doing in here?"

Laughing, I lean back. "C'mon. Surely I haven't changed *that* much over the years."

Melvin frowns and then squints for a better look. I'm thrilled when recognition kicks in. "You gotta be shitting me," Melvin swears.

"Ah. So you do remember me. I feel a little better. After all, you did put a baby on me."

"Oh, fuck. Not this shit again," Melvin says, rolling his eyes. "I thought I made it clear to you not to bring your ass out to my house again."

"Yeah. I remember how you didn't like anyone disturbing your precious wife about your criminal life, right, *Cousin Skeet?* I flash him a smile. "Well, I wouldn't worry about anyone bugging your wife ever again."

Melvin's expression evaporates. "What the fuck is that supposed to mean?"

"Ask her yourself." I nod for him to turn around.

Instead of following my direction, he stares at me.

"Go ahead. Look."

Finally unable to resist, Melvin does a slow turn toward the leather sofa behind him. There sits his precious wife, Victoria, slumped over with a bullet hole in the center of her forehead.

"Victoria!" His body deflates as he races to his dead wife. The second he touches her, she flops over against his chest. "Oh. My god. Noooo," he cries out in anguish. He holds her for a long while, before easing her back against the sofa like he's handling a delicate flower.

"Touching. If I didn't know any better, I'd think that you actually gave a shit about somebody else."

Melvin jumps to his feet and charges toward me.

POP!

A bullet slams into his right shoulder and he spins around. "Aaaargh!"

"I suggest that you slow your muthafuckin' roll, Captain."

"You're a dead bitch."

"Maybe. But not today," I tell him. "And certainly not by you."

"What the fuck do you want?"

"Who said that I wanted anything?"

Melvin's face goes from angry to incredulous. "Then why are you here?"

"I'm settling *all* my old debts."

He shakes his head. "You're crazy."

"That's what those doctors kept telling me. I have a lot of people to thank for that—but instead of my letting shit slide, I've decided to stop playing the victim. Only I'm not doing that forgiving and forgetting bullshit. I'm going biblical. Eye for and eye type of shit."

The color drains from his face. "Oh, God, Christopher. What did you do to Christopher?"

"Relax. He's fine. You don't think that I would hurt my own grandson, do you? He is my grandson, isn't he?"

Melvin grunts.

"I guess we should be grateful that he's not some kind of retard or something, seeing how his mommy and daddy are brother and sister."

"Stop that! Stop that!"

"What? Are you still denying the truth?"

"You wouldn't know the truth if it bit you in the ass," he seethes. "If you've harmed one hair on his head, I'll . . ."

"What? You'll do what?" I cock my head at him. "Haven't you figured out how this is about to go down—or do you need me to draw a picture?"

"What? You're going to take my grandson just because your old girl, Dribbles, stole your baby? Hell. Did you ever think that the boy was better off?" he rambles off. "Who the fuck puts a baby in a goddamn oven? Your apartment was trashed and you was strung the fuck out. You should be happy that somebody stepped in and raised that boy. Smokestack stepped up and Mason turned out to be a fuckin' good man. A true muthafuckin' soldier. I'm glad your ass never got the chance to know him before they put him in the earth."

"Dead? My baby is dead?"

Melvin throws back his head and laughs. "Yeah. You didn't know about that, did you? Your precious Mason was killed by his big brother Terrell. That's a Shakespeare tragedy for you."

Each explosive revelation is like being hit by a Mack truck.

When Melvin finishes his tirade, he's glaring at me while I remain in shock.

"Dribbles stole and raised my baby?" I ask, standing up. "You *knew* where my baby was the whole time—and you left me in that jail?"

Now was the time to take all that shit back, but Melvin threw up his head and talked down his nose at me—like he's always done. "So the fuck what? You weren't doing shit but pissing your life away. Locking you up probably saved your life, but do I even get a fuckin' thank you card?"

"Oh. I'm sorry. Thank you." *POP! POP! POP!*

I walk around the desk and jam my finger on the trigger. *POP! POP! POP!*

Melvin jerks around on his feet until I empty my clip in his ass. When I stop he collapses to the floor with a river of blood streaming out of his mouth and chest, but I'm not satisfied.

"You sick muthafucka. How could you do that shit to me? How could you!" I drop to my knees next to his body and proceed to pistol-whip his ass until my arm grows tired and I'm covered in his blood.

My baby is dead. I've lived with that possibility for over twenty years. I accepted it. At least, I thought I did. But now that I know for sure, I slip into mourning all over again. *Terrell killed his own brother? No. Say it isn't so, God.*

The cool reserve that I've worked so hard to maintain is gone and I'm racked by grief. I roll off Melvin's dead body, sobbing.

Thump!

I jerk my head up to see a little boy in Batman pajamas, staring wide-eyed back at me. "Christopher."

I move to get up and the boy takes off running. "Wait, Christopher. Come back." I leap to my feet and take off after the kid toward the front door.

"Christopher, I'm not going to hurt you." I give chase. "I'm your grandma."

He opens the door and collides into someone on the other side just as they're about to knock.

"What the . . ." The woman's head whips around to see the boy blow past her.

For me, time slows as I attempt to slow down, but I'm also having a minor heart attack when the woman turns back toward me while standing beneath the porch light. I know those blue eyes anywhere.

"Dribbles."

47

Ta'Shara

"All is well." That's all that Profit ever says nowadays. Somehow we both have made it through hell only to become ghosts in our own lives. If you can call what we do now as living.

I don't.

Love sustains our hearts while revenge consumes our souls. It's been months since the Vice Lords lowered their leader, Fat Ace, into the ground. And since then, Profit hasn't missed a Saturday where he would come out to his brother's grave to shed a few tears and give the proper respect.

Him and Lucifer.

They are a solemn pair; Profit with his broadening shoulders and mounting muscles and Lucifer with her growing belly. More than once people have mistaken them for a couple and more than once I've wondered if I'm out of place for remaining by his side. I can't bring a smile to his face or hope to his heart anymore—hell, I can't even do that shit for myself.

There is chaos in the streets. The Gangster Disciples and Vice Lords have the entire city on lockdown. The minute the sun goes down, scared citizens run into their houses and lock up their shit. The rest of us spill into the streets, hunting each other down like animals.

And I'm no different.

Once I dreamed of escaping this life, these streets, and now they *feel like a second home. While Profit busts his ass making moves, I'm right by his side, proving how much I deserve to be his ride-or-die chick. If I don't do it, another bitch will.*

It's not to say that I don't have to watch my own back. I've racked up plenty of enemies in a short time.

I close my eyes while the rain pelts my body. Add the cold February wind and you'd have three potential Popsicles on the verge of catching their deaths. At long last, Lucifer is the first to turn away from the gray tombstone to slosh her way back to the waiting vehicle. I glance over at Profit and have to reach out for his hand to try to bring him back to earth with me.

"Baby, let's go." I might as well be talking to myself because I'm sure that my words don't penetrate. Stepping back, I gently tug his hand. After a few tries, he turns toward the car.

"It's time," he says, barely above the sound of the accelerating rain. "I'm ready."

His words are like an ice pick to my heart. It's not that I didn't know that this moment was coming. I did. It's that the stakes are so high and, being honest, the odds are stacked against us. After all, Python is a legend out here, and his killing Fat Ace has elevated him to icon status.

"Are you sure, baby?" I ask.

Profit pulls his hand from mine so that he can walk to the other side of the SUV and climb in behind the wheel.

Sighing, I climb into the vehicle as well without looking into the backseat where Lucifer stares out the window toward Fat Ace's grave. I don't know why I thought that Profit and I would resume our conversation, but after he turns over the engine and pulls off, I see that I'm sadly mistaken.

During the drive back to Ruby Cove, there is just the soft, steady whirl of the car's heater, struggling to fill the thickening silence. Again, I find myself stealing glances over at Python and seeing the same rock-hard expression, the same intense stare, and the same raw anger.

I understand that anger. I've lived with it for months now . . . and I'm exhausted. I twitch in my seat, wanting to say what's on my mind, but not in front of Lucifer. Then again, the times that she's not with us are few and far between. She has taken it on herself to train Profit to get him ready for some big showdown that they both claim is inevitable.

For months now I've watched Profit train. Nearly all the bullet holes LeShelle had scarred him with are now covered with tattoos; five stars, bunny rabbits, pyramids, but most importantly the name MASON stretched across his heart.

Niggas eyeball him and whisper about how he should take Fat Ace's place as the people's leader. Others still think the title belongs to Lucifer, pregnant or not.

We turn down on Ruby Cove and pull up outside Lucifer's crib. When she doesn't jump out, Profit turns to look back at her. "We're here."

He says it gently enough to jar her out of her little world. And without saying a word, she climbs out of the vehicle.

I watch Lucifer as she slowly walks toward her house. That's going to be you if anything ever happens to Profit. I've lost count how many times that thought has crossed my mind and each time that ice pick chips another huge chunk away from my heart.

"Baby, we need to talk," I say, turning back around in my seat.

Profit sucks in a small breath as he cruises down to Da Club-ten minutes out.

Since he doesn't stop me, I take it that his silence is a cue for me to spit out whatever it is I got on my mind. The problem is that I have so much that I don't know where to start. "Let's just leave," I say.

I reach across the seat and take his hand into mine. "I know and understand that you want—"

"No." He looks over at me. "I don't want to do anything. I need to murk that ugly nigga Python. He still slithering around out there and killed my brother." Venom seeps into his voice. "I know blood don't mean shit with you and your family, but it's a little different with mine."

That jab hurts.

"Smokestack will be out soon. Let him handle it."

Profit pulls his hand from mine. "What the fuck? Do you think your nigga is a punk or some shit? You want me to run out of this city with my dick tucked in between my ass and let other niggas fight my battles?"

"No. That's not what I meant."

"That is what you meant. Be woman enough to admit it."

"WHAT?"

"Don't think that I don't know that you've been plotting and planning to dump this emotional bullshit on me. Your heart has never truly been down for this shit. You're walking the walk and talking the talk but it's all bullshit. Your heart ain't VL. You ain't no true Flower."

"How the fuck can you say that shit to me? After what I've been through to be with you? What we've been through. Now your entire world is running with the Vice Lords? Shit. Whatever happened to us not wanting to be sucked into this street bullshit?"

"My fucking brother died that's what happened! All that other shit is squashed. If you're down, you're down. If you're not . . ."

My shock grows. "If I'm not what?"

Profit jerks his gaze away.

"No. Finish your muthafuckin' sentence. If I'm not what, Profit? You want me to go? Leave? Then maybe you and Lucifer can hook up since clearly she's the fuckin' kind of bitch you like?"

"Ta'Shara—"

"No. Fuck you, Profit!" I jerk the car door open and race through the pouring rain and into Da Club. However, the minute I run in, an army of guns jerk up and point at me. Two seconds later, Profit runs in behind me.

"Ta'Shara, I didn't mean . . ." He freezes, seeing that we're surrounded. He goes for the gun on his hip.

"Ah. Ah. Ah. Ah," a low baritone warns. "I wouldn't do that, if I was you."

Profit stops, waits, and then heeds the warning and let his hands fall back to his sides. "What the fuck y'all niggas want?"

A man steps forward. My eyes are instantly drawn to his big, bulky frame donned in ink black. But it's the man's face and that damn forked tongue slithering across his thick lips that get my blood boiling and my hands balling into tight fists.

Python smiles as he locks gazes with Profit. "Hey, Superman. I heard that you've been looking for me."

"Then you heard right," Profit growls, his hand still itching to go for his gun.

Python's thick, rubber-band-like lips spread while he flicks his forked tongue at us. "Well, here I am. Speak your mind."

"I'm not interested in talking. I want you dead."

"A lot of muthafuckas want that shit. What makes you so special?"

"I'm going to be the one that actually does it."

Python snickers. "Is that right?"

"That's right."

The room grows stifling hot while I feel myself choke on the tension. I don't know what Profit is thinking, baiting this muthafucka while we're outnumbered.

Python lets the words hang in the air for a long time while his black gaze burns a hole in Profit's skull. Just when I'm ready to beg one of them to say something, Python's smile returns. "Well, what do you say that we go ahead and settle this now?"

"What—so your boys can do your dirty work?"

"Nah. Just me and you—some old-school cowboy shit."

I don't like the sound of that. "Profit, don't." I tug on his arm, but he shrugs me off.

"Your boys are just going to let me kill you and then walk away?"

Python's smile widens. "Sure. You have my word."

He's lying. "Profit, don't do this."

"Then let my girl go first," Profit negotiates.

Python's gaze slithers toward me and I physically become ill. "A'ight. Deal."

"No! I'm not leaving." I grab Profit, but then someone else snatches me by my waist. "Let me go! Profit! PROFIT!"

He refuses to look at me.

I kick and scream as I'm dragged to the door. "PROFIT! PROFIT! PROFIT!"

"PROFIT, NOOOOOO!"

"Baby, baby. Wake up!" Profit rattles me by my shoulders.

I bolt up in bed, unable to catch my breath.

"Baby, what is it?"

I'm confused by the darkness and unable to remember where I am.

"T?" Gently, he pulls me over into his arms. "You must have had a bad dream."

A dream? The graveyard, the rain, Lucifer being pregnant—all a dream?

"But it all seemed so real." *Maybe it's of things to come.* Python's sinister face surfaces in my head and then the next thing I know, I dissolve into tears.

48

LeShelle

The moment the Douglases' house comes into view, my clit starts thumping. Every light in the place is out and from what I can tell there's no nosy neighbors milling about. My only concern is my girl, Kookie, twitching in her seat.

"What the fuck is up with you?" I snap

"Nothing," she lies, looking around again. "Are you sure that you want to do this?"

"I have a debt to settle," I tell her, shutting off the engine and killing the lights. "And I always settle my debts." I peek over my shoulder to see my babysitters pulling up behind us. "Let's do this."

We climb out of the car, pop open the trunk, and hand out gas cans over to June Bug and Kane. At least they know how to follow orders.

Kookie still looks jittery as shit.

"Don't tell me that you're scared."

"Bitch, please. How many times I done rode dirty with your ass? How are you going to ask me something like that?"

"Then what's up?"

She shakes her head and spits out that lie again, "Nothing."

"Well all right then. Grab a can."

I remember the kind of bullshit locks the Douglases have

on the house and I get past them easily. It turns out that they haven't changed the security password since I moved out. *Stupid muthafuckas.*

"Nice place," Kookie whispers, looking around.

I press a finger to my lips and then direct June Bug and Kane to splash off around on the bottom floor, and then direct Kookie to follow me upstairs. I head straight to Ta'Shara's bedroom, feeling my clit pump in double time. Outside the door, I set down the gas can and pull out my gun.

I got you, bitch. Opening the door, I flip on the light switch. The room is empty.

What the hell? I walk into the room and look around. I check the closet and under the bed before turning to Kookie. "I thought you said that she was released."

Kookie shrugs. "That's what I heard."

My cell phone rings. *Damn.*

Shit!

I rush to shut it off, but it's too late. There's a rustling down the hall.

Fuck!

"Ta'Shara, is that you?" Tracee races out of the master bedroom to Ta'Shara's room. When she spots my ass, she gasps and pulls up short.

"Surprise." I level my gat at her.

A second later, Reggie comes rushing in behind her, tugging on his robe. He doesn't look up until he crashes into his wife's back. "What the *fuck* are you doing here?"

"I thought it was past time for us to have a little family reunion." I smile as I edge closer to them. "Where's Ta'Shara?"

Neither one of them speaks.

"Don't make me shoot you."

Tracee swallows. "She moved out with her boyfriend."

"Oooh. Did she now?" My blood pressure climbs. "Tell you what—why don't we go back into your bedroom?" I wave my gat, but neither one of them moves.

POW!

A single bullet rips off the lower lobe of Reggie's ear.

He jerks back with a roar. "Aaargh!"

"REGGIE!" Tracee rushes to her husband.

"He's fine," I tell her, bored by her melodramatics. "It's just a little bee sting." I gesture to my own chewed off lobe. "Believe me. He'll live." *For a few more minutes.*

"Now move your asses."

Growling through his pain, Reggie glares like he wants to put paws on me. I laugh in his face and then blow him an air kiss. "You don't want to look at me like that. It's turning me on."

"You're fucking crazy," Tracee says, shaking her head. "Ta'Shara was right about you."

My smile melts off of my face as an image of Ta'Shara charging toward me flashes in my head. *"DIE, BITCH. DIE!"*

Pain rips through my chest as if those damn needles are stabbing me all over again.

"LeShelle," Kookie hisses and elbows me.

I snap out of my trance and then try to shake the whole thing off.

June Bug and Kane's heavy footsteps hit the stairs and at the sight of my new goons, the Douglases finally scramble toward their room. That shit kind of hurt my feelings. *Am I not scary enough?*

I follow them into the room but then I'm thrown off guard when I see Tracee going for something on the nightstand.

"Watch out!" Kookie bumps me out the way just as Tracee spins and fires.

POW!

Kookie falls back.

What the fuck? I return fire and manage to shoot the gun out of Tracee's hand.

"TRACEE," Reggie roars and dives for his wife.

June Bug and Kane rush in with chromes cocked and ready to blast.

"DON'T SHOOT," I order in time before they turn the Douglases into Swiss cheese. There's not going to be any merciful killings on my watch. I want this shit to go down as slow and painful as possible.

I glance over at Kookie. "You cool?"

A red flower blooms at the side of her blue shirt while she nods bravely. "I'm good," she pants, leaning against the door.

Reggie pulls his wife into his arms. "What the fuck do you want with us?"

I return my attention to him and smile. "I need you in order to send a message to my snitching sister. Don't take any of this shit personal." I flash one last smile and then order June Bug and Kane, "Tie them down to the bed."

"What?" Reggie looks alarmed as the men come at him.

They scrape for a while. But Reggie is no match for these raw dawgs. After delivering a few body blows, the Douglases are tied down. I even stroll over to the bed and check the rope. "Nice and tight." I take my gun and slide it down Tracee's face.

"Pleeaassse. Don't do this," she begs. More fat, watery tears roll down her face.

They look so perfect that I can't help but lean down and lick one up.

"Nice and . . . salty." I wink. "Delicious."

I stand up and go and retrieve my and Kookie's gasoline cans from the hallway. "Do it up," I tell June Bug and Kane, handing them cans.

They splash that shit everywhere: the curtains, the bed—across the carpet.

"Ohmigod. Ohmigod," Tracee sobs.

Reggie tries to console her, but he sounds as scared as she is.

Once the gasoline starts burning my nose, I edge back toward the door.

"Please, LeShelle don't do this. Please don't."

"I'm sorry, but I have to. Let's roll."

"LeShelle," Kookie says, slumped onto the floor. "I think I'm going to need some help."

June Bug steps forward.

"Leave her," I tell him.

Kookie's eyes widen. "Wh–what?"

I squat down next to her. "I have a question for you. Why was McGriff doing an unauthorized drug pickup with Python's connect the night he died?"

"What?" She looks confused. "How would I know?"

I shake my head. "See now. I'm not quite buying that. You wanna know what I think?"

"LeShelle, please—"

"I *think* that you and McGriff were tryna make moves while Python and I were underground, tryna hustle your way onto the throne."

"Girl, don't be silly." Sweat beads along her hairline. "You know me and McGriff would never do anything like that."

"That's just it. I *do* know you—and I know that you're the kind of bitch who would stab her own momma in the back if it would get you ahead."

"LeShelle, don't do this," she pants heavily.

I stand back up and shake my head. "You'd think that of all people, you would know that I'm not the bitch to cross." I glance over at June Bug and Kane. "Let's go."

"LeShelle, wait," Kookie cries out.

"I'LL SEE YOU IN HELL," Reggie roars at my back.

"I'm sure you will. I'll be the bitch sitting on the throne." I toss him one last wink and then head out. Downstairs, I listen to their cries while I take a final look around. "A little gift from me to you, Ta'Shara."

I light a match.

49

Shariffa

Lynch is on that blue diamond shit tonight and beating my G-spot like it fucking owes his ass some money. Sweat glazes our bodies until we look like a pair of chocolate doughnuts in the center of our king bed. He looks so good that I can't stop running my tongue over his chest. He's both salty and bitter at the same time and I can't get enough.

"Say that shit again, baby," he growls, grabbing my wrists and pinning them over my head. "Tell me I'm the king."

The corners of my lips curl upward as I throw my pussy back down on the dick. "You're the king, baby. All those muthafuckas are going to fall dead at your feet and you're gonna rule it all."

"Fuck, yeah!" Lynch's hips shift into overdrive.

"Ahhhhh, shit." My nut grows in the center of my clit, so I lock my legs around his waist and prepare for another blastoff. My baby doesn't disappoint. In the next second, the power of his thrust sends my ass flying to the moon. Even as I'm drifting among the stars, Lynch's insatiable ass is still drilling. At times like this, a bitch is glad to have backup.

Trigger slides up from behind Lynch and nibbles on his neck. "My turn, your highness."

Lynch chuckles, releasing my hands and pulling out of my wet drenches. "Bring your fine ass over here." He grabs her by the hair and jerks her in between us.

Trigger plays her role to the hilt, giggling like a teenager and going with the flow when he plants her face in between my legs.

"Clean my baby up for me," Lynch orders while repositioning himself behind her onion ass.

Our threesome party is nothing new and we keep the shit to ourselves. I can't have too many bitches knowing that I allow this shit to go down. Bitches would take it as permission to toss all kinds of miscellaneous pussy at him whenever they came around him. That ain't what this is. We do what we do, but we do it together. Those are the damn rules and I choose which bitch joins the party. I chose Trigger's ass because she ain't sloppy with her shit. We've been doing this for a couple of years and not one time has she opened her mouth about this. She even pinch-hitted when I was big as hell with the twins.

Lynch would wear her ass out and then roll over with me. For us, the arrangement is perfect.

"Oh." I fist the sheets as Trigger's small tongue dips down for a rim shot.

"Is she hookin' you up, baby?" Lynch asks, spreading Trigger open and sliding through her back door.

"Oh, yes," I praise my girl while squeezing my breasts together. While she does her thing, I lock gazes with Lynch.

He grips Trigger's waist and starts drilling again. Our party goes on for hours. We stop only a couple of times to rehydrate. That's the problem with those damn blue pills. A bitch got to be ready to put in work.

Sometime after three, we all pass out in several wet pools in the sheets with our limbs entwined. A cell phone rings.

And then another.

And another.

What the fuck? Exhausted, I pry one eye open and try to find the source of all that ringing only to discover that I'm buried beneath one of Lynch's musky armpits.

One by one, the ringing stops—only to start up again.

I shove Lynch off of me, waking him up.

"Who in the hell?" Lynch lifts his head and starts looking around.

Trigger is the last to stir.

We scuffle around and I answer the first phone I come across. "Hello?"

"Lynch, man. There's some disturbing shit down here at Crunk's Ink. I think you need to get down here, man."

"Wait. Hold on." I shove the phone toward Lynch while he's shoving my phone at me. "Hello," I try again.

"Girl, Shariffa. Our asses are in fucking trouble," Shaqorya hisses. "You need to get down here to Crunk's Ink."

"Whaaat?" the three of us say at the same time and then glance at each other.

"I mean it, girl. Get your ass down here." *What the fuck is going on?*

"All right. I'll be there in a few minutes," I tell her while I hear Lynch tell his caller the same thing.

Clearly, something is up. Our scramble to get up and get dressed is like a bad, three-ring circus. We leave the kids with Lynch's momma and then pile into the chromed-out Range Rover, armed to the teeth. Any shit could be up, so best to be prepared. When we arrive at Crunk's Ink, there is an army of Grape Street Crips piled outside the door.

Shaqorya and Brika break away from the crowd and rush me and Trigger.

"What the fuck is up?"

Brika shakes her head, looking pale as shit.

Shaqorya grabs my hand like I'm going to need the support. "Girl, you gonna need to prepare yourself for this one.

Crunk's sister came out here when he was a no-show for a family dinner. You ain't gonna believe what the fuck she found."

"What? Spit it out."

"No. This is some shit that you gotta see."

These silly bitches got the hairs on the back of my neck standing up. "Fine. Damn." I push past my girls in time to follow Lynch to the door. I'm already suspecting Crunk has been put down, but that can't be all. These muthafuckas have seen dead bodies before.

The moment I walk through the door, my world is flipped upside down. I take in the scene, but there's so much blood that I can hardly process it all. Hanging and spinning around from the ceiling fan is Crunk's head with his dick shoved in his mouth. On the walls, my and each of my girls' names are written in blood. "Oh, shit." My gaze then bounces around to see body parts lying everywhere. In the right corner, a pair of legs are propped against the wall, while the feet are sitting in a chair. Arms, torsos, hands—all tossed around like garbage.

"What the fuck?" It's the sickest shit I've ever seen.

While I'm standing there with my mouth hanging open, Trigger taps me on the shoulder and then points up at the ceiling.

I glance up and see the Vice Lords' five-pointed star and the letter L. There's no mistaking who left this calling card. "Lucifer."

50

Momma Peaches

I'm not going to die in this room, goddamn it. I keep saying this shit, but my doubt is growing stronger every day. There have been times that I was on the brink of begging Alice to put a bullet through my brain. I've lost count of how many nights I've suffered beatings at her hand, but even that hasn't defeated me. I've tried to think of some MacGyver shit to get me out of here, but I keep falling flat.

I always knew that my sister never forgave me for what happened to her, but I never thought the girl would do no shit like this. I've been locked down many times in my life, but this beats all I've ever seen.

Currently, I'm on the third day of my hunger strike and my mind is getting a little clearer, but the pain in my belly remains strong. I am drifting to sleep when I hear the sound of an engine. A few seconds later, tires crunch over gravel.

Where is she going? Peeling my swollen eyes open, I'm able to make out that it's nighttime. The moonlight has managed to filter through the dirty, barred window. I grab my splintered prosthetic leg. It doesn't fit like it's supposed to, but it still does the job in getting me over to the window so I can look out. I make out the red taillights as the van pulls away from the house.

Alice rarely leaves the house, and this is the first time she ever left at night.

Frustrated, I grip two of the bars and shake them. To my surprise, one of them snaps off into my hand. I'm so stunned, that I'm stuck staring at it like it's a foreign object. Finally I look at the ends and see the tips rusted through.

Once the shock is over, I'm filled with a sudden hope and excitement. I pull and tug on the other bars and manage to get two more to snap off. But all that shit dies when I then try to open the window. It's painted shut and refuses to budge.

"Please, Lord. Please." I shove my entire weight up on the wooden pane and then howl in pain when my hand slips. I pull back and see three large splinters in the palm of my hand. "Fuck!" I snatch them out of my hand and then glance down at my shackled foot. What the hell am I thinking? I'm not going to be able to get out through the window anyway.

Hit by another wave of hopelessness, I drop to the floor and rest my head against my knee. *I'm not going to die in this room. I can't.* I cringe when another painful cramp hits me. I hold my breath until it passes. When it does, I'm dizzy as hell and wonder whether I have the strength to climb back into bed.

Lifting my head, I stare at the twin-size bed. The longer I do, the more it looks like a coffin. "God, if you're up there, I swear I'll change my ways if you could do some kind of miracle. I'll go to church. I'll stop smoking weed. I'll even leave all them hot boys alone. Please, just . . . help an old woman out."

I wait, hoping for some kind of sign to let me know that the Big Man is listening. I hold fast for about twenty minutes. *Give up. Alice is never going to let you out of here alive.*

That shit floats around my head for a bit while I keep staring at the bed—then it dawns on me that I'm actually staring at the wire bedsprings.

Wire.

"Shit." I struggle to get off the floor. When I do, I rush to the bed and flip the mattress up to stare at all the coil springs. "God is good." I get busy pulling and untwisting one of the springs. It's hard and it takes some time, but I'm finally able to break off a piece to use on the metal bracelet around my good leg. I haven't seen a lock yet that I can't pick and less than a minute later, this one is no different.

I smile for the first time in months as I wobble toward to the door. Once I hear the lock disengage, I still hold my breath while I pull it open. Despite my hearing Alice leave, I still creep through the dark basement worried that she'll jump out of a corner at any second. I feel my way around until I trip over the bottom staircase.

"Keep it together, old girl. You're going to get out of here." It's the first time I believe it. My eyes wet up as I reach out and brace myself against the shaky rail. Hell, it feels like the mutha-fucka is about to break off in my hands, but I can't help but rely on it to help pull myself up the stairs.

By the time I reach the top stair, I'm a sweating and cramping mess. I go for the doorknob and then stop before opening it. What if Alice has an accomplice and that mutha-fucka shoots first and asks question later? I ain't scared of no fight, but I would prefer to be strapped to have a fighting chance.

Fuck it.

I open the door and cringe when the hinges squeak like it's hooked up to a sound system. When no bullets start flying, I go ahead and creep into the main house that is just as dark as the basement. I'm hit with a foul odor that has me gagging. Hell, I didn't think anything could smell worse than I do. Slapping a hand over my mouth, I waste no time getting my creep on tryna find the front door. When I locate it, I hear the sound of tires crunching gravel again.

Shit. She's back.

I back away from the door as headlights flood the side windows. *I'm not going back down that hole. I can't. I won't.* Jerking away, I scramble to find a place to hide, but there's very little furniture in the living room so I rush into the next room, hit something hard and crash onto a wet linoleum floor, snapping my prosthetic leg and busting the other side of my lip.

Pain explodes in every part of my body.

The car engine shuts off.

That awful stench is all over me. My stomach seizes up and I gag over my own tongue. *What the fuck is that?* I cover my nose with the back of my hand and try to just breathe out of my mouth. I turn to see what I stumbled over, but my eyes must be playing tricks me because it's a body and . . . is that a knife sticking out of it?

What the fuck?

Two doors slam shut.

How many crazy people are in on this shit? Panicked, I reach over and snatch the knife out of the body and then scoot and wiggle my way back out of the kitchen. I find a nook behind some kind of table and grandfather clock. I have no idea how this shit is about to go down, but I'm feeling my confidence trickle back into my veins with this knife in my hands.

Despite all the crazy-ass bullshit, I still love my sister, but I'll gut her like a fish in order to end this nightmare. The wait stretches for an eternity and fear mixes in with my confidence.

"C'mon. C'mon. C'mon." I'm impatient to get this shit over with. If I'm going to die, then I'm going to die, but at least now I ain't going down without a fight.

"Move, bitch!" Alice yells from outside.

"Please, Alice," a woman begs. "You don't want to do this."

What the hell is going on?

"Oh, I definitely want to do this," Alice seethes. "You stole my baby and then let my ass rot in jail while you played momma. Where the fuck do you get off?"

What? I lower the knife while I try to wrap my head around what I'm hearing.

"Alice, I'm so sorry. At the time we thought that it was the right thing to do—what was best for Mason. For God's sake, you put that child in the oven."

"Liar!"

POW!

I jump and then wait to hear what happened.

"I'm sorry. I'm sorry," the woman sobs. "It seemed like the right thing to do at the time. You were high out of your mind."

"Said the crackhead to the other crackhead."

"It was Smokestack's idea!"

"And you always did do what that high, yellow nigga told you to do, didn't you, Dribbles?"

Dribbles? There was really someone named Dribbles?

"What about me?" Alice rants. "Do you know what that shit did to me? We were friends. You had to know that they locked my ass up. That rat bastard police captain is your nigga's brother!"

Captain Melvin Johnson flashes in my head. *He was involved with Mason's disappearance? Alice had been telling the truth the whole time.* All kinds of feelings trip up in my chest. I climb out from my hiding place and scoot over to the window and peek out the venetian blinds. I make out a thin, blond woman visibly trembling with her hands up.

"And now my baby is dead. I'll never get the chance to see his face, never get the chance to tell him that I'm his *real* mother."

Mason is dead? That small ball of hope drops like a stone.

"You're wrong," Dribbles says. "Mason did know."

"What?"

Clearly both me and Alice are thrown for a loop.

"I told him on his eighteenth birthday. I thought he deserved to know the truth. I told him everything. About you, your family, but—"

"But what?" Alice's voice chokes up.

"He . . . he didn't want to have anything to do with you. At that time, he considered me and Smokestack his parents and the Vice Lords as his people. Smokestack molded him to take his place and that's what he did."

Smokestack? *That would mean Mason is . . . Fat Ace?* I can't stop shaking my head and listening to this wild story.

There's a moment of stunned silence and then Alice shakes her head. "You're lying. What did you tell him?"

"The truth."

"Liar!"

POW!

Dribbles screams as she flies back and hits the hard, graveled road.

"Get up," Alice shouts.

The woman sobs, clutching her bloody shoulder.

"GET THE FUCK UP."

"I'm going. I'm going." Dribbles struggles to get back onto her feet. "Please, Alice, don't kill me. I swear I told him the truth, but he said his allegiance was with the Vice Lord Nation and that he never wanted to talk about it again. So we didn't. But he knew the truth, about you, your sister . . . and his brother, Terrell."

"No. No. I don't believe you. You're lying. You turned him against me."

"Alice—"

"Shut up! I'm tired of talking."

Dribbles snaps her mouth shut.

"Now move."

"Where are you taking me?"

"Over by that big oak tree," Alice tells her calmly. "I've been digging two graves for my sister and ex-lover, but now I think I'm going to put you in one of them."

Dribbles doesn't move.

"Or I can shoot you right here and now," Alice warns.

Crying and snotting, Dribbles finally shuffles one foot in front of the other toward the side of the house. Once they are out of view, I pull back from the window with my head spinning with so much information. There's no use trying to absorb it. It's too much. How long have Python and Fat Ace been beefing—and all this time Mason knew Terrell was his brother?

I can't believe it.

I don't want to believe it.

"I gotta get out of here," I whisper. I probably have a few minutes at best before Alice returns to the house. After that, it's either me or the poor bastard in the kitchen that's going into that other grave by the oak tree.

Struggling to get back onto my feet, I keep hold of the knife and make my way toward the door. Once there, I creep out onto the porch and then hop like a muthafucka to that van, praying the whole time that the Lord got one more miracle and Alice left the keys in the ignition.

She did. *Praise Jesus!* "I promise, Lord. I'm going to church every Sunday." I lock the doors first and start the van.

To my right, Alice and Dribbles spin around. I have two seconds to think about my next move.

POW! POW! POW!

The passenger window explodes.

Heart racing, I shift the car into drive and pull a hard right toward Alice.

POW! POW! POW!

I duck as bullets slam into the front window.

Dribbles turns and jumps into one of the graves while Alice stubbornly holds her ground while emptying her clip into the van's windshield.

Tears burn and flood my eyes. "I'm so sorry, Alice."

POW! POW! POW!

The SUV plows into Alice head on and then crashes into the big oak tree behind her with a sickening *thump*. At the same time, the vehicle's air bags explode in my face and knock me out cold.

51

Ta'Shara

"Shhh, baby. Stop crying," Profit says, gathering me into his arms. "Everything is going to be all right."

I close my eyes and allow him to pepper the top of my head with kisses. As much as I love the warmth of his body, I can't stop my tears from washing his chest. "I think I made a mistake," I blurt out.

Profit pulls back and looks at me confused.

"Maybe I should go back to the Douglases. I never wanted it to go down the way it did. They have done so much for me. They believed in me when no one else did. I can't help but feel there has to be a better way to handle this situation."

Profit gently places his hands on both sides of my face and then tilts it up so that he can look me in the eye. "You're just upset. You had a bad dream. It's going to be all right."

"Yes, but—"

"No buts. Your folks don't understand us. They don't *want* to understand. They're too heated over what they *think* they know."

That doesn't make me feel any better.

"Look, baby. We'll just give them some time. They love you, they'll come around."

"I don't know. I've already put them through so much."

"Give it time." Profit kisses the tip of my nose and then releases me and I lay my head back down against his chest so that I can breathe in his scent. I'm still tryna get used to lying in his bed—in his house—on Ruby Cove. It's another world over here and every Vice Lord I've crossed looks like they'd rather put a bullet in my head than to speak to me.

"Give them some time," Profit keeps telling me, but I don't think I'll live long enough for any of them to accept me. But there's a part of me that says "fuck them." I'm not here for them. I'm here because my place is beside my man.

Profit presses me back against his cotton sheets and feeds himself from my hungry lips. His hands are as soft as feathers as they drift down the side of my body and roam over the curves of my hips. Some ugly images try to surface, but Profit's tenderness keeps them at bay.

Days ago, I thought that I could never be intimate with a man again. I couldn't imagine my body wanting a man to enter where there had been so much pain. But here I am, unable to get enough of all that Profit has to offer. I'm drunk from the taste of him and the feeling of him stretching me open has me high.

We're not fucking.

We're making love—on a level that I never knew existed.

He understands me. He loves me. He *is* me.

We are one.

I lose track of time as each stroke drives me closer to insanity. The tears rolling from my eyes go from sadness to joy. I never want this to end. I never want to climb out of this bed, out of his arms—ever again. The whole world can go to hell with all its heartaches and pain.

When our lips finally rip apart, Profit buries his head in the crook of my neck. He can barely hold back his release. I can tell by the way his body tenses that's he waiting for me.

My body quakes. In no time, I'm digging my nails into his back, thrashing my head among the flat pillows. My breath trips up in my throat while out of habit I try to restrain my cries.

"Don't hold back. Let it go," Profit pants, reminding me that my foster parents aren't about to bust in the door. I'm free to fully express myself.

Two strokes later, I'm screaming at the ceiling with an explosive release.

Profit follows my lead and releases a roar that almost blasts my eardrum open. I can feel his hot seed explode within me. He collapses until he catches his breath. When he rolls onto his side, he pulls me along with him into a nice, warm cuddle. I don't mean to fall asleep, but I must have because in the next second, I am opening my eyes and the room is pitch dark and Profit's light snoring buzzes in my ears.

Smiling, I ease my head back and gaze up into Profit's face. He looks like a sleeping angel. He's so handsome and peaceful that I don't want to wake him. I wonder what it would be like to wake up next to him fifty years from now. Will we be just as much in love then as we are now?

Your love is going to turn your gangster into Prince Charming and you'll ride off into the sunset and live happily ever after. Ain't that the fairy-tale bullshit that you keep telling yourself?

Reggie's voice rings in my head while I wrestle with my emotions. How in the hell am I ever going to get out of this city when I'm in love with a man who is married to the streets?

But I can't let him go.

"I love you so much," I whisper, stretching up my neck and brushing my lips against his.

"I love you, too," Profit answers.

"You're awake." I gently smack him on the shoulder. "Big faker."

He laughs as his long, black lashes flutter open. "Frankly, I thought I put you out for the count. This must mean that you're ready for round two." He rolls me onto my back and starts peppering my collarbone with kisses. "I could make love to you forever."

"Don't talk about it—be about it."

"You mean like this?" he asks, gliding easily through my pink walls. Round two becomes an Olympic sport. Each of us tests the limits of our stamina and endurance. It doesn't take long for sweat to drench our bodies. By the time we collapse it's from exhaustion and dehydration.

"Damn, girl. You're like a drug."

"You took the words right out of my mouth." We share a laugh and then just smile at each other.

"I'm so happy you're here," Profit says, cupping my face. "This is where you belong."

An image of Tracee and Reggie flashes in my mind and my smile melts from my face. When I attempt to drop my gaze, he holds my head in place.

"Give it some time, Ta'Shara."

I nod even though the situation still doesn't feel right. *I made a mistake.*

"Fuck, T. Don't say that you *really* want to go back," he says, jumping right into the conversation I'm having inside my head.

"I don't want them to hate me."

"They don't hate you," Profit says. "If anything, they hate me. I'm the thug that soiled their perfect daughter."

"I'm *not* their daughter . . . and I'm far from being perfect."

"You're wrong. I've seen how they look at you. How they care *for* you. In their eyes you are their daughter—and you are perfect."

Tears race at a clip down my face. "Then I *have* to go back."

Profit closes his eyes with open anguish.

"Please don't be mad at me," I beg. "It'll just be for a little while—long enough for me to convince them how we truly feel about each other. They'll come around. It's like you said. They're just heated right now." I hold my breath while Profit shakes his head.

"I don't believe this shit," he swears, pulling back.

"This doesn't change how I feel about you—how I feel about us."

"If your parents have their way there will never be an 'us.'"

"Then they won't get their way—but I'm sure I can get them to come around. We just have to go about this another way."

Profit grinds his teeth. "All right. If this is what you *really* want to do, then I'll take you back."

"You're not angry, are you?"

"What do you think?"

"Don't be. I love you. It's all going to work out. I promise."

"Look. I'm not going to force you do anything. You want to go back then I'll take you back. You want me to wait for you, then I'll wait. In the end, I'm always going to be here for you, Ta'Shara."

Tears spill over my lashes.

"Thank you, baby." I brush another kiss against his lips and then watch him turn away from me to climb out of the bed. As he does so, my already broken heart finds a few more pieces to shatter.

While we shower and dress in complete silence, I'm too afraid to speak and he's looking like he doesn't want to hear anything else I have to say. I don't think he's angry as much as he's heartbroken.

Profit loads my bags back into the car and then avoids meeting my gaze when he climbs in behind the wheel. I stare out of the window and listen to the soft whirl of the car's air conditioner as we coast off of Ruby Cove. When I think I'm about to break down, I feel Profit's hand cover my own.

"It's cool, baby. I understand you gotta do what you gotta do. I'm just disappointed, but I'll get over it."

"It'll only be for a few weeks."

"And if they *don't* come around?"

I pause, hoping that it doesn't come to that. "Then it's their loss—but I have to give it a try."

"I'm going to hold you to that." He tosses me a wink and a smile, but before I have a chance to return it, it melts off his face. "What the fuck . . .?"

I turn my head to follow his gaze only to get the shock of my life.

Big, bright orange flames shoot up toward the black sky while red and white lights strobe in front of the place where my house is supposed to be.

No. No. This is some mistake. We have to be on the wrong street or something. That's not my house.

But then the tears come and my vision goes to shit. "Stop the car."

"Ta'Shara, baby—"

"STOP THE FUCKING CAR!"

Profit slams on the brakes while I bolt out of the door. "TRACEE! REGGIE!" I take off running toward the house. *They're not in there. Please, God. Don't let them be in there.* "TRACEE! REGGIE!"

"Ta'Shara, wait up," Profit yells. His long strides eat up the distance between us even as I shove my way through the city's emergency responders.

"Hey, lady. You can't go in there," someone else shouts and tries to make a grab for me.

As I draw closer to the front porch, Profit is able to wrap one of his powerful arms around my waist and lift me off my feet. "Baby, stop. You can't go in there."

"Let me go!" My legs pedal in the air as I stretch uselessly for the door. "TRACEE! REGGIE!"

Profit drags me away from the growing flames.

Men in uniform rush over to us. I don't know who they

are and I don't care. I just need to know one thing. "Where are my parents? Did they make it out?"

"Ma'am, calm down. Please tell me your name."

"WHERE ARE THEY?"

"Ma'am—"

"ANSWER ME, DAMMIT!"

"C'mon, man," Profit says. "Give my girl something."

The fireman draws a deep breath and then drops a bomb that changes my life forever.

"The neighbors reported the fire. Right now, I'm not aware of anyone making it out of the house. I'm sorry."

"NOOOOOOO!" I collapse in Profit's arm, and he hauls me up against his chest so that I can sob it out. I wail as my very soul is being ripped out of my chest. As I tighten my arm around Profit's neck, I'm able to make out a familiar car through my fat tears.

"Oh. My. God."

"What?" Profit pulls me back, but I can't take my eyes off of what I'm seeing.

He turns and follows my gaze. I can feel his entire body tense.

There, across the street sitting behind the wheel of a burgundy Crown Victoria, is LeShelle. A slow smile spreads across her evil face. She forms a gun with her hand and then pretends to shoot at us.

We're next.

Dear Reader,

I want to take a moment and thank everyone for embracing my *Divas* series. The warm response has been both surprising and overwhelming. When the idea came to me to write about the female gangs in my hometown, I never dreamed that the story would take on such a huge life of its own. What was once thought to be a trilogy has grown to become a full-fledged hood soap opera. When I sat down to write *Gangsta Divas,* I had every intention to end the series, but then I blew past the word count and was only halfway through the outline I'd set for the story. After too many sleepless nights, blown deadlines, cuts, adds, more cuts, and trying my editor's patience to the max, I had to accept that the series has to continue. So I hope that you will continue this journey with me.

Also, I want to take a moment to make clear that I do not advocate, condone, or encourage the behavior, lifestyle, and violence my fictitious characters engage in. Though some storylines are inspired by real headlines and personal experience, and a good dose of creative liberties, this series is meant for entertainment purposes only—not unlike books about vampires, serial killers, and magical wizards.

I hope that you enjoyed this latest installment and I look forward to your responses.

Best of love,
De'nesha Diamond

GANGSTA DIVAS

De'nesha Diamond

ABOUT THIS GUIDE

The questions that follow are included to enhance
your group's reading of this book.

Discussion Questions

1. LeShelle's ruthless revenge seems to know no bounds. Why can't she let this battle between her and Ta'Shara die?

2. Ta'Shara ignores the voice of reason from Reggie. Do you believe that she's doing the right thing by following her heart?

3. The truth about Alice and her babies' fathers is finally revealed. Were you surprised? With the sexual liberties of today, what do you think of the probability of some sexual partners being related?

4. LeShelle has finally gone from wifey to wife. Do you think that what she went through to get the title was worth it? Have you ever had to do something to prove your love to a man?

5. No one is more dangerous than a woman scorned. Do you believe that Shariffa can lead her new set to be real contenders to take over the street game?

6. Python is emotionally invested in the loss of his baby brother, but it's revealed that Mason has known for some time that he's related to his nemesis. Why do you believe that he chose the Vice Lords and his fake parents over his real family?

7. How do you feel about LeShelle burning the Douglases in their home? Has her vengeance reached a point of no return?

8. Lucifer sustains a lot of losses in this installment. Since she was only in the game to be Mason's ride-or-die chick, why do you think she refuses to step off the throne and let her brother rule in Mason's absence?

9. Much of the theme of the *Divas* series is about the betrayal of family. Have you ever experienced betrayal from your own family?

10. After decades of fights, Momma Peaches and Alice finally have their last face-off. Do you think Alice's tragic end could have been avoided?

A sneak peek at

BOSS DIVAS

Coming soon from Dafina Books

Lucifer

"Is it done?" My mother's voice floats out to me the moment I walk through my door. She doesn't even flinch at the sight of my bloody clothes. "Is it done?" she asks again, pushing up from a chair.

Her hands are clamped tight at her sides and her eyes are bloodshot red from hours of crying. "I got one of them—and the names of the others. It's just a matter of time."

Momma thrusts up her trembling chin and nods at me. "Good." She doesn't seem to know what to say next. After a long, awkward silence she creeps toward me and the door.

"You're such a good daughter," she says, throwing her arms around me.

My breath catches and unexpected tears rush my eyes. It is the praise that I'd been waiting for, but didn't know it. Slowly, I lift my arms and wrap them around her thin frame and squeeze.

The connection feels odd, but good at the same time. When we pull away, I'm embarrassed about the tears streaming down my face.

"Maybe you should go and tell your brother tomorrow," she says.

I'm confused for a moment and then understand that she wants me to visit his grave. "I will."

She nods and then shuffles out of the house to her place down the street. I watch her go, wondering if we're now going to grow this new bond.

At long last, I close the door and make my way up the stairs. In the bathroom, I strip out of the bloody clothes and shove them into a plastic bag. Once in the shower, I make the water as hot as it can get and accept the pelting punishment.

First Mason. Now Juvon.

It feels as if someone has snatched the ground from up under me and I'm in a constant state of falling. I don't like the feeling. Now, after all I've been through, I don't know that I even want the throne anymore.

I slide my soapy hands over my body, but I keep settling it over my small belly. Pretty soon, I'm not going to be able to hide the truth from the soldiers—then what?

More challenges to the throne?

I suck in a deep breath and am suddenly hit with a wave of pure exhaustion. Tears splash over my lashes, but I feel safe in my tiled chamber to let it out. Thirty minutes later, the water has cooled and my tear ducts are drained.

I shut off the shower, wrap a towel around me, and gather the bag of clothes to take downstairs. There's a metal barrel out in the backyard. I'll toss them in and start a small fire to burn the evidence. I might even grab a beer and just watch the flickering flames while I try to think out my next move.

But halfway down the stairs, a noise catches my ear.

"Hello?"

The staircase is pitch dark and I don't have a weapon on me. I should rush back up and rectify the situation, but I don't. I continue to creep down the stairs at a snail's pace with the hair standing at attention on the back of my neck.

"I know someone is in here," I say, tryna make out any figure in the semi-darkness. I feel the heavy weight of someone's gaze.

If I make it to the living room, there's a .45 on the table next to the bar. I reach the bottom stair and think I detect someone breathing in the direction of the dining room. I drop my bag and make a mad dash for the table.

When my hand closes on the gun, a voice cracks like a whip out to me. "Willow, wait. It's me."

I freeze—my heart squeezing out of my chest. *It can't be.* Slowly, I turn back around. This time, I'm able to make out a large, familiar frame as it steps forward into a pool of moonlight.

I jump at the grotesque and hideous sight. After my initial shock, my gaze roams over the ugly black-and-red burns covering a pulpous face. My gut churns, but I'm finally able to lock gazes with the figure's one brown and one milky-white eyes. In the next second, my heart explodes with joy. "Mason."